Extraordinary Quests for Amateur Witches

ALSO BY KAYLA COTTINGHAM

Practical Rules for Cursed Witches

My Dearest Darkest

This Delicious Death

Extraordinary Quests for Amateur Witches

KAYLA COTTINGHAM

DELACORTE PRESS

Delacorte Press
An imprint of Random House Children's Books
A division of Penguin Random House LLC
1745 Broadway, New York, NY 10019
penguinrandomhouse.com
GetUnderlined.com

Editor: Hannah Hill
Cover Designer: Ray Shappell
Interior Designer: Cathy Bobak
Production Editor: Colleen Fellingham
Managing Editor: Tamar Schwartz
Production Manager: Tracy Heydweiller

Library of Congress Cataloging-in-Publication Data is available upon request.
ISBN 978-0-593-81401-7 (trade) — ISBN 978-0-593-81403-1 (ebook)

The text of this book is set in 11.3-point Adobe Garamond Pro.
Interior chapter opener art and ornaments used under license by stock.adobe.com

Manufactured in the United States of America
1st Printing

The authorized representative in the EU for product safety and compliance is Penguin Random House Ireland, Morrison Chambers, 32 Nassau Street, Dublin D02 YH68, Ireland, https://eu-contact.penguin.ie.

To the golden children and the scapegoats

Slicetooth Mounta
Iceweave Coven Castle
Pelumbra Estate
Havensbridge
Wyvern Spri
Pinwhistle Forest
Gellingham
Shui City
FENSHI
Yarrowport
ESPERONA

Celdwyn
Lake of Whispers
Raven's Roost
Wrenlin's House
Gabriel's Edge
Dothering
Silverside Lake
Bea Cottage
Kitfield
Port Lorring
irrorveil Woods
MERIN SEA

CHAPTER ONE

As the first snow of the year began falling on the golden city of Gellingham, Kieran Pelumbra was hours away from unintentionally upending the entire course of his life.

He, of course, wouldn't have guessed that at the time. For him, it was like any other Friday since his move to Celdwyn's capital city. He'd woken to the piercing ring of his alarm clock just before the sun rose, thrown on his wrinkled uniform, and shuffled off through the frigid air on his way to the Witch's Brew Café. The morning rush had seemed endless; due to the café's proximity to the Library of Curses, most of their clients were, predictably, witches.

None of them, however, was the witch Kieran was not-so-patiently waiting for.

As each new customer walked through the door, a silver bell rang overhead. Kieran couldn't help but tear his attention away from the customer ordering to see if maybe, just maybe, a familiar face would appear. As the minutes ticked by, though, only the regulars and a few tourists stopped in. He examined the clock on the wall as the hands moved far too quickly toward nine a.m. That was the start time of said familiar face's shift at the library, which meant that after nine hit, it was pretty much a guarantee he wasn't stopping in.

When the clock's arms landed on twelve and nine, Kieran let out a long, strained sigh.

"Is making a mocha really that much of a hassle?" the customer in front of him asked, incredulous.

Kieran jumped at the sound of the voice. "What? Oh—no, I'm sorry. Just distracted. I'll have that for you at the bar in a moment."

As Kieran turned to the espresso machine, his coworker, a blond woman in her early twenties named Sylvia, shot him a sideways look.

"Hoping Ash will come in?" she guessed.

Blood rushed to Kieran's cheeks. It had been six months since Kieran started dating Ash Bartelle, an apprentice librarian at Gellingham's famed Library of Curses. Their relationship hadn't started in earnest until just after Kieran's deadly family curse broke last spring, thanks to his best friend, Delilah Bea. After a brief period of travel around the country, Kieran, along with his twin sister, Briar, and Delilah, her girlfriend, had decided to move to Gellingham. For Delilah, it had meant the opportunity to become a professional cursebreaker. For Kieran, it had meant a chance at pursuing the handsome librarian he'd fallen for on their first trip to the city.

Everything had clicked into place. The first few months of

dating Ash had been some of the most exciting of Kieran's life. The boys had explored the city together, trying all kinds of new foods and checking out the historic sites Ash had such an intense love for. The relationship had been fun, and easy, and Kieran had looked forward to seeing it grow every day.

Until the summer ended, anyway. As soon as autumn arrived, Ash's apprenticeship kicked back into full gear, taking up most of his time. At first, they'd managed to still see each other. Their meetings were brief but enjoyable. But as the city grew colder, the stretches between meetings got longer and longer until . . .

Kieran loaded a scoop of ground coffee beans into the espresso machine, cranking it until it clicked into place. "He's probably just trying to save money—you know how it is. Apprentices don't make much, and rent's expensive."

Sylvia's lips pressed into a line. "Doesn't stop all the other apprentices from stopping in every morning."

Kieran opened his mouth to shoot some comment back at her, but then Sylvia turned on the frother, which let out a loud hiss as she dipped it into the milk. That, paired with the rumble of the espresso machine, made it too loud to do anything but watch the machines work. Espresso slowly began to spit into a small white cup, and the milk began to bubble and steam, giving off a warm aroma.

When the machines finished and the noise quieted, Sylvia asked, "When did Ash last come in?"

Kieran had to hold back a wince. "Oh, well . . . Lauren said he's been coming in in the afternoons pretty frequently. He's less busy then, I think."

"In the afternoons . . . when you're not working?"

Kieran turned even redder. "Maybe we could talk about something else? The closers haven't cleaned the floors since Wednesday—"

"Kieran, come on. While you stare at the door like a war widow waiting for a soldier who'll never come home, I'm picking up the slack. I think I deserve a little honesty."

"Honesty about what?"

"Face it, Kieran: He's avoiding you, and it's messing with your head. A *lot.*"

Kieran tensed. His stomach twisted, and bile crept up his throat. "No, he's not. He's just . . . got a lot on his plate."

Sylvia cocked an eyebrow. "How long has it been since you last saw each other?"

Kieran flinched. The answer wouldn't have been so hard to wrap his head around if he hadn't been literally counting the days. Especially since one day had turned into three, then five, then a week, and then . . .

"A month," Kieran admitted, forcing himself to focus on mixing thin curls of chocolate into the espresso and milk, melting them down the moment they hit the steaming liquid. "Give or take."

"A *month*?" Sylvia repeated in horror. She shook her head. "Kieran, if someone you're in a relationship with doesn't talk to you for that long, it's not a good sign."

"So?" he shot back, tone more venomous than he'd intended. "Some couples just—you know—talk less than others. How often do you talk to Raya?"

"Every day," Sylvia replied without missing a beat.

Kieran blinked. "Seriously?"

Sylvia nodded. "Sometimes it's just a five-minute call to check in, but yeah. If they didn't talk to me for a month, I'd assume they were dead or . . ."

Kieran asked the question before the growing anxiety tightened his throat too much: "Or what?"

"Or they were breaking up with me."

Kieran recoiled as if he'd been slapped. He quickly righted himself, clearing his throat. "Well—that's just your relationship, right? It's not like that for everyone. Plus, for the record, Ash called me yesterday *and* we're getting dinner tonight, so maybe you're overthinking it."

"*I'm* overthinking it?" Sylvia repeated, trying not to laugh. She crossed her arms over her chest. "Kieran, come on. You gotta be realistic about this. A relationship where you don't communicate isn't much of a relationship at all. You deserve to feel like a priority in your partner's life."

Kieran's eyes went to the floor. "He's just . . . busy, okay? I can't blame him for that."

"We're all busy, Kieran. What matters is who we make time for."

Sylvia took the finished mocha from Kieran as he stood in silence, staring out at the door again. While she called the customer's name and set the mug on the bar, Kieran exhaled through his nose.

She doesn't know what she's talking about.

She doesn't know us.

That afternoon, Kieran returned home to the shoddy little apartment he shared with Briar and Delilah. He was tired enough that he passed out face-first on the couch and slept for nearly an hour before the sound of Delilah rifling through the kitchen cabinets stirred him from his post-work nap haze. He moaned, just faintly, and Delilah stifled a chuckle.

"Sorry to wake you," she said as she pulled down a mixing bowl from one of the higher cabinets. Now that his eyes were open, Kieran spotted tins of flour and sugar lined up neatly on the counter. Delilah continued: "I'm meeting some potential clients this evening, and I wanted to make them some enchanted biscuits as a sort of . . . preview of my magic. Might help sell them when it comes to hiring me to break their curse."

Kieran sat up, rubbing his bleary eyes with the inside of his forearm. "Oh, it's okay. I should have gone to my room."

"But it's too cold in there?" Delilah guessed, shooting him a wry smile over her shoulder as she pulled her brown curls into a ponytail.

In response to her repeating his frequent grievance, Kieran muttered, "Maybe."

Delilah laughed, then turned back to her baking. Ever since they'd moved in together, near the end of summer, she'd made an effort to fill the run-down apartment with things that made it feel more like a home and less like a refuge for wayward mice (which they had seemingly evicted, though Kieran wasn't holding his breath). Whether it was covering up the scuff marks on the hardwood floors with mismatched rugs, hanging thrifted art over cracks in the walls, buying curtains for the windows that frosted over on the inside on cold nights, or tending to the menagerie of plants she'd tucked into nearly every nook and cranny, she always had some kind of project going. In the beginning, Kieran had tried to help, but whenever he'd found decorations or furniture he liked, they were far out of his budget.

When it came down to it, he was pretty much broke. Which, for someone who grew up in one of Celdwyn's richest families, was somewhat of a jarring experience.

Just then, the front door flew open, making Kieran jump. Carrying two massive grocery bags was his twin. Briar shook red hair out of her eyes as she came in—in the last few months, she'd let it grow from a buzz cut into a choppy mop that hung around her ears. She sidestepped into the shared living room and kitchen area, dropping the grocery bags on the counter beside her girlfriend.

"They didn't have the berries you wanted, so I got chocolate chips instead," Briar explained, shrugging off her oversize black coat. Kieran noticed a dusting of snow on the sleeves, flakes sticking to the fabric and to Briar's hair and eyelashes.

"Of course your replacement for fruit is chocolate," Delilah said with a laugh. She bent down and kissed Briar on the mouth, all tenderness. The tension that had been in Briar's shoulders melted away, and she made a faint, contented sound as she wrapped her arms around Delilah. Delilah lifted Briar off the ground, setting her on the counter and deepening their kiss.

This continued for a long, painful second before Kieran interrupted: "So, did you need me to put those groceries away, or . . . ?"

The girls broke apart, Briar blushing while Delilah giggled and tucked a loose curl that had escaped her ponytail behind her ear.

"Sorry, Kier," Delilah said.

"Consider it payback for the last time I caught you and Ash on the couch." Briar snickered. She hopped off the counter and went back to the groceries, pulling things out of the brown paper bag and passing them to Delilah. "How is he, anyway? Haven't seen him around in a few weeks."

If there had been anything left of Kieran's good mood, it vanished. The last thing he wanted to talk about after Sylvia's confrontation this morning was Ash. Sure, he knew their relationship wasn't exactly . . . perfect, per se, but what relationship was?

Theirs, muttered a deeply unhelpful voice in Kieran's head as his eyes went from his sister to Delilah.

Kieran sighed through his nose. It wasn't that he wasn't happy for them—of all the people he knew, Briar and Delilah may well be the most deserving of an easy, loving partnership after what they'd been through. Both had seen themselves as doomed by their respective family curses—Briar cursed to siphon Kieran's magic away until it killed him and turned her into a monster, Delilah to never find true love. The fact that they'd found each other and broken each other's curses was something of a miracle. Plus, seeing his sister and his best friend so happy together was genuinely wonderful. It was the kind of love people wrote poetry about and used to decorate the pages of storybooks. Warm, patient, and understanding.

And despite himself, for all that he loved the two of them, it made Kieran wildly, painfully jealous.

Not that he'd ever admit it out loud. Those feelings were reserved for the poetry he penned late at night in his poorly insulated, too-cold bedroom, wrapped in layers upon layers of blankets like a fabric cocoon. He'd found it was a good way to distract himself from the sound of the girls' giggling make-out sessions, which the paper-thin walls did little to dampen.

The kind of sessions he rarely had with Ash anymore. But that, again, wasn't something he'd say out loud. Some feelings, he thought, worked better as poetry.

"Ash has been a bit, ah, busy—but we're actually meeting up for dinner tonight downtown," Kieran explained, doing his best to keep the smile on his face. "He wants to talk to me about something."

Delilah gasped. "He does? What do you think it is? Moving in together?"

"Oh—um—it's a little early for that, don't you think?"

Briar scoffed, jabbing a thumb in Delilah's direction. "Are you forgetting we rented this place after being together for, oh, a month and a half?"

"Your love broke two ancient curses within a few weeks of each other," Kieran argued. "Your timeline is a little different from that of most relationships."

Briar and Delilah exchanged a look. Delilah said, "That's . . . a fair point. Regardless, I'm sure it'll be something exciting. I'll buy us champagne to celebrate when you get home."

"Tell him we say hi," Briar agreed.

"Will do." Kieran stood up from the couch, shaking out his blond curls where they hung around his shoulders. "I'll be in my room getting ready if you need me."

With that, he left, doing his best to ignore the sinking feeling in his gut.

Later that evening, Kieran pulled his royal-blue scarf tighter around his face as he hustled down the street in the direction of the restaurant Ash had invited him to. The golden skyscrapers of Gellingham framed him on either side, creating something of a wind tunnel. The snow had gone from a light dusting to a flurry of fat flakes that stuck to Kieran's eyelashes as he hunched to avoid the wind. He was used to snow, generally speaking—the Pelumbra family's estate was located high in the Slicetooth Mountains, which meant he'd seen a lot of snow in his childhood—but that didn't mean he liked it.

The yellow glow of the streetlights guided him to a little hole-in-the-wall shop promising PIPING-HOT RAMEN and CHEAP MEAT SKEWERS, according to the wooden signs hanging outside. Kieran shouldered the door open, stepping inside along with a gust of snowy wind.

A few people crowded around small tables glanced up at him, including Ash, who sat at a table in the far back of the restaurant. He stood from his chair and waved Kieran over. Kieran shrugged off his coat as he crossed the slightly sticky floor past the chef, who was in the midst of laying out bowls of steaming ramen on the counter for the waitstaff to grab. The walls were decorated with colorful graffiti, some seemingly done professionally while other bits had clearly been drawn by patrons. The whole place smelled of grilling meat and spices, and it made Kieran's mouth water.

Ash offered Kieran a shaky smile as he came to the table and draped his peacoat over the back of his chair. Ash Bartelle was nineteen, a slim boy with warm brown skin and eyes like wildflower honey. His tight curls had been shaved short since the last time they'd seen each other, exposing his high cheekbones. He'd elected to wear his glasses that evening and was still dressed in his classic witch's robes from his job at the Library of Curses.

"I was worried you got lost in the storm," Ash said, squeezing Kieran's arm. Kieran instinctively began to lean in to give him a peck on the cheek, but Ash pulled away at the last moment, playing it off by adding, "I was about to send a search party."

Kieran's throat tightened. *It's probably nothing. He just wants a little more space today, I'm sure. Or he's worried he smells bad or something—I'm overthinking it.*

Kieran unwound his scarf from his neck while he shrugged. "I'm still getting the hang of navigating around here. But the snow didn't help, in my defense."

Ash laughed at that, but as Kieran sat down, he couldn't help but notice how Ash's smile didn't reach his eyes. Kieran's grin drooped. When Ash had mentioned meeting up to chat about something important, Kieran had done his best not to overthink. Which, of course, had led to a night of tossing and turning in bed and having to put his head between his knees to keep from hyperventilating. Suddenly, that anxious energy that had stuck to his ribs the night before solidified into a noticeable weight in his chest.

A few minutes later, a waiter stopped by and took their order, barely giving Kieran time to pick a random item off the menu. Once he'd left, Ash ran a hand back over his buzzed hair, as if trying to steady himself. "So, um," he began, "it's been a little while since I saw you last. Anything . . . exciting going on?" Kieran stared down into the tiny clay cup of jasmine tea that Ash had poured for him, watching a few loose leaves float around inside. "She's been working on creating a version of ledrith for defensive magic instead of offensive, and the Council was really impressed. She passed, obviously. Not that anyone's surprised."

"That's— Wow. Really incredible." Ash blinked, seemingly a little taken aback. "It's not often you hear about witches creating entirely new forms of spellcasting, especially when it comes to something like combat dance."

Kieran shrugged, forcing a smile. "Well, you know my sister. She's, ah . . . better at magic than most."

Better than me, certainly, he stopped himself from saying.

"And what about *your* Calling?" Ash asked. "Have you decided what you're doing?"

Kieran tensed. Ash had been asking about that since Kieran moved to Gellingham. Because both Kieran's and Briar's existence had been a secret up until recently, the Witches' Council had granted them an extension on their Callings, the magical test they needed to pass to legally wield magic in Celdwyn. Naturally, Briar's Calling only took a week to complete instead of the usual six months, as she'd planned it out for months beforehand. Since then, she'd been planning to join a ledrith gym in hopes of teaching her techniques to other witches.

Which was all fine and good, of course. But it didn't make Kieran feel any better about the fact that his extension was about to run out and he still had no idea how to prove that he was worthy of being a witch.

Kieran rubbed the back of his neck sheepishly. "Uh. Well— you know my poetry? I—I was thinking maybe I could write a book of poems and they'd all be different spells. So people could pick a different poem and get a little enchantment for whatever they need that day."

"Oh!" Ash smiled, but his mouth seemed a bit lopsided and there was a wrinkle in his forehead. "That sounds . . . nice."

Kieran nearly winced. He'd shown Ash a few of his poems in the past, and the reception had been . . . tepid. There'd been a lot of polite nodding and suggestions for other poets to check out to help "hone the craft" in a way that was, perhaps, a bit less "melodramatic"—all Ash's words, of course. Kieran didn't know what he was talking about. His writing was *raw.* It was *evocative.* He'd just figured Ash's taste was different from his.

Kieran crossed his arms and sank a little lower in his seat. "I'm still brainstorming."

Thankfully, after a few more minutes of small talk, the waiter returned with their orders. With his bowl of miso pork ramen in front of him, Kieran was able to at least refocus on that instead of Ash's forced smiles and overly sunny questioning.

Something was off. It had been off for a while, Kieran knew, but this was the most pronounced it had ever been.

Maybe he's just nervous about what he wants to talk about, Kieran thought. *It could be something positive.*

As Kieran neared the end of his ramen, Ash broke the silence. "I forgot to ask—how's everything in the apartment?"

Kieran deflated. If Ash kept stalling, Kieran would have to lie down and stare at a wall for a few hours.

"Great," Kieran said, voice coming out a bit more cutting than he intended. His fingers tightened around his chopsticks, and he averted his eyes. "It's great. I get to spend my days watching my sister and my best friend be madly in love with each other while you and I haven't so much as talked in a *month.* Nothing makes a house a home like burning jealousy, right?"

Ash's fake smile finally faltered. Kieran hadn't realized how red his own face had become, and how his heart sped up as he ranted. He tried to even out his breathing and avert his eyes while Ash studied his expression. The other boy let out a sigh.

"Look," Ash said, nervously fiddling with his napkin in his lap. "Kieran, this is . . . part of the reason I wanted to talk."

Kieran's stomach dropped. *Shit, shit, shit.*

"Sometimes it feels like all we talk about is Briar and Delilah," Ash explained, his voice weak. Kieran's eyebrows shot up as Ash added, "Because you can't stop comparing our relationship to theirs. Hell, you can't stop comparing *yourself* to them—to everyone, really."

Kieran blinked. He didn't know how to respond. If he was being honest with himself, he did, perhaps, have a tendency to compare himself to others, but that wasn't his fault. The Pelumbras always held themselves to high standards. A Pelumbra was supposed to be the smartest, most attractive, and most powerful witch in any given room. To be anything less than that reflected weakness. And because of his former curse, he'd spent far too much of his life being seen as weak.

"So . . . what?" he finally replied. "You want me to not talk about them so much?"

"No, Kieran, I—"

"Because—listen—I can work on it—but sometimes it's hard when—"

Ash blurted, "I think we need to take a break, Kieran."

The entire world screeched to a halt. For a beat, Kieran just stared at him. Ash refused to look at him, instead staring into his empty ramen bowl as if he might discover in it a portal out of the restaurant.

Kieran's ears rang, and his entire body went numb. Throat dry, he croaked, "A *break*?"

"That's why I wanted to meet up," Ash said after another pause, doing his best to look anywhere but into Kieran's eyes. "I think we both need to reevaluate this relationship. Just . . . take a step back and really think about what we want. Because if you're stuck on being the same as Briar and Delilah, this is never going to work. I can't be what you want."

"Wait, hold on, I never said I wanted—"

"I'll need a few weeks before we talk it over." Ash set his napkin on the table and stood up. "Until then, let's not make this harder than it needs to be. I should get going."

"Ash, wait! Can't we just—?"

"Goodbye, Kieran."

The other boy shrugged on his coat, and all Kieran could do was watch him leave the restaurant and disappear into the snow.

Kieran remained at the table for so long, staring blankly into space, that eventually an employee came over to ask if he was okay. After muttering something about being fine, he stood. His knees felt like jelly, barely able to support him. Numb, he pulled on his coat and wound his scarf around his face.

This has to be a nightmare, he thought as he headed to the door, pushing through to outside. A gale of snowy wind immediately hit him, and he winced. *A really cold nightmare.*

A thick layer of snow had covered the street in the last hour. The sidewalks were empty, the only sound on the wind the distant ding of the trolley bell. It was eerie to see downtown so empty, and a shiver—half from cold and half from trepidation—ran down Kieran's spine. He hunched, arms crossed to try to keep the heat in. Snowflakes hit his exposed nose and stung the bare skin until it turned red. Each step felt like a battle. It didn't help that Kieran had gone out in a pair of leather loafers, which were now soaked through and almost certainly ruined.

However, none of that could pierce the words playing on repeat in Kieran's mind: *Let's not make this harder than it needs to be.*

Kieran winced. Ash hadn't even given him a chance to explain himself. How long had he been considering this? Weeks? Months? They hadn't been speaking for a while, but still. Kieran had truly thought it was just because Ash was busy, not because he needed to reevaluate their relationship.

The back of Kieran's throat tightened. Tears welled in his eyes.

I'm a fool, he thought, sniffling. He wiped his nose, and his sleeve came away damp. *A stupid, self-centered fool. Maybe I don't deserve Ash.*

Maybe I don't deserve anyone.

A sob caught in Kieran's throat as he rounded the corner, just a few feet from home now. He was almost glad everyone else in Gellingham had decided to spend the night inside so no one could see what a mess he was. Despite himself, he couldn't help but imagine Briar's and Delilah's faces when he told them. Delilah would give him a tight hug while Briar berated Ash for dragging out the inevitable. And then, when night fell, he'd have to listen to them through the paper-thin walls of their apartment whispering about how sorry they felt for him.

Tears wet his cheeks, immediately going cold. *I really am pathetic, aren't I?*

He was so wrapped up in his misery that he failed to notice the soft crunch of footsteps approaching him from behind.

Something heavy slammed into the back of his head.

A flash of pain shot through Kieran's skull as starbursts exploded across his vision. He let out a strangled scream and staggered, barely catching himself before he slipped and fell into the snow. He spun around. Standing a step behind him was a massive, shadowy figure, his eyes the only part of his face exposed.

And in his hand was a glinting silver knife.

"Your wallet," the figure demanded, flipping the knife around so it hung poised in the air, aimed at Kieran's throat. "Now."

At some point in his life, Kieran had heard the phrase *fight or flight* to describe one's reactions in a moment like this. He'd never had to give much thought to which he'd do, seeing as he'd spent nearly his entire life safely tucked away at his family's estate. Dangerous situations tended to be something he avoided. First, because he had the same body type as most telephone poles, and second, because he was an awful witch.

So awful, in fact, he couldn't even think of a single spell he could cast to defend himself. He found himself unable to fight and much too terrified to flee, which left him one option:

Freeze.

"Did you hear me? Turn out your pockets!" the figure bellowed, his face so close Kieran could smell the liquor on his breath.

"Okay, okay!" Kieran reached into his coat pockets and turned them inside out, revealing them to be empty. Little did the attacker know that Kieran didn't own a wallet. Buying one was on his to-do list, along with learning how to use defensive magic and limiting his crying sessions to his bedroom. "L-look, I make coffee for a living. You should really find someone else to steal from."

"Bullshit—you're dressed like all those fuckers knocking back whiskey highballs downtown," the figure snarled. "If I have to ask again, this knife is going into your throat."

Kieran's eyes darted to the knife. He saw a slice of his own reflection staring back at him, pulse jumping in his throat. His brown eyes were bloodshot from crying, tears and snot streaming down his face. His mind scrambled for what to do. He had a few extra bills in his back pocket, but considering that his attacker thought he was rich, giving him the cash equivalent of a day-old pastry probably wasn't going to satisfy him. He could scream for help, but that would likely earn him a stab wound. Briar had tried to teach him a little ledrith, but the first time he tried to throw a punch at a weighted bag, he bruised his knuckles so bad he hadn't tried since.

Or, a quiet voice in his head whispered, *you could just let him stab you. At least then you wouldn't have to deal with all this anymore.*

Then again, that's a bit dramatic, the more logical half of his brain argued. *After everything that's happened this year, I deserve to at least die in a way that's a bit more dignified than bleeding out in the street. Preferably, old age. Or at least doing something interesting, like walking a tightrope between skyscrapers or whatever.*

Kieran reached into his back pocket, pulling out the few bills he had and held them out. "Th-they're yours. I don't have anything else—I swear."

The attacker snatched the money from Kieran's hand. He examined it with narrowed eyes, which darted back to Kieran's after a second. "I don't take kindly to insults, kid."

The knife rose. Air caught in Kieran's throat.

Well, he thought, screwing his eyes shut as he braced for pain, *worth a try.*

He waited. One breath, then two. Then three. After four, Kieran thought, *If you're going to stab me, at least have the decency to be quick about it.*

There was the sound of a wet *smack,* then a choking gasp quickly followed by a heavy *thunk.*

"Kieran! Move!"

Kieran cracked a single eye, only to discover his attacker's body sprawled on the ground in front of him. The attacker's eyes darted around wildly while the rest of his body slowly became more and more encased in a layer of ice, all stemming from a snowball thrown at his back. Behind him stood Briar and Delilah, Briar with another snowball in her hand and Delilah's eyes glowing bright green with magic.

Kieran didn't need further prompting. He moved to run toward them, but after a second's hesitation, he reached down and plucked his money from his attacker's icy hand. Then he sprinted for Delilah and his sister.

"Go inside," Briar instructed Delilah and Kieran. "Call the

police. I'll keep an eye on him until they get here in case that spell wears off."

Delilah put a protective hand on Kieran's arm and nodded to Briar. She ushered him toward the apartment, and Kieran followed, keeping his head down. His heartbeat rattled in his ears.

"We heard you scream and came as fast as we could," Delilah said as they ducked into the front entryway for their apartment. "That asshole messed with the wrong witches."

Kieran nodded numbly, mind whirring as Delilah locked the door behind them and they started for the stairs. He paused, glancing over his shoulder again just to make sure no one had slipped in after them. The staircase was empty. He was safe.

And once again, he had Briar and Delilah to thank for that. Just like all the other times he'd been too weak—and useless—and pitiful—to take care of himself.

Kieran swallowed the lump in his throat before running after Delilah toward their apartment.

CHAPTER TWO

That night, long after the mugger was taken into custody, Kieran sat at his bedroom window watching as snow covered up the tracks on the sidewalk. Delilah had fawned over him for hours, stress baking until Kieran had had to politely inform her that fifty mini cupcakes were plenty when it came to eating his feelings. Briar, meanwhile, had paced the living room, muttering about how they should probably move to a safer neighborhood once she had a steady job. The whole time, Kieran had sat under a pile of blankets, staring at a wall despondently.

The only positive thing about the whole evening was that the girls were so caught up in the attack that they completely forgot to ask about Kieran's date.

He let out a sigh, turning away from the window. He'd tell them in the morning. Luckily, he had the day off tomorrow, so at least he didn't have to worry about putting on a fake smile at work while he took coffee orders.

Kieran stood. His room was still bare six months after he'd moved in. He'd gotten the smaller of the apartment's two bedrooms, but it still had enough space for a bed, a desk, and a little reading nook in the corner by the window. His bed was a tangle of sheets and pillows, while his desk was covered in stacks of books and old cups of coffee. He shoved them out of the way as he sat in the creaky old wooden chair he'd snagged off the curb when they first moved in.

He knew he wouldn't be able to sleep, so he might as well get something done in the meantime. Hopefully, something that would help him get his mind off the fact that this might well have been in the top ten of worst nights of his life thus far.

It's just a break, Kieran reminded himself. *He could change his mind and take me back.*

The mere thought felt hollow.

Kieran sighed, then reached to where his coat hung over one of the bedposts and withdrew a small leather-bound journal from a pocket. It was his book of poems. He'd only started writing a few months ago when Delilah had asked him which form he wanted his magic to take. Up until then, he'd always envisioned himself doing something elegant and sophisticated, but he'd never actually picked anything. After a few miserable days trying to learn how to play the violin, and a few more smearing watercolors in a sketchbook with the skill of a drunk toddler, he'd elected to go with poetry. After all, being a tortured poet felt right: He could get his feelings out and cast spells all in one fell swoop.

Granted, he hadn't quite gotten the whole *spellcasting* part down yet—each time he'd tried to weave magic into the words, he'd been unable to focus enough to summon magic and write at the same time. He figured it would come in time as he honed his craft. Writing first, magic second.

Kieran cracked open the journal to the next clean page. It stared back at him as he took a pen from a jar at his side and chewed absently on the end. He decided to start with just writing down each snippet of thought that had been on repeat in his mind all evening. Everything Ash had said at the restaurant, the fear Kieran had felt when the attacker had pointed the knife at him, and ultimately the self-loathing that bubbled up from both.

Kieran Pelumbra: world's worst witch and even worse boyfriend.

Tears welled. Kieran felt a strange sensation in his chest, almost like the twinge of something alive between his ribs. He tapped his pen against the page, staring at the words before him.

He flipped to a new page and began to write.

As soon as the lines were on the page, the sensation in his chest became stronger, engulfing him in warmth. It was strange but pleasant. The more Kieran wrote, the better he felt. He'd kept everything bottled up for so long that letting himself finally *feel* was more freeing than he'd anticipated. While he'd written plenty of poems, something about this one was different. This one felt . . . *alive.*

He worked at it, picking out the knots in the words, for hours. For the first time since he moved in, his bedroom didn't feel frigid. The air had an almost palpable electricity and warmth to it. Kieran's hand moved quickly, slashing through words and rewriting new ones in their place. It was raw, and painful, but freeing.

This is how art is supposed to feel, he thought.

As the sky outside began to turn pink with the sunrise, Kieran sat back in his chair, staring down at the page before him. He finished it with a title, nodding to himself.

Better Off, he'd written, *by Kieran Pelumbra.*

You met me downtown on a snowy night,
But a blizzard could never be as icy cold
As what you said to me:
"I can't be what you want."
But how can you know
What my shattered heart yearns for?
Have you considered that what I want
Is a life where I deserve you?
Instead of this one, where I'm nothing
But a whisper on the frigid winter wind—
Imperceptible, barely a memory—
To you, the only man I've ever loved.
Maybe in a different time, sooner than later,
When I'm worthy of your tender heart,
When I'm confident, sure, and skilled,
You can see me again
And I'll be something better than the boy
You left downtown on a snowy night.

He liked it. There was still work to be done to polish it, but it felt good to express his feelings honestly. It helped that the weight that had been hanging heavy inside him seemed to have dissipated as he worked, and for the first time in hours, his shoulders relaxed. Kieran stood, closed the book, and took a deep breath.

I'll talk to Ash when I wake up, he silently promised as he crawled into bed. *And apologize for everything. Maybe I can convince him that I can change and stop comparing myself to others so much.*

And maybe then he'll decide we don't need a break.

The moment he shut his eyes, Kieran fell into a heavy, dreamless sleep.

The next day, after scraping together a few hours of sleep, Kieran woke up with a new sense of purpose. Sure, Ash seemed set on leaving him for being an insecure ass, and yes, he'd had to depend on his sister and her girlfriend to defend him from a mugger, but that was yesterday. New dawn, new day, and all that. He could fix this.

Kieran caught the trolley near their apartment and took it across town to the Gellingham Library, better known as the Library of Curses for its sweeping collection of cursed scrolls, tomes, and slates. Cursewriting had long been illegal in Celdwyn—with magic removal being the typical punishment for witches who defied the Council—but the library was still one of the most bustling hubs for witches in the world. Ash's apprenticeship there was a testament to how good he was at what he did.

The only downside was that witches who had yet to pass their Calling weren't allowed inside. Which meant that for half an hour, Kieran stood outside the front entrance, shivering in the snow, waiting for Ash's shift to end. The entire time, he rehearsed what he was going to say: *I'm so sorry for making you feel like you weren't enough for me. I swear I'll be better. Just give me a chance.*

When Ash finally appeared, Kieran's heart leapt. The other boy had shadows under his eyes, and Kieran wondered if maybe he'd had trouble sleeping last night too. *Maybe he was having second thoughts about the break.*

"Ash!" Kieran called, waving a hand in the air. "Wait up!"

Ash, however, didn't turn. He was heading toward the trolley, seeming not to have heard Kieran's shout. Kieran cursed under his breath, then jogged to catch up with him, careful not to step wrong on the cobblestones and twist his ankle.

"Ash!" he tried again. The other boy didn't so much as look up at the sound of his voice, staring ahead. Kieran felt a stab of hurt—he knew they hadn't exactly ended on the best of terms last night, but Ash's flat-out ignoring him seemed a little juvenile. "Hey!"

Kieran was right next to him now, but despite his saying Ash's name a few more times and waving a hand at him, Ash didn't respond. Kieran's forehead wrinkled. *Is he really that mad at me?*

"Ash, come on," Kieran said, walking beside him. They had reached the crosswalk, and Ash checked both ways before heading forward. As he turned his head to the right, he looked Kieran directly in the face.

Still, he didn't react. He simply stepped into the crosswalk, unfazed.

"Ash, seriously!" Kieran reached out and grabbed his shoulder. "Can we just talk—"

"Ah!" Ash yelped at Kieran's touch. He flipped around, pressing a hand to the spot where Kieran had touched him. His eyes darted back and forth, passing over Kieran more than once. He muttered under his breath, "What was that?"

Kieran blinked. *Huh?*

In lieu of a better idea, Kieran reached out and poked him. "Hello?"

Ash jumped again, eyes widening. He said, "Okay, this isn't funny. Whoever that was, show yourself. I'm not sure how you managed an invisibility spell, but you got me."

Invisibility spell? Kieran hadn't cast anything of the sort. At least, not on purpose. And it wasn't as if other people hadn't seen him today—Delilah had said goodbye to him when he left the apartment, and the ticket taker on the trolley had given him a dirty look as he'd dug through his pockets trying to find his trolley pass for a few moments too long. He hadn't successfully managed to cast a spell that did more than a create a few sparks, well . . . ever. The closest he'd ever gotten was when he was writing—

His stomach dropped.

Poetry.

"No," Kieran muttered under his breath. He reached into his coat pocket, pulling out his poetry notebook. Last night *had* felt different. The way the words had flowed, the way he'd tapped into a well of emotion in his chest and it had been so cathartic. Could that have been . . . ?

He flipped through the pages desperately, his hands starting to shake. He found the page he'd written last night, eyes darting over the words as dread clamped its teeth around his heart. He willed the words not to be there as he remembered them. *There's no way,* he thought. *I'm not* that *inept at magic that I'd . . .*

The thought halted as he read the second stanza.

Imperceptible, barely a memory—/ To you, the only man I've ever loved.

Kieran's heart plummeted. He hadn't written a poem last night.

He'd written a curse.

After hopping off the trolley from downtown, Kieran sprinted the entire way back to the apartment.

Delilah's a cursebreaker—she'll know what to do, he reminded himself, narrowly avoiding an icy patch on the sidewalk as he rounded the corner to their apartment. He tried not to think about last night as he passed the spot where he'd been attacked—yet another reminder of the fact that he was an absolutely horrid excuse for a witch.

And, apparently, an unintentional cursewriter. The thought cut like a spike directly through his ribs.

He ran even faster.

When he reached the front entrance to the building, he took the stairs two at a time. As their door came into view, he didn't pause to notice the neat line of shoes outside. He hopped around as he pulled off his boots, throwing them down before he shoved his way inside.

"Delilah!" he cried as he burst into the living area, nearly slipping as his socks slid on the hardwood. He caught himself and added, "I fucked up *so bad*—"

He closed his mouth, though, as three strangers turned to face him.

They were all sitting at the table in the dining room, steaming mugs of tea in front of them. There were two men and a woman, and all three appeared to be around his parents' age. Kieran immediately recognized the golden sun-and-moon clasps that held each of their cloaks in place around their necks.

His voice died in his throat.

Why are three members of the Witches' Council in my house?

Delilah and Briar sat side by side across the table from them, Delilah with her hand on Briar's thigh under the table. At the sight of Kieran, Delilah perked up. Considering the sheer number of baked goods laid out on the table, she had clearly panicked.

"Oh, good, you're home," Delilah said. She forced a smile and gestured to the people seated at the table. "We have guests."

"They wanna talk to you about your Calling," Briar said, cutting to the chase.

"Right now?" Kieran blurted out before he could stop himself. He glanced at the older witches. "N-now isn't a great time."

"We'll be quick," the woman said. She stood, revealing a purple cloak with silver-threaded star details across it. She had brown hair streaked with gray, and a pair of round glasses on her nose. Her skin was papery pale—so much so that Kieran could see the veins in her wrists as she gestured at the other two witches. "It's nice to meet you, Kieran. My name is Tilda, and these are my associates, Franklin and Gerard. We've come to officially give you your Calling."

"Apparently in big cities there isn't a whole Calling ceremony as there is in my hometown," Delilah explained with a shrug. "They just need two witnesses."

"B-but I thought I still had time on my extension!" Kieran said. "You said that we had six months before . . ."

He trailed off, the math suddenly clicking in his head. Six months.

Exactly how long it had been since he and Briar had received their extension.

". . . Oh," he concluded. "Right. Never mind."

Tilda nodded. "Anyway, I'm sure you're aware of how this all works. Despite your extension, this will function like any other Calling appointment. We members of the Witches' Council are here to ask you if you'd like to be assigned a task by the Council or if you'd like to pose your own. Obviously, your case is unique in the sense that your circumstances prevented a traditional Calling up until this point, but today we'd like to change that."

"So, Kieran Pelumbra," one of the men said, his voice pinching a bit on the name *Pelumbra.* Kieran couldn't exactly blame him, considering the family's recent fall from grace in the magical community. "Do you have your own task? Or would you like one assigned?"

Kieran was reeling. What was he supposed to do? His first thought, naturally, was to propose breaking Ash's curse. But if he mentioned that, how would he keep it a secret that *he* was the one who placed it on him? They'd take away his magic in a heartbeat if they knew—so that option was out. But then again, if he did anything else, how would he have time to figure out how to break the curse on top of his Calling?

Unless . . .

Unless there was a way to end the curse without breaking it in the traditional sense.

Before he could give it more than ten seconds' thought, Kieran met Tilda's eyes and announced:

"I propose my own Calling task," he said, trying and failing to keep the edge of desperation out of his voice.

"I want to create a panacea."

CHAPTER THREE

Everyone in the room stared at Kieran as if he'd grown a second head.

Instantly, his mouth went dry and his stomach twisted. But the words were said, and he certainly couldn't back out now—even if his brain was begging him to make a running leap for the window just to escape, broken bones and glass cuts be damned.

Tilda tapped a finger on her chin, studying Kieran. For a second, Kieran expected the witches to tell him his proposal was simply too far-fetched.

It probably was. Panaceas were generally thought of as fictional. Kieran had only ever heard of a single true one—water from a hot spring run by the Hammonds, Delilah's family on her paternal side—and its source had long since dried up. The idea of even the most experienced witch finding a way to create a magical cure-all was borderline impossible.

Much less an amateur like Kieran, who could barely spark enough magic to light a candle.

Meanwhile, Delilah and Briar shared mirrored expressions of horror. Delilah mouthed, *What are you doing?* while Briar seemed lost in her own mind, skin having gone pale as she stared blankly ahead. A spear of guilt went through Kieran's heart—as a child, Briar had unwillingly been the test subject of a number of fake panaceas at the hands of their aunt Wrenlin, and Kieran knew how uncomfortable the concept of them made her.

After a long, pregnant pause, Tilda nodded.

"Tilda," one of the male witches—the one called Gerard—said, his eyes rounding, "we can't in good conscience—"

"Why not?" Tilda asked. She gestured to Kieran with a graceful wave of her hand. "This is a son of the great Pelumbra family. The *head* of the family, no less. It seems like an apt task to me."

It occurred to Kieran as Tilda spat out his family name that he was dealing with a slightly more complex situation than he'd anticipated. This woman *definitely* hated his family. Which wasn't an uncommon sentiment—the Pelumbras had been one of the most powerful and influential families in Celdwyn before their downfall six months ago, when the blessing that had given the family supernatural luck broke along with the twins' curse. Before that, the Pelumbras had gotten away with nearly every con and scheme they could dream of, which had made them a lot of enemies. Only now were they facing any consequences for their actions as money drained from their accounts and the court of public opinion turned sharply against them.

Gerard seemed to hesitate, but based on his defeated expression, Kieran got the sense that Tilda was the one in charge. After a moment, the witch sat back in his chair, nodding.

"I agree," he said. He turned to the other man, who was much shorter and had a substantially smaller frame. "Franklin?"

Franklin chewed on his lower lip. He shot Kieran a pitying look as he sighed. Despite that, though, he said, "I do as well."

"It's decided, then," said Tilda as she met Kieran's gaze again. "Kieran Pelumbra, your Calling task is to create a panacea, which we will test for authenticity upon delivery. If you are unable to complete this task in six months, your magic will be taken away. Do you understand?"

Well, Kieran thought, swallowing the lump of dread in his throat, *I guess I won't have to worry about any more accidental curse-casting, since I'm about to kiss my magic goodbye.*

"Y-yes," he stammered, ignoring the way Delilah's jaw dropped and Briar looked about ready to throw something at him. "I understand."

"Then it's settled. Consider this the first day of your Calling." Tilda bowed her head and gestured for her fellow witches to follow her. "We'll take our leave."

The men stood, following Tilda to the door. Franklin cast a look over his shoulder, gently shaking his head. While the others walked out, he said, "Best of luck, Mr. Pelumbra."

He shut the door behind them.

The second the witches left, Briar wheeled on Kieran, her face turning red. "What were you *thinking*?!"

Kieran rubbed the back of his neck sheepishly. "Well . . . if I'm being honest, I . . . kind of . . . wasn't?"

"*Clearly!* Kieran, you're going to lose your magic!"

"And?" Kieran said, voice cracking on the word as tears pricked. Something about his sister's tone made his throat feel like it was closing up. "I can barely use magic as it is! Whenever I try to cast a spell, nothing happens, and when I cast unintentionally, I mess up *horrifically.* You know what happened last night? I accidentally cursed Ash! If anyone deserves to lose his magic, it's me!"

Delilah, who had been about to interrupt, went stock-still. She blinked, mouth hanging open. At her side, Briar looked as if she was on the verge of incredulous laughter.

Briar shook her head. "You *accidentally* cursed Ash? *How?*"

Kieran tilted his head back and moaned. After a beat, he launched into a full rundown of the last twenty-four hours: Ash asking to take a break, then the attack, and how he'd felt so pitiful and useless that he thought poetry would help him cope. How he'd misconstrued the act of channeling magic into his words as the thrill of artistic expression and cursed his probably-soon-to-be-ex boyfriend into being unable to perceive him.

"And now," Kieran finished, voice choked with tears, "I just have to wait six months, fail my Calling, and accept that I was never meant to be a witch in the first place."

"Do you not even want your magic?" Briar asked in horror.

"Of course I do," Kieran admitted, shoulders falling. "But . . . maybe my losing it isn't the worst thing in the world."

"Well—let's not get ahead of ourselves," Delilah quickly said before Kieran could break down in tears. She stood up and pulled him into a hug, which Kieran accepted with a sniffle. As she patted his back, she said, "You know, Klaus has been working for months on making a panacea using the magic vein in the Pinwhistle Forest. Maybe I could call him and see if he'd be willing to talk you through his progress."

Kieran pulled away from the hug, ears pricking at the mention of Delilah's famous cursebreaker father, Klaus Hammond. Kieran had been positively starstruck the first time they'd met. During his childhood, he had seen Klaus in newspapers and heard his voice over the radio talking about all the complex, powerful curses he'd managed to break. He was known for helping everyone with their curses, from Celdwyn's common folk to other nations' royalty. He was charismatic, handsome, and extremely skilled.

And also, something of a fraud, seeing as all his cursebreaking prowess had been fabricated. Klaus had spent decades using a panacea to break those curses, making his clients swear never to speak of how he helped them. Recently, though, his panacea had run out. Hence, his journey to the woods outside Gellingham to look for a new one.

Kieran asked, "You think he'd help me?"

"Generally speaking? No, he's way too selfish for that. But if I ask him to?" Delilah shrugged. "He's been pretty desperate to win me over ever since he realized that he's been a terrible father. So if I frame it as a favor for me, he'll almost definitely say yes."

Kieran let out a sigh, his shoulders relaxing. "That would be a massive help. Thank you."

"Anytime. I do, of course, apologize in advance for the fact that you'll have to deal with my father, but what can you do."

"I'm sure it'll be fine. I just appreciate the help," Kieran said. He pivoted to his sister, who sat at the table worrying at a hangnail. "And, Briar, I . . . I know that panaceas are kind of a touchy subject—"

Briar held up a hand to stop him. "Just promise me something, okay?"

Kieran closed his mouth. He nodded, eyebrows raised in question.

"Don't . . . don't try to use anything on Ash unless you're *positive* it's an actual, functioning panacea, okay?" Briar wrapped her arms around herself, absentmindedly touching a raised pink scar on her arm. "Promise me that."

"I promise," Kieran said without hesitation. "I would never do what our aunt did to you, Briar. I swear. I'd give my magic any day before I hurt someone else on purpose."

"Good. Then I'll help you however I can." Briar cracked her knuckles. "Happy to punch anyone who looks at you funny."

"Me too," Delilah agreed—though she quickly added, "About the helping part. I try not to punch people unless absolutely necessary."

Briar snorted a laugh. "Don't want to break your thumb again?"

"I thought we agreed not to bring that up," Delilah shot back.

"Thank you," Kieran cut in before the two of them could go off on one of their usual flirting-by-mocking tangents. "Really. I can't express how grateful I am to have both of you in my corner."

"You're certainly stuck with us," Briar replied.

"I'll call up Klaus now and see if I can set something up." Delilah squeezed Kieran's arm. "It'll be all right, okay? We'll figure this out—just as we did before with your curse."

At that, Kieran felt the closest thing to relief he'd experienced in days.

The next day, Kieran found himself staring up at the trailhead at the lowest point of the Pinwhistle Forest, outside of Gellingham.

The once-verdant trees had turned spindly with the onset of winter, and the forest was covered in a blanket of fresh snow that glittered in the sunlight. Squirrels and chipmunks sprang between tree branches, knocking off little puffs of snow. Red cardinals darted through the air, chasing each other between long, dripping icicles hanging off the trees. Rabbit and deer tracks dotted the snow, along with boot prints from hikers. The sky was a cloudless blue.

The only *not*-beautiful thing was the trail, which, while mostly clear of snow, was composed entirely of mud and ice.

"Well." Kieran exhaled, holding fast to the walking stick he'd brought. It had been a gift from Ash, who was a much stronger hiker than he was. "This'll be fun."

It was, indeed, not fun.

It took Kieran nearly two hours to reach the rendezvous point Klaus had told Delilah about over the phone. In that time, he'd fallen twice. Both times he'd managed to divert into the snow, so while he'd avoided becoming completely mud-crusted, his pants and coat were damp. If the last few days had taught him anything, it was that maybe, just maybe, he should consider moving to a more tropical locale.

Luckily, he soon came upon a tall, imposing man with familiar dark curls graying at the temples and a salt-and-pepper beard. He was dressed in outdoor gear that was clearly worn from use, and his hair was longer than it had been a few months ago. The rugged mountain-man look suited him.

"There's the little Pelumbra princeling," Klaus announced as Kieran came to his side, trying not to pant too loudly from the exertion. That he'd somehow done this hike six months ago when he was cursed and dying was beyond him.

"Don't worry," Klaus added, "you haven't kept me waiting too long."

Kieran hadn't been worried about that in the slightest, but whatever Klaus needed to think to stay happy was fine with him. "Good to see you, Klaus. Delilah says hi and hopes you're doing well."

"Did she say that?" His brown eyes lit up a bit. "How kind of her. You'll have to let her know I echo the sentiment."

"Of course." Kieran smiled. Delilah hadn't actually said that, but Kieran knew how to play to rich men's egos. He'd watched his parents do it nonstop for nearly seventeen years. While luck had been a big part of the Pelumbra fortune and reputation, their charisma hadn't hurt either.

"Well, no reason to wait around here." Klaus used his walking stick to point off into the woods. "Come with me and I'll explain everything on the way to the vein."

Kieran nodded and followed the older man, doing his best to listen as he launched into an overly detailed description of his last six months of work. A solid amount of the lecture involved how he'd made himself comfortable and at home in the woods, which mostly amounted to the fact that he'd paid to have a cabin built near the vein. Kieran did the usual wow-how-great-that's-wonderful spiel while only half listening—at least until he moved on to the actual important part: the magic vein itself and its potential ability to create a panacea.

"While I know where it is, *getting to* the magic is much more of a challenge," Klaus explained. "It's hidden underground, and anytime I get too close, the vein reacts by sending strange creatures after me. And while I'm quite adept at combat magic—obviously—I'm only one man versus a sentient magic vein and its myriad unpleasant creatures."

Kieran glanced up—he'd been doing his best to watch his feet so he didn't get caught in any roots or snowdrifts. "You think it's *sentient*?"

"Very much so. There are mushrooms around it, and if you inhale their spores, you start hearing odd whispers. I've taken to inhaling them on purpose, and I've started to get much clearer communications. Mainly being told to stay away, but it's a good start."

Kieran blinked. *What is the likelihood that Klaus is high on mushroom spores all the time rather than the vein actually being sentient? To be determined.*

"The other issue," Klaus continued, not stopping to read the horror written all over Kieran's face, "is that I'm not the only one out here trying to convince the vein to let me near it."

That caught Kieran's attention. "Oh?"

"There's a man named Elias Barclay who found out about it and has been nearly as tireless as me in trying to extract the magic," Klaus grumbled. Kieran noticed a twitch in his jaw. "He's the CEO of a company in the city—made a fortune off new and inventive magical cures for various illnesses. I suspect he thinks that if he can gain access to the panacea, he can add it to his list of products and double his profits."

"It sounds like you don't care for him much."

"Not at all," Klaus said, eyes narrowed. "On top of trying to steal the glory of my magical discovery, he's also incredibly self-centered. Seems to enjoy the sound of his own voice over anything else."

Kieran elected to ignore the irony of that statement. "Has he made any progress?"

"No more than I have. The only real move he's made recently is hiring an assistant. Some kid from Shui City—I don't even know his name. Seems to be more of a glorified bodyguard, if you ask me."

As Klaus maneuvered over a fallen log, Kieran paused for a moment, boots crunching to a halt in the snow. "Humor me: You didn't bring me along just to try to level the playing field with Elias now that he has an assistant, did you?"

"Of course not!" Klaus said, not looking back to see whether Kieran made it over the log or not. He simply pushed ahead, nearly snapping a tree branch into Kieran's face by accident. "That's absurd. I couldn't care less about what *Elias Barclay* does."

Kieran had to stop himself from laughing. *Sure, Klaus.*

"Well, enough about that—we're almost there." Klaus waved a hand ahead. "Brace yourself, Karen. This is powerful magic."

"It's actually pronounced *Kieran*—"

"Right, just as I said. Now, come along—we've business to attend to."

Kieran hadn't exactly known what to expect when they reached the vein, but it wasn't the lush, summery tableau they came upon in the middle of the snowy forest.

Giant pinkish mushrooms stood tall at what must be triple Kieran's height, colorful bunches of smaller mushrooms collected at their base. Strange midnight-purple dragonflies with eight wings flittered through air that was shimmery with mushroom spores. Bright-green moss covered the ground, and the snow on the trees around the edges of the vein was half melted: The branches that reached over the vein were still leafy while the others stood dormant and snow-dusted. It was like an eternal spring contained within a small strip of land.

As he stared, Kieran thought he saw a flicker of movement from the ground, but when he turned his head to examine it, it was nothing but mossy earth. *Strange.*

"Impressive, right?" Klaus put his hands on his hips as he surveyed the scene. "The way raw magic impacts the environment is fascinating. To think how powerful it will be once I tap into it . . . it's dizzying."

Kieran tore his gaze away from the moss and shot Klaus a sideways look. "How, exactly, do you plan to create a panacea once you've tapped the magic vein? Have you done it before?"

"Well," Klaus started, straightening his coat as he led Kieran to the moss-covered ground. It was springy under Kieran's feet, almost like walking on a plush blanket. Klaus continued: "That's a very good question. It's . . . something of a mystery. No one really knows what form raw magic takes. Whether it's some sort of liquid or perhaps a gemstone—all that knowledge has been lost to time. So the real question is, what is it and how do we refine it? But we won't know until we reach the inner part of the vein."

Kieran cocked an eyebrow. "Which you plan to . . . dig up?"

"Theoretically," Klaus said. He gestured to a particularly large clump of blue, green, and pink mushrooms that sprouted out of the ground in a grand bouquet. "That's the last place I tried to dig. I created a slim, handheld device that can bore a narrow hole in the earth, and my hope was to disturb the vein as little as possible. Unfortunately, even with the addition of an invisibility spell, the vein's creatures still found me and drove me away before I dug more than a few feet."

"How many ways have you tried to get to the vein so far?"

"Last week I reached attempt seventy-three," Klaus said, sounding almost proud. When Kieran's face went pale, Klaus quickly justified, hands gesticulating wildly, "It's all part of the scientific process! And, well, now that you're here to help me, I have the advantage of a witch who might be able to help fend off the vein's creatures while I work."

Kieran did his best not to openly laugh at that. "You want *me* to fight off magical creatures?"

Klaus cocked an eyebrow. "Is that a problem? Your twin seemed quite adept at fighting, so I assume you had similar training."

"Um. About that—"

Before Kieran could finish, though, a new voice boomed through the woods, calling, "Well, now, look who it is! My dear friend has returned."

Kieran and Klaus turned to find a pair of figures approaching them. One was a short, stout man with his arms outstretched as if he were going to embrace them. He wore a clean, pressed pair of slacks and a crisp black coat—he would have looked more at ease having a martini at a five-star hotel bar than in the woods. He appeared to be in his early fifties, with a light, ruddy complexion and gray-streaked, neatly trimmed brown hair. He also lacked much of a neck, lending him the likeness of a posh turtle.

"Elias." Klaus said his name like a chore he needed to cross off his to-do list. "What a surprise."

"A pleasure as always, Klaus." Elias's eyes fell on Kieran. "And who is this?"

"This," Klaus said, gesturing to Kieran with a flourish, "is my new assistant, Koren."

Typically, Kieran would have quickly correctly the misnomer. But he hadn't processed anything Klaus had said, nor Elias.

Because the boy standing at Elias's side may well have been the most attractive person Kieran had ever laid eyes on.

He was a few inches shorter than Kieran—who stood just shy of six feet—with a slim, muscular build. His skin was pale but gold-toned, his piercing eyes so dark brown they appeared black. He had shiny jet-black hair parted in the middle and trimmed so it barely tickled the shell of his ears. His face was a mix of delicate features—a straight, short nose and pinkish lips—paired with sharp cheekbones and a slim, angular jaw. He wore a simple slate-gray woolen trench coat and had his hands tucked in the pockets. Based on his stony expression, he had little interest in the introductions at hand.

Kieran's heart thumped hard against his ribs.

Elias stepped up, blocking Kieran's view of the other boy, and offered a hand to shake. Kieran had to pause for a moment to remember what he'd been doing, then took the hand. Much to his surprise, Elias yanked him forward. Kieran stumbled just as Elias clapped Kieran on the back as if they were old friends. The pat of his heavy hand felt more like a smack than a kind gesture.

Kieran tensed as Elias pulled back, a smile on his face. Nothing about it, though, seemed friendly. "Nice to meet you, Koren."

"Oh, um—it's Kieran. Kieran Pelumbra."

"Pelumbra, hmm? Been hearing that name in the papers a lot recently." Elias chuckled, trying to meet Kieran's gaze even as his focus wandered back to the other boy. "So sorry about your family's . . . misfortune. I will miss the estate parties."

Realizing that Kieran was not paying attention to him, Elias added, "Ah, yes. This is my assistant, Sebastian Feng. Sebastian?"

"It's a pleasure," the boy said in a voice as smooth as silk. For the first time, he met Kieran's gaze, nearly making his heart leap from his chest. Sebastian bowed his head politely to both Kieran and Klaus, a greeting Kieran recognized as being more common in places like Shui City, where most people had ancestral roots in the neighboring country of Fenshi.

"How nice that you finally have some help for your experiments," Elias went on, returning to his pissing contest with Klaus. "It's been so sad seeing you alone out here on your knees in the dirt day in and day out."

Kieran tried and failed to hide his bemused expression, his nose wrinkled and eyebrows furrowed. He wasn't sure, but he could have sworn that the corner of Sebastian's mouth twitched toward a smile as he held in a laugh at the older men's absurdity.

Kieran's stomach fluttered. *This guy is definitely not your average assistant.*

"Well," Klaus shot back, fingers twitching at his sides, "I've always been the sort of man who isn't afraid to do things himself. I'll have you know, I've made great—"

Suddenly, the sound of a branch snapping cut him off. Sebastian stepped into action immediately, moving in front of Elias with his arm out. Kieran's head snapped toward the sound just in time to catch a flash of movement. Not a small movement either.

That was all the warning they got before something massive crashed through the woods, claws aimed at their throats.

CHAPTER FOUR

Kieran barely had time to jump out of the way as a mushroom-covered monster soared over his head.

The creature in front of them was massive, standing roughly twenty feet tall and made largely of mud, moss, and mushrooms. It looked to be a mix of a giant toad and something more predatory, with clawed toes and no visible eyes—only a wide mouth full of sharp clay teeth. It had swung first toward Kieran and Klaus, but as soon as it missed, it doubled back toward Sebastian and Elias. It opened its mouth and let out a gurgling roar before swiping at them.

Klaus cried, "Run!"

Kieran floundered, turning to find Klaus already sprinting in the other direction. Someone cried out. Kieran whipped around to find that Sebastian had pushed Elias to the ground just as the creature took a swing at him. Elias ducked his head and managed to avoid getting hit.

Sebastian held out a hand to him, saying, "Come on, we have to—"

Just then, the creature roared and jumped at them, hitting Sebastian with a hard *smack.* He went flying, landing limply in a heap not far from Kieran. Sebastian moaned, lifting himself up onto his elbow as he struggled to stand.

Elias, meanwhile, screamed shrilly and scrambled to hide behind a mushroom.

The creature spun back toward Sebastian with impressive speed, given its size. Sebastian was still on the ground, his expression dazed. Kieran wondered if he'd hit his head on impact. He didn't seem to notice that the toad creature was descending on him, its moss-covered tongue lolling over its sharp teeth.

It lifted a clawed arm toward Sebastian, readying another blow.

In that moment, time seemed to slow to a crawl, the scene appearing to Kieran as if in flashes: The creature's claws glinting in the sunlight. Sebastian trying to blink his vision back into focus. Blood seeping from a cut on his forehead.

If Kieran didn't do something, he realized, he was going to watch that monster tear Sebastian to ribbons.

Which was why, despite the screaming part of his brain telling him to run, Kieran grabbed a rock from the ground and launched it, full force, at the toad creature. As the rock left his fingers, he felt a spark of magic in his chest—the same sensation that had gripped him while writing the curse poem.

The rock struck the creature hard in the side of the head, embedding itself. For a second, it didn't seem to make a difference. Kieran's heart dropped from where it had climbed up his throat.

But then the rock exploded like a loose grenade.

The toad creature shrieked as chunks of mud and moss rained down around it. A huge crater was left in the side of its body, revealing a network of pale roots inside, not unlike the ones Kieran had seen in the soil when pulling flowers out of their pots to be replanted. Its head swung back and forth wildly, sending more clumps of dirt and mushrooms flying.

Kieran was momentarily taken aback. *I . . . did that? I did that!* Then, bolstered by the realization, he waved his arms in the air. "Hey! Over here! Come get me!"

Kieran turned on his heel and ran as the toad roared once again, leaping to follow him. Glancing over his shoulder to check on Sebastian, Kieran saw that the boy had struggled to his feet and was swaying in place.

Well, at least he's up, Kieran thought, arms pumping at his sides. *Now I just have to—*

In a flash, the creature hit him with a bone-shattering *smack.*

Kieran sputtered a choked yelp as his body rolled across the moss. The wind flew out of him. He came to a halt beneath a giant mushroom, head swimming as he gasped for breath.

Okay, he thought, blistering pain zigzagging through every nerve in his body. *Maybe that was a stupid move.*

"Kieran!" Klaus shouted from the woods. "Don't fight it! Just come this way and I'll—"

Kieran didn't hear the last part. Because at that moment, as he tried to haul himself up, the toad creature took another swipe at him, claws first.

And stabbed him straight through the ribs.

For a second, the pain didn't hit him. Instead, he was just staring at the creature, trembling in terror. Its open mouth waited to devour him, muddy saliva dripping from its teeth. The claws were still inside Kieran, holding him aloft like a rag doll. He felt warmth on his skin as blood began to leak from the puncture wounds, wetting his side. Before the rattling agony of a punctured lung hit him, he glanced back.

Sebastian was staring at him, pupils blown out, with a hand clapped over his mouth.

Well, Kieran thought, *at least I went out finally being able to help someone other than myself. Ash would be proud.*

Kieran's body slipped from the toad's claws, landing hard on the ground. As his vision swam, he caught the briefest flash of movement in front of him. It almost looked like someone opening a hidden, moss-covered trapdoor in the ground.

Oh, good, he thought, vision going dark at the edges. *Death hallucinations. That's a new one.*

A gnarled hand reached out to grab him. He felt it wrap around his collar, yanking him forward.

What in the—

Everything went black.

"Now, that," a croaking, feminine voice said, "was quite a sight."

Kieran's eyes flew open. He sat up with a gasp, expecting pain from the toad creature's claws piercing his flesh. Instead, he just felt . . . tired and heavy, as if his body were made of iron. Even opening his eyes and sitting up was a fight.

What he saw, though, immediately distracted him from his current physical state.

He was lying in a creaking wooden bed, the sheets well-worn and patched with random scraps of fabric. He found himself in a strange combination of a rabbit's burrow and a studio apartment. Instead of standard walls, there was tightly packed dirt, and bright green moss acted as a carpet. Mushrooms and huge pinkish crystals clung to the earthen walls, all glowing with faint light. Dried herbs hung from the ceiling, and around the moss coating the ground bounced motes of bluish light, as weightless as balloons, occasionally ricocheting off each other and squeaking with dismay. Other pieces of furniture looked as if they had grown out of the ground itself, with roots connecting them to the floor. A fire in a stone woodstove at the other end of the room crackled, spitting smoke through a hollow stone pillar that went into the ceiling.

The most notable feature of this strange home, though, was the woman in front of him.

She looked to be in her late eighties, with a hunched back and deep wrinkles. Her skin was light brown, and her glossy black hair was tied back in a braid. She had huge milky-brown eyes and round glasses that sat on the edge of a stubby nose. She wore ragged patchwork clothes, along with a cape made of moss, and atop her head was a floppy pointed hat decorated with mushrooms.

She leaned over Kieran, examining him. Her eyes looked enormous behind her round spectacles. "Are you alive, little witch?"

"Gah!" Kieran gasped, lurching back. His head swung around. "What's going on? Where am I?"

"That's no way to greet the person who just saved your life," the old woman said. She used a walking stick to gently poke Kieran's side. "Have some respect for your elders."

"What? You . . . saved my life?"

The old woman gestured to his side. "Sure did. Wasn't easy either. Took me nearly three hours."

Kieran looked down to find his coat shredded where the toad monster's claws had sunk into him. The skin underneath, though, was unblemished. He poked at the spot where the toad's claws had stabbed his lung; it didn't even ache.

"I thought that wound was going to kill me," Kieran admitted, still poking at the skin.

"It would have," the woman agreed, nodding her head. At the widening of Kieran's eyes, she explained: "You'll have to excuse the vein—it's been temperamental these last few months. Especially since those men started trying to steal my magic."

Kieran's head cocked to the side. "*Your* magic? Forgive my ignorance but . . . who exactly are you?"

The old woman let out an inelegant snort. "Verbena Dropleaf, the Witch of the Woods. I've spent my whole life protecting this vein, just as my mother and her mother and her mother before her did. It's been our sacred duty since the first witch was gifted her magic from the earth. I know this vein's magic like no one else alive."

"Well, erm . . . it's an honor to meet you, Verbena. I'm Kieran." He dusted off his clothes as he straightened up. "How . . . did I get here?"

Verbena pointed to a ladder leaning against the wall. Tilting his head up, Kieran realized that it led to a wood trapdoor in the ceiling. "Luckily, that toad dropped you right by my front door. I pulled you in before any of the other men could notice."

Kieran blinked. So he *had* seen movement in the moss when he and Klaus arrived—it must have been this woman watching them. Regardless, it was hard to believe a woman of Verbena's age and stature could have managed to haul him inside, but again, if she had some kind of connection to a magic vein, who knew what power she had at her disposal.

Kieran cleared his throat. "I should thank you for saving me, then. Considering the week I've had, I really thought I was a goner."

Verbena, however, didn't seem interested in harping on that fact any longer. "I have a question for you."

"Oh, um—go ahead." *What in the world could a powerful witch like her want with someone like me?*

"That boy up above," she said, inclining her head as she gazed at Kieran. "From what I saw, you'd never even met him before. He's a stranger to you, yet you nearly died for him. Why?"

Kieran thought back to the image of Sebastian lying there in the dirt, clearly too hurt to protect himself. He pursed his lips as he mulled it over. He thought of the silent scream on the other boy's lips and the terror in his eyes.

Well, Kieran thought, *no sense lying.*

"I guess . . . I know how it feels to be helpless," he explained, eyes wandering to his hands. He remembered how they'd grown skeletal before Delilah broke his fatal curse. He'd been able to see every vein and joint through the papery skin—an ever-present reminder that he'd been flirting with death. "And for a long time, I dreamed about the day some hero would come along and save me."

He looked up, meeting Verbena's huge eyes. He saw himself reflected in her spectacles, shoulder-length blond curls a mess and clothes stained with drying blood. Still, he looked a thousand times healthier than he ever had before. He wasn't stick thin or gaunt as he was before his curse broke, and his cheeks had filled in. His skin was no longer pallid and cold to the touch. He just looked like a normal almost-eighteen-year-old.

He took a breath. "Not everyone gets that. But I did. So it seemed right to try to be that for someone else."

"How brave," Verbena mused. She rubbed her chin ponderously, staring up out of the corner of her eye. "Or stupid."

Kieran sputtered a laugh, shrugging. "Maybe both?"

"Perhaps," Verbena agreed. She drummed her fingers on her walking stick. "One more question, then: Why did you come to my vein in the first place?"

Kieran hesitated, gnawing on his lower lip. The last thing he wanted to do was piss off the witch who'd saved his life. But if she had the magic to do that, he probably couldn't get away with lying. Besides, he was a terrible liar.

So, in an avalanche of words, Kieran explained the situation with Ash, his Calling, and the Witches' Council. The old woman listened to every word with a look of mild interest, nodding along. Even when he admitted he wanted to use the magic for himself, she didn't flinch.

After he was done, Verbena stared at him for a long moment,

as if mentally mapping the expression on his face. He nervously tucked his hair behind his ears, averting his gaze. *She's probably not gonna like all that.*

But to his surprise, Verbena said, "I could help you create a panacea."

Kieran jerked back. "Wha— You can? Really?"

"Of course. I know more about this vein's magic than anyone, don't I?" She tapped her walking stick on the ground. "And you certainly seem more deserving than those other dreadful men."

Kieran's eyes brightened.

"But," Verbena said, holding up a gnarled finger, "my help doesn't come for free. In exchange, I need you to complete a little something for me. A quest, so to speak."

"Quest?" Kieran blinked. He hadn't heard of something referred to as a *quest* since the last time he borrowed one of the adventure novels Briar read under the breakfast table when she was taking a break from her usual smut.

Verbena nodded. "While I have an ancestral connection to this vein, the magic has become . . . unruly of late. I still have some power over it, of course, but nothing like I used to. You see, the magic will fully obey someone only if they wield a very special item: the Scepter of the Woods."

Kieran's eyebrows shot up. "A . . . scepter? Kind of like a magic wand? I haven't heard of a witch using one of those since my great-grandparents were alive."

Verbena shot him a sideways look, expression stormy. "Are you calling me *old,* Kieran?"

Kieran paled and stammered, "N-no, of course n—"

Verbena, however, immediately broke her glare and began to cackle, pointing at Kieran's horrified expression. "Heh! Look at you. So concerned. I jest—it's no secret that my joints ache and my eyes and ears have nearly given up on me. After all, that's how I lost the scepter in the first place."

"Oh—did you lose it around here? I know there's a lot of snow, but maybe a tracking spell could—"

"Alas, it is not here any longer. I used to be able to patrol these woods day and night, concealing evidence of the vein's power. But in my old age, I've become far less adept at hiding the vein and its magic. I missed a whole section of the vein that had become overrun by magic-infused mushrooms. After those were found, rumors of a vein began to spread among local witches. As more arrived in the forest, it became harder to avoid them. One day, when I thought I was alone, I used the scepter to channel the vein's magic. Unfortunately, I didn't sense the eyes on me. After that, the thief merely had to follow me home."

"A thief? Did you see who it was?"

Verbena barked a laugh. "Nosy, aren't we? The answer to that question is irrelevant—what matters is that I was forced to break the scepter into pieces in order to save it—and the vein—from my would-be thief. I used the last of its magic to scatter the pieces throughout Celdwyn. Since then, I've waited for a hero brave—or perhaps stupid—enough to look for them. Once they've been reunited, they'll return to their original form. Whoever wields the scepter will be able to use the vein's magic at will."

Kieran's eyes widened. "So . . . if I can find the pieces and return the scepter, you'll be able to make me a panacea?"

Verbena nodded. "Indeed. First, you must retrieve the Hilt from the bottom of the Lake of Whispers. Then uncover the Stave hidden in Mirrorveil Woods in the south. Finally, persuade the Iceweave Coven of the Slicetooth Mountains to relinquish the Crown. If you succeed in bringing them together once more, I will aid you in your Calling to break your lover's curse."

Kieran's head swam as he tried to remember all these details. He'd have to travel all over Celdwyn to do what she said, not to mention how many complicating factors might come up while retrieving the pieces of a scepter. He'd need transportation, money, moral support—all things hard to muster up in the six months allotted for his Calling.

But then again, this may well be the only way to create a panacea in, perhaps, the entire world. Really, what choice did he have?

"Okay," Kieran said, mostly to reassure himself. "I accept your quest."

A warm smile broke across Verbena's face. She was missing a few teeth. "Then we're in agreement. Return here once you've reformed the scepter, and the panacea will be—"

Suddenly, she paused, her face paling as her eyes focused on something on Kieran's shoulder. "Oh *no.*"

"What?" Kieran glanced down at his shoulder, twisting it around so he could see the back. Just then, he spotted a small golden beetle on his back. It appeared to be made of clockwork parts, all of which spun as its wings began to buzz. "Ah!"

"That's a listening bug!" Verbena growled. She gripped her walking stick and began jabbing it at Kieran. "Someone left it on you! Kill it! Before it can return to its master and tell them of this conversation!"

"Shit!" Kieran slapped a hand toward the bug, but it buzzed, darting out of the way. He hopped out of bed, trying to clap his hands around it as Verbena chanted for him to kill it over and over. "Shit, shit, shit!"

Kieran stumbled over the mossy floor as he chased the bug across the burrow, jumping to try to smash it between his hands. Before he could, it flew into the fire in the woodstove. Kieran watched in horror as it shot up the chimney.

As Kieran cursed under his breath, he suddenly remembered earlier when Elias had clapped him on the back. "That asshole's trying to spy on me and Klaus!"

"You see why I do not trust easily," Verbena said, wagging a finger at no one in particular. "This kind of power leads men to do terrible things, my young friend. It seems your quest just got a bit more complicated."

Kieran cursed again under his breath. "I should find Klaus—maybe he can help."

"Perhaps it is best to get going," Verbena said, pointing to the trapdoor. "But please: I implore you not to let that man find my scepter. I suspect that his intentions are anything but pure."

"You can say that again." Kieran nodded to Verbena. "Anyway, thank you for saving me, Verbena. I promise I won't let you down."

With that, Kieran made his way to the ladder, said his goodbyes, and headed back up to the surface.

CHAPTER FIVE

When Klaus and Kieran finally got back to Gellingham that night, Briar and Delilah were waiting for them in the living room.

"Kieran!" Delilah cried as she leapt up from the couch, Briar close behind her. She crossed the room and threw her arms around Kieran before he could so much as shrug off his coat. As she squeezed him, she felt the tears in his coat. She pulled back, gently touching one ripped, copper-stained spot. "What in the world happened? Are you okay?"

"I'm fine—I promise. The coat is the only casualty." Kieran glanced down at it again, frowning. "Shame, really. I quite liked it."

"I'm also uninjured," Klaus volunteered, despite the fact that no one had asked him, "for the record. The monster failed to touch me."

"Monster?" Delilah's gaze flicked to her father. "What in the world are you talking about?"

"Long story," Kieran said, gesturing to the couches. "We should sit."

The girls exchanged a look before nodding and heading back to the seating area. Klaus and Kieran joined them, and for the next while, Kieran broke down the entire afternoon for Delilah and Briar: meeting Elias, risking himself to save Sebastian, and, ultimately, Verbena's quest. The entire time, Delilah stared at him, gaping, and Briar's eyes got wider and wider. When he finished, Briar and Delilah looked gobsmacked.

"So if Elias heard all that with his listening bug," Kieran added, rubbing his chin in thought, "then I suspect I'm not going to be the only one searching for the scepter parts. And Elias is a powerful man with a *lot* of money at his disposal. I . . . can't exactly say the same."

"Then we need to get going as soon as possible," Delilah said.

Kieran's eyebrow shot up. "We?"

"Obviously," Briar echoed, nodding. "You think we'd let you go on some huge, dangerous journey alone? Come on, Kieran, you know us. Where you go, we go. We're like those bonded kittens at the shelter who can't be adopted separately."

"Well, you'll need funding for that much travel," Klaus quickly cut in. He met Kieran's gaze. "I've spent nearly six months competing against Elias. He's a horrid little rat man with horrid little rat schemes. And I'll be damned if I don't at least give you a leg up in beating him to the punch."

"That's all fine and good," Delilah shot back, "but I doubt it's just professional rivalry motivating you. You want a panacea too."

"Of course," Klaus said, shrugging. "But that can be discussed once Kieran has the scepter. I may be ambitious, but I also know when to pivot. Right now, you're my best bet, Kieran Pelumbra."

Kieran quickly held up his hands, eyes flicking around the

room at the three of them. "L-listen, this is all great but—this is a *massive* undertaking. We have no idea what to expect from any of these places, much less what it'll take to get the pieces of the scepter once we're there. It could be really dangerous, especially considering I'm . . . not exactly great at magic."

"All the more reason to bring us," Briar pointed out.

"She has a point," Klaus agreed.

Delilah nodded. "I'm with Briar on this one."

Kieran let out a breath. He loved Briar and Delilah very much, but they were two of the stubbornest people alive. He suspected that even if he did want to go alone, it was unlikely he could persuade them to stay behind. Plus, with Klaus's funding . . .

"Well," Kieran said, rubbing his sweaty palms on his pants, "looks like I need to make a few phone calls, but other than that . . . I guess we'd better start packing."

And as Delilah and Briar whooped and cheered, a small smile crossed Kieran's face.

He might just have a chance.

That night, Kieran sat on the couch in the living room staring at his book of poetry. Part of him wanted to write—to get his feelings out—but he feared he might accidentally curse someone else. It was a pity, because he had some great ideas from the day. Something about how love was like a growth on his heart that couldn't be removed, just like the mushrooms on that toad monster. *I can't believe Ash called me melodramatic.*

As he rubbed a thumb across the blank page, the phone began to trill.

Kieran perked up. *Is it Ash? Did he hear that I nearly died? Maybe the thought of losing me made him realize what a terrible mistake this break is. Perhaps he wants to beg for my forgiveness? Although, then again, he won't be able to hear me—*

"Pelumbra-Bea residence," Kieran said into the receiver.

"Hello," said an unfamiliar voice. It was deep and resonant but gentle, demanding the listener's ear. "Is this Kieran? It's Sebastian Feng. We met in the woods this afternoon?"

"Oh! Y-yeah—this is Kieran. I'm . . . surprised to hear from you," Kieran said, at a loss for how else to put it.

Sebastian sounded almost amused at that. "Are you? You saved my life. Calling to say thank you seems like the least I can do. I'm just glad you were easy to find in the phone book."

Kieran wrinkled his forehead. Part of him wanted to wave off Sebastian's statement about saving his life, but of course it *was* true. Sebastian would have been ripped asunder without Kieran's help. Still, Kieran couldn't help but tilt his head to the side in question. "What about Elias?"

Sebastian paused for a moment. "What about him?"

"You work for him—isn't it, I dunno, bad form to reach out to the enemy? Or are you trying to get information out of me because your listening bug is gone?"

Sebastian was silent. Then, completely out of the blue, he snorted.

"Enemy?" he repeated. "You've misjudged me, Kieran. Elias is my employer—I do what he asks and he pays me, end of story. I

couldn't care less about his professional rivalries. In fact, that's part of why I wanted to call you."

Kieran's eyebrows shot up. "Oh?"

"Elias has already started hiring mercenaries to help him get that scepter," Sebastian said, his voice even. "It won't be long before he sends them after you."

Kieran's face drained of color. "That sounds . . . bad?"

"Indeed." Sebastian cleared his throat. "You'll need to be stealthy if you want to find it. Elias has a lot of money, and he's going to do everything in his power to get that panacea."

Kieran tried to swallow, but his mouth had gone dry. He'd figured Elias would try to get the scepter, but mercenaries? People didn't hire mercenaries unless they wanted to dispose of someone permanently.

After a long, pregnant pause, he set his book down on the side table beside the couch. "I . . . appreciate the warning," Kieran said, nodding to himself. "I didn't know Elias was quite so . . ."

"Bloodthirsty?" Sebastian hummed softly to himself. "Greed does that to people."

Kieran looked down at his hands. He knew that all too well—the Pelumbra family's greed had driven them to all kinds of immoral deeds. It seemed Elias wasn't all that different from his family in that sense.

After a beat, Kieran asked, "Are you . . . going to keep working for him?"

Sebastian took a moment to consider it. "I . . . suppose. I don't know. As I said before, I work for him because he pays me. Until I find someone else who needs my skill set and has a salary for me, that's what I'll do."

"What if *I* hired you?"

For the first time in the conversation, Sebastian sounded genuinely shocked. "Excuse me?"

"I mean, I can use all the help I can get." Kieran shrugged. Perhaps he was going out on a limb, but if Elias was hiring mercenaries, he was going to need more than just Briar and Delilah to protect him. "If it's money you need, I can work something out with Klaus. Plus, having someone around who has worked for Elias might be just what we need to get a leg up on him."

Sebastian paused, sounding nonplussed. "You're . . . serious? You haven't even seen my résumé."

Kieran laughed. Sebastian sounded so overly formal that Kieran had to wonder whether he was trying to sound more grown-up on purpose or he was just like that. "I suppose that's true. Any highlights I should know about?"

Sebastian went quiet for a moment as he considered it. This line of questioning seemed to have chipped at his assuredness. Kieran got the sense that he'd practiced this phone call beforehand but hadn't considered something like this happening.

Finally, all business, Sebastian said, "I excelled in school, particularly in the sciences. I finished my education two years early with perfect test scores, and I've worked since then. I know how to chart the stars, survive in the wilderness, and decode cyphers. And I'm trained in self-defense. If you need additional information, I can furnish letters of recommendation from my former employers."

Kieran had to stop himself from laughing—he hadn't expected Sebastian to take this so seriously. It was strangely endearing. "Well, that makes one of us. Maybe you can show me a few things. Anyway, I'll have to talk to the others, but I think it's safe to say you've got the job if you want it. What do you think?"

Sebastian considered it. "I'll . . . have to let you know. Perhaps I can call you once I've had a chance to think about it?"

Kieran smiled. "Sounds like a plan to me—we'll be leaving Gellingham on Wednesday, so you have until then to decide. But I think you'd be a great fit."

"I appreciate that. And . . . thank you again for today. I don't know many people who would risk their own lives for a total stranger like that."

Kieran shrugged nonchalantly. "All in a day's work, I guess. I should get to bed, though. Talk soon?"

"I'd love to." Sebastian coughed, as if he'd blurted the phrase out too quickly, and cleared his throat. "Er, anyway, ah—sleep well, Kieran. I'll be in touch."

Before Kieran could even say goodbye, the line went dead.

A few days later, Kieran, Delilah, and Briar returned to the airfield where they'd first landed in Gellingham six months ago.

Delilah and Briar had both been in good spirits as they'd gathered their travel bags in the living room that morning, seemingly unaware of Kieran chewing his lip and staring at the phone in the kitchen. He had been waiting for it to ring for days as he worked out the logistics of their trip, from putting in his resignation notice at the coffee shop to working out payment details with Klaus. Whenever he returned home, he'd ask Delilah or Briar if the phone had rung, and aside from Delilah getting a few calls from her cursebreaking clients, it hadn't. It seemed that Sebastian had decided not to take the job offer.

Kieran told himself it didn't matter. They'd be just fine with their usual crew—Delilah and Briar were capable witches, and they had a skilled pilot, to boot, but it would have been nice to have Sebastian's insider knowledge.

And those diamond-cutting cheekbones, a traitorous voice in his brain offered.

Not that I care about those, he argued with himself. *Ash's cheekbones are just as nice, obviously.*

"Hey!" Delilah said, breaking Kieran out of his thoughts. "There it is!"

Kieran looked up to find their old aeroship parked on the frost-covered grass. The aeroship was shaped like a traditional sailing ship, with two massive red balloons attached to the top. Its metal wings hung off the sides, with springy webbing between them that helped push air down during takeoff. The crow's nest, Briar's favorite former haunt, looked out over the airfield and miles beyond.

"There they are!" came a familiar voice from the top deck. A short, round-faced person with chin-length black hair and gold-toned skin waved at them. They wore an oil-stained vest over a rumpled white shirt—their usual uniform. "Long time no see!"

Kieran craned his neck to see the ship's pilot—and new owner—Ariel Zhang grinning at him. After they'd broken the curse, Kieran had sold Ariel the ship he'd initially stolen from his parents. While the sale wasn't technically legal—Kieran would have needed the official paperwork for that—he'd had little interest in trying to maintain the thing after the curse broke, and Ariel had always wanted their own ship to travel the world. Ariel had paid him enough to help him start his life in Gellingham, then took off into the skies for a new adventure.

Kieran had been lucky they'd been willing to sign on as the pilot for this quest. Granted, he'd offered a sizable salary from Klaus's money, but still.

"Ah, our little friends have returned!" cried a second voice. A tall, tan-skinned man with a carefully manicured undercut leaned over the edge of the ship, his big brown eyes bright and his smile warm. "Oh, how I've missed locking my liquor cabinet."

"That was one time!" Briar shot back from below.

Santiago Luna, the Pelumbra family's former personal chef and Ariel's partner, let out a booming laugh. "Glad to see you haven't changed, Briar."

Shortly after, Ariel and Santiago extended the gangway, and came out to give their friends hugs and express how much they'd missed them. Ariel ruffled Briar's hair, commenting on how it had grown out, and Santiago clapped Delilah on the back. Seeing them made the trepidation that had begun to churn in Kieran's stomach subside somewhat. While Ariel and Santiago were only in their mid- to late twenties, they were as close to parents as he, Briar, and Delilah had had on their cursebreaking journey last spring. He'd found himself missing being able to ask them questions like how to make scrambled eggs or not shrink wool sweaters in the wash.

Santiago squeezed Kieran's shoulder. "I heard you got yourself into a bit of a situation, my friend."

Kieran sighed. "That's one way of putting it."

"Let's head in—you can tell us more while I get us in the air," Ariel said, gesturing toward the gangway. "I had Santiago set up your old rooms with clean sheets—"

"Kieran—hold on a moment."

At the sound of the unfamiliar voice, the five of them turned just as someone crossed the frosty grass, headed in their direction. At first, Kieran didn't recognize him. He wore a gray woolen coat, his hands in the pockets, and a pair of leather shoes that would have looked more appropriate at a business meeting. On his back was a large pack, clearly meant for travel. As he came closer, he brushed dark hair from his face, revealing a black eye and a bruised jaw.

"Sebastian?" Kieran said, taken aback by the boy's sudden appearance. "You came?"

"Wait, *the* Sebastian?" Briar asked. "This is the guy you saved?"

"Oooooh—now I get it," Delilah said. She lowered her voice and leaned closer to Kieran, whispering behind her hand conspiratorially. "He's *very* pretty."

Kieran shot her a wide-eyed look as his cheeks flushed. "That's not—"

As Sebastian came to a stop, Kieran's words stopped behind his teeth. Up close, he saw a cut through Sebastian's eyebrow crusted with dried blood, and more of it stuck in his hair. Kieran had assumed the injuries were left over from the attack in the woods, but now that he looked closer, it was clear these had happened within the last few hours.

"Goodness—are you all right?" Kieran asked, rushing up to meet him. His eyes darted over Sebastian's body, looking for more wounds. The coat and long pants covered most of his skin, but he did seem to be walking with something of a limp. "What happened to you?"

Sebastian swallowed thickly. His lower lip was busted and swollen. "Nothing of import."

"*Nothing of*— You look like you've been through a meat grinder!" Kieran reached out, unsure of whether a touch would be comforting or unwelcome, and wound up pulling back. "Who did this? Elias?"

At the sound of the man's name, Sebastian flinched. He quickly recovered. "That's beside the point. Though it's safe to say I'm no longer working for him. As such, I came to accept the job, assuming the offer still stands."

"Job?" Santiago asked, eyebrows nearly at his hairline. He shot a look at Kieran. "Perhaps we should be focusing on getting our new friend a first aid kit and some stitches instead of employment?"

"I offered Sebastian a position on the ship since he's worked with Elias," Kieran explained. "I figured we could use all the insider information we can get. That said, I didn't expect Elias to react to Sebastian's resignation like *this*."

Sebastian shook his head. "It looks worse than it is."

"Like hell," Briar scoffed. "Look, I've been in my fair share of fights, and those aren't light injuries. You must have really pissed someone off."

Sebastian winced, and his fingers instantly went to his neck, where Kieran could see the slimmest line of purple bruising poking out from under his collar. Kieran wondered how much worse the injuries were beneath his coat.

"Please," Sebastian said, seeming to fight to keep his voice even. He was doing a good job of it, but nonetheless, Kieran had to assume he was in a great deal of pain. "I swear I can be useful. I won't let this get in the way."

It took Kieran a moment to realize what Sebastian was getting at. Did he really think that Kieran would rescind the offer just because he was injured?

"Oh! Of course you're still welcome. As long as no one has any objections."

There was a long pause as the rest of the crew exchanged looks, and Kieran found himself waiting for one of them to chime in. But Briar was silent, and Santiago and Ariel were too busy whispering to each other about how they were going to treat Sebastian's injuries with the supplies they had on the ship. Delilah, meanwhile, covered her wrinkled nose with her hand. Kieran cocked a brow at her, but she didn't seem to notice; she was staring at Sebastian as if he'd sprouted a few extra eyes. Kieran made a mental note to ask her about it later.

Finally, it was Briar who piped up: "It's up to you, Kieran. It's your Calling."

Kieran chewed his lower lip. It seemed obvious that Sebastian needed help, but Delilah's reaction seemed strange—did she know something he didn't? But then again, nothing about the boy's words seemed untrue. Technically, it was possible that Elias could have sent him to be a spy. He could have hurt Sebastian intentionally to make his leaving seem more convincing, sure. But at the same time, Kieran doubted injuries as severe as Sebastian's were merely intended to be a cover-up. Like Briar had said, they looked like they'd been inflicted by someone who was livid, not calculated. Plus, Sebastian genuinely seemed like he wanted to help them beat Elias and pay Kieran back for saving his life.

And he's also probably one of the most attractive boys I've ever laid eyes on, he thought. *Not that that matters, of course. Boyfriend and all. Ex status pending.*

He sighed. *If this bites me in the ass later, I'll just have to deal with it then.*

"Okay," Kieran said, nodding. "Consider yourself the newest member of the crew, Sebastian."

Sebastian let out a breath. "Thank you, Kieran. Truly. Once again, I owe you."

"Well," Ariel said, jutting their chin toward the ship, "on that note, let's get this kid some bandages and this aeroship in the sky. We've got a lot of ground to cover."

Exchanging looks, the crew nodded, then boarded the ship for departure.

Returning to the aeroship after six months away felt a bit like coming home.

As the engine kicked on and the metal wings beat, lifting them into the air, Kieran quickly settled into his old room. Delilah and Briar elected to share Briar's old one. Sebastian took Delilah's old room, kitty-corner to Kieran's. Once Kieran had finished unpacking his trunk of clothes and other items, he went straight to Sebastian's door.

After a few knocks, the door opened and Sebastian appeared on the other side. He'd taken off his coat, revealing a crisp white button-down shirt with the top two buttons undone. His face was clean, and the cut by his eyebrow was bandaged. All in all, he looked better physically, though Kieran knew it had to have been traumatizing to take a beating like that.

"Hi," Kieran said, immediately cursing the way his voice cracked as he said it. He cleared his throat. "Are you feeling better?"

Sebastian nodded. "Do you think you could help me find ice? I want to try to get the swelling down."

"Sure—I'll show you the lay of the land. And offer proper introductions to everyone now that you've had a chance to get fixed up."

"I'd appreciate that. Apologies again for all this." He gestured to his face, cringing. "I didn't plan on such a dramatic entrance. I assure you it's not how I typically present myself."

"Hey—it's okay. We've all had our fair share of cuts and bruises." Kieran waved his hand dismissively. "Plus, it's nice that someone else could take a turn at a dramatic entrance. Usually, it's just me getting made fun of for wearing too many frills."

Kieran expected a laugh for that, but Sebastian simply nodded and stared at him for a long beat, then two, still all business.

Kieran pursed his lips. *Tough nut to crack, I suppose.*

"Your fashion sense is quite flashy," Sebastian blurted out, realizing that he'd been silently staring for a few seconds too long. His cheeks filled with color, and he averted his gaze, adding, "It's, ah . . . nice."

Kieran smiled at that, offering a small flourish with his ruffled sleeve. He'd had a taste for the ostentatious since he was a child, especially when it came to clothing, and he had no shame in showing it. "I'll take that as a compliment. Come on. I'll give you the grand tour."

He gestured for Sebastian to follow, and the other boy shut his new bedroom door behind him, barely making a sound. Compared to the way Briar and Delilah moved around without regard for the noise they made, it was almost jarring to meet someone who strove for silence.

Kieran pointed out his own room as well as Briar and Delilah's. He figured he could save their introductions for last, since he could hear them laughing through the door and didn't want to interrupt. Instead, he led Sebastian out onto the main open-air deck.

"It's chillier now than it was the last time," Kieran said with a laugh as Sebastian instantly tensed at the cold. When Sebastian shot him a questioning look, Kieran added, "It's my second time traveling aboard this ship. Last time was with my friend Delilah—the tall girl with the curly hair you saw earlier—for her Calling in the spring."

Kieran looked around at the tables and chairs set up around the perimeter, facing the open sky. Since the last time he'd been aboard, Ariel and Santiago seemed to have started using the deck for storage, judging by the stacks of wooden crates he saw there. "But with the right coat, this deck is great for stargazing. I come out here a lot when I can't sleep."

Sebastian tilted his head to examine the aeroship's balloons and crow's nest. "It seems . . . quiet. I can't hear the wind at all."

Kieran explained: "My great-aunt Adelaide traveled with us

the last time, and she wove us a spell to keep the wind away so we could stay outside without its being too loud to speak."

Sebastian's eyebrows rose. They were thick and black like his hair, with a sharp angle that gave his resting face an intimidating look. "I've heard that all the Pelumbras are witches. Is that true?"

Kieran nodded. "Yep. For the last two hundred years or so, they haven't allowed any nonmagical folk to marry into the family. Don't want to accidentally dilute the bloodline."

" 'They'?" Sebastian repeated, cocking his head. The cold had begun to turn his cheeks and the tip of his nose pink. "You're a Pelumbra. Do you not associate with them?"

Kieran nearly laughed. "Oh, definitely not. If it hadn't been for Delilah, I'd be dead because of them. My twin too—she's the redhead who's attached to Delilah at the hip. But that's a long story for another time. Let's get out of the cold."

Sebastian gratefully nodded and followed Kieran to the stairs that led to the lower decks. Kieran took them two at a time, practically bouncing with excitement at getting to show off his home away from home. He showed Sebastian the kitchen—where they got some ice for Sebastian's split lip—then the study and the dining room while recounting a few stories from the previous journey, like finding Delilah in Kitfield, her hometown, and persuading Briar to join them in Port Lorring. Sebastian nodded as he took it all in, his eyes seeming to map out every corner of the ship.

Although he offered nods and one-word responses to show he was listening, Sebastian wasn't much of a talker. He seemed much more concerned with whatever was going on in his head. Kieran was generally good at reading people, but Sebastian's face and voice gave very little away. *Then again, he's probably anxious about Elias. Maybe he just needs to get his mind off it.*

Kieran decided to take that as a challenge.

"But enough about me," Kieran said, gesturing to the stairs to the lowest deck. He sat on the banister and used it to slide down to the bottom while Sebastian followed stiffly behind him using the stairs. "Tell me about yourself."

Sebastian pursed his lips, considering the request as he looked around the deck. It was the one in which Kieran spent the least amount of time. It boasted two rooms: the observation deck—a mostly window-enclosed room with a view of the clouds and the land below the ship—and the bedroom that Ariel and Santiago shared. Kieran led Sebastian toward the observation deck.

Following Kieran to the big open room at the back of the ship, Sebastian finally asked, "What would you like to know?"

The day was cloudless after Gellingham's recent snowstorm, and they could see all the way to the ground. Ariel had spent the few days before picking them up researching the best way to the Lake of Whispers, which was only a two-day journey to the east, in the direction of the sea. Now they were passing over the villages outside the city, the pale-green Gell River winding through them like a massive serpent.

"Hmm," Kieran considered, stroking his chin. "Well . . . how did you wind up working for Elias Barclay?"

"Nothing very exciting," Sebastian explained, stepping closer to the windows to get a better view. His shoulders, wider than Kieran's, were tense. "He was hiring, and I was looking for a job. His was the best-paying one I could find."

"Saving money for something in particular?" Kieran pushed. He hoped he didn't sound nosy, but then again, it seemed as if getting Sebastian to open up was going to require a bit of prying.

Sebastian paused, as if mentally weighing the words hanging on his lips. Finally, he said, "Not really. I mostly just send money to my younger sisters in Shui City."

"It must be hard to be far from your family," Kieran said, hoping it might push him to share more. "Are your parents around?"

"No. They've both passed." Sebastian stuck his hands in his pockets, not meeting Kieran's eyes. "It's just me and my sisters."

"It sounds like you had to grow up really fast," Kieran said, standing beside Sebastian as they gazed down at the landscape. He wondered if he was too close, but let the thought go when Sebastian didn't move away. If he squinted, Kieran could just see the edge of Shui City, and he wondered if Sebastian was thinking of his sisters now.

Sebastian nodded but didn't say anything more.

Silence overtook them, and Kieran immediately felt itchy. Some people, he knew, were comfortable with silence, but he certainly wasn't one of them.

He blurted out, "So how, um, old are you exactly?"

Sebastian stared at Kieran for a long beat. Kieran's heart rate picked up. That stare was enough to make Kieran sweat, although not necessarily in a bad way.

"Pardon me for asking," Sebastian said, "but is this a . . . job interview? I can't say I've prepared, so my apologies—"

"What? No!" Kieran had to hold in a laugh. "I'm just trying to get to know you, Sebastian."

"As an employee?"

Kieran sputtered a giggle. "As an employ—? No. Listen, I know I offered you this job, but that doesn't mean I'm your *boss.* It doesn't work like that on this ship. Me, Delilah, Briar, Ariel, Santiago—we're not coworkers. We're . . . kind of a weird little family. Obviously, you don't have to be best friends with all of us, but it would be nice to get to know you. If you want."

"Oh. I . . . suppose I misread that." Sebastian looked away, seemingly trying to hide the blush that had spread across his cheeks. "Sorry—I'm out of practice when it comes to casual socializing. Elias is the only person I've talked to for months now, and he preferred that I limit our conversations to work topics."

"Seriously? What an asshole."

For the first time since Sebastian had boarded the ship, Kieran had managed to coax a smile out of him. Kieran brightened at the sight of it—Sebastian's resting expression was quite severe, so even a small smile softened him significantly. It took him from intimidating to roguishly handsome. Especially with the way his hair hung slightly in his nearly black eyes, which glinted in the sunlight. And how white his teeth were behind those pouty, pale-pink lips.

Not that Kieran noticed that, of course.

Sebastian said, "It's all right—it's behind me now. Plus, I can safely say I prefer it here already. And, ah—to answer your question—I'm eighteen. My birthday was last week. You?"

"Seventeen," Kieran admitted, tearing his eyes away before his thoughts could spiral. "I'll be eighteen in a few months. You know, old witches' tales say people born in the winter are supposed to be extra ambitious and mysterious."

Sebastian flexed his eyebrows. "Well, I'm no witch. I don't know that the old tales apply to me."

"I—um—I know some nonmagical folks don't feel comfortable around witches," Kieran said, doing his best to tiptoe around his real question. "You, um . . . you wouldn't happen to be . . ."

"I'm not afraid of you, if that's what you're asking," Sebastian said, folding his hands in front of him—apparently something of a nervous habit. "You don't seem the type to get angry and curse me because I forgot to say please and thank you or whatever it is that earned people curses back in the day."

Without meaning to, Kieran cringed.

Sebastian raised an eyebrow.

"Sorry," Kieran muttered. "It's, ah . . . Long story."

"You seem to have quite a few of those."

"I guess we'll have plenty of time to get into them now that you're along for the ride." Kieran nodded toward the door. "Would you like to see the control room? I can properly introduce you to Santiago and Ariel. After that, my sister and Delilah should be done with . . . whatever they're doing."

"Lead on."

After their conversation, Kieran led Sebastian back upstairs to the control room, where Ariel and Santiago were chatting about where they should stop to restock supplies. Their introductions were pleasant, Ariel asking Sebastian a thousand questions about who he might know in Shui City until they found a mutual acquaintance, seeing as Ariel had grown up there as well. Santiago kept shooting Kieran meaningful looks, which Kieran ignored. Sure, Sebastian was handsome, but that wasn't why Kieran had agreed to let him on board. On the contrary, he knew exactly how hard it was to trust a total stranger in a situation like this; he'd asked the very same of Delilah less than a year ago, after all. It felt, in a strange, cosmic way, like paying it forward.

The sun was setting by the time they got upstairs to swap introductions with Briar and Delilah. Briar answered the door, trading a quick greeting with Sebastian, which felt less like pleasantries and more like Briar wanted them to leave her alone. Delilah, however, hopped up from their shared bed and came to the door to introduce herself and took over the conversation, much to both twins' relief. Briar excused herself while Delilah had a brief exchange with Sebastian about what he thought about the ship, if he was settling in okay, and how she'd drop some sweets off at his door after she did some baking later.

Once they'd exchanged nice-to-meet-yous, Delilah quickly reached out and snagged the corner of Kieran's sweater.

"Can I talk to you for a second?" she asked. Her tone was calm, but Kieran caught a flash of something darker in her eyes.

"Sure." To Sebastian, Kieran added, "I can grab you when dinner's ready?"

"I would appreciate that. I might go back to the observation deck for a bit—take in the view." Sebastian nodded to them. "See you all later."

Kieran waved as Sebastian exited, only stopping when Delilah pulled him inside, closing the door behind him.

As he stumbled in, Delilah said to Briar, "I seriously might throw up from the smell—can you light those candles I brought?"

Briar dutifully went to Delilah's trunk by the foot of the bed and dug out a bunch of candles, which she lit with a spark at the tip of her finger. Kieran watched in horror as Delilah took deep breaths through her mouth, looking paler than normal. Kieran had seen her like this only once before, and it had been . . .

Well, when they met. And the stench of his former curse—the kind that only Delilah, a rare type of witch who could smell magic, could sense—had overwhelmed her.

Kieran's stomach dropped. He started, "Is Sebastian . . . ?"

"Cursed? I don't know. I've never smelled anything like it," Delilah replied, eyes closed. Her forehead was wrinkled, nose scrunched up, and lips turned down in a frown. She went to one of the tables of candles and wafted the scent toward her.

"Do you think it's dangerous?"

Delilah pinched the skin between her eyebrows and shook her head. "It's just so . . . different from anything I've ever smelled. At first, I thought I was smelling the blood on him, but it's worse than that. It *stinks,* like he bathes in gore every night."

"What kind of curse would cause that?"

Delilah shook her head. "I don't know. But honestly? It . . . scares me. All of a sudden, I felt like I was looking at an animal whose behavior was just off enough to hint that it had gone rabid."

"He's not *rabid,*" Kieran scoffed. "He's *terrified.* And rightfully so. Wouldn't *you* be scared if someone tried to kill you this morning? Cursed or not, he needs help. And who are we to turn away someone with a curse? It'd be awfully hypocritical."

Delilah bit her lip, considering her words. Softly, she said, "Just . . . be careful, all right? Maybe I'm paranoid, but something here seems . . . off."

"Only time will tell," Briar offered.

Kieran looked over his shoulder at the door, thinking of Sebastian heading down to the observation deck. To add a powerful curse on top of the fact that he was supporting his family? He couldn't even imagine. Kieran exhaled a breath.

I have a lot to learn about Sebastian Feng.

CHAPTER SIX

Dear Ash,

I don't know when—or, really, if—I'll ever send this letter, but I can't sleep and I figured that I could at least get all this off my chest in the meantime. I'll come right out and say it: I miss you. I miss cuddling on your couch while we listen to the radio. I miss seeing your smile when you walk through the door of my café every morning. I miss kissing you as we lie in bed and fall asleep to the city noise. I may not physically be in Gellingham now, but my heart is still there with you.

I'm on my Calling, which I'll tell you all about when I'm finished. ~~since the only way you'll ever see me again is if I break this curse.~~ My first task is retrieving the hilt of a magic scepter from a lake. Easy, right? We're going to land tomorrow evening, so I've been practicing my magic. I managed to light a candle, which is a great start! Nothing else really worked, but I'm not overthinking it. I'm sure it'll just be a quick in and out before we're back on the aeroship and coasting to our next stop. I'll be home before you know it, Calling complete and you and I back on track!

~~Who am I kidding? There's no way I can do this. We're over, it's done, I'm screwed. I'm sure I'll probably come up with some stupid idea that'll get me killed at the very first stop because I'm supposed to be the leader of this whole quest and meanwhile I can barely lead myself to the bathroom to brush my teeth every morning. Sure, it's great to have Sebastian along, but if I don't get myself killed doing something stupid, his former boss will likely do it for me. Verbena should have let that toad monster eat me. Would have been kinder than letting me fumble my way to an untimely death.~~

~~Love~~ Yours,
Kieran

The next morning at breakfast, Sebastian withdrew a map from his pocket and spread it out on the table, much to everyone's blinking surprise.

"This is a copy of Elias's intended path to each scepter part's location," he explained as he used his teacup, plate, and silverware to hold down the corners of the map. "I did my best to copy it from memory, so I may have missed a few notes, but it should help us avoid any run-ins with his mercenaries."

Ariel looked up from adding too many sugar cubes to their coffee. Their narrowed eyes slid over to Sebastian's side and scanned the map. They took a loud sip of coffee and nodded, fingers drumming on the table.

"These are the most direct routes to each place," they said. They reached into a vest pocket and withdrew a compass, a protractor, and a pencil and began making marks on the page. "Not much of a surprise that he'd be wanting to reach each location as quickly as possible. Any idea when he left?"

"He's a half day behind us," Sebastian said, and pointed to an upscale part of Gellingham on the map. Kieran had never been there, but he knew that's where Klaus Hammond lived, along with most of the city's gentry. "He was planning to leave his mansion in the evening after he'd met up with the mercenaries. So we've got a head start, but his mercenaries could easily catch up if they have smaller, faster aeroships."

"So we have to decide whether to risk attack or to delay our progress by taking a slower, roundabout path," Kieran realized aloud. He rubbed his chin, noticing he'd developed a bit of stubble overnight. He made a mental note to shave before its embarrassing patchiness became more apparent. "What do you think, Ariel?"

"Honestly? I might just stay on the fastest path and see if we can outrun them," the pilot said, tapping their lower lip with their pencil. They shot Delilah and Briar a look. "How do you feel about fighting some mercs?"

"It's been a while since I've taken my anger out on someone trying to kill me. Might be fun," Briar said, taking a bite of bacon. She used the strip to point at Sebastian. "How about you? You have any combat training?"

Sebastian's face didn't change as he said, much to Kieran's shock, "Yes."

Kieran asked, "Er, self-defense, right? You mentioned that on the phone."

Sebastian shrugged, all nonchalance. "My father wanted to make sure his kids could defend themselves. He taught me and my sisters a few useful things before he passed. I didn't escape Elias without leaving him with a couple bruises."

"Ooh!" Briar chuckled, flexing her eyebrows as she took another bite. "I like you."

"I'd rather not fight anyone if at all possible," Delilah cut in, shooting a chastising look at Briar, who just snorted. Unfazed, Delilah continued: "But keeping our head start seems more important for now—at least until we know more about what we're dealing with."

"I agree," Ariel said. They met Kieran's gaze. "You get final say, kid. What do you think?"

"I, um . . . I . . ." A lump rose in Kieran's throat. Leadership wasn't something he felt particularly comfortable with, especially when he was in a room with someone like Delilah, who, historically, was great at it. She was fair and rational. Really, she should be the one to—

You're doing it again, Ash's voice said in his head. *Comparing yourself to other people. Just as you always do.*

Much to his surprise, Sebastian cleared his throat beside him. Their arms were only a few inches apart on the table, and he closed the distance to nudge his elbow against Kieran's.

He said, "I trust your judgment."

Heat blazed in Kieran's face. *He . . . trusts me?*

"Uh—yes," Kieran blurted. He coughed, trying to cover up how suddenly he'd spoken. *It's going to be a miracle if he doesn't notice how red I am.* "I, um, I think we should stay on this path. We'll get to the Lake of Whispers tonight and have time to investigate the area and figure out how to get to the Hilt."

Agreeing, Ariel pointed to the map. "There's a town called Raven's Roost at the edge of the lake. Santiago and I can stay here to refuel while you kids poke around. The locals probably know more about the lake."

"Right. Let's do that." Kieran glanced between Sebastian, Briar, and Delilah. "Ready to do a little investigating?"

While Briar and Delilah just nodded, Sebastian said, in a voice that was all velvet and honey, "Looking forward to it."

Kieran's traitorous heart did a backflip in his chest.

I am in serious trouble.

"Is it just me or is the lake . . . steaming?" Kieran asked.

Kieran, Delilah, Briar, and Sebastian stared out at the small town of Raven's Roost as the final rays of sun set into the lake. They'd landed about an hour before, leaving Ariel and Santiago on the aeroship while they explored. The town was lit by golden streetlamps that scented the air with the aroma of burning oil. A faint mist hung around them, seeming to rise from the ground, where snow had begun to melt. The streets themselves were slush-slick cobblestone, and mostly devoid of cars. There weren't many people out, but the few who were had their heads down as they made their way down the street.

Beyond them, however, was the looming shadow that Kieran could only assume was the Lake of Whispers. It was unlike other lakes he'd seen; this one appeared to be situated in a shallow crater, with jagged rock edges that stuck up around it like teeth. Light from Raven's Roost bounced off the steam rising from the lake, giving it an almost ghostly glow in the waning light.

"It must be a geothermal spring," Delilah said, hands on her hips. "They're a lot more common in the north. Though I've never heard of one that size."

"Fascinating," Kieran said. He gestured to the town. "Maybe we can ask the locals about it. What do you say we try the pub?"

Everyone nodded in agreement—Briar a bit more enthusiastically than the others, muttering that she'd kill for a drink—and they followed the path before them into town.

As they began their trek down the main street, Kieran let his eyes wander. The whole town was drenched in a plume of golden mist, obscuring the townsfolk's faces until they were close enough to reach out and touch. As they did, Kieran couldn't help but notice that upon looking at him, each person seemed to bow their head and hurry in the other direction. After the third time it happened, Kieran subtly checked his reflection in a window. *Must be the horrible stubble.*

As he tried to meet his own gaze, though, Kieran felt a chill come over him—the shopwindows they were passing were covered in posters featuring sketches of people both young and old. Above the sketches was printed a single word: MISSING.

Kieran reached over and tugged Delilah's sleeve. "Am I hallucinating, or are there at least twenty missing-persons posters on that shopwindow?"

Delilah ground to a halt. She gave Kieran a questioning look before her gaze swept over the window. She took a step closer, hesitantly, as if one of the illustrations might jump out and bite her. Her lips moved as she read each of the names, and the color drained from her face.

"They're all recent," she said, gray eyes rounding. "But I can see more tape marks around them, which makes me think there have been more than just these in the window. That . . . can't be a good sign."

Above them on one of the rooftops, a crow let out a sharp caw, and Kieran nearly tackled Delilah in terror. She withheld a laugh while he cursed under his breath.

"Let the record show, I hate it here," he squeaked.

"Hey!" Briar called from up ahead, waving a hand. "Come on, I see a pub!"

Delilah offered Kieran a sympathetic arm pat before speeding up to reach her girlfriend. He had to jog to catch up, eventually falling into step with Sebastian, who waited a few paces behind Briar and Delilah.

"This place seems . . ." Sebastian started, making eye contact with a flock of crows that had assembled atop a boarded-up store that looked as if it had once sold antiques. His lips twitched toward a frown. "A bit unsettling."

"Understatement of the century," Kieran grumbled. "The sooner we can get the Hilt and get out of here, the better."

Sebastian nodded his agreement.

Not long after, the sign for the local pub, the Sunken Soul, came into view. It hung askew from a metal rod and creaked faintly in the wind. Through the window, Kieran could see that the entire place had hardwood flooring and matching wood paneling on the walls, the only breaks in color coming from old portraits nailed to the wall. People crowded around tables and squeezed in at the bar, sipping from steins of golden ale. In the corner, some young women played darts, but that seemed to be the most exciting thing going on. *One of these people must know something about the Hilt.*

Briar pushed the door open and held it for the others. A little bell rang overhead as they stepped inside, and every eye in the pub immediately turned their way.

Kieran's skin crawled. Every person in the pub had gone silent, staring at them as if they'd come in and fired off explosive spells in every direction. While a few stopped after a beat, most just kept looking. Others whispered behind their hands while some not-so-subtly pointed at them. Anxiety tightened Kieran's throat. Suddenly, he had a newfound understanding of how zoo animals must feel.

Seemingly unruffled, Briar said, "Looks like there's room at the bar over here. Come on."

As they waded deeper into the pub, more of the stares fell away, and Kieran remembered how to breathe again. Townsfolk scooted away from the four of them as they took the last group of open seats at the bar. Kieran took one between Delilah and Sebastian.

"Could I get a whiskey?" Briar asked the bartender. "On the rocks?"

The barmaid—an older woman with thick, gray-streaked black hair and brown skin—turned at the sound of Briar's voice and cocked an eyebrow at her. Silently, she grabbed a bottle off a shelf and poured the contents into a glass, then pushed it in Briar's direction.

"Water's fine for me," Kieran said, knowing that his incredibly low tolerance for alcohol would catch up with him if he wasn't careful. Delilah nodded in agreement and asked for the same.

"I'll have the house red," Sebastian said.

The barmaid was silent as she poured everyone their drinks and slid them across the bar. She wrote out the tab for each and passed it to them, still not speaking a word.

Before she could turn away, Kieran cleared his throat. "So, um—sorry to distract you while you're working, but we're new in town, and I was hoping to ask a few questions about the lake."

The barmaid blinked at him as if that was the dumbest statement she'd ever heard. Color flooded Kieran's cheeks as she drawled, "It's a lake. Not much else to know."

"Is it a warm spring?" Delilah asked. "We saw steam rising when we came in."

The barmaid nodded. "Yup."

They waited a beat for her to continue, but it seemed that was all they were going to get out of her on the subject.

She began to reach for a dirty glass to clean when Briar took a big swig of whiskey, sighed, and said, "All right—let's cut to the chase: We're looking for a magic-imbued item that's supposed to be in the lake. Part of a scepter. You familiar with it? Know how we might get to it?"

For the first time, the barmaid's face changed. Her eyes widened for a moment, her fingers tightening around the glass she'd picked up. For a second, Kieran could have sworn he saw her lip tremble.

In a quieter voice, she said, "Unless you're looking to die, you're better off leaving that lake well enough alone. That's witch stuff, and we don't trust witches here anymore."

That, it seemed, was her final word on the subject. While Kieran sat agog, she turned and walked to the other side of the bar to take an order from some surly-looking men. Kieran turned to see Sebastian's reaction, but he was just sipping his wine.

"Well, that was ominous," Briar grumbled.

Delilah pulled her hair back from her face, twisting it around as if she were going to put it in a bun. Kieran recognized it as a nervous habit that tended to get worse the more anxious she grew. "What do you think she meant by *witch stuff*?"

"No idea," Kieran muttered. "But something tells me we might want to lay off on any magic until we learn more."

"I suspect we may need to change our approach," Sebastian said, using his thumb to wipe a droplet of wine from his lip. He set his empty glass down. *That was fast,* Kieran thought. "I . . . have an idea, if you're willing to let me take the lead."

"At this point, I'll do anything," Kieran admitted.

Sebastian nodded, then said, "Briar, Delilah—maybe see if you can strike up a conversation with any amenable townsfolk here. In the meantime . . . Kieran, would you mind coming with me?"

"Me?" Kieran blinked. "Why?"

"I have a plan that I suspect might work better with just the two of us." Sebastian nodded toward the pool tables and dartboards at the back of the pub. "Any experience with darts?"

Kieran thought back. He'd never played. But he'd done a lot of archery as a child on the Pelumbra estate and had always had good aim, so maybe that would translate to darts. If not, well, what did he have to lose? Other than an eye, maybe.

"No, but I can certainly try."

"Right, then." Sebastian nodded to the girls. "We'll be back shortly."

"Sorry to interrupt, ladies. Mind if we join you?"

The two women playing darts paused their conversation, turning to find Sebastian smiling warmly. They looked to be in their early twenties at most and shared a likeness that made Kieran think they might be sisters or even twins. Both had straight blond hair, blue eyes, and pale skin and wore heavy woolen dresses to keep out the cold. One had the flush of someone who'd had a bit too much to drink, while the other seemed sober.

"I don't recognize you," the sober sister said, swirling sparkling pink wine around in her glass. "You tourists?"

"Tourists." The drunker girl laughed. "No way. What tourist would want to come to a horrible place like this? They must have family here or something."

"We're just passing through," Sebastian replied breezily. "Thought we'd try our hand at mingling a bit with some kind locals like yourselves before we head out tomorrow. Learn about the town, get a sense of what there is to do around here—you know. I'm Sebastian, by the way, and this is my friend Kieran."

The drunker one scoffed. "You think we're *kind*?"

"I suppose that remains to be seen." Sebastian ran his hand

back through his hair, offering her a wink. "I probably shouldn't just assume that every beautiful woman is kind, should I?"

Kieran's stomach flipped as the color drained from his face. *Is he . . . flirting with them? He's definitely flirting with them. Shit, does that mean he wants* me *to flirt with them? Because he's made some wildly incorrect assumptions about me if he thinks I'm well-versed in wooing women. The last girl I kissed was my mother when I was five.*

"Well, aren't you smooth?" The drunker girl laughed, not seeming to notice Kieran's internal meltdown. "But you're not gonna have much luck mingling around here. Nobody *wants* to be in Raven's Roost anymore."

Her sister immediately shot her a sharp look, and it was obvious she'd said too much. The drunker sister rolled her eyes.

"*What,* Deena?"

Before the more sober woman—Deena—could respond to her sister, Sebastian cut in: "It sounds like this place has a bit more going on than meets the eye."

"What's it to you?" Deena asked, though she didn't sound accusatory as she said it—more wondering why in the world Sebastian would even be interested.

He shrugged. "Just a sense I got. We were thinking of checking out the lake tomorrow before we leave, since it's a warm spring, but no one we've met wants to tell us about it. Why is that?"

Deena froze and quickly shot her sister a look before she could say anything. "It's a . . . touchy subject."

Sebastian just chuckled. "Well, fair enough. But what if we made a friendly bet on it?"

The drunker sister barked a laugh. "A bet? What kind of bet?"

"Lila," Deena warned.

Sebastian hooked a thumb toward Kieran. "How about a few rounds of darts? If Kieran and I can beat you, we get to ask you one question about Raven's Roost and you have to answer truthfully."

The drunker sister, Lila, broke into a grin. "Sure. But I should warn you, we're *very* good at darts. Maybe the best in town. And I might ask a little favor if we beat you."

"Ask away."

"If we win"—Lila giggled—"you have to give me a kiss."

Sebastian gave another smile that didn't quite reach his eyes. "I think I can handle that."

Kieran's hands turned clammy. He suddenly wondered if he'd misread Sebastian. Did he only like women? Not that it mattered, of course. It wasn't as if Kieran cared who Sebastian kissed. They'd just met, after all, and Kieran had Ash. Kind of.

So why did he have to fight to stop his jaw from clenching and his fingers from tightening at his sides?

"Well, then." Lila dimpled, fluttering her eyelashes. "Get ready to lose, pretty boy."

Lila tossed her hair and went to retrieve the darts from the board. As she did, her sister shook her head, letting out a sigh as she crossed her arms over her chest. If Kieran had to guess, this was far from the first time Lila had agreed to a challenge like this and dragged Deena along with her. Part of him wanted to commiserate with her, but that would probably blow his cover if he was, in fact, supposed to pretend he had any interest in flirting with women.

Meanwhile, Sebastian met Kieran's gaze. He offered a quarter smile and flexed his eyebrows.

An entire kaleidoscope of butterflies fluttered to life in Kieran's stomach.

Lila returned with the darts the next moment and passed three each to Kieran, Sebastian, and Deena. Jutting her chin toward the board on the wall, she explained: "Let's keep it simple: The team with the highest combined score wins the round. Best two of three. Ready?"

Kieran and Sebastian nodded, and Lila turned back to the board. She narrowed her eyes and held her tongue between her teeth as she lined up the shot. She flicked her three darts at the board, landing them all in the twenty- and eighteen-point slivers of the board. Kieran's eyes widened while Sebastian nodded. Lila giggled and lifted her skirt to curtsy before sidestepping to let her sister take a turn.

"Not bad," Sebastian said.

"And that's after four drinks," she said with a wink.

Kieran's jaw twitched. *Why do they keep winking? Do they think winking is attractive? I certainly don't. It looks like they have dust in their eyes, and eye irritation is serious business.*

Deena took her turn, landing one shot in the twenty-point sliver while her others flew somewhat askew. She cursed as Lila tallied up their points and retrieved their darts to give Sebastian and Kieran their turn. Kieran found himself going next, lining his shoes up with the strip of tape on the floor.

He weighed the dart in his hand. *If I mess this up, we're out of leads and I have to watch Sebastian kiss some random girl. Oh, I'm so fucked. I've never even done this before! I should just tap out now—feign stomach problems. Well, not* feign, *exactly. I do think I might actually puke—*

Just then, Kieran felt a gentle nudge against his hand. He glanced down to find Sebastian's pinky brushing his own, so softly it was almost imperceptible. Kieran tried to look at him, but he was facing the other direction, chatting with the girls. Still, the touch was there, like a secret whispered between the two of them.

Kieran inhaled, lifted the dart, and flicked it forward with his wrist.

It hit the dead center of the bull's-eye.

Lila gasped, breaking the focus of their conversation. Deena let out a low whistle. A small smile warmed Sebastian's face.

Feeling their eyes on him, Kieran threw his other two darts, bolstered by the first shot. They didn't hit the bull's-eye, but he did manage to get them in the green circle outside it. As each one hit with a satisfying *thunk,* his smile grew wider, his back straightening. There was a lightness in his chest he hadn't felt in a long, long time.

"Damn," Deena muttered while her sister just gawked. "Well done."

Kieran bowed, eyes and smile sunny. "Thank you."

"Gonna be tough to follow that," Sebastian said. He slid into Kieran's spot in front of the tape line. Lining up his shot, he told Kieran, "You're very impressive, Kieran Pelumbra."

Kieran's face warmed. "Oh, no, I mean—I'm sure it's just beginner's luck."

In lieu of immediately responding, Sebastian threw all three of his darts in quick succession.

Bull's-eye.

Bull's-eye.

Bull's-eye.

Kieran's jaw dropped.

Sebastian shot him a sly smile. "I guess we make a pretty good team."

CHAPTER SEVEN

"So, basically," Kieran explained to Delilah and Briar, "we need to find the village witch."

Back at the aeroship, Kieran sat in the study with the two of them. Briar was nursing a glass of water, having had a few too many drinks. Delilah was beside her, petting her short ginger pixie cut as they sat beneath a blanket on the green velvet couch. Briar leaned up against her, eyes heavy, seemingly seconds away from falling asleep. Kieran sat alone across from them with a cup of tea.

Sebastian had elected to stay at the pub for a while longer, even after they'd been able to repeat their success at darts and won easily, much to Deena and Lila's horror. After a bit of prodding from Sebastian about their deal, he'd gotten Lila to admit the truth: The missing posters all over town, the fear in the residents' faces—it was all because of the village witch.

"Lila told us that the lake was perfectly safe until six months ago," Kieran continued, setting his tea down on the ornate side table. "But the townsfolk think someone cursed it. Now it seems to be drawing in townsfolk and drowning them. That's why they call it the Lake of Whispers: It *speaks* to people. And it doesn't stop until . . . well . . . the listeners drown."

"Great," Briar slurred, nuzzling closer to Delilah. "Cursed lake. Just what we need."

"Like some kind of siren song?" Delilah asked. "I've read about stuff like that in books but never heard of it happening in real life. Do you think the Hilt is involved?"

Kieran nodded. "Dunno—maybe. Lila didn't know anything about the Hilt. Her only advice was to try to find the village witch. Apparently, she lives on the other side of the lake and hasn't come to town since the lake started killing people. Everyone assumes she had something to do with it."

"Any word on whether the village witch is dangerous?" Delilah asked.

Kieran shrugged. "Lila said she was much loved before the curse. Now no one gets close to her cottage. So . . . I guess we won't know until we go."

Delilah raised her eyebrows. "Is that your plan? To go see her?"

Kieran paused. Once again, leadership had been foisted upon him, and he very much didn't enjoy it. He felt himself moving to ask Delilah her opinion, but really, wasn't that exactly what Ash would expect him to do? Just go with the flow and hope someone else figured it out for him?

Kieran pursed his lips. *If I want to get him back, I have to start taking control of my life.*

Finally, Kieran nodded. "Yeah. First thing tomorrow, let's all head over there. If we're going to find the Hilt, we have to figure out what's going on with the lake first. And who knows, maybe she's really nice outside of the whole cursing-lakes thing."

Delilah and Briar exchanged a doubtful look, but neither tried to argue. Finally, they nodded.

Hopefully, Kieran thought, *I'm not leading us into a trap.*

Later that evening, after Delilah and Briar had gone to bed, Kieran headed to the upper deck and stared out across the airfield.

He sighed, leaning against the banister at the front of the ship. He looked out toward the Lake of Whispers with its teethlike rocky edges. At this time of night, it was little more than a shadow in the distance, taunting him.

Ever since his conversation with Delilah and Briar, he'd felt that he was on the verge of a panic attack. In his life, he'd made exactly one big decision on his own: stealing the aeroship from his father and running away from the Pelumbra estate to try to break his curse. The only way he'd managed it was because of sheer desperation: If he'd stayed, he'd be dead.

Since then, he'd been perfectly happy to let others take control. Leadership was something that simply did not mesh with his brain—he hated making mistakes, hated being seen as a failure. Pelumbras were raised to be perfect. They were strong, bold, capable leaders who valued logic over emotion.

So, in summary: everything Kieran wasn't.

He let his forehead press against the tops of his forearms where he leaned on the banister. *I have to be better. Stronger. Less likely to cry and throw up at the slightest inconvenience.*

He lifted his eyes just enough to look up at the stars. At least it was a clear night, so his view wasn't bad. The moon hung heavy above him, a waning gibbous. *I'm so out of my depth.*

"Needed some air?"

Kieran let out an inelegant shriek as he whipped around to find Sebastian standing behind him. He clapped a hand over his chest, trying to catch his breath. Sebastian just wordlessly looked at him, his expression even.

"You scared me," Kieran said, trying to smooth his coat. Absently, his hand went to his hair to make sure none of his curls had decided to stick straight up. "Sorry, um—back already? Did you . . . have a nice time?"

Sebastian huffed out a small laugh. "I got what I needed."

"From one of those sisters?" he blurted out. Thankfully, it came out sounding like pure curiosity instead of an accusation. Kieran was just so surprised—he hadn't taken Sebastian for the type to have casual relationships with women at small-town pubs.

Sebastian nodded. "Yes, Lila. Nice girl. I suspect she'll have quite a hangover tomorrow."

Kieran's nose wrinkled. "She did drink a lot. Likely too much to be sleeping with anyone, don't you think?"

"I— What? No, no, I wasn't talking about intimacy," Sebastian said, dropping the word so casually that Kieran had to pause to process what he'd actually said. "I would never."

"Wait, what were you talking about, then?"

Sebastian fluttered his fingers, but otherwise didn't react. "I was asking her for more information about the lake. I thought it might help us tomorrow."

Kieran immediately paled. "Oh. Oh, goodness, I'm so sorry—I shouldn't have just assumed. I guess I noticed how you seemed to have a connection and thought—"

"It's okay, really." Sebastian held up a hand to stop him. "You're just trying to look out for people. It's a commendable trait." While Kieran groaned and let his head fall back to the banister, Sebastian added, "I'm glad my performance was convincing, though."

"Performance?" Kieran lifted his head just a bit. "You mean . . . you weren't attracted to her? But—you seemed so . . ."

"Earnest? Charming?" Sebastian shrugged. "I try, even if it doesn't come naturally."

"What do you mean?"

Sebastian made his way to Kieran's side, leaning forward on the banister. He stared out at the lake, dark eyes flickering in the moonlight. "It's all scripted, trust me. I use the same couple of lines, smile at them, nod when they're speaking, make eye contact—it's just going through the motions so people see what they want. Left to my own devices, I fear I can be quite . . . awkward. In social situations."

Kieran sputtered a laugh. Immediately, he thought of their first interaction on the ship when Sebastian had mistaken Kieran's trying to get to know him for a job interview. Sure, the other boy was a bit stiff and overly formal when he didn't know what to say, but Kieran found it charming in a strange way.

"Well, you did an excellent job of faking it this evening. In my opinion." A little prickle in Kieran's chest made his pulse begin to race faster. As casually as he could, he asked, "So I guess . . . you don't actually fancy women, then?"

"I do," Sebastian said. For a moment, Kieran's heart dropped before the other boy added, "Occasionally. Not as much as the alternatives, however." Kieran wasn't sure, but he could have sworn he saw him lick his lips. Sebastian added, eyes still trained straight ahead toward the lake, "What about you? You didn't seem particularly enthused by Deena."

Kieran had to stop himself from snorting—he'd always figured it was obvious, but maybe not. "Oh, no, I don't like women." When Sebastian cocked an eyebrow at him, he quickly corrected, "I mean—of course I *like* women—as friends! Just not, um . . ." He searched for the right word. ". . . carnally?"

Sebastian sputtered a laugh while Kieran turned beet-red. He covered his face with his hands. "I should stop speaking, shouldn't I?"

"Carnally," Sebastian repeated under his breath, biting back his smile. "Eloquently put."

Kieran moaned, hair falling into his eyes as his head slumped. "Sorry—words and I aren't exactly on the best of terms."

"Oh?" Sebastian turned and leaned his back against the banister so he could get a better look at Kieran. At the feeling of Sebastian's dark eyes on him, Kieran immediately felt heat begin to climb up his neck. "Why do you say that?"

Kieran opened his mouth, then paused. He'd only known Sebastian for a few days. If he had any sense at all, he wouldn't go spilling his secrets to the first person who'd made him feel decent about himself since his series of unfortunate, self-inflicted events. Plus, there was Sebastian's curse to worry about—clearly, he was keeping that secret. Not that Kieran blamed him—even now, he hated talking about his own former curse—but it did raise a flag. Still, there was something about him that made Kieran feel like the two of them could be something more than just colleagues on this quest. Perhaps . . . confidants.

Especially since he really, genuinely seemed to have faith in Kieran. *Even if it is misplaced.*

"Because," Kieran explained, "the whole reason I'm here is I wrote a stupid poem that accidentally put a curse on my boyfriend."

For the first time since Kieran had met him, Sebastian looked genuinely surprised. He studied Kieran's face for a moment as he considered what he'd said. His lips parted, then closed again. His arms crossed over his chest as his eyebrows settled halfway to his hairline.

Finally, he met Kieran's gaze again and settled on "Care to elaborate?"

Before Kieran knew it, he had fallen into an in-depth recollection of the last week of his life, including every detail he could think of from the almost-breakup to the mugging and his realization that he'd cast the curse. The entire time, Sebastian just watched him, barely seeming to react. His dark eyes seemed to almost stare through him, reflecting the silvery moonlight. Kieran found himself trying not to make eye contact—half because of his embarrassment over the situation and half because Sebastian's stare was so unflinching.

Kieran concluded, "So . . . yeah. If you want to run for the hills now, I'd understand."

Finally, after being entirely silent through the whole explanation, Sebastian said, "I appreciate your telling me. Most people I know wouldn't have the courage to own up to a mistake like that."

Kieran shrugged. "It's the least I can do, after everything."

Sebastian tilted his chin to get a better look at Kieran's expression, and Kieran took that moment to once again get a good look at him: skin moon-pale and smooth, a sharp contrast from his black hair and eyes—the concept of chiaroscuro made flesh. He was, genuinely, breathtaking.

"Could I speak plainly for a moment?"

Kieran's heart thumped. "Sure."

"I've made plenty of mistakes in my time," Sebastian admitted. His gaze fell. "Far be it from me to judge you for yours. But—and I don't say this to try to discount your guilt, but . . . cursing Ash to not be able to perceive you isn't *that* bad."

Kieran choked. "I— *What? Not that bad?*"

"As far as curses go, yes." Sebastian shrugged. "It's not like he's rotting from the inside out or turning everyone he touches to dust. Obviously, any curse is less than ideal, but it's not like you intentionally hurt him. I'm just saying . . . perhaps you deserve a bit more grace."

"Now, *that's* a new one," Kieran muttered. "You do realize cursewriting is illegal, right? I committed a crime."

"Ah, of course. And such a dangerous one, at that. How will I ever survive an encounter with this dangerous witch and his wicked rhyme schemes?"

Kieran rolled his eyes, knocking his elbow against Sebastian's. "Since when do you tell jokes?"

"I'm just saying, it could be *much* worse." The faint smile that had warmed Sebastian's face faded, and for a moment, a shadow passed over his eyes. "Trust me."

Kieran studied him. Was this a reasonable moment to ask about his curse? It was taboo, sure, but maybe Sebastian wanted to talk about it—

Before Kieran could open his mouth, Sebastian straightened from where he'd been leaning on the banister. He tucked a loose piece of inky black hair behind his ear. "But I should get to bed. I take it we're speaking to the village witch tomorrow?"

"That's the plan." Kieran sighed. "Hopefully she doesn't try to kill us on the spot."

"Well, I'll do my best to make sure that doesn't happen." The corner of Sebastian's lips lifted in a quarter smile. "See you tomorrow, Kieran."

In that moment, Kieran caught sight of a small reddish stain beside Sebastian's mouth.

Without a second thought, Kieran reached out, brushing his thumb over the smudge to wipe it away. Sebastian's eyebrows shot up as Kieran pulled back and explained, "Sorry, it's just—you had a little wine stain by your lip."

Sebastian, for a moment, froze as if he'd been hit. Then his shoulders relaxed, and he rubbed his sleeve across his mouth.

"Thank you," he said, voice muffled by his sleeve. "I'll, ah, wash up. Good night, Kieran."

Kieran barely had a chance to wish him good night before Sebastian rushed back to his cabin.

The village witch's shack sat on the other side of the Lake of Whispers, and it took Kieran and his friends nearly forty minutes just to skirt the edge of it. The air was cold enough that they could see their breath, and Kieran wrapped his arms around himself to keep in the warmth. Frost turned the pine trees' needles a silvery green that sparkled in the light from the rising sun.

Kieran probably would have appreciated the beauty of the wintry scene if he weren't running on less than three hours of sleep. He'd spent the night tossing and turning, considering everything that could go wrong. He felt unprepared, exposed, and extremely nauseated.

But I can't fail him, Kieran reminded himself, thinking of Ash's smiling face. *I can't.*

As the sunrise turned the sky pink and orange, they came upon the witch's home. It was nestled among a copse of towering pine trees—easy to miss if you weren't looking for it. Smoke rose from the chimney, so it was clear someone was inside, even though the windows were dark. Frost coated the stone pathway up to the front door, and Kieran took care not to slip.

As they came to the door, Kieran spotted a wooden sign nailed to it. It read: MAGICAL SERVICES DISCONTINUED UNTIL FURTHER NOTICE. SORRY. COME BACK LATER.

Kieran stood with arms akimbo. "At least she's polite enough to put out a sign. People like that don't usually begin interactions by trying to kill you."

"The sign is, however, explicitly telling us to leave," Briar pointed out.

Kieran waved his hand dismissively at his twin. "Semantics. Anyway, let's get this over with."

Before his nerves could get the better of him, Kieran reached up and rapped on the wooden door. He immediately took a step back—part of him was afraid that simply touching the door might trigger some sort of poison needle or fireball to shoot out at him.

Nothing happened.

She's clearly inside, Kieran thought, crossing his arms. *She can't ignore us forever.*

Once again, he knocked. "Hello? Is anyone home?"

"We're closed!" a voice called back. It was feminine but hoarse, as if she hadn't spoken to another person in days. "No magic until further notice!"

Kieran called, "We're not here for spells! We just want to talk!"

"Did you hear me? I'm not taking clients! Go home!"

Kieran leaned back on his heels, frowning. There went his theory about the village witch being polite. He glanced over his shoulder at Briar and Delilah, hoping one of them would provide some advice, but they both looked just as perplexed as he was. He took a breath before turning back. *Should we bust down the door? She has no choice but to talk to us if we break and enter—*

Kieran felt a hand on his shoulder and found that Sebastian had come to his side. He cleared his throat and called, "We're here about the lake! We might be able to fix it, but we need your help. We think it has something to do with a magical artifact. Please—there are lives at stake."

This time, the witch didn't immediately respond. Kieran

shot Sebastian a sideways look, cocking an eyebrow. In response, Sebastian whispered, as if reading his mind, "Something tells me she's not going to take kindly to our beating down the door, hmm?"

Kieran opened his mouth to argue but closed it as he realized Sebastian was right. *You're telling me he has nice hair* and *common sense? The nerve.*

Just then, the door let out a small *click* and opened the tiniest sliver. A single green eye appeared in the gap, a dark thumbprint beneath it from lack of sleep.

"Y-you know about the artifact?"

Kieran's eyebrows shot up. "You mean the Hilt? Yes. We were sent here to get it."

The witch inhaled sharply. "So . . . you know about the lake too?"

"It's luring townsfolk in, and no one knows why," Sebastian said plainly. "And they seem to think you're involved."

Kieran quickly cut in, "B-but we don't believe that, obviously."

"You should," the witch said, voice cracking. "It's my fault."

Kieran's mind whirred as he tried to think of a nice way to say it probably wasn't her fault, but he never got the chance. The next moment, seemingly out of nowhere, the witch behind the door sniffled and then burst into tears. Sebastian's brow furrowed while Delilah and Briar exchanged a wide-eyed look.

Ever so gently, Kieran reached out and pushed the door the rest of the way open. It revealed a short, stout woman with auburn hair and freckles who appeared to be in her early twenties. She wore a stained dress, and as soon as the door was open, the smell of body odor began to seep out. Clearly, she hadn't showered in some time.

She snorted up phlegm, rubbing tears from her eyes. "A-are you serious? About helping me?"

Kieran had to actively stop his lip from curling at the smell. The witch was short, and Kieran could see over her head into the shack. Dirty dishes were piled on different surfaces, along with unwashed clothes and moldy, dying potted plants.

Doing his best to keep his voice even as he breathed through his mouth, Kieran said, "We can certainly try."

"Perhaps we could speak inside?" Sebastian offered, seemingly unfazed by the scene before them.

The witch sniffled, then nodded and stepped aside.

"Come in. I'll tell you everything."

The witch's name was Hattie Pren, and for the first time in a while, Kieran was starting to think he'd finally found someone who was having an even worse few months than he was.

After some quick introductions, Hattie led Kieran, Sebastian, Briar, and Delilah to a seating area in front of a wood-burning stove on the left side of the shack. Kieran was grateful for how quickly he went nose-blind—it was quite clear that Hattie hadn't been taking care of herself or her home for some time now. The four stood and watched as Hattie moved to grab the piles of clothes on her couch, hastily tossing them onto her nearby bed. Hesitantly, everyone took a seat while

Hattie tucked herself into a rickety old rocking chair next to the stove.

"So," Kieran said, breaking the silence after a beat. *Great leadership. Keep it up.* "You've been closed for business for a while, eh?"

Hattie looked down at her hands. "It's been six months since I got the town into this mess."

"You know," Sebastian said gently, "you don't seem the type to curse a lake into luring townsfolk to their doom. I'm . . . assuming that was a mistake?"

At Sebastian's assessment, Hattie's pale, freckled cheeks turned pink. Kieran had to stop himself from rolling his eyes. *Socially awkward my ass. Sebastian could woo a wall if he smiled at it long enough.*

Hattie nodded. "I've only been the Raven's Roost village witch for a year or so. Before that, my dad oversaw helping all the townsfolk. He was the most talented potion maker this side of the Slicetooths. His brews could cure everything from cramps to baldness.

"He died unexpectedly—had an allergic reaction while he was out in the woods where no one could help. Suddenly, I was supposed to take over as village witch, but . . . I never wanted the job. I just wanted to work on my inventions in peace."

"Inventions?" Kieran repeated. "What do you mean?"

"Just little things, mostly." Hattie reached into her dress pocket and withdrew a small metal tube that had several joints soldered together so it could twist and bend. As Kieran squinted at it, he realized it had a small triangular head with metal eyes. It took him a beat to put two and two together and realize it was a tiny metal snake.

"I channel my magic through toy making," Hattie went on. She tapped the snake's head twice, and suddenly it began to slither up her arm. Delilah let out a shriek she was barely able to contain by slapping a hand over her mouth. Briar, meanwhile, laughed with glee. Kieran, admittedly, was more on Delilah's side—he didn't want to be on the receiving end of a rusty bite from a magically animated toy.

Sebastian pointed at the snake. "Fascinating. What's its purpose?"

"Purpose?" Hattie blinked. "Um. Companionship, I suppose? It's not sentient or anything, but it's nice to feel like there's something else here." She looked down at her arm where the metal snake had wrapped around her biceps like a bangle. "I get kind of . . . lonely out here all by myself."

"So you create children's toys to fill the social void where friendship used to be?" Sebastian said, perhaps not realizing how cutting the words were. Hattie jerked back while Kieran had to withhold a laugh. *Ah. His script ran out. Now I get it.*

Before Hattie could try to defend herself, Kieran jumped in: "I think what he means is there's a whole village on the other side of the lake. Why not go see them?"

Hattie hung her head, a few pieces of her auburn braid falling into her eyes. "Well . . . I guess it makes sense to tell you. See, legend has it that there's a benevolent spirit that lives in the lake. Making an offering to the spirit is supposed to grant small wishes, so for centuries now, the townsfolk have been leaving things on the shore for the creature. For generations, their wishes came true.

"When my father passed, I spent a lot of time wandering the woods, trying to walk off the grief." Hattie's fingers tightened where they rested atop her thighs. "During one of those walks, I found the hilt of something embedded in the ground. I'd walked that path a thousand times and never once seen it until that morning. The second I touched it, I knew it was *very* magically charged. I decided it must be some sort of . . . good omen. I thought maybe if I offered it to the spirit, I could wish to speak to my father one last time." She sniffled. "To get closure."

"But something went wrong," Kieran said, mostly to himself.

Hattie nodded. "The spirit came to take my offering and swallowed it whole. Suddenly, its entire body changed. It used to be a cute little thing, and now it was morphing into a monster. I barely got away."

"So the Hilt is . . . inside the spirit's stomach?" Briar asked. She withheld a gag and turned to Kieran. "Ugh. That's gonna be nasty work. Glad it's your problem."

"Always appreciate the support, Briar." Kieran sighed.

"Not inside," Hattie corrected. She pointed to the center of her forehead. "It's become something like a horn. If you could pull it out . . . there's a chance the spirit might go back to normal. Stop all this pointless death I've caused."

While tears began to shine in Hattie's eyes, Sebastian nodded. "Pulling the Hilt out sounds easier said than done. We'll need a way to block the siren-song thing Lila told us about, and a way to defend ourselves from attacks. Perhaps beeswax for earplugs and bait to distract it?"

"We won't be able to get to it if it lives underwater, though," Kieran pointed out. "Unless anyone knows a spell to give us gills."

Kieran looked in Delilah and Briar's direction, but both shook their heads. His shoulders wilted. *Shit.*

"I . . . actually may be able to help with that part," Hattie said. She rose from her seat. "Hold on."

She crossed to a wooden workbench tucked into a corner of the room. Random wood and metal pieces were scattered across it, along with some leather strips and tools. She opened a drawer and dug around for a moment before withdrawing a small device. She brought it back to the others and held it out for them to see. It looked a bit like a face mask, with a metal frame that could cover the nose and mouth and a leather lining to help it conform to the wearer's face. Another leather strip went around the back to secure it in place around the wearer's head. The front had a few small holes in the front, seemingly to let air in.

"It's a little different from the toys I usually make," Hattie explained, turning it over in her hands. "It's a mask for breathing underwater. If you can attune your magic to it, it'll transform the water you inhale through the front into air."

Kieran's and his friends' eyebrows all shot up.

"Really?" Briar asked. "Have you tested it?"

"I mean—kind of." Hattie rubbed the back of her neck sheepishly. "I . . . haven't been brave enough to try it in the lake. B-but it worked when I stuck my head in the sink! Granted, I only took a few breaths, but . . ."

"Scientifically speaking," Sebastian said, mostly to Kieran, "that's barely more than a hypothesis."

Kieran opened his mouth to agree, but just then, a loud commotion started outside. It sounded like people screaming, though Kieran hadn't seen any on their walk to Hattie's home. As he wondered where the sound might be coming from, thundering splashes echoed from the lake. Instantly, everyone in the cottage jumped to their feet and ran to the windows.

Outside, two boats floated atop roiling waves, bobbing back and forth as a gigantic tail slapped the water beside them. It was scaled and covered in frills. A few men dressed in skintight black swim garments were in the water. They thrashed wildly, trying to get back to their boats. One of them was only inches away from the boat ladder when a clawed hand the size of a car reached up, grabbed him, and yanked him underwater.

"Are those men mad?" Hattie squeaked, wrapping her arms around herself. "What in the world are they doing?"

"They're not townsfolk?" Keiran asked.

"No—those have to be Elias's mercenaries," Sebastian said, voice cold. His eyes narrowed into a glare. "They're here for the Hilt."

Kieran's throat immediately closed. *They caught up? Does that mean Elias is here?*

"There's the spirit!" Hattie cried, pointing as the water began to ripple. "Look!"

At that moment, a huge head rose from the depths. The creature reminded Kieran of an otter but had the scaled body of an aquamarine serpent. Huge tangles of algae hung off it. It might have been sort of cute if it weren't for the eight beady black eyes and the gnashing, serrated teeth. It was impossible to tell how large it was with part of its body submerged, but based on what he'd seen, Kieran assumed it had to be larger than the aeroship.

And there, in the middle of its forehead, was a shining metal horn.

Kieran gasped, pointing. "That's the Hilt!"

Just then, a tiny aeroship coasted by the spirit's head. It had a bubble-like glass window that revealed the pilot inside. As she got closer to the creature, the glass split and retracted into the body of the ship. The pilot reached an arm out of the cockpit, one hand on the wheel. Her fingers were inches from the Hilt.

The creature thrashed. Its head slammed into the ship, smashing its buzzing left wing to bits. Smoke burst from the machine as it began to tailspin. The pilot's scream was loud enough to reverberate across the lake.

The ship crashed into the water, swallowed by the foaming waves.

With a screech, the spirit plunged its head into the lake. Its entire body arched above the waves as it dove, and Kieran saw several turquoise fins flash in the dawn light as it disappeared into the depths.

"Oh, no fucking way," Briar said quietly. She turned to look at Kieran. "We're not going out there—right?"

In any other situation, Kieran would have immediately agreed with her. That thing was hungry for blood and wasn't going to stop until all of Elias's men were dead. But then again . . .

They were serving as an *excellent* distraction.

Kieran turned to Hattie, heart racing in his ears. "How do I attune my magic to that breathing device?"

She stammered, "Y-you just hold it and channel your magic into it as you would a paintbrush o-or a ball of dough. You'll feel when it connects."

"Are you *mad*?" Briar gaped, completely ignoring Hattie. "That thing is going to kill you if you go out there!"

"She's right," Delilah said, shaking her head furiously. "There has to be another way—"

"I'll help you," Sebastian cut in. When the girls spun on him in horror, he went on, pressing a hand to his chest: "Whatever you need, tell me. You saved my life before—let me repay the favor."

"Oh, so you both have death wishes! Fantastic!" Briar met her twin's eyes. "That thing will rip you apart, Kier. Just admit you're out of your depth, and we'll come up with a different plan."

"Out of my depth?" Kieran frowned and shook his head. "If it were you, you'd charge in there without a second thought!"

"Sure, but that's because I've been practicing combat magic my entire life, so I can defend myself! You, on the other hand, barely know anything *about* magic! What are you going to do if it attacks you, huh? Write a sad poem? Because that went *swimmingly* the last time."

Kieran flinched as if she'd punched him in the jaw. He'd always known how little Briar thought of his competency with magic—she was, admittedly, right—but she'd at least had the decency to keep it to herself until now.

Voice gentle, Delilah started, "Briar, come on—"

"You know what?" Kieran took the breathing mask from Hattie's hand, using it to point at his twin. "Screw you, Briar. I'm going to prove you wrong."

With that, he stormed toward the door, leaving the others slack-jawed behind him.

CHAPTER EIGHT

The back of Kieran's throat burned as he left Hattie's and stormed toward the woods, letting the trees swallow him until he was out of sight. He grasped the breathing device in one hand and held his other in a fist at his side.

Don't cry, he chided himself, even as the tears slid from the corners of his eyes. *Don't you remember what Father used to say? Pelumbra men are the brave ones. Not the ones who cry the second someone doubts them.*

He swiped a sleeve across his face. Ahead of him, the lake had gone deceptively placid. The two boats floated, unmoving, in the calm water. Most of the mercenaries had been able to get back onto them. Two of them were shouting about whether to follow the spirit into the water, while a third man refused to so much as touch the lake again. For now, it seemed, the spirit had elected to lie in wait.

Good, Kieran thought, gripping the breathing device. *Gives me time to attune to this. Then I'll make Briar eat her words.*

Near the edge of the water, Kieran stopped. He looked down at the device, holding it with both hands. It seemed simple enough. He could feel a spark of magic already in it—it was like a wick, and he merely needed to provide the flame. It should be easy. He didn't even have to cast a true spell, just tap into the well of magic in his chest and channel it.

So simple. Any witch could do it.

So why couldn't he, no matter how hard he focused, seem to be able to summon anything but more tears?

Kieran's fingers tightened around the device. His hands had begun to shake. Briar's face hung in his mind's eye, staring him down as if he was the most useless creature alive. Not far behind was Ash, shaking his head in disappointment, knowing full well that Kieran wouldn't even be able to do this if he had ten more years of magical training. His curse would never break, and he'd never take Kieran back.

Pathetic, useless—

"Kieran, wait."

Kieran sniffled and looked up to find Sebastian jogging toward him, hair fluttering in the breeze. Kieran desperately tried to rub the tears out of his eyes, but it was useless. Even if he could stop them, his red face and sniffles would have been obvious.

"Briar's right," Kieran said, looking down at the device. "This was a terrible idea. I can't even prove her wrong, because—because—"

"Take a breath," Sebastian said plainly, putting a hand on his shoulder. The warmth of it immediately made Kieran look up. Sebastian continued, unfazed by Kieran's tears, "If you want to do this, I can help. The spirit is hiding—if you can swim to it, I can distract Elias's men. You might be able to use this as an opportunity to surprise it and take the Hilt while it's focused on the mercenaries."

"But my magic—" Kieran blubbered.

Sebastian squeezed his shoulder. Suddenly, his other hand was clasped over Kieran's, heat from his palm pressing into Kieran's skin. Kieran inhaled sharply. It was enough to make the tears stop.

"You're panicking," Sebastian said. He grasped Kieran's hand tighter. "You just need to focus. Close your eyes and breathe with me. Understood?"

"I—I can't—"

"You can." Sebastian moved his other hand so both of his cradled Kieran's. "Listen to me: Inhale for one . . . two . . . three . . ."

It took Kieran a second to really hear what Sebastian was saying over his panicked heartbeat. His mind was moving a million miles an hour, the world around him nothing but an impressionist blur. But then, slowly, he began to follow along. One long inhale, hold it for three seconds, then exhale. Once, twice, three times.

"Now," Sebastian said, "focus on your magic. Take a minute to find it, then really, really focus. Don't rush."

Kieran nodded, screwing his eyes shut. His thrumming pulse began to slow. The woods around them had gone quiet, as if even the birds were holding their breath. He focused on his breathing for a couple more seconds, then on feeling his magic.

When he'd tried to find it a moment ago, the feeling had been too subtle to grab hold of. Now, though, Kieran could sense the tiniest spark of it deep in his chest. He let his head hang as he visualized giving the spark more oxygen, fanning it with enough force to feed it, but gently enough to keep it from slipping back into the void. All the while, Sebastian held on to his hands, bowing his head toward Kieran's so they were nearly touching. The sensation was electric, skittering over Kieran's skin with warmth.

When he opened his eyes, he found that his hands had begun to glow with subdued silvery light.

Sebastian smiled at him. "Well done."

At those words, Kieran felt a zing of power rush through him, and the light coming off his hands glowed brightly, pulsating like a star come to life. After a second, it shrank back, revealing the breathing device in his hands. Now, though, Kieran could feel the magic within it as if it had come into focus after being nothing but a blur.

A smile broke across his face. "I-it worked!"

Sebastian gave Kieran's hands one last squeeze before he let them go. "I knew it would. Now, Hattie has a boat tied up near the shore. I'll row us to the center of the lake and drop you off as close to the spirit as I can. Then you get the Hilt, and I'll hold off Elias's men. Deal?"

"Deal." Kieran gazed into Sebastian's eyes, feeling a lightness in his body he hadn't felt in a long time—something like courage.

"All right," Sebastian said. "Let's go."

It didn't take long for them to haul Hattie's boat to the water and push off. Sebastian held one oar in each hand, effortlessly paddling them toward the middle of the lake, where Elias's men lay in wait. He'd taken his jacket off to stay cool, revealing a black long-sleeved shirt that clung to his arms. Kieran did his best not to stare as his muscles flexed with each row.

Halfway to the center of the lake, the steam from the warm water below became a cloud of mist that got thicker by the moment.

"Do you think the spirit is doing this?" Kieran asked, watching as Elias's boats became more and more obscured by the mist.

Sebastian shrugged. "Maybe. I don't know much about spirits."

"Guess that makes two of us."

The closer they got, the faster Kieran's heart beat. The breathing device hung around his neck, and he'd stripped down to his white undershirt and shorts. The chill bit at his exposed skin, but the warmth coming off the lake negated some of it. He rubbed the gooseflesh on his arms and worried at his lip.

Once they were a few yards from the other boats, Sebastian brought the boat to a stop. This close, they could hear the mercenaries talking, but the men didn't seem to have noticed their approach, thanks to the mist. Aside from the conversation, the only sound was the gentle lapping of the water against Kieran and Sebastian's boat.

"One more thing," Sebastian whispered. He took Kieran's hand and pressed something into it. Looking down, Kieran saw that it was a small ball of yellowish wax. He cocked his head in confusion, and Sebastian said, "Beeswax. Use it to make earplugs before you go in. That way, if the spirit tries to lure you with its song, it'll be easier to shut out."

Kieran pulled his hand back, meeting Sebastian's dark eyes. "Smart. Thank you."

Sebastian nodded. "Of course. Best of luck. I'll take care of everything up here."

I'll take as much luck as I can get. "Appreciate that. I . . . guess I'll be off, then."

Sebastian nodded. "See you on the other side."

Before he could allow his thoughts to unravel, Kieran balled up the wax, stuffed it in his ears, put on the mask, then slid out of the boat and into the lake.

It swallowed him whole.

As soon as his eyes adjusted, he stared around in awe. The water was crystal clear and warm. Instantly, the tension melted away, and he kicked forward. Hesitantly, he opened his mouth and inhaled, ready for the water to fill the breathing device and send him into a coughing fit.

Nothing happened. He took a deeper breath, and all he got was air.

That's a relief, Kieran thought. *Drowning would be an inglorious way to die after all this.*

He kicked and descended deeper. The bottom of the lake seemed miles away, growing deeper and darker as the sun struggled to shine through. The lakebed was rocky; the boulders were sharp and foreboding. Massive green stalks of feathery kelp rose from the bottom, undulating with the gentle tide. A few small brown fish darted in and out between them, reminding Kieran of birds in a forest—the kelp was thick enough, he realized, to constitute one.

At least it's kind of pretty, he thought as he swam closer to the nearest patch of kelp, reaching out to touch a pale green frond. *Hopefully it's not all gross and slimy.*

Upon running his finger over it, Kieran discovered that it was, in fact, very gross and slimy. He wrenched his hand back, shaking it out as if he'd touched a damp piece of food on a dish he was washing.

Never mind. I hate it here.

Kieran kept a steady pace, kicking toward the bottom. His arms and legs burned from the effort, and his breathing had become a bit heavier, but he was fine otherwise. So far, so good.

The water pressure grew stronger, and he felt it hammering on his eardrums. Still, he swam deeper, and the water grew warmer as he descended. A chill went up his spine—where in the world could the spirit be hiding?

Then he heard a whisper. "Stranger?"

Kieran stopped. At first, he wasn't sure if he'd heard someone say the word out loud or if he'd thought it. His eyes darted around. There was kelp on all sides, swaying ever so gently. As his gaze flitted left to right, he caught a brief flash of a brownish fin. While it was the wrong color to be the creature he'd seen, it was much too large to be a regular fish.

"A stranger?" a different voice said behind him. Kieran whipped around to see another fin disappearing into the kelp. "Here to visit us?"

He reached up to try to press the beeswax deeper into his ears, but as the voices became louder, he realized it was no use: They were in his head.

Just ignore them, Kieran thought, kicking forward. The bottom still felt so far away, and his muscles were screaming for him to take a break. *They're not real.*

He kept going, pushing himself as a third voice began repeating the same thing as the others. "Stranger? Stranger here?"

Not real, Kieran repeated to himself, over and over. *Not real, not real.*

Slowly but surely, the bottom came into focus. He was nearly there. His eyes combed over the rocks, looking for anything resembling the creature he'd seen up above. But it was just rocks. Rocks, and the holdfast roots of the kelp clinging to the bottom. It didn't help that it was so dark. Every rock looked the same. Every one except—

There, at the very bottom of the lake, was the head of an enormous beast, its long, serpentine body curled under it, half hidden by rocks. Its eight eyes stared straight ahead, seemingly unaware of Kieran floating above it. Its scales had changed color to blend in with its surroundings, making it almost impossible to spot. But the metallic glint of the Hilt embedded in its forehead was enough to command Kieran's gaze. Holding his breath, Kieran gently kicked closer, doing his best to disturb the water around him as little as possible. His pulse quickened as he hovered directly above the Hilt.

As he reached for it, something touched his foot.

He whipped around as glinting green scales brushed by him. It was almost too dark to see what the creature was, except that it was long and skinny, with a fish tail and a more humanoid top half. Long, spindly fingers reached for him from all directions. He felt something else brush his hand.

"Stranger," the voices chanted. "Stranger, stranger!"

More scales and more fluttering touches created a blur of

movement around Kieran. With a shout, he swatted at them. His hands rippled straight through them, as if they were nothing but projections of light.

But if they're not solid, how can I feel them touching me? he thought in horror.

More and more fish creatures swept closer, even as Kieran's hands waved blindly through the water, trying to fight them off. All the while, they screamed "Stranger, stranger!" in high-pitched, almost childlike voices. He saw flashes of sharp teeth inside their too-wide mouths. The cacophony made Kieran want to grab his blond curls and rip them out just to feel something in his head that wasn't screaming.

As panic gripped him, a new sensation hit: claws. They were no longer simply touching him but swiping at him, the skin splitting beneath long, bony fingers. Blood rose from the cuts, staining the water red around him. As the creatures swam through it, their words began to change.

"Kieran," they said, instantly paralyzing him. "Kieran's come to see us. Come to stay!"

How had they learned his name?

"Get away from me!" he howled, his voice turning to bubbles. He tried to kick them away. He was nearly within grabbing distance of the Hilt, the spirit just below him, but that didn't matter. His heart was drumming a panicked beat against his ribs, and his throat seemed to be closing up on him.

Suddenly, the lake spirit's head turned, and all its eyes looked straight into his.

Kieran's entire body went cold.

"Kieran?" asked a gentle voice. "Are you okay, my darling?"

Kieran blinked. Suddenly, all the creatures were gone. In their place was a familiar woman, her red hair streaming around her in the water. She had the same sharp chin, pouty lips, and big eyes as Briar, though there was something cloyingly sweet about her smile that Briar could never replicate.

Camilla Pelumbra, Kieran's mother.

She wore a white dress with pink and blue flowers stitched into the neckline. Kieran remembered it from his childhood—she'd worn that most days, not caring when it got dirty as she sat in her garden and stared out at the mountains for hours at a time. Kieran's father would always promise she was just relaxing, but Kieran knew it was more than that. His mother smiled only when she had something to prove; the rest of the time, she had that same faraway look in her eyes, as if she were simply too numb to feel anything but emptiness.

For a moment, a cocktail of emotions overloaded the logical half of Kieran's brain. It had been half a year since he'd seen his mother's face. He hadn't spoken to her since the curse broke, even though there were days when he had to fight the impulse to call her up and chat. That was the hardest part of their estrangement. He'd always been closer to his mother than anyone else in his family, even though she'd been overly coddling and rarely spoke about anything other than herself.

As a child, though, Kieran hadn't cared about that. He'd been her favorite, and it had made him feel good. Even when he'd realized, years later, that her favoritism wasn't so much a love of *him* as it was a love of how the family treated her for having him. She was the tragic mother, doomed to lose her only son to the family curse, which had made her a martyr among the Pelumbras. That kind of attention had fueled her for years, even at her most depressed.

For a second, staring at her floating there in the water, all Kieran wanted was to throw his arms around her. Despite himself, he missed her. He missed the way she'd always made him feel special and talented and *good*.

Everything he hadn't felt since the curse broke.

"Mom?" he whispered.

"It's okay, my sweet boy." She floated closer to him, reaching out a hand to smooth his hair as she always had when he was a child. "It's just us now. I've got you."

As Kieran looked into her eyes, the world around him seemed to blur. The fear that had gripped at him moments ago was gone. While part of him screamed to look away, to escape, it was growing quieter by the moment. In fact, that part of him wondered why the idea had even occurred to him. Why had he ever thought some scepter hilt was important when his mother was right here?

"I missed you," Kieran admitted.

"I know." His mother's arms encircled him, hugging him tightly. She felt warm and steady, an anchor holding him safely in place. He sank into her embrace, squeezing his eyes shut as she whispered, "I've missed you too. And I'm so, so sorry for everything that happened."

That, however, made Kieran pause.

He'd always wanted to hear those words come out of his mother's mouth. Even in those final moments in the basement of the Pelumbra mansion, when Delilah had broken the curse, part of him had been silently begging her to apologize. To admit that she'd been wrong about how she treated her children, to own up to the pain she'd caused both twins. Because then, maybe, he could still have a mother.

But she hadn't. Because part of her, Kieran knew, simply couldn't.

This isn't real.

Kieran blinked, and all at once, the scene around him came back into focus. Where his mother's arms had been before was only kelp. It was wrapped around his arms and legs, and a piece was beginning to encircle his throat.

And staring directly into his eyes, barely a foot away, was the enormous head of the lake spirit. Its jaws were open, massive teeth poised to bite Kieran in half and swallow him.

Instantly, he thrashed, tearing at the kelp with his fingernails. The stalks around his legs clamped down harder, and he swore he heard a faint, shrill scream as he ripped off the one on his left wrist. He grabbed the one around his throat and tore it off, more shrill screams filling his head as he did. They were all in his mother's voice now, begging him to stop.

The spirit's jaws opened wider, preparing to consume him.

"Wait, wait!" Kieran cried, voice muffled by the breathing device. "Stop! I can help you!"

The spirit hesitated. Kieran couldn't be sure, but recognition seemed to show in its eyes. Maybe it could understand him. It had, after all, been granting the townsfolk's wishes for years—it would make sense that it would be capable of listening, even in this corrupted form.

Which is probably my only shot at getting out of this.

"Hattie explained to me that you've spent centuries helping this town," Kieran told the spirit. It hadn't so much as blinked since he'd first opened his mouth, making its stare even more intimidating. Still, Kieran continued, "That's a long time to spend taking care of others. Maybe you could let someone help *you* for once. If you do, I swear I can fix this."

Suddenly, the lake spirit paused. Its mouth closed slightly, and there was something . . . confused about its expression. As if it had never considered that someone might want to help it.

"You must be lonely down here, huh?" Kieran said. As he spoke, the kelp began to loosen around his limbs, withdrawing into the water. "All this time, you've been alone. And you must have felt extra lonely after the scepter's magic changed you. Is that why you lured the townsfolk down here? Because they stopped leaving you presents and you got sad?"

The spirit let out a small whimper. Its mouth closed all the way now, and it hung listlessly in the water, as if all the anger had been drained out of it. Now it just seemed . . . broken.

Ever so gently, Kieran reached out and touched its otter-like snout. "I understand. I used to be lonely too. My family treated me like there was something wrong with me for something I couldn't control. You're the same, aren't you? You're not a monster—you're just angry they abandoned you."

The spirit bowed its head, whimpering again. Kieran rubbed its scaled cheek.

"I might be able to help you change back," Kieran said. "You just have to let me pull that Hilt out of your head. Is that okay?"

The spirit regarded him, unsure. After a moment, though, it drifted closer to him, its head bowed and the Hilt just inches away. Kieran swallowed his terror past the pulse pounding in his throat. He grabbed hold of the Hilt.

It slid free of the creature's head with a burst of light.

The creature let out a sharp cry. At first, a rush of terror flashed through Kieran. *Did I hurt it? Is it about to swallow me whole?*

Then, though, its body began to glow, shrinking before Kieran's eyes. By the time it was finished, the spirit had been reduced to the size and shape of a regular river otter, but with scales and fins like a blue-green fish.

It was, for lack of a better word, adorable.

The spirit made a delighted clicking sound, swimming in a circle before barreling toward Kieran. He yelped as it slammed into his chest, nuzzling into the front of his undershirt and squeaking happily.

Kieran's heart was still racing, but he felt the fear begin to ebb. Gently, he reached out, letting the spirit rub its head against his hand. He scratched the side of its head, a small smile on his face. It may have lured townsfolk to their deaths, but it was under the influence of the Hilt when that happened. Considering what Hattie had said about its having served the town for so many years, he doubted that it posed much danger now.

Still petting the creature, he let his eyes slide to the Hilt in his hand. It was brilliant silver, heavy and solid to the touch. Even in his grasp, it seemed to fizzle with magical energy, as if it could spring to life at any moment.

I did it, Kieran realized through the din of the spirit chirping its thanks. *I actually did it.*

The moment he relaxed, the psychic strain hit Kieran. His limbs felt like jelly, and it was all he could do to go limp and hang in the water. As his head began to pound with a powerful migraine, the lake spirit grabbed hold of his shirt. It held the back of it like a mother cat with the scruff of her kitten, webbed feet flicking as it lifted him toward the surface.

As the light returned and Kieran's vision began to swim with a painful, bright aura, the surface came into view above him. Moments later, his head broke the surface.

He gasped for air as a familiar voice said, "Kieran!"

He looked up just in time to see Sebastian on the rowboat, reaching out for him. Kieran wearily held out his hand. It was barely enough for Sebastian to grab it and haul him halfway into the boat. With a bit more wriggling, Kieran sprawled out, pulled the breathing device off, and gasped for air.

"I got it," he whispered gently, holding up the Hilt.

"I knew you would." Sebastian reached out and gently touched his wrist. "Now let's get to shore before Elias's mercs realize I cut the fuel lines on their boats."

That was all Kieran needed to hear before he passed out, the Hilt held tightly against his chest.

CHAPTER NINE

Kieran awoke sitting in a hot bath.

He sat up with a start, eyes darting around. It took him a moment to realize he was in Briar and Delilah's bathroom, seeing as their room was the only one on the ship with a bath. He glanced down and found he was still in his underclothes. His wrists and ankles were wrapped with angry red marks that stung as Kieran moved. He held up his arm and realized that the shape of the kelp fronds had been pressed into it. When he gently touched his neck, he recoiled as the raw skin stung at his touch. The kelp hadn't cut him, but he was definitely going to bruise.

Not to mention the absolutely seismic headache rocking his skull.

But, he reminded himself, *I'm not dead. So that's a win.*

He stood shakily and stripped off his wet underclothes before grabbing one of the clean towels that Delilah kept under the sink. After drying off, he tied it around his waist so he could head back to his room and put on eight or so sweaters before burying himself in a pile of blankets and, hopefully, napping for the rest of the day. Maybe then his headache would go away.

As he went to the door, it occurred to him that the Hilt was nowhere to be seen.

"Shit," he whispered. *"Shit!"*

Without thinking, Kieran flew from the bathroom and, finding Delilah and Briar's room empty, ran in search of one of his shipmates. He darted onto the top deck—empty as well. He did, however, quickly discover that they were no longer docked in Raven's Roost: They had taken off again.

Kieran took the stairs two at a time before bursting into the dining room. He skidded to a halt in front of the table, where four pairs of eyes turned on him at once.

"Ah," Sebastian said. At the sight of a towel-wrapped Kieran, the boy's face went from stony and unreadable to wide-eyed and bright in a second. "You're . . . awake."

His eyes drifted from Kieran's face down to his bare torso before immediately flicking back up again.

Kieran's entire body seemed to blush bright red all at once. Ariel and Santiago were also at the table, trying and failing to contain their laughter, while Briar pressed a finger into her temple as if this was the most exhausting day of her life. Delilah was nowhere to be seen—at least for a second, until Kieran heard her voice behind him.

"Oh, you're up! I was just grabbing some ice packs to put on those red marks all over you to try to bring the swelling down."

Kieran turned to find Delilah holding two cheesecloth bags

wrapped in twine in each hand. Which was all fine and good, but now he was nearly naked in front of the entire crew, looking as if he'd gone absolutely out of his mind.

Before he could linger on that thought too long, he cried, "The—the Hilt! I had it when I was in the water, but now I can't find it—"

"I put it in your sock drawer," Briar said. When Kieran glanced back at her, it occurred to him that everyone sitting there was in the middle of eating lunch. From the looks of it, Santiago had whipped up some of his classic paella, which explained the pleasant spicy scent in the air. Almost instantly, Kieran's stomach growled.

"Wh-what about Hattie and the spirit?" Kieran asked.

"Hattie was doing a ritual when we left to honor all the souls you released from the lake," Delilah explained. "It sounded like they'd been trapped down there with the spirit for a while now. Once you removed the Hilt, they all floated to the surface and vanished."

Kieran thought back to the lake. "Is that what all those little fish monsters were? Ghosts?"

Delilah repeated, "Fish monsters?"

"Oh, right. Long story." Kieran waved a hand as if to dismiss the thought. "I'll tell you later. And the spirit?"

For whatever reason, at the mention of the spirit, Santiago rolled his eyes melodramatically. Ariel covered their mouth with a hand to stifle laughter, while Delilah bit back a smile.

Before anyone could explain their reactions, Kieran heard a series of little chirps from down the hall. He turned just in time to see a small, scaled otter creature bounding toward him. It was about the size of a house cat, with a long, thick tail that moved like a serpent. The spirit took a running leap, and Kieran barely had time to hold out his arms before it landed in his embrace and nuzzled him under the chin.

"She jumped into the rowboat right after you passed out," Sebastian explained. "Hissed at me every time I tried to move her. Looks like you have a new friend."

The spirit chirped again as Kieran absently scratched her under the chin. She had no scales there—just short, velvety fur. "But what about Raven's Roost? Isn't the lake spirit supposed to grant their wishes?"

"Doesn't seem like she wants to do that anymore," Delilah said. She came to Kieran's side and gently patted the spirit between the shoulder blades. "Right, bud?"

The spirit chirped excitedly, pressing her forehead against Kieran's breastbone.

His eyebrows furrowed. He'd never had a pet before, much less one that was a former lake monster and wish granter. He had no idea how to care for her, but then again, she seemed both sentient and powerful enough to do that for herself. Maybe she just needed a friend. Kieran could certainly use more.

"Well," he said, "I guess we'll have to think of a name for you if you're going to be traveling with us, hmm? How about . . ."

"Seaweed?" Briar joked, gesturing to the red marks on Kieran's neck.

"Perhaps a bit dark," Santiago started. "Although, accurate in that that creature *killed dozens of townsfolk*—"

"Oh, come on," Delilah argued, wagging a finger in the spirit's direction as if tempting her to pounce on it. "She was all mixed up because of the Hilt's magic—she wasn't in her right mind. I don't think she'd hurt a fly now."

"You don't know that," Santiago argued, shooting the creature a look. "Best-case scenario, that creature is going to creep into our beds at night and eat our toes. I don't want to consider the worst case—"

"As long as we stay on her good side, I suspect we'll be fine." Kieran chuckled. "Right, Seaweed?"

The spirit nuzzled closer to Kieran. She made a noise somewhere between a cat's purr and a squeak, and Kieran added, "Aw! See? We're friends now."

"Fine," Santiago grumbled, "but I'm not feeding it, and when it gets peckish for toes, don't say I didn't warn you."

"Anyway," Ariel said, drawing the group's focus away from their new friend, "we're heading south toward the Mirrorveil Woods now—it should take us a week and a half to get there."

"Any sign of Elias's mercenaries?" Kieran asked.

Ariel shook their head. "Not since the lake. Sebastian's cutting the fuel lines on those boats meant they were still trapped out there when we left. Gave us a great head start."

Kieran offered Sebastian a small smile. "Thanks for that."

"Of course. Anything to slow Elias down." Sebastian nodded, his eyes once again drifting to Kieran's bare chest before snapping back up to meet his eyes. "Hopefully, it . . . helps."

Seaweed hopped out of Kieran's arms, exposing his torso again. *Well,* he thought, glancing down at his slim form and nearly hairless chest, *this has been properly humiliating.*

He cleared his throat, crossing his arms over his chest. "In that case, I might just . . . go get dressed."

Delilah held out the ice bags. "Take these. You were shivering when we first brought you back, hence the hot bath, but if you've warmed up enough, you should really give them a try."

"Thank you, Delilah," Kieran said as he took the bags. "You're a lifesaver. I'll, uh, be back shortly. Ideally, a bit more decent."

With that, he turned for the stairs, the spirit on his heels, and told himself that he was imagining Sebastian's eyes burning a hole in his bare skin.

Kieran spent the rest of the day napping on and off in a cocoon of blankets, Seaweed curled up against him like a cat. His head still hurt, but the silence was helping. As he lay there under the blankets, watching the sun shining through the white sheet he'd pulled over his head, he kept thinking about what he'd seen in the lake. There was his mother, of course, but that was a whole other ordeal to unpack. Instead, he thought of all the spirits who were finally released from their watery grave. Where had they gone? Into some kind of afterlife? Did their families know they were free?

He hoped so, genuinely. Even if he hadn't gone to Raven's Roost specifically to help the townsfolk, it still felt good to know he'd done something for all those people. Maybe he'd just barely managed to channel his magic into Hattie's breathing contraption to do it, but he had, hadn't he? He supposed he was something of a hero.

Maybe his magic wasn't a total loss after all.

That night, after most everyone had gone to bed, Kieran lifted Seaweed off his lap, set her down on a bed of pillows to sleep, and went to the kitchen to make himself tea. Back at the Witch's Brew Café, he'd occasionally mix his own tea blends for customers. He'd gotten quite skilled at finding good pairings for blends. This time, he took dried chamomile flowers, sweet and bitter fennel seeds, and licorice root and crushed them together using a mortar and pestle. Then he combined them in a small cheesecloth pouch and placed it in his mug. When the water was boiling, he let it cool for a moment so it wouldn't burn the flowers, then poured it over the teabag, added honey and a few drops of vanilla extract, and took a quick sip. Once he'd decided it was to his liking, he headed up the stairs toward his room.

As he passed the study, he saw a flash of red hair—his sister—then paused when he realized there was no Delilah.

That's odd, he thought. *I almost never see Briar without Delilah these days.*

The twins hadn't really spoken since their spat at Hattie's. Briar's words still stung whenever Kieran played them back in his mind: *You, on the other hand, barely know anything* about *magic.*

At that moment, Briar lifted her head, noticing Kieran lingering outside. She had been reading a book with a yellow-eyed woman on the cover. At the sight of him, Briar jumped, closing the book as if she'd been caught doing something illegal.

"Oh. You're awake." Briar put the book down, then gestured at Kieran's throat as he took a seat on one of the green velvet couches facing her. "Do you want to . . . sit? Your, uh, strangle marks look better."

Kieran couldn't help but snort at her crass description of his wounds. "Thanks. Icing them really did help—"

Before he could finish, Briar burst out, "Also, I'm sorry."

Kieran blinked. "Oh."

"For this morning," she clarified. She kept her gaze focused elsewhere, careful not to meet her brother's eyes. "I was a jerk. I just—I was really worried about you. After seventeen years apart, the thought of losing you to some lake monster was . . . a lot for me to handle. I never had any kind of blood family I cared about before you."

That gave Kieran a moment of pause. Instantly, the image of his mother floating in the lake came back to him, and his expression fell. He always did his best not to bring up the past with Briar, worried that it might stir up bad emotions. After all, she'd had it worse than he had, being raised by their abusive aunt, Wrenlin, in the woods outside Gabriel's Edge. Even if Kieran's childhood hadn't been great, it didn't hold a candle to what Briar had survived.

Still, he didn't know who else he could really talk to about what he'd seen in the lake. He was growing closer to Sebastian, but that felt like a lot to dump on someone he'd just met. And talking about mom stuff with Delilah was tough sometimes—not because she wasn't a good listener or sympathetic (she was very much both), but because her own mother was such a lovely person, it felt . . . wrong, somehow, to bring up the subject with her. As if he'd be angling for pity when he wasn't.

So, despite their unspoken rule not to bring it up, Kieran said, "Speaking of, um, upbringings . . . I saw our mother down there. In the lake."

To his relief, Briar didn't immediately wince as she usually did when someone mentioned their parents. Instead, she chewed her lower lip for a moment before saying, "I assume it wasn't really her?"

"No—definitely not." Kieran stared down into his tea, watching as a few tiny flower petals that had escaped the bag sank to the bottom of the mug. After a moment, he decided to take a seat on the couch next to his twin as he continued: "I think Seaweed made a vision of her to try to keep me down there. For a minute, I fell for it too. That's why I have all these marks—the kelp tried to grab me."

There was a long pause as Briar mulled over his words. She rubbed her thumb over the corner of her book, her expression far away.

Finally, she took a breath. She didn't make eye contact as she asked, "Do you miss her?"

That was a loaded question. But then again, they'd already waded this far into the discussion—no point backing out now.

Kieran took a sip of tea, then shrugged. "It depends on the day, honestly. I never miss our father, or really anyone else in the family barring Adelaide and a few cousins I used to play with when I was little. Father was gone nearly all the time doing business as the head of the family. When he was home, he only made me feel inadequate. I wasn't strong or powerful or, well, *masculine* enough for him. He preferred to avoid me. But Mother . . . she and I were always close. Or, at least, her version of close."

Briar's eyebrows furrowed. "What do you mean, 'her version'?"

Of course Briar wouldn't know. She hadn't grown up with their mother. She'd only met her once after their birth, and it was the night that Delilah broke the curse. She hadn't spent the first seventeen years of her life constantly navigating their mother's moods and trying to win her favor.

Not as Kieran had.

He sighed. "Our mother . . . Well, her mind doesn't work like yours or mine does. I don't think it's intentional. I suspect it's how she was born. She's always been preoccupied with herself, first and foremost."

When Briar cocked an eyebrow at him, Kieran continued: "So, for example, from our mother's point of view, you and I weren't her children. We were just . . . tools she could use as bragging rights, I guess. Which meant that when you were born with your half of the curse, I think she treated you the way she did because she considered you . . . imperfect. Like your existence meant she was imperfect too. Meanwhile, I was doomed to die, and therefore I helped her become a sympathetic martyr to the family. If she could pretend you didn't exist and focus on loving me, then everything would be fine."

"But . . . that's not real love. That's just using you as a prop for her own self-interest."

"I . . . Yeah. I guess that's true." Kieran set his tea down and met Briar's eyes. "When I was down there in the lake, the vision of her apologized for how she had treated me. That's how I knew it couldn't be her. Our mother has never, and will never, apologize."

His voice grew quieter. "Even if I wish she would. Part of me misses her version of love, even if it wasn't good."

Briar nodded. "As a child, you'll take any love you're given." She rubbed at her eyes, and for a moment, Kieran wondered if she was holding back tears. "I felt the same way about Wrenlin when I was little. I . . . I get it."

"I'm not sure it's fair to compare," Kieran said. He pulled his knees up onto the couch and sat cross-legged. "Wrenlin was a monster. At least our mother cared about me, in her own twisted way."

Briar shook her head. "Trauma isn't a competition, Kier. What happened to both of us is wrong. Just because it was different doesn't mean that it didn't royally fuck us both up. You're allowed to be mad. I certainly am—on both our accounts."

"It really isn't fair, is it?"

"No, it isn't fair, and that's what gets me." Briar sat up straighter, and Kieran could sense that what she was about to say was something that she'd been holding in for a long, long time. "You know what makes me feel like a terrible person? Just how jealous I feel when I see other people who have what I don't. People with normal families where love isn't a commodity. It's why I can't talk about stuff like this with Delilah."

Kieran's eyebrows shot up. He'd always pictured her and Delilah's relationship as perfect—they never fought and always seemed happy. But then again, he was seeing it from the outside.

"I know, I know, it's terrible." Briar ran her hands through her hair. "I shouldn't be jealous of my own girlfriend for having a mother who loves her unconditionally. But sometimes I see them together and all I can think is *Why didn't I get that? Didn't I deserve it?* And I know that makes me a bad person—"

"I don't think it does," Kieran cut in. He met his sister's eyes. "We did deserve it. Honestly, that's part of why I miss our mom. It's not so much that I miss *her* as much as I miss the *idea* of her. The idea of a parent who loves unconditionally. Coming to terms with the fact that we'll never have that is . . . horrible, if I'm being honest."

"It is! It's fucking horrible! And it's so hard to explain to someone who hasn't been through it!" Briar was nearly laughing now, hands thrown in the air. "I can't believe we didn't talk about this sooner. I feel like I've been sitting here for months hating myself for being so bitter, because I didn't feel like I could talk to you without dredging up the past."

"Me too." The back of Kieran's throat tightened. He took a deep breath, staving off the tears that threatened to push through. "I guess that's another thing they took away from us, isn't it? We never got to be real siblings. But at least we can now, right?"

"Right." Briar nodded, rubbing her eyes. Kieran wasn't sure he'd seen her cry more than once or twice, so it was a little jarring to see her tearing up. "Not to be all gross and sappy or whatever but . . . I'm really glad you ran away from home, Kieran. That must have taken a lot of guts, all things considered. Ultimately, you saved both of us."

"Delilah definitely did a lot of the heavy lifting there," Kieran said, rubbing the back of his neck sheepishly.

"Come on, give yourself a little more credit. Delilah wouldn't have even met us without you. You're more capable than you think."

Kieran mock-gasped. "Was that a *compliment*? Since when do you give compliments?"

"When they're earned—so don't get used to it." Briar stood up and held out her arms. "I'm going to offer you a hug now, but only if you swear never to speak of it."

Kieran got up and threw his arms around his twin, squeezing her. "Thanks, Briar. I really appreciate it."

"Likewise." She let go of him and then, seeming not to know what to do with herself, punched him a little harder than needed in the arm. "Just don't get used to this corny stuff. It's not my style. Maybe your new boyfriend can help you with that."

Kieran blinked. "New . . . boyfriend?"

"Oh, come on, I have eyes." Briar used her thumb to gesture toward the upper deck. "Sebastian? The guy who can't stop staring at you all the time? Honestly, it's hard to tell if he wants to kiss you or take a bite out of you."

Kieran immediately felt his cheeks turn pink. "What? No, no—I barely know Sebastian. And, sure, he's very handsome and all that, but I have a boyfriend."

"You mean the one who basically dumped you and made you walk home in a blizzard all alone so you got mugged outside our apartment? Be realistic, Kier."

"He couldn't have known that was going to happen! And, sure, it was a little . . . sudden. But that doesn't mean I'm just going to give up on him!" He paused for a moment, his mind unhelpfully conjuring up the image of Sebastian catching him while he swooned like an old-timey maiden. He quickly shook his head to dislodge the thought. "Ash and I dated for six months. He was my first kiss, the first person I ever thought about sleeping with—"

Briar's blue eyes widened. "You never slept with Ash?"

Kieran didn't think it was possible, but his face managed to feel even hotter. "Well—I mean, I—uh—"

"I'm not shaming you. I'm just surprised."

"I guess I wasn't ready to take that step." Kieran felt as if he was about to fold in on himself like the world's most pathetic origami crane. "Maybe that makes me . . . immature or whatever. But I was scared I'd do something wrong and then Ash would break up with me and—"

"You know what? That's none of my business." Briar reached out and patted his shoulder. "Do what you feel is right. Just . . . don't get so caught up trying to glue together the pieces of something broken that you forget to look around and see what's right in front of you."

Kieran frowned. "What's that supposed to mean?"

"You're smart—you'll figure it out." Briar grabbed her book off the couch and gave Kieran a nod. "I'm heading to bed. But . . . thanks for this. It's nice to know I'm not alone."

Still stuck on what she'd said, Kieran agreed, "Likewise."

With that, Briar bid him good night and retreated up the stairs. Slowly, Kieran sank back down on the couch and held his cooled cup of tea between his hands.

I, he decided, *have a lot to think about.*

CHAPTER TEN

Dear Ash,

I'm not sure if I'll get around to sending that first letter I wrote you, or this one, but I suppose I just need to get a few things off my chest.

I think, maybe, it would have been better to have talked a bit more before deciding to take a break. I never even had a chance to explain that I do want to change. It feels a little unfair, if I'm being honest. If we can't talk about these things now, how can we expect to in the future?

Anyway, that aside, I guess I just wanted to say I miss you and I hope we can talk soon. I finished the first step in my Calling, which means I'm one step closer to seeing you.

~~*Hopefully, you'll be able to see me, too.*~~

Yours,
Kieran

The next few days on the ship passed in relative calm as the crew made their way toward the Mirrorveil Woods, in southern Celdwyn. The Hilt remained tucked into Kieran's sock drawer. A few times, he pulled it out and examined it, doing his best to ignore the way his new lake spirit friend hissed at it. Even just running his fingers across the gilded filigree was enough to feel the magic buzzing inside.

In a strange way, it brought him back to the moment he'd had with Sebastian when he'd been able to attune to Hattie's invention. He was so new to summoning his magic on purpose that the feeling of it was still novel to him. It had been so warm and electric—a sculpture waiting to take shape, and all he had to do was mold it.

Maybe, he'd thought later as he stroked Seaweed's head where it rested on his thigh, *I should give it another shot.*

The next morning, Kieran was up before the sun rose. He figured if he was going to try using his magic, it would be best to practice before anyone else woke up and started giving him unsolicited advice. Whenever he'd asked Delilah or Briar for help in the past, their methods of casting had always felt so specific to them. They had their ways of doing things that worked for them, because they'd both had years and years to refine their process. Kieran had tried their methods, sure, but nothing had worked for him.

I just have to find my own way of doing things.

He slid out of bed, Seaweed hopping off his chest, where she had fallen asleep, and squeaking with annoyance. The spirit lingered at his feet, weaving between his legs as he dressed. Then he grabbed his poetry notebook before heading out to the top deck, Seaweed on his heels. The sky was just barely beginning to brighten, the clouds cottony and languid as they floated by. A chill hung in the air, and Kieran could see his breath. He pulled his coat tighter around him as he took a seat at a table. Seaweed hopped up and wrapped herself around his neck like a scarf, warm against his skin. For a spirit who had technically killed dozens of people while under the Hilt's control, she was quite affectionate.

Kieran gave the spirit a few pats as he laid the notebook out in front of him and opened it to a blank page. Words from the page before were imprinted onto the blank space—the letter he'd written Ash last night.

Kieran found himself mindlessly tapping his pen against the page. He'd barely given any thought to how he wanted to cast if not through poetry. He'd drawn a lot as a child, but he'd never gotten very good at it. Reading and writing had always been what called to him most.

Maybe I could try writing something other than poetry.

He shivered a bit in the cold, even with Seaweed's added body heat. What he would give for a nice fire to sit in front of.

Hmm.

Kieran pressed the pen against the page. He thought back to his childhood, seated on a fur rug in front of a fire on the Pelumbra estate. Warmth rose from his chest as he began to pen a description of the memory. He wrote about the gentle popping sound the wood made as it burned and the faint vanilla scent of the smoke. He described how the rug had felt so soft beneath him, and how his mother's hand had gently ruffled his hair.

As he did, he noticed a faint silver glow sparking off the tip of his pen. Seaweed chirruped excitedly at the sight. He did his best not to let this distract him—the moment he stopped focusing on his writing and got caught up in the casting, he was sure his magic would retreat to where it lived in its well within his chest.

Just as he finished the description, a familiar voice asked, "What brings you out here so early in the morning?"

He turned to find Sebastian behind him, wearing his wool coat with a red scarf. His hair was wet, as if he'd recently stepped out of the shower.

"Oh! Um—just practicing magic." Kieran gestured to the notebook as Sebastian closed the distance between them. Kieran continued: "Decided to give prose a chance."

"May I?" Sebastian asked, pointing to the notebook.

Kieran immediately stiffened. What if the spell didn't work? Worse yet, what if Sebastian thought the writing was bad? What if he'd miswritten something and it could somehow harm Sebastian? What if—?

He cut himself off, handing the notebook to Sebastian. He did his best not to tense up as Sebastian's eyes darted across the page. *You'll never improve if you don't open yourself up to feedback.*

"Oh, wow," Sebastian said as he finished reading. After a moment, he gently pulled the scarf from around his neck and unbuttoned his coat. "That's lovely. I don't even need this anymore."

He laid the coat on the seat across from Kieran, who felt blood rush into his cheeks. "It . . . worked?"

"Assuming you were hoping to mimic the feeling you described here? I'd say so." Sebastian handed the notebook back. "I like your writing style."

Kieran felt a genuine rush of warmth at that. Ash had always been a bit critical of his poetry, so it was nice to get a compliment on his prose. *Maybe I should have been focusing on that all along.*

"Thanks." Kieran tucked a gold-blond curl behind his ear. "What brings you out here so early anyway?"

Sebastian bit back a smile. "Promise not to panic?"

"Why would I—?"

Just then, Sebastian withdrew something silver from his belt, casually flipping it around his fingers with a grace Kieran hadn't seen before. After a moment, Sebastian held his arm up, hand bent back near his ear, and launched the object into the air with a flick of his wrist.

As it hit one of the ship's nearby supply crates with a clean *thwack,* Kieran realized what it was: a small silver knife. Without thinking, he let out a squeak. Seaweed too was spooked enough by the sound that she hopped off Kieran's shoulders and ran off before disappearing through the door. Honestly, he didn't blame her.

"Is—is that a knife?" he asked, pointing to it, knowing full well that it was.

"Indeed." Sebastian went to the crate he'd thrown it at. With his coat off, he was left in short sleeves, and Kieran could see his defined muscles clench as he pried the knife free. *Oh, goodness.* Then Sebastian turned and closed the distance between himself and Kieran. For a second, Kieran's heart rate picked up before Sebastian held the knife out to him hilt-first.

"It's one of my throwing knives," he said, watching as Kieran's eyes traced the curve of the blade. "It's an old hobby. Sometimes I practice to clear my head."

Kieran swallowed the lump in his throat. "Your hobby is *throwing knives*?"

Sebastian shrugged. "One of them, yes. My father was a bit paranoid about self-defense. I've never thrown one *at* someone, mind you. Just unsuspecting crates and trees and whatnot."

Kieran wasn't sure, but he could have sworn he saw Sebastian flutter his fingers as he said it. Hadn't he done that before as well, on the deck after he stayed to chat with Lila? Was it a nervous habit?

"I could show you how," Sebastian said, nodding to the crates, "if you like."

Kieran weighed the knife in his hand. He'd never considered learning that type of skill. Not that anyone had ever offered to teach him; all the self-defense or combat skills he'd seen were magic-based, like Briar's ledrith. It was—among witches—the more socially acceptable thing to do. Using a weapon felt taboo.

Maybe I'm being too judgmental, Kieran thought. *Briar has ledrith; Sebastian has knives. It's not like he's going to throw one at my throat because I can't pass him the salt fast enough at the dinner table.*

Before he could think himself in circles too much, Kieran met Sebastian's gaze and said, "Sure, why not?"

Sebastian huffed out a laugh. "Color me surprised. I didn't take you as the sort to try something like this."

Kieran shrugged. "I'm trying to be a little more . . . spontaneous these days."

"Well, who am I to argue, then?" Sebastian gestured for Kieran to follow him. "Come on. We'll start a little closer. Make things easier."

Kieran bit his lip but followed, briefly glancing over his shoulder in case any other crew members were around. Briar wasn't likely to give him any grief for something like this, but he could see Delilah and the adults doing so. The knife felt heavy in his hand.

He swallowed that feeling. *I have got to stop worrying so much about this sort of thing.*

Sebastian stopped about eight feet from the crates. He pivoted and said, "Copy my stance. It's not all that different from how you throw darts, ultimately. Are you left- or right-handed?"

"Left."

"Perfect—so put your weight on your left leg and put your right foot in front of you . . ."

Sebastian kept talking about proper stance and throwing technique, but Kieran found that, despite himself, he was far more distracted watching the way Sebastian grew more animated as he spoke. Seeing the way his eyes lit up and hearing his voice rise in the moment was . . . strangely gratifying. As if Kieran was finally peeling back a layer to see what was underneath Sebastian's even-keeled demeanor.

"Understand?" Sebastian asked, snapping Kieran back into focus.

"Oh, um—yeah. Got it." Kieran tried to remember what Sebastian had just said about holding the knife. Apparently, this one was handle-heavy, so he needed to hold the blade to throw it. He held his arm aloft as Sebastian had shown him, glancing at him to make sure he'd done it correctly.

Sebastian reached over and gently guided Kieran's arm into a slightly different position. His skin was cool. Kieran's eyes met his for a flashing moment, and he found himself drawn to the parted curve of Sebastian's pale lips.

Sebastian cleared his throat, stepping away. "You can go ahead and throw now."

"Oh! Oh, right, of course." *Get it together, Kieran.* He tore his eyes away from Sebastian's lips to look back at the crates.

Just like darts, he reminded himself, trying to let his shoulders relax. *Just aim and throw.*

Kieran took a breath, narrowed his gaze on his target, and threw the knife.

Much to his shock, after one turn in the air, it smacked directly into the crate and stuck. He gasped, a childlike smile brightening his face.

"Nicely done," Sebastian said, grabbing Kieran's shoulder and giving it a little shake. "You're a natural."

"Really?" Kieran laughed a little, mostly out of shock at his performance. "I've never been a natural at anything."

"Maybe you just weren't trying the right things." Sebastian went to one of the ship's tables, where he'd laid out four other knives. He brought one to Kieran and said, "Wanna give it another shot? These yellow pine crates are perfect for this sort of thing—soft enough to pierce but not so flimsy they break."

Kieran took the knife. "You know what kind of wood these are?"

Sebastian's entire face lit up all at once. His tone was bright, and he spoke faster than Kieran had ever heard him. "Sure. Yellow pine's the most common in Celdwyn for this sort of thing. Unlike what this ship is made of—that's mostly teak. Beautiful construction too. Did you know teak has natural chemicals that prevent rot? And it's the strongest and most durable wood on the planet—it's fascinating, really. And it's high in oil . . ."

All Kieran could do was stare as Sebastian continued. This was the person he'd been so intimidated by at first? Who had seemed so stiff and overly formal? And now he was . . . waxing poetic about types of *wood*?

I can't believe it, Kieran realized. *He's as weird as I am.*

And for whatever reason, something about that made Kieran's stomach flutter.

"Not to mention, some scientists think the oldest teak tree on the planet is probably six hundred years old. Can you imagine how many generations of people have seen it grow? It's humbling to consider." Sebastian paused, just then seeming to notice Kieran's shell-shocked expression. Sebastian went quiet, sheepishly rubbing the back of his neck. "Oh. My apologies. I tend to get a little . . . carried away when it comes to wood."

When it comes to wood! Can he hear himself? Kieran couldn't hold in a laugh. *Oh, this is incredible.*

"What?" Sebastian asked.

"Nothing! It's nothing. It's just . . ." Kieran shook his head, still trying and failing not to giggle. "I don't know. When I first met you, you seemed so . . . aloof. I guess it's nice to know you're as weird as the rest of us."

"Weird? Wood knowledge isn't *weird;* it's useful."

"Sure." Kieran chuckled. "If you're a beaver, or a particularly ambitious woodpecker."

Sebastian crossed his arms, incredulous. "If that's what you think, then I guess I won't show you any of my whittling projects."

"Whittling projects?" Kieran repeated, his voice going so high it nearly cracked. He sputtered a laugh. "You're joking. You whittle?"

"I'm a multifaceted person," Sebastian said, deadly serious. A few days ago, Kieran would have been intimidated by the sudden tone shift. Now he realized that it was for comedic effect.

"It all involves knives, though," Kieran pointed out. "So not *that* multifaceted."

"You say that now, but I think you'd be quite impressed by my handmade spoons. They're birch. Do you want to hear my birch facts?"

"Desperately," Kieran near-cackled. "Talk dirty to me."

That finally broke Sebastian, and the two dissolved into laughter, Kieran nearly doubling over. As soon as Kieran thought Sebastian was done, he would supply another fact with clinical seriousness—"Did you know you can identify silver birch by their pendulous branches?"—and send Kieran into an entirely new fit of laughter. Soon, Kieran had to sit on the ground, clutching his sides. His stomach hurt from laughing. Sebastian sat beside him, chuckling along in a feedback loop that didn't seem close to stopping anytime soon. Kieran wiped away tears, trying to catch his breath.

"You," Kieran said, "are not what I expected, Sebastian Feng. Consider me pleasantly surprised."

Sebastian just shrugged, his smile almost smug. "I could say the same about you. I . . . really enjoy your company, Kieran."

"Likewise." Kieran bumped his shoulder against Sebastian's. "Thanks for showing me the knife-throwing tricks. Maybe we can set up a target and have a competition one of these days. If, of course, there's suitable wood for that on board."

"I'm sure I could figure something out," Sebastian said. Not looking at Kieran, he casually added, "For you, at least."

Kieran's pulse quickened. There was something so . . . human about this side of Sebastian. He'd been remarkably handsome before, sure, but there was something about this moment that Kieran couldn't exactly put his finger on. As if he'd only been seeing a fraction of Sebastian before and a new piece had fallen into place.

"You know, I would like to see those spoons sometime," Kieran said.

"That's a very high honor. I don't show my spoons to just anyone." Kieran felt something brush his hand and glanced down to find Sebastian's pinky touching his. "But you're well on your way."

Kieran's heart nearly leapt out of his chest. Sebastian's touch was electric. He hadn't had that sensation in months—not since Ash had last touched him.

He stiffened, just slightly. Even as he did, though, all he could think of was what Briar had said to him last night:

Don't get so caught up trying to glue together the pieces of something broken that you forget to look around and see what's right in front of you.

That night, as the moon rose high in the sky, Kieran couldn't sleep. His mind had become a tangle of thoughts—about their impending arrival in the Mirrorveil Woods to get the Stave, about Ash back home, and finally about Sebastian and the scintillating look in his eyes that afternoon. Really, his only focus should be on the Stave, but . . . he couldn't help it.

He took out his notebook, stared at the page, and debated how he could explain this to Ash. *Hello, darling! I had another great day devoting myself to fixing our relationship. Sure, my heart has started racing every time I lay eyes on another boy. And yes, he's started showing up in my dreams, just as you used to. But that probably means nothing!*

Kieran moaned into his pillow, nearly waking Seaweed next to his feet, where she'd taken to sleeping. *How in the world do you go from loving someone to fantasizing about someone else a week later?*

It was love, wasn't it? Kieran had said so, once. He and Ash had been in the middle of kissing beneath Ash's sheets when he'd said it. Sure, it had been the first time anyone had ever touched him that way, but he'd definitely felt *something* strong. It *had* to be love. And yeah, sure, the other boy hadn't responded—which had hurt Kieran's feelings a bit—but he'd figured Ash just needed more time.

Three months later, he still hadn't gotten there.

Kieran's jaw worked as he stared at the ceiling of his bedroom. Even in the later days of their relationship, Ash had never fully opened up to him. Sure, he knew about Ash's family and the mining partnership with the Pelumbras that had ruined their lives, but beyond that, he'd run into something of a wall. There had always been something surface-level to the way they spoke. It was always the same questions: *How's your magic training? Anything new at the library? How are Delilah and Briar?*

At the time, Kieran had considered it comfortable. He knew what to expect when he was with Ash. They had their routines and plans. It was all very . . . safe.

And he liked safe, of course. He needed safe, to some degree, after everything he'd been through with his curse. Kieran wasn't the type who liked surprises or did things spontaneously most of the time. The knife-throwing with Sebastian that morning was probably the most spontaneous thing he'd done since . . . well, deciding to run away from home to break the curse.

Maybe there's something to be said for taking risks, he thought.

With a sigh, Kieran sat up, deciding he'd go make himself a cup of tea to help him sleep. He threw on the silk bathrobe he kept on his bedpost and tied it around his waist, yawning. Sliding on his sheepskin slippers, he shuffled out of his room and into the hall.

As he did, he couldn't help but notice that the door to Sebastian's room was ajar. *He probably can't sleep either. Maybe I'll run into him.*

He didn't hate that idea.

Carrying on, Kieran made his way out onto the top deck, bracing as a rush of cold air blew past him. With a shiver, he started toward the stairs leading belowdecks.

Just then, though, he caught a flash of movement out of the corner of his eye.

Kieran whipped around in time to see a shadow vanish behind the stack of crates they'd thrown knives at earlier. He immediately went rigid. Was it a bird that had landed on board? He'd seen ravens and crows occasionally hanging out on the top deck before flying off into the sky, so that wouldn't be too unusual.

But then again, that wouldn't explain the unmoving white shape on the ground where the shadow had just been.

Kieran tugged the tie on his robe a little tighter. As he approached the shape, he called out, "Hello? Someone there?"

No response. As he got closer to the shape, though, he realized what he was looking at: a seagull, its wings splayed out but unmoving. It was definitely dead, but it took Kieran a second to realize what had killed it.

The bird's neck had been pierced with something sharp, and dark red stained its white feathers. Kieran's eyes widened as he bent down next to it. There was still blood leaking from the wound. Whatever had killed it must have just done so. Kieran suspected it would still be warm to the touch.

Before he could question that, though, a shadow passed overhead.

At first, Kieran assumed it must just be a cloud. But as he craned his neck to get a better look, his heart nearly stopped.

It was another aeroship.

Kieran's throat closed. *Shit, shit, shit—!*

Before he could so much as shout for help, six ropes suddenly dropped from the sides of the other ship. It was much smaller than this ship, perfect for flying without detection. Shadows climbed over the sides and slid down in a flash. Heavy boots hit the deck all around Kieran as they came to a halt. The figures were all in black and armed with blades that glinted in the moonlight. Kieran straightened from the dead gull with a gasp.

"Evening," the nearest one said, holding his saber out in Kieran's direction. "You must be Kieran."

Kieran—not sure what else to do—threw up his hands. "Who? I don't know anyone named Kieran. M-must be on a different aeroship."

"Cut the shit," another figure behind him said. Kieran felt something poke against his back. A cold burst of horror ran up his spine—it had to be a dagger.

"Now, no one needs to get hurt," the first speaker continued.

"Really, we're not interested in getting blood on our hands if we can avoid it. We just need the Hilt, and we'll be on our way."

Well, no point in lying, I guess. "Did Elias Barclay send you?"

"Indeed. He sends his regards." The first speaker stepped close enough that Kieran could smell his breath. "Now, why don't you go get that for us?"

Kieran glanced around him. There were five of them and one of him—there was no way he could take them. He could scream to try and get Briar and Delilah's attention, but with a knife about to slide into his back, that wouldn't do him much good. It didn't help either that he could feel his attacker's breath on his neck. There was no getting out of this.

What other option did he have?

"F-fine," Kieran started to say. "Just, um, please put your weapons aw—"

Suddenly, Kieran heard a sickening *crack* behind him. The mercenary let out a choked sound, and the knifepoint fell away from Kieran's back. He whipped around just in time to see the mercenary land flat on his face on the deck, unmoving—

With a single throwing knife lodged directly in his brain stem.

"Kieran!" Sebastian cried. *"Move!"*

All hell broke loose.

CHAPTER ELEVEN

As four armed men ran at him at full speed with swords drawn, it occurred to Kieran that he might actually vomit in terror.

Before he could, Sebastian stepped in front of him. He held a knife in each hand, arms tensed as he prepared to throw. He looked over his shoulder, meeting Kieran's eyes as he pointed to the dead man with the knife in his spine.

"Take his sword!"

Kieran's voice came out a strangled squeak: "And do *what* with it?! I'm in a *bathrobe*!"

"I don't think you have a choice—" Sebastian suddenly broke off and cried, "On your right! Duck!"

Kieran spun to find a saber headed for his throat. He was barely able to dodge before it sliced through his windpipe. The blade flew past as Kieran scrambled back.

Before the attacker could get any closer, Sebastian flicked a knife in his direction; it landed squarely in his shoulder. The man stumbled backward as he pressed his fingers to the wound, howling in pain. Another mercenary weaved around him, sword held aloft as he let out a war cry.

Kieran bent down and pried the sword from the dead man's hand, brandishing it just in time as another mercenary swung at him. With a yelp, he blocked the attack. The swords clanged so hard against each other that he felt the vibration all the way up his arm. He jumped back, dodging a blow.

Kieran felt something else: the burn of magic welling in his chest, begging to be released. His brain clawed for the few ledrith moves Briar had shown him. How did you shoot a magical blast at someone? Kick–ball change–fourth position–relevé? Wait, no, that was the beginning of a pirouette—

The mercenary roared and charged at him again, sword aloft. Acting purely on instinct, Kieran planted his slipper-clad foot, then twisted his arms around with a flourish. He stabbed the sword forward, bathrobe fluttering around him.

And while the blade landed nowhere near his attacker's heart, the bolt of lightning that shot out from the tip of it did.

The mercenary's muscles all locked up at once. He fell to the ground, shaking as flickers of electricity skittered across his body. While he seemed momentarily paralyzed, he was thankfully still alive. Kieran coughed out a shocked gasp. He looked down at the sword, realizing that it had acted like a conductor for his magic. Maybe he could use that again to his advantage.

Behind him, Kieran heard a choking sound. He spun to find Sebastian prying one of his throwing knives from the quivering body of another dead mercenary, blood burbling from the wound and staining Sebastian's hands. Sebastian stood stock-still. His lips were parted, and he seemed to be breathing through his mouth. He looked . . . pained. As if the blood on his hands was disgusting enough to make him sick.

He was so distracted he didn't seem to notice the mercenary running up behind him.

"Sebastian!" Kieran cried. "Behind you!"

Still, he didn't react, his eyes locked on his bloody hands. Without thinking, Kieran dropped the sword and sprinted to Sebastian's side. The attacker inches away, Kieran did the only thing he could think to do.

He tackled Sebastian to the ground.

The two of them rolled over each other once, landing with Kieran atop Sebastian. Kieran had his arms around the other boy, clinging to him as if his life depended on it. Sebastian's body felt stiff against him, and Kieran could feel Sebastian's breath against his neck, ragged and pained. Kieran let go just enough to lift and look the boy in the face, desperate to make sure he was okay.

"Kieran," Sebastian said, voice choked. His eyes were rounded, pupils blown out so any trace of brown in them was swallowed up by darkness. Kieran wasn't sure, but it seemed as if he was trying not to open his mouth too much. "Y-you have to get away from me. *Now.*"

Just then, something sharp pressed against the side of Kieran's neck. It bit into his skin just enough to cut. A hot bead of blood bloomed from the wound before it slid down his throat.

It dripped down onto Sebastian's pale cheek.

He went rigid, holding his breath.

"Look at the mess you've made of things, Sebastian," the mercenary standing over them said, blade poised to slice through Kieran's throat. "This is no way to repay the man who offered you a cure for your little affliction. Or does your new friend not know about that yet?" He chuckled. "Guess he's about to."

The next moment, the mercenary sliced his blade across the side of Kieran's neck. It wasn't deep enough to kill, but hot pain flared from the wound nonetheless. Kieran gasped as blood poured freely. It rained down, spattering Sebastian's face with crimson.

In an instant, the boy's entire visage twisted into something horrifying.

His eyes flashed open to reveal glowing red irises. Suddenly, a second pair of smaller eyes opened below that, then another and another, until six additional red eyes had opened, framing his natural ones on either side of his temples down to his cheekbones. His lips parted to reveal that his upper and lower canines had sharpened into fangs, along with the incisors beside them. At his sides, his fingers twitched and bent as they turned black and curved into hooklike points, almost like a spider's legs.

Kieran, for once in his life, was entirely speechless.

"Hey, you!" a voice cried from across the deck. "Get away from them!"

A bolt of greenish light shot across the deck and over Kieran's head, striking the mercenary who'd cut him. The man screamed, bloody sword clattering to the ground as he reeled back, hitting the ground paralyzed. Kieran smelled something—cloth, maybe—burning.

Delilah and Briar sprinted in their direction, eyes and hands glowing with the sparks of magic. Both were in their nightclothes. Briar's hair was sticking straight up where she'd been sleeping on it. Delilah's braid was coming undone, and from the scowl on her face, it was clear that she was far from happy to see their uninvited guests. Briar shot an electric bolt at another mercenary, paralyzing him. That left two paralyzed, one dealing with a stab wound in his shoulder, two dead at Sebastian's hand, and the final one, who'd cut Kieran's throat, on fire behind him.

Before Kieran could process the whole situation, Sebastian hissed below him. His hands shot up, shoving Kieran away with enough force to send him flying. Kieran's back collided with the mercenary still shouting and patting at his burning clothes. They both fell in a heap, Kieran barely able to push the man off before the fire could spread to his bathrobe.

Sebastian put his hands behind his head, rocked back on them, and then launched himself onto his feet. At the sight of him, Delilah gasped while Briar let out a low whistle. Kieran wasn't sure, but Delilah seemed to mouth, *So that's his curse.*

One of the paralyzed mercenaries finally regained momentum, scrambling to stand. He was looking at Sebastian in horror, eyes wide. He sprinted for the ropes hanging from the tiny ship that had brought them, screaming.

Before he could get there, though, Sebastian sprang at him with uncanny dexterity. His clawlike fingers hooked into the man's arms, stopping him in place. In seconds, Sebastian's fangs were in the mercenary's neck. The black-clad stranger let out a piercing scream as Sebastian began to drink from the wound, blood wetting the lower half of his face.

"Retreat!" cried the man with one of Sebastian's knives still in his shoulder.

"But the Hilt," the one Kieran had paralyzed said, just now starting to move again.

"Are you a fool? Even Elias can't pay me enough to die." The stabbed man ran for the nearest rope, shouting, "Hurry!"

The remaining mercenaries all made a run for the ship, limping and clearly injured. Kieran made eye contact with Delilah, unsure whether he should do something to stop them, but Delilah shook her head. Each mercenary grabbed a rope and was lifted into the air. They vanished into the tiny aeroship, and with a tinny, buzzing sound as its wings began to beat like a hummingbird's, the ship took off into the sky.

There was a beat before the man Sebastian had been drinking from hit the ground, dead. Sebastian stood over him, panting, his front completely crimson-stained. After a moment, he looked up, the extra eyes closing and vanishing from his face while the fangs shrank to normal teeth. The last thing to change back was the glow in his eyes, which went out like snuffed twin candles.

While Kieran, Delilah, and Briar all stared at him, slack-jawed, he held up his hands in surrender.

"If you'd prefer to restrain me," Sebastian said, head hanging, "I would understand. Just please give me a chance to explain myself."

"Are you . . . lucid?" Briar asked, the evenness of her tone contradicted by her ledrith stance.

"I am," Sebastian confirmed, "at the moment."

"At the mo—?" Kieran started.

Delilah cut him off by clearing her throat and shook her head before he could continue. "I think it's about time we had an emergency crew meeting."

Not long after, Kieran, Briar, Delilah, Ariel, and Santiago all sat around the dining room table, facing Sebastian as if he were on trial. Delilah sat beside Kieran, dabbing at the cut on his neck with gauze. It wasn't deep enough to need stitches, but she wanted to try to use some of the first aid skills she'd learned from her mother to at least patch it up so it didn't get infected. Kieran winced each time the gauze touched him—he didn't have a particularly high threshold for pain.

"You're fine," Delilah promised, dropping the red gauze in a bowl. "It's just the salve. I'm almost done."

Kieran kept a stiff upper lip—whimpering only a tiny bit—as Delilah finished applying the salve and bandaged the wound.

Sebastian, meanwhile, looked terrible. His hair was matted with dried blood, and while he'd been able to wipe most of it off his face, dried copper-red stains remained around his mouth. He kept his face down, not making eye contact with anyone.

Kieran frowned. Seeing him so disheveled was like a kick in the stomach.

"So," Ariel started. They spoke through a yawn, adding, "What happened? Why is this kid covered in blood? Better yet, why is there blood all over the top deck?"

"All over?" Santiago repeated, the color draining from his face.

"Didn't have time to clean it up after I threw the dead mercenaries overboard," Briar said casually as she took a seat across the table from Kieran. When all heads snapped to her, jaws agape, she held up her hands. "What? We passed a lake back there, so they landed in water. That way I didn't accidentally kill anyone out for a late-night walk by dropping a corpse on them from the sky."

While Sebastian nodded as if he completely understood, everyone else still just stared.

Briar sighed. "Would you rather I had left them there for a sky burial?"

Delilah waved her hand. "I suppose what's done is done. Kieran, you're the only one who saw everything. What happened?"

Kieran chewed his lower lip. He wished he'd had a chance to speak to Sebastian alone before this. He sensed that he knew him better than everyone else on the ship, and it might have been a bit easier to understand what had happened without an entire jury sitting around to judge. In a strange way, Kieran wanted to protect him, even though Sebastian had been the one ripping someone's throat out in front of him.

With a sigh, Kieran took them through the evening—how he'd gotten up to get tea, found the dead gull on the deck, and then been ambushed by mercenaries.

"Sebastian saved me," Kieran added, making sure to emphasize the statement. "If he hadn't thrown a knife in that mercenary's neck, I'm not sure my head would still be attached to my shoulders."

"Sure, but he also looked ready to drain you dry," Briar pointed out, making Sebastian flinch. When he did, Briar cocked an eyebrow at him. "You know, it would have been nice to know about your diet *before* we decided to share close quarters."

A muscle in Sebastian's jaw twitched. "Generally speaking, creatures who subsist on blood aren't thought of as trustworthy or likable. I wanted the job, but if Kieran thought I was liable to eat you, I doubt he would have offered it to me. I . . . thought I could keep it a secret."

"Subsist on blood?" Santiago repeated. He seemed as if he was going to laugh, the concept was so absurd. "What, are you some kind of vampire?"

"No," Sebastian said. He paused. "Well. Maybe, in a sense."

Kieran's eyebrows shot up. He'd read books about vampires before—but those were just stories. Anything supernatural like that in the real world had some kind of magical root, like a curse. It wasn't as if there were storybook immortal, undead vampires running around draining virgins in the dead of night. Right?

He felt his face drain of color. *Does Sebastian know I've never slept with anyone? Is that why he's been so keen to get to know me? To lure me in and drink my delicious virgin blood?*

"It's a curse, isn't it?" Delilah asked softly.

Sebastian nodded, voice quiet. "Yes. I . . . hope you won't think less of me for it."

Everyone at the table exchanged a look. It occurred to Kieran that Sebastian didn't know everyone's history. He probably assumed they thought of curses as an unspeakable taboo, as most people in Celdwyn did.

Kieran didn't particularly enjoy thinking of his own former curse—not only because of the social taboo but because if he dwelled in the memories too long, he'd start to remember the feeling of his body wasting away day by day. And that didn't even take into account how it had turned Briar into a literal monster every few nights.

If anyone could understand an ounce of what Sebastian was going through, it was them.

"Curses are familiar territory for us," Delilah said simply. She gestured to everyone at the table. "Other than Ariel and Santiago, we've all had one. We . . . get it."

Sebastian's eyes immediately went to Kieran, who whispered, "I'll tell you later."

"What exactly is your curse?" Briar asked, barreling across the unspoken social boundary with her usual grace and delicacy. "You drink blood and have extra eyes sometimes?"

Sebastian's only reaction was to pause and stare, as if he'd never heard it put so plainly. "Simply put, yes. I still feel regular hunger and thirst, but food and water are never enough. If I don't consume blood, I can't control whether I turn into what you saw on the top deck. Generally, animal blood is enough. I've been catching birds on the top deck the last few nights—like that gull you found before the attack—and that's been fine. But when that mercenary cut your neck, Kieran, I . . . lost control. I'm so sorry you had to see that."

Briar scoffed loudly, and Delilah immediately shot her a burning look. Briar whispered, "Come on, I've seen worse in the mirror."

Delilah just sighed.

"Oh." Kieran blinked. "That's . . . good that animals' blood works. Better than people's."

"So we have another curse to deal with—that's all fine and good," Ariel said, yawning loudly behind their hand. They shook their head, as if trying to get the sleepy fog out of their brain. "But it's also the middle the night, and I'm exhausted. I can change our route again before bed to try to shake off any more potential attackers, but how do I know I'm not going to get drained in my sleep?"

"Ariel, come on—" Kieran started.

"No, they're right. I understand." Sebastian sighed. "If it makes you all feel better, you're welcome to lock me in my bedroom until you decide what to do. I should be fine for a few days after draining that man. Plus, the doors are hickory—even in my other form, I can't break them down."

"You know what kind of wood the doors are made of?" Briar repeated, wrinkling her nose.

Kieran nearly snorted. "Oh, he knows *a lot* about wood, trust me."

Everyone at the table stared at him in horror.

"I—I mean literally! He whittles! Goodness, get your minds out of the gutter. Anyway, locking him up feels wrong—"

Despite the situation, Sebastian managed a small laugh at that. "It's okay, Kieran. Really."

"We could always vote," Briar offered. "Everyone in favor of locking Sebastian in his room until we figure out what to do next?"

Everyone at the table other than Kieran and Sebastian raised their hands.

Kieran crossed his arms. "Fine. But let the record show, I think this is overkill."

"I guess we can decide that if we get to the Mirrorveil Woods in one piece," Ariel said. "Now, I need to go to the control room and change our path. The rest of you should get to bed."

With that, everyone nodded, and Kieran worried at his lower lip with his teeth. It was wrong to imprison Sebastian, wasn't it? He'd made it this far without hurting any of them—why would he now?

As if reading his mind, Sebastian shot Kieran a soft look. "Really, it's okay, Kieran. I'll be fine."

Kieran pursed his lips, frowning. But after a moment, he realized he had no other choice but to agree.

Even if he hated it.

CHAPTER TWELVE

Kieran spent the rest of the night tossing and turning in bed, unable to sleep with the adrenaline still coursing through his body. Every creaking sound and innocuous *thump* from the ship's hull turned into another troop of mercenaries come to kill him. When he did finally fall asleep, he had nothing but nightmares of swords against his throat and gleaming red eyes.

When he woke, dawn had just begun to break. He felt wide awake. Realistically, he should try to get a few more hours of sleep, but he wasn't sure if he'd be able to. Not with the way he'd fallen asleep thinking of Sebastian and woken up to the image of him with blood in his hair and the most shame-stricken expression Kieran had ever seen.

I should check on him, he decided. *If I were him, I'd want someone to talk to after last night.*

Kieran got dressed, tied his hair back with a piece of twine, and crept out into the hallway. He could hear snoring coming from

Delilah and Briar's room. Having lived with them for months now, he was all too familiar with the fact that they were both extremely deep sleepers, which was probably a good thing considering how loudly Delilah snored and how much Briar talked in her sleep.

Kieran quietly went to Sebastian's door. Light shone out from underneath—either he was awake or he'd slept with the lights on. Kieran pressed his ear to the door, listening for movement. Indeed, there was the faint sound of humming, paired with a *scrape, scrape, scape* sound Kieran didn't recognize. The humming, though—he knew the melody. It was the tune of a love song Kieran had heard on the radio many times, the lyrics telling the story of a young man who fell in love with a traveling witch. Kieran loved that song. For a second, he just waited, listening to the low vibration of Sebastian's voice.

Kieran raised his hand to knock, then stopped. Perhaps he should bring a sort of peace offering. *I could try to catch him a bird to drink from. Then again, I don't know how to catch a bird, much less kill one.*

Just the thought of slaughtering a bird made the back of his throat tighten. *Okay, maybe not something with a heartbeat. He does still drink normal things along with blood, right?*

Coffee, Kieran decided. *I'll make coffee.*

Downstairs in the kitchen, Kieran brewed himself a coffee, then paused, wondering what Sebastian might like. He seemed to enjoy sweeter foods. Nodding, Kieran poured steaming coffee into a mug, leaving room at the top. He grabbed some cinnamon and sweetened condensed milk, mixing them into the coffee. Then he spooned in a bit of frothed milk, topping it with a sprinkle of sugar and more cinnamon. It smelled absolutely divine—sweet and creamy and bold all at once.

When he was done, he brought both mugs back upstairs, careful not to spill on his white shirt. Once he was back in front of Sebastian's door, it occurred to him that he didn't have a free hand to knock. He went with his first instinct and gently kicked the door three times.

His heart raced. He couldn't exactly pinpoint why—he wasn't scared of Sebastian, even after last night. And he wasn't usually the type to get nervous talking to people. But there was something about Sebastian that made his knees feel like jelly.

Just like how you used to feel about Ash, a traitorous voice in his head whispered. *He's the one you should be thinking about.*

Kieran chose to ignore that.

After a pause, Sebastian called from inside, "Sorry—it's, ah, locked from the outside with magic."

Oh, right, duh. Forgot about that. I really do need more sleep. Kieran's eyes darted around the frame, looking at what spellcasting method could have done that, and found a small rune painted beside the handle. *Probably Briar's doing,* he decided. *Delilah rarely uses runes.*

"Give me a second," Kieran called back. He set the mugs on a side table below an oil painting in the hallway, then used his fist to rub away the ink. As he pulled away, he heard a lock click. "Okay, should be good."

Kieran grabbed the mugs as Sebastian opened the door. He was dressed far more casually than usual, wearing just black undershorts and a tight, sleeveless dark-blue shirt instead of his usual put-together businesswear. His arms and legs were exposed, and it became exceedingly apparent to Kieran that Sebastian was quite fit. He was muscular in a lithe way, defined but not bulky. His hair had been washed but hung messily in his eyes. His shirt rode up a bit, exposing the divots above his hip bones and a small dusting of hair beneath his belly button.

Oh, shit.

Kieran broke into a cold sweat as the blood seemed to drain from his brain and venture downward all at once. His thoughts became a string of curse words as he tried to distract himself with mental images of other things—a boring passage from a book he'd read, the Celdwynian national anthem, the concept of taxes—to little avail.

Hoping to draw attention elsewhere, he shoved the mug in his left hand directly into Sebastian's face. "I made you coffee!"

Sebastian blinked. He reached up, his fingers brushing Kieran's as he took it. The touch sent an electric jolt through Kieran that only made things worse.

Well, if there was any question about my inability to stay focused on Ash, that's gone out the window.

"Oh—thank you. That's . . . very thoughtful. Did you want to sit down for a bit?" Sebastian hooked a thumb back toward the little sitting area beneath his window. There were two chairs and a small table, identical to the ones in Kieran's room. "I . . . assume you have questions about last night."

"I— Yes!" Kieran's face was absolutely burning. "Sitting down, great call."

Sebastian cocked an eyebrow at him for a moment but thankfully didn't comment on the fact that Kieran had turned the color of a ripe tomato. Kieran took a seat, scooting the chair in and silently thanking whoever had built this table for saving him from a deeply awkward situation. While he did his best to steady himself, Sebastian sat down across from him, taking a sip of coffee.

"Mmm," he said, pulling it away from his lips. A bit of foam stuck to his upper lip. Kieran inwardly cursed at how cute it looked as Sebastian added, "This is *lovely.*"

"I'm a barista back home in Gellingham," Kieran explained, finally feeling as if he could breathe again. *I'm overthinking it. Definitely just overthinking it.* "Whenever I get bored at work, I start throwing stuff together to make new drinks. That's one of my favorites."

"Well, I'll have to start coming to your coffee shop when this is all over," Sebastian said. He took another sip, then paused. "Assuming you'll have me, of course. I'd completely understand if you'd rather not invite someone with a condition like mine into your place of work."

Kieran's forehead wrinkled. If there was one thing he was familiar with, it was self-loathing, but that didn't make it any easier to swallow coming from someone else. It made him want to reach across the table and put his hand over Sebastian's just to reassure him that he wasn't afraid of him.

But I won't, Kieran told himself. *Because I have Ash.*

"It's a curse," Kieran finally said, shaking off those thoughts. "Trust me, I know from experience how terrible they are. I'd never judge you for something like that."

"Shouldn't you?" Sebastian asked. "You saw what happened. I nearly attacked you last night. I could have killed you."

"But you didn't," Kieran pointed out. His fingers went to the bandage on his neck for a moment. "That has to count for something."

Sebastian worried at his lower lip, sitting back in his seat. He cradled his mug like something precious, sighing. Dawn sun streamed in, making his long lashes cast shadows across his cheekbones. He was, genuinely, one of the most beautiful people Kieran had ever seen.

"I wasn't always like this," Sebastian said, thumb rubbing the side of his mug in circles. "It's only been . . . six months, maybe? I've gotten better at controlling it since I was first cursed, but it's never easy. The thirst is always there in the background, like an alarm in my brain that never turns off. It gets quieter but never goes silent."

Kieran sipped his own coffee. "You were cursed that recently? That's terrible, Sebastian. Have you considered going to the Witches' Council for help?"

Sebastian shook his head. "No. The person who put it on me . . . Well, their magic is very strong. I doubt the Council could do anything."

"What do you mean?" Kieran narrowed his eyes. "Was it a famous witch or something? Because even they can fall. My family's a great example: After the curse on me and Briar broke, the blessing tied to it broke too, and their supernatural luck vanished. That's why they're in every paper for a newly discovered scandal each week."

"Not exactly," Sebastian said. "It's, ah. It's a long story. I'd rather not get into it. It's not easy for me to think about."

"Oh—that's okay." Kieran rubbed the back of his neck sheepishly. "I don't love talking about my curse much either, even though it's broken. You don't have to share more than you're comfortable with."

Sebastian's nearly black eyes met Kieran's. There were bruise-like marks under them—it occurred to Kieran that Sebastian probably hadn't slept at all last night after everything. "Maybe . . . maybe I can share a little about mine, and in exchange, you tell me a little about yours?" Sebastian suggested.

Kieran considered it. "I think I can handle that."

Sebastian nodded. "My curse is atypical. It wasn't written, so it can't be broken by examining a text. When I was searching for a cure, I realized my best chance was to find a panacea, so I connected with Elias because I heard he was trying to get one from the magic vein in the Pinwhistle Forest. He told me that if I acted as his research assistant, he would give me a panacea to break it once he unlocked the vein's secrets. It was good too because it meant I was staying at his camp in the woods. That meant I could still send my sisters my earnings to take care of things while keeping them safe . . . from myself."

"But you left Elias," Kieran pointed out. "How will you get a panacea now?"

A silence spread out before them, and as soon as Kieran said the words, he saw Sebastian tense. He had to study him for a moment before it occurred to him what the answer to his question was.

"Oh." Kieran's eyebrows shot up. "Sebastian, listen, this whole

scepter thing is already a long shot. Obviously, it's not going to stop me from trying, but if I do get that panacea—"

"You want to use it on Ash," Sebastian finished. He stared off to the side, refusing to meet Kieran's eyes. "I know. If you get the panacea, you're the only one who can decide what to do with it. I swear I won't do anything to jeopardize your plan. I owe you too much."

Kieran bit his lip. On the one hand, he did feel obligated to fix his mistake with Ash. But on the other hand, all Ash's curse did was make Kieran invisible to him—Sebastian's was completely, catastrophically life-altering. Was it morally worse to let Sebastian suffer to keep his promise to Ash, or to leave Ash cursed in favor of helping someone he'd known for less than a month? Ultimately, he knew it was something to consider, though perhaps after he actually *got* the panacea as to not put the cart before the horse.

Plus, even if Sebastian *said* he supported Kieran's desire to save the potential panacea for Ash, he didn't necessarily mean it. Kieran wasn't naive—even if Sebastian did consider himself indebted to Kieran, Kieran couldn't help but feel a niggling *something* in the back of his mind. If only there were something he could do to confirm whether or not Sebastian was being forthright with him. Perhaps a spell, or maybe something he could look out for in his body language—

Something like a tell.

Kieran paused. *Wait a minute. There was that thing back on the deck the other night when he got back from the pub with Lila. He had the red stain on the side of his mouth, and when I asked what he'd been doing with Lila, he did that little finger flutter. If I'm right . . .*

"Can I ask you something?" When Sebastian nodded and

waited for him to continue, Kieran asked, "The other night in Raven's Roost when you got back late . . . that wasn't wine on your lip, was it?"

Immediately, Sebastian's shoulders tensed. He reached up toward his mouth, as if the red smear were still there, tattooed into his skin. Then he exhaled, gaze dropped.

"No point in hiding it now, I suppose." He pushed his inky hair out of his eyes, letting it slide through his fingers. "No, it wasn't. After you left, Lila invited me to join her behind the pub. I went with her and . . ."

He winced. "The curse gives me a lot of adaptations to work with. The extra eyes can see body heat, which makes it easier for me to find prey. And there's venom in my saliva, so when I bite someone, I can use it to make it feel . . . positive for whoever I'm drinking from. Lila didn't realize I'd bitten her until I'd already had my fill and let her go. But—I didn't kill her, I swear. She just walked away a little woozy. The venom makes the puncture wounds heal quickly, so by the time she went back inside, the only evidence was that blood on my lip."

Kieran watched Sebastian's hands as he spoke. No finger flutter. So he had been lying the other night, but not now.

I knew it.

"I do keep to animals most of the time, though," Sebastian said, seeing Kieran's expression. "I swear. It was just . . . after a few days up here with nothing but seabirds, I knew I needed something a little more substantial to make sure I was in control of myself for the next leg of the journey. Lila just happened to be in the wrong place at the wrong time, and I—"

Kieran held up a hand to stop him. "As long as you didn't hurt her, I can't exactly blame you. Though, if I'm being honest, I'd feel a lot better if you promised to stick to animals while we're traveling together."

"Of course." Sebastian nodded. "I can do that. We just might need to plan ahead a bit more with our stops."

No movement from his hands. *He's telling the truth. Which probably means he was serious about respecting my wishes for the panacea if it comes to that.*

"Okay. Good. I'm . . . glad we settled that." Kieran nodded. "I'll see if I can convince the others to let you out of here once we land. Thanks for telling me."

Sebastian nodded, taking another sip of his coffee. "Of course. Now it's your turn. Tell me about your curse."

"It's a pretty long story," Kieran warned.

Sebastian gestured around. "Not much else to do in here other than whittle more spoons."

"Right. Good point." Kieran took a breath. "Well, it all started when Briar and I were born . . ."

Kieran spent the next hour or so recounting the details of his curse to Sebastian. He'd meant to keep it short, but as soon as he started, it was like he couldn't stop. He described how the curse had been placed on his family hundreds of years ago by the first witch who had married into the family only to discover her husband had been unfaithful and impregnated a village girl with twins. She'd written the curse so that each generation, starting with her husband's love children, a set of twins would be born, one twin doomed to die while the other slowly stole their sibling's magic and became a monster. His family, however, had chosen not to break it, as it had been come with a blessing as well: So long as the curse remained, the Pelumbra family would have supernatural luck that kept them wealthy and prosperous for generations.

Then he got into the specifics: how it had felt to watch himself wither away in the mirror, growing bonier and paler by the day. He described how he'd been forbidden from using magic at home, forced to watch his cousins' lessons before inevitably being caught and dragged away by his father. He even shared the bit about Briar's half of the curse, which Sebastian seemed to be heartened by—knowing he wasn't the first person on the ship to deal with an involuntary monstrous change seemed to comfort him somewhat. And finally, Kieran covered how Delilah had broken the curse when she admitted her feelings for Briar in the Pelumbra basement all those months ago, bringing the twins back from the brink.

The whole time, Sebastian had listened with an empathetic ear. In a strange way, Kieran found telling his story cathartic. He didn't talk about the curse much, and it felt good to get it off his chest with Sebastian.

"Is that why you don't use magic often?" Sebastian asked. "Because you were never trained?"

Kieran swallowed thickly, then nodded. "It's . . . almost like not knowing how to read. Everyone around me learned to do it so early that it's become second nature to them. The fact that I struggle just to summon magic at all makes me feel . . . inadequate. Like it's too late and I'll never be able to catch up."

Sebastian considered this. Ever so gently, he touched Kieran's arm, making him snap to attention. Sebastian offered him a quarter smile.

"I think," he offered, "you're more capable than you think. You just have to give yourself the grace to get back up after you fall instead of getting stuck on tripping in the first place."

"Maybe," Kieran scoffed, "but it's not like anyone's there to help me stand up again, metaphorically speaking."

"I would," Sebastian said, "if you asked."

Initially, Kieran dismissed the statement with a laugh, and the conversation soon turned to other things. By the end, though, he couldn't stop thinking about what Sebastian had said. As the next few days passed and they approached the Mirrorveil Woods, Kieran found himself repeating it over and over in his head.

Magic had become something shameful to him—proof that he was a lesser witch than Delilah and his sister. He'd felt embarrassed going to them for help, especially knowing that they pitied his lack of experience so strongly. But perhaps Sebastian was right: He would never improve if he was too embarrassed to try.

And maybe what he really needed was help from someone else.

Each of the following nights, Kieran opened his journal and tried his hand at penning more spells. Seaweed sat by his side, piping with excitement every time Kieran's eyes and hands began to light up with the faint silvery glow of his magic. It was helpful, in a way—it felt a bit like the spirit was doing her best to encourage him. Poetry magic still seemed risky, whereas prose felt more straightforward. With prose, Kieran didn't have to be as worried about his magic misfiring due to overwrought phrasing or homophone slipup.

Each morning after, Kieran found himself at Sebastian's door with fistfuls of spells he'd written the night before. He needed all the help he could get with the Mirrorveil Woods creeping closer and closer with each sunrise. Thankfully, Sebastian was more than happy to act as Kieran's magical guinea pig and spell editor. He would read the spells over, telling Kieran where the magic was most effective and where he might be able to tighten things like sentence flow and word choice to make his writing more concise and the spell stronger. The more direct the writing style, the more easily the magic came through.

It wasn't much, but it was a start.

It did also help Kieran's stomach churn a little less, days later, as he watched the Mirrorveil Woods come into view from the window in the lower observation deck.

The forest below them was like nothing Kieran had ever seen before. The pines were tall and thick with strange, shimmering silver bark. At first, Kieran thought they had colorful images painted on them. Then one of them moved, and a little orange fox darted in and out of the trees. At the sight of it, Seaweed began to chirp excitedly.

The bark wasn't colorful—it was reflective, like mirrors. The stripes of color he saw in the trees were the reflections of the descending aeroship and the cloudless blue sky. *Incredible.*

He withdrew his notebook from his pocket, itching to commit the image to writing. He scribbled out a few sentences, speculating as to how he could leave marks on the trees to remember his path. Almost immediately, he felt the warmth of magic begin to rise from his chest, asking to be poured into the words. The silvery glow of it wove around his fingers, creeping toward the pen.

He hadn't even had to try to summon it. In his memory, the

only time he'd been able to cast so easily had been by accident when he wasn't fully in control of his magic. At the realization, Kieran felt the unexpected prick of tears in his eyes. At his side, Seaweed stood on her back legs, gently pawing at his trousers with a flicker of excitement in her black eyes.

I'm actually doing it.

"Hey, Kier! Ariel and Santiago want us to meet in the control room!"

In an instant, the magic vanished. Kieran turned to find Delilah standing by the door to the staircase. She smiled and nodded toward the stairs.

He tucked the notebook back in his pocket. "I'll be up in a minute."

Delilah nodded and vanished up the stairs.

Kieran glanced back down at his hands, grinning.

Maybe there's hope yet.

Ariel landed the ship in a meadow of silvery-green grass that fluttered in the breeze. This far south, winter rarely yielded more than the occasional frost and gray skies, and even with the cold, tiny glasslike flowers poked up from between the grass. They reminded Kieran of buttercups that had turned translucent.

After the ship was in place, the crew—excluding Sebastian—met up in the control room. While they waited for everyone to arrive, Kieran found himself staring out at the woods, his pulse beginning to speed up.

"I've never seen anything like this." He glanced over at Delilah. "Have you been here before? We're only a day or two from Kitfield."

She shook her head at the mention of her hometown. "No. This is super remote—I think it's at least twenty-five miles from the closest town. Though, growing up, I heard rumors about this place. Mostly that the reflections make it hard to navigate, so people avoid it. It's easy to get lost when the only thing you can see is yourself."

"At least it's not underwater," Kieran muttered.

"You say that now, but I've heard plenty of stories about people who get lost in these woods and get trapped for so long that their own reflection starts to drive them mad."

A shiver ran down Kieran's spine. "Ah. How charming. Verbena really knows how to pick exciting locales, doesn't she?"

"If I didn't know better, I'd say she was trying to get you killed," Briar said.

"Let's hope not," said Kieran.

Just then, Ariel and Santiago entered the control room. Ariel said, "Good, you're all here. I need to tell you something."

"Woods are haunted?" Briar guessed.

"Hell if I know. The woods aren't my concern." Ariel glanced at Santiago, who reached out and squeezed their shoulder as they explained: "After that last attack in the middle of the night, I called a few of my pilot friends to see if they'd be willing to update me on any sightings they might have of Elias's ships." Ariel gestured to a map of Celdwyn they'd pinned to the wall beside the controls. They took a tack and jabbed it into the text indicating an airfield not too far from their own location. "One of them got back to me about thirty minutes ago—they spotted Elias's mercenaries about half a day behind us. They seem to be hanging back for some reason."

"Needed to refuel?" Kieran guessed.

Ariel shook their head. "That's what I thought at first, but then I got another call." They took a second pin and jammed it into the map even closer to their location. "There's a smaller scouting aeroship right behind us. I saw it last night for a few seconds before it ducked into the clouds."

"They're . . . spying on us?" Briar asked. "So they can . . . what? Strike once we've rested? That seems stupid."

The gears clicked into place in Kieran's mind. He straightened and shook his head.

"No. They're waiting to see if we can get the Stave."

"What?" Briar blinked at him. "Why would they want us to get it?"

Kieran reached down to where Seaweed was curled up near his feet. "Think about it—they were totally unprepared back at the Lake of Whispers. Seaweed decimated them."

The lake spirit trilled at the sound of her name, hopping up on the table before using Kieran's shirt to climb his torso. She wrapped around his neck like a scarf. Kieran gently patted her head and added, "They went in blind and failed spectacularly. On the other hand, they did manage to sneak on board the other night. Even if we beat them, that was only a fraction of their manpower. If a scouting ship is watching us, they can launch an attack exactly when we're not expecting it—and then finish what they started the other night."

"When we're not expecting it? What are you talking about?" Briar asked.

"When Kieran gets the Stave," Delilah realized aloud. She swallowed. "If they wait to attack until we have the Stave, then they don't have risk losing more men to the magic woods *and* they can take the Hilt at the same time. From there, they just have to convince the Coven to give up the final piece, which I'm sure they feel confident about. After all, Elias is a charismatic businessman—that kind of negotiation will be easy for him. As long as they have the first two pieces when that happens, it'll pretty much seal the win for them."

"Exactly," Kieran said.

"I fear he's correct," Santiago said to Ariel, who had begun chewing their lower lip. "What's our best chance to avoid them?"

"Speed," Ariel responded plainly. Their eyes fell on Kieran. "It's up to you, kid, but our best chance might be getting in and out of these woods before they can catch up. But that does mean rushing in without much of a plan."

"These woods will eat us alive," Delilah shot back, gesturing outside. "We need something to lead us back once we're inside, otherwise we'll get lost out there."

"Screw that—we have magic!" Briar argued. "I'm sure we can figure something out on the fly. If time is of the essence, we should just go now."

"That would be reckless," Delilah reasoned.

Briar threw her hands up. "Maybe we need to be reckless!"

"It's too much of a gamble," Delilah shot back.

"Stop it," Kieran said, holding up a hand to stop Delilah and Briar's quarrel. "Arguing won't help."

"You still need to make a decision, though," Briar pointed out. "You're the leader here. What do *you* want to do?"

Kieran froze. If Elias's men were on their heels and they waited too long, it would be his fault for not diving in immediately. At the same time, if they headed out now, they'd be totally unprepared. *And my magic doesn't work well on the fly.*

"Well?" Briar pushed.

"I—" Kieran tried to swallow but found his throat dry. With all his crewmates' eyes on him, he felt like their gazes were burning holes in him. It made him want to curl up in a ball and hide, but that wasn't an option.

"Kieran . . ." Delilah started softly.

"We don't have a lot of time," Ariel reminded him.

Briar started, "Which is why we should—"

Kieran slapped a hand against the table. "One hour!"

Everyone stopped. Kieran could barely contain his breathing, which wasn't a good look for someone with limited time to decide. He continued: "Give me an hour to think about it. That way, we'll still have a few hours to find the Stave, and I might be able to come up with a plan so we're not just winging it. Okay?"

The others all looked at each other, as if too stunned to speak after Kieran's outburst. Finally, Delilah began to nod.

"I still think—" Briar started.

Kieran stood, cutting her off. "I," he said, avoiding their gazes, "will be on the top deck figuring this out. We'll meet back here in an hour."

With that, Kieran turned for the door, exiting the control room before his panic consumed him.

Up on the top deck, Kieran did his best to quiet his racing heart.

I was not made for leadership, he thought as he counted to ten, trying to steady himself. Seaweed sat on his shoulders, nuzzling his throat. *What I would give to still be rich enough to hire people to solve my problems for me.*

He rested his chin on his arms as he gazed out at the woods. He really didn't have any ideas; he'd just wanted to get out of the control room before he panicked. Listening to people argue always made him anxious. Briar had inherited only a fraction of their father's short temper, but—and he'd never say it out loud—she reminded Kieran of him when she dug her heels in, as she had before. It wasn't her fault, by any means—she certainly wasn't anything like William Pelumbra in the areas where it mattered—but the reminder had been enough to make Kieran feel like the air was getting sucked out of his lungs.

I'll figure something out, he thought. *I have to. Just need to calm down first.*

Kieran took a deep, cleansing breath. As nice as it was to have Seaweed to comfort him, part of him longed to have someone wrap their arms around him and tell him it was going to be okay. For a moment, he thought of the way Ash used to tuck Kieran's curls behind his ear and trace the shape of his jawbone with his finger.

He'd be so disappointed, Kieran thought with a sigh, *knowing I can't even come up with a simple plan.*

Just then, a flicker of movement in the trees caught Kieran's eye. Seaweed too stiffened and let out a low growl. At the edge of the meadow, someone stepped out into the open.

Kieran straightened as he realized he was looking at a child with a head of short blond curls and pale-pinkish skin. While he couldn't see the child's face, his size made Kieran guess he was only seven or eight years old.

The child glanced around, arms wrapped around himself. His shoulders were trembling, and Kieran got the sense it wasn't from cold. *Poor kid looks terrified. Plus, if what Delilah said about how isolated this place is true, he must be really lost.*

"Hey!" Kieran cried, waving his hand in the air to get the child's attention. "Up here! Are you all right?"

The child looked his way for a second, then yelped, turned on his heel, and sprinted into the woods.

"Wait—no! Come back! I can help you!" Kieran glanced frantically side to side, looking for some way to follow him. He couldn't let a child run deeper into these woods if he was already lost—that could be a death sentence. He quickly spotted a coiled length of rope that had been tied to the ship's rigging.

Oh, this is deeply stupid, Kieran thought. *I'm going to regret this.* Still, he wouldn't be able to live with himself if he didn't at least try to help.

Kieran grabbed the rope and tossed it overboard, then tugged on it to make sure it was tied solidly to the rigging. When nothing budged, he nodded.

"We're going down," Kieran warned Seaweed. "Hold on." Hands tight on the rope, he hoisted himself over the edge of the ship, then slid down.

Aside from a bit of rope burn on his palms, Kieran landed unharmed on the silvery grass. Seaweed leapt off his shoulders, landing beside him. He could just barely see the reflection of the little boy in the trees up ahead, running away from him. Kieran took off as quickly as he could, hopping to avoid a few rocks and a fallen tree. He and Seaweed dove into the trees, Kieran shouting for the boy to slow down.

The boy either didn't hear him or chose to ignore him. Kieran chased after him, leaving the meadow behind. He caught sight of the blond curls up ahead, then took a sharp turn to follow them. A few steps later, he saw them again to his left.

No, he realized, staring at the tree. *That's a reflection. Gotta make sure I'm chasing the real thing in here.*

Kieran kept going, breath turning ragged and muscles aching from exertion. The cut on his neck throbbed. He rubbed the bandage with a wince, catching sight of his own reflection in the trees. He looked a bit disheveled and sweaty but passable. Certainly not scary enough that this child should still be running away from him.

Just then, he heard a branch snap.

Kieran's head whipped around. Up ahead, the child had halted in a small clearing. Kieran's hand dropped from his neck, and he jogged to close the distance.

Finally, he thought. The boy had his back to him, staring ahead into the woods. Kieran caught sight of his reflection in the trees, then paused. There were two of him.

"What in the world—?" he started to say.

At the sound of his voice, the child jumped. He didn't run this time, though. Trembling, he turned around, meeting Kieran's eyes. Instantly, Kieran froze. This wasn't just any child lost in the woods. Not with those mismatched blue and brown eyes, the pointed chin, round cheeks and long, straight nose. And while it was clear that the child was at least ten years younger, Kieran knew exactly who he was looking at.

Himself.

CHAPTER THIRTEEN

Before Kieran could process the appearance of his younger self for more than a few seconds, he vanished into thin air.

Kieran spun around, hunting for the child. All he found was a fun house of mirrored trees, reflecting his grown-up self back at him. Seaweed too looked spooked; the spirit pawed at a tree, seemingly perplexed by the appearance of her own face in front of her.

It occurred to Kieran then that he'd gone much deeper into the woods than he'd intended. The canopy was thick enough overhead that it blocked out most of the sunlight, making it impossible to use it to navigate back to the ship. Anxiety balled in his stomach, growing heavier by the moment.

He was *definitely* lost.

"Shit," he breathed, his own wide eyes and color-drained face staring back at him from every angle. How could he have been so stupid, running into the woods recklessly like that? Clearly, there was some magical element to them if they'd lured him in with the younger version of himself. How was he supposed to get out if the woods were *sentient*?

Before the panic could fully set in, though, Kieran heard the burble of voices nearby. Seaweed stood up on her hind legs, ears perked. Kieran felt a flicker of hope and quickly headed in that direction. Maybe if there were other people here, they'd know how to get out.

But then again, what if it was another trick the woods were playing on him? Or worse, some of Elias's men, come to find him and steal the Hilt?

Not like I have much of a choice, Kieran thought. *I'm already lost. I might as well try.*

Kieran and Seaweed stepped as silently as they could into the trees. He couldn't help but notice the lack of animal sounds here; it was as if the birds knew not to land among the pale mirrored branches. At least the silence made it easier for him to locate and creep closer to the voices. It didn't take long before he'd found his way to another clearing.

Inside it was a group of people all dressed in black. Kieran jumped, thinking they might be more mercenaries, before he realized it wasn't black combat clothing—it was formalwear. Specifically, he noted, mourning clothes that were common in the north. He tiptoed closer, realizing as he approached that he couldn't make out their faces for some reason.

"At least," a man said as he wrapped his arm around the woman next to him, "we know this is what he'd want."

Kieran frowned. It occurred to him as he came up behind them that they were crowded around a large object set on a pedestal—something velvet-lined on the inside, its lid open. A coffin, Kieran realized.

This was a funeral.

The woman broke down in tears, putting her face in her hands. Kieran's brow furrowed—he knew that cry. And he knew the man who had spoken just now.

His mother and father.

Kieran was standing directly behind them now, maybe an arm's length away, while Seaweed lingered behind him. His mother's shoulders shook as she wailed, his father patting her shoulder in an attempt to soothe her. Suddenly, their faces were reflected all around him in the trees, along with those of the other people in attendance. They were all Pelumbras, Kieran's cousins and aunts and uncles, some of whom he'd known well and others who had moved away from the estate and rarely returned. He even recognized Wrenlin, Briar's former caretaker, staring into the coffin with her lips pressed firmly together and a scowl on her face. Her black dress was ratty and moth-bitten, her red hair messily pulled into a braid away from her hawklike face.

"A shame," Wrenlin said, though her voice didn't hint at any sort of empathy. "Neither the first nor the last, sadly."

She didn't sound sad at all. If Kieran were a slightly less composed person, he might break her nose for everything Briar had told him over these last six months about her upbringing. Wrenlin deserved worse.

His mother's weeping drew Kieran's gaze back in her direction. She'd put her hands on the side of the coffin, using it to support her. As she leaned forward, Kieran saw over her into the box. Immediately, his throat felt as if it was about to close.

Lying inside the coffin, dressed in an ill-fitting blue suit, was Kieran himself. This version, though, he recognized all too well. Just six months ago, he'd looked like the slightly warmer version of this corpse: Gold-blond curls limp. Cheeks and eyes so sunken in that the skull beneath was all too visible. Lips chapped and cracked. Skin papery white and nearly translucent, mottled blue veins peeking through the surface. Every bone protruding, the muscle wasted away. Despite the suit he wore, it was impossible to ignore just how skeletal he'd become.

"I'm glad it didn't end like this," a small voice at his side said.

Kieran glanced down and jumped at the reappearance of his seven-year-old self—the one who had drawn him into the woods in the first place. The littler Kieran stood beside him, his eyes wet. He didn't seem to notice Seaweed gently nuzzling his ankle. He was sniffling, the tip of his nose and cheeks pink. This version still had one brown eye and one blue eye, the blue one glowing faintly—the ever-present reminder of the curse that had once consumed him. This young, though, he hadn't started to wither away yet.

"What's going on?" Kieran asked, wincing as he caught another glimpse of his corpse-self. "Obviously this isn't real, and neither are you. Are you a spirit of the forest trying to speak to me?"

"No?" his younger self said, looking a little confused and offended by the question. It was cute, in an odd way. He looked as if he was about to stomp a foot down in the grass, cross his arms, and demand that Kieran apologize to him. "I'm you. Isn't that obvious?"

Kieran was almost inclined to laugh. He'd forgotten how serious he'd been as a child, always trying to fit in more with the grown-ups than with his younger cousins. While his cousins learned magic and played in the rolling hills and woods around the estate, Kieran had been with his mother, joining her for all her afternoon teas and brunches with family as if he were little more than a charming accessory for her to show off.

"All right, then," Kieran said, deciding that arguing with his younger self wasn't likely going to get him anywhere. Regardless of whether the forest *had* somehow created a reflection of his younger self he could speak to or if it was some other spirit disguised as him, he suspected that his only way out of this place was to figure out what it wanted. "If you are, well, *me,* then why show me this?" He gestured to the funeral, cocking an eyebrow.

Little Kieran's shell-pink lips curved into a frown. "This is what everyone always thought would happen to us. I wanted to show you because you haven't been very nice to us recently, even if you should be. You saved us."

"Nice to—? Oh."

Kieran paused. It occurred to him that the child-version of himself was, in a weird way, trying to thank him for preventing this future—the one where he was nothing but a sacrificial lamb to his family members. It was what was supposed to have happened. A foregone conclusion. The fact that it hadn't . . . Well, there was a lot to unpack with that.

"We're not done yet, though," little Kieran said. "Come on."

He took off running into the woods, the funeral scene vanishing in an instant. Seaweed immediately raced after him, chirping with concern. Kieran choked on what he'd been about to say, calling, "Wait! Tell me what you want!"

When he got no reply, he let out a sigh, then chased after his younger self. He was fast, so Kieran had to hurry to keep up. Deeper into the forest they went, leaping over fallen trees and stones, still not a single bird or small animal to be seen. Kieran felt a shiver come over him but shoved it down.

Finally, his younger self skidded to a halt. Seaweed squeaked just as another vision flickered into existence in a new clearing. In this one, Kieran saw himself at thirteen. He'd started to grow out his hair so it hung around his chin, his face soft and childlike in contrast to a recent growth spurt that had made him nearly as tall as his mother. He had his arms crossed and his eyes pointed at the floor.

Looming over him was his father. Kieran bore more of a resemblance to him than to his mother, but his father was all sharp edges and heavy muscle. He kept his curly blond hair cropped close to the scalp and had a short, trimmed beard. Everything about him was well-kept, from his appearance to his reputation. Only the best could be expected from the head of the family.

"I heard from your uncle that he caught you spying on your cousins' magic lesson this afternoon," Kieran's father said, his face giving little away. "This isn't the first time either. Tell me, Kieran, what are my expectations for you?"

"To enjoy the time I have," Kieran's thirteen-year-old self whispered. "To not distract myself with things that aren't meant for me."

Kieran felt his stomach twist. He remembered this—vividly. It wasn't a memory he particularly enjoyed reliving, much less seeing played out in front of him like some sick piece of theater. Seaweed too was growling in William's direction.

"Correct," the vision of his father said. "Practicing magic will only expend what little of it you have. You'll only cut your time shorter if you try it."

"But, Father," the younger Kieran said, his voice cracking. He sounded on the verge of tears. "I'm a witch. I want to know how to do the things that everyone else can! I'm the only one in the whole family who doesn't know how to cast—"

"And you're also the only one in the family who was born with such a special purpose," his father cut in. He reached out, putting a hand on young Kieran's shoulder. Kieran winced: From the outside, the gesture might look comforting, but he was all too familiar with it. It was a power play on his father's part, meant to hold him in place if he tried to draw back or run. "You have so little time, Kieran. Do not waste it on something that will only cut it shorter."

At Kieran's side, he heard a sniffle. He glanced down to see that Little Kieran had begun to cry, wiping tears away with his fists. Kieran's chest ached. Despite the years that had passed since this moment, it still made him want to cry too.

"He wanted me to stay weak," he said to no one in particular. Little Kieran and Seaweed looked up at him as he continued: "That was his plan all along. Keep me uneducated in magic and complacent so there was no chance I'd be able to defy him. No chance I'd defy the family." He sighed. "And I'm still weak. I guess he succeeded at that in the long run."

Little Kieran frowned at him. "You're not very nice, you know that?"

Seaweed chirped in agreement.

"Not very—what?" Kieran wrinkled his forehead. "I'm just saying—"

"Come on," Little Kieran said, snapping his fingers. The vision in front of them vanished. "You're still not getting it. Follow me."

"Still not getting what?" The younger boy ran off again, Seaweed on his heels, and Kieran groaned. "Oh, *come on.*"

He ran to catch up. He wished he could see the sky better—time was beginning to feel a bit too nebulous for his taste, and not being able to track the sun wasn't helping. He could have been following his younger self for minutes or days—he couldn't be sure.

Anxiety tightened his throat again. If he was gone for too long, it would give Elias time to catch up with them. All he knew was that running through the brush had scraped up his exposed skin, and the wound on his neck still throbbed whenever his heart rate rose.

Finally, Little Kieran stopped. He waved Kieran over as a new vision appeared before them, reflected all around in the trees.

Kieran recognized it instantly. This was himself eight months ago, wearing all black as he prepared to run away. He was minutes from heading to the Pelumbra airfield, where the aeroship he'd decided to steal with Santiago, Ariel, and Adelaide was parked. The curse had begun to progress, leaving him pale and thin but not yet withered, as he'd been in the funeral vision. In his hands, he held either side of a large portrait.

"Remember this?" Little Kieran asked.

Kieran nodded. "It's the night I ran away—I was terrified. I was so sure I was going to get caught. But at that point, I knew it was either run away or just . . . die. So I ran."

In the vision, the other Kieran held the painting up. It was a familiar one—a portrait of Kieran with his parents, all dressed in finery. None of them were smiling. Kieran remembered the afternoon they'd spent sitting for it—how his mother had kept standing up to correct the painter, her annoyance palpable. *Make Kieran look like he's sitting straighter. Make my waist narrower. Could my husband be taller?* All the while, Kieran had sat silent, his father behind him like an evil entity ready to spirit him away if he so much as breathed wrong.

"They got that made to use at my funeral," Kieran said, feeling his shoulders sink. "Father had noticed that the curse had begun to impact me physically, so they wanted the painting finished before I got worse. It was a way to memorialize me before I even died."

In the vision, the other Kieran withdrew something from his pocket—a steak knife, stolen from the kitchen. Gritting his teeth, he stabbed it into the portrait, ripping it down the canvas so it tore with a satisfying *rip.* He hacked at it until he'd cut a triangular piece free: the painted image of himself, sitting with his back straight and hands folded neatly in his lap.

He stared at it for a moment, a scowl on his face. Kieran remembered the way rage had bubbled up inside him at the sight—physical proof that his parents had long given up on keeping him alive, if it had even been a priority in the first place. His entire life he'd been the perfect martyr—so kind, so giving, so patient.

And he was tired of it.

The other Kieran crumpled the painted image of himself in his hand before tossing it sideways into the roaring fireplace. He flipped up his black hood as the flames licked up the side of his painted face, turning it to cinders.

He shot the burning image one more look before whispering, "I'll never be you again."

The vision vanished, the last ashes of the image the final thing to go. Kieran felt as if he'd had the wind knocked out of him. To see all those versions of himself back-to-back, pain and loathing tingeing each of them, was overwhelming.

All he'd wanted when he ran away was to get away from that. To be the master of his own destiny. To be someone who wasn't just the family sacrifice.

To be anyone other than Kieran Pelumbra.

Little Kieran tugged Kieran's sleeve, and when he looked down, he found the child crying. Seaweed let out a small whimper at the sound.

"Is that still what you want?" Little Kieran asked. "To not be me anymore?"

The words felt like needles driven straight into Kieran's chest. He thought back to telling Delilah soon after they met that he wanted to distance himself from who he'd been. At the time, it had felt like the most practical solution. Burn his old self with the fury of a forest fire so something new could grow in its place.

But nothing had. Just an emptiness that only seemed to spread and spread.

"I . . . I don't know," Kieran admitted.

"You don't have to be me," Little Kieran said. He reached into the waistband of his pants and withdrew something silver. "If you don't want to."

The child held it out to Kieran, and with a start, he realized what it was: a long staff with a pointed end, sharp enough to stab. Kieran reached out and carefully took it, immediately feeling an electric hum of magic coming off it. At the sight of it, Seaweed jumped back, bristling and hissing. Kieran's breath caught in his throat as he realized what he was looking at.

This was the Stave.

Little Kieran's arms dropped as Kieran turned the Stave over in his hands, eyes wide. The boy was sniffling, trembling slightly. Kieran's eyes flicked back to him, but the child wouldn't meet his eyes.

"All you have to do is put it through my heart," Little Kieran said. He was doing his best to keep a stiff upper lip but wasn't particularly successful. "And I'll be gone. You can be whoever you want."

Kieran opened his mouth but closed it again. Was that what he wanted? To truly be able to start over? He'd wanted that so badly when he'd first fallen for Ash. Ash's family had hated the Pelumbras, and Kieran had felt even more inclined to change his identity because of that. If he could just reinvent himself—be someone else—then maybe he could be happy. Not a body in a coffin or an angry teenager or a crying little boy.

Kieran's hand tightened around the Stave. It felt heavy and cold against his palm. Seaweed squeaked in alarm at his feet.

Little Kieran sniffled. "Please make it quick."

Kieran blinked as tears welled in his eyes. He raised the Stave, his pulse quick. His eyes went to Little Kieran, with his chubby cheeks and teary eyes. He'd been so small back then. He'd believed that his mother truly loved him and he was special. Sometimes, in secret, he'd use a tiny spark of magic to make the flowers bloom early, a smile breaking across his face every time he saw their petals unfurl. He'd been innocent. Happy.

Before everyone had failed him.

It had never been his fault. All those moments that had broken him down, one after another, had been because of other people's selfish desires. He'd never been enough for any of them. Not his mother, or his father, or even Ash, if he was being honest. Ash was just another person in the long line of people who had looked at him and decided that there was nothing permanent about Kieran Pelumbra.

With a shuddering breath, tears streaking his cheeks, Kieran dropped the Stave.

His younger self barely had time to blink before Kieran bent down and threw his arms around him, pulling him tightly against his chest. The little boy stiffened for a moment before he melted into his older self's arms, crying quietly against his shoulder. Seaweed too hopped up, snuggling between the two of them.

"I'm sorry no one stood up for you," Kieran said, ruffling the boy's hair. "And no one was there to step in when things got bad. I wish I could go back in time and protect you from them. You didn't deserve that. Nor did you deserve the way I acted like it was all your fault. I just didn't want to face how much it hurt to think about the past. I thought if I was someone else, then maybe I wouldn't feel so broken anymore, but . . . I'm never going to be someone else. I'll always just be Kieran."

"Maybe that's not so bad," the child in his arms whispered between sniffles.

"Yeah." Kieran squeezed him even tighter. "Maybe it's not. Not if I get to give you the life you always deserved. I . . . just have to figure out what exactly that is."

"Thank you." The little boy nuzzled his face deeper into Kieran's shirt, holding on to him as if he was the only thing keeping his feet on the ground. "I love you."

"I love you too. And I'll make you proud someday," he said. "I promise."

The little boy squeezed him back. "You already have."

The next moment, the weight against Kieran vanished. He opened his eyes to find himself alone in the trees, save for Seaweed squeaking at his side. Below him on the grass sat the Stave, framed by the silver-green grass. He reached for it, careful not to let it get close to Seaweed, who shied away from it as if it were a flame. Kieran saw his own face mirrored back in its surface, eyes red from crying.

But after everything, it was still him. And maybe that wasn't so bad.

CHAPTER FOURTEEN

In a stroke of luck—or perhaps his child-self's mercy—Kieran had wound up barely thirty feet from the meadow where he'd first entered the forest. It took him only a few minutes of walking to spot the outline of the aeroship through the trees. Feeling as if he'd been wrung out like a wet towel, he trudged back, holding the Stave with a delicacy one might reserve for a baby bird instead of a weapon. Seaweed sat on his shoulders, whiskers twitching as she seemed to sense something in the air.

Kieran came to a dead halt when he saw what was waiting for him in the meadow.

Three small airships, barely larger than cars, sat parked in the grass around his own. The gangway to his aeroship had been lowered, and two men dressed in black stood on it, chatting. Kieran spotted two more on the upper deck, while a few more were standing around the other aeroships. A bit of smoke rose from the top deck. Kieran heard voices coming from the open door to the ship as well—none of which he recognized.

"Try picking the lock on that door up top again," one of the men on the gangway called. "If you can't, we'll have to take an axe to it."

"And the hostages?" called another voice.

"We've got four subdued," the one who Kieran guessed was in charge said. "They're tied up on the lower deck. Still no sign of Sebastian, though."

"Elias has a real chip on his shoulder about that kid," another mercenary said. "He's gonna be thrilled to get him back. Finish what he started."

Kieran's pulse quickened. He ducked into the trees, doing his best to hide himself and Seaweed as the two mercenaries on the gangway headed for one of the small aeroships.

It sounds like Briar, Delilah, Santiago, and Ariel are tied up on the observation deck, Kieran thought, peering around the tree again. His fingers tightened around the Stave. *And if they can't get into the crew cabins, that means Sebastian's probably still locked in his room.*

Kieran counted the men again. There were six total out here in the meadow, and at least two more on the upper deck. There was no way that Kieran and Seaweed could take eight men in a fight, even with the magic he'd been practicing the last few days. But if he could free the others and try taking the men out one by one, they might have a chance.

That does require me to sneak inside, though, Kieran realized. He glanced down at himself. He was wearing a loose white tunic tucked into shimmery high-waisted sapphire-blue pants—not the subtlest of outfits. He surveyed the mercenaries again. All of them wore the same black long-sleeved shirts and pants, along with black cowls drawn over their heads to hide their faces.

An idea dawned on him.

Kieran surveyed the glade. All the mercenaries appeared to be men, or at least taller people with their chests bound. Most were bulkier than Kieran, but as he peered closer, there was one leaning against a small aeroship whose build seemed similar to his. He was a bit separate from the group too, inspecting what appeared to be a bit of damage to the side of the ship.

A smile crept up Kieran's face. *Perfect.*

As silently as he could, Kieran crept through the trees, skirting the edge of the meadow. He overheard a few more shouts from the top deck, telling the others that lock picking wasn't going well and to bring the axe. At that, a few more of the men went inside, but the slimmer one remained where he was.

Kieran came to a crouching halt about ten feet from him. He had his cowl down, his back facing Kieran as he tinkered with the ship. Seaweed curled her little toes tighter around Kieran's shoulder. In a strange way, that helped him focus.

Kieran reached into his pocket, withdrew his journal, and began to write:

> **Darkness without so much as a shape to take turned to inky blackness across the senses. A void that consumes all within, sight and sound, paralyzing each limb in tandem.**

Kieran was nearly done with his spell when a different mercenary called, "Quinn, you coming? They want you to try the lock up top before they break the door. They're worried those witches might have trapped it so if we break it down, it could trigger a spell."

"Just a minute," Kieran's target—Quinn—called back. Kieran made a note of how his voice sounded. It was bit higher-pitched than Kieran's, with a nasal quality. "We won't have a getaway ship if I don't fix this."

"Well, better get it done quick, because the boss is pissed."

Quinn scoffed. "I'll see you up there in five."

Much to Kieran's relief, the other mercenary raised his hand and whistled for the others to follow him. The men around the ships all stood at attention, then jogged to follow him inside.

Leaving Quinn alone.

Kieran waited ten seconds, then thirty, then a minute for the other mercenaries to disappear. The tip of his pen still glowed with silvery light as he tucked it back into his pocket. Quickly, he tore the page from his journal, then folded it into a tiny plane.

He flicked it at Quinn, who looked down as the paper landed at his feet.

"The hell?" he muttered. He glanced around and, not seeing Kieran, called out, "You're needed on the ship! Quit messing around with—whatever this is." His eyes scanned the page. "*A void that consumes* what—?"

Just then, a shadow passed over his face, and his eyes went entirely black. He sucked in a gasp as his body convulsed, eyes rolling back into his head. He hit the grass with muscles rigid.

Kieran patted Seaweed's head. "Well done, us."

The spirit squeaked excitedly in response.

Kieran rushed out and grabbed Quinn's shoulders, Seaweed jumping off him to help. Using their combined strength, Kieran and Seaweed hauled Quinn's body into the woods. Kieran's arms strained at the weight, but he managed to pull him back five, ten, then fifteen feet so they were obscured by trees. Kieran bent down and pulled the cowl from his face to reveal a pale-skinned man in his early twenties with a peach-fuzz mustache and goatee that made Kieran wince. *And I thought my facial hair was bad.*

Kieran quickly checked Quinn's pulse—he was out cold but not dead. *Thank goodness.*

"My apologies," Kieran said as he began unbuttoning the man's shirt. "Necessary evil and all that."

Not long after, Kieran had stripped off his clothes in exchange for Quinn's. He pulled the cowl over his face, along with a strip of fabric that covered his nose and mouth. It smelled a bit of old cheese, but he elected not to dwell on that too much.

"Seaweed, keep an eye on things out here," Kieran whispered. When the spirit squeaked with annoyance, he added, "You're a bit . . . conspicuous, bud. They'll know I'm not Quinn if I show up with a teal otter."

Seaweed seemed to consider this, ears drooping.

"I'll give you a sardine after."

Seaweed straightened with a squeak, eyes bright.

"Thought so." Kieran tried to fight the terror—or, more likely, bile—climbing up from his stomach into his throat. He tucked the Stave into his waistband. "I'll be back."

Doing his best to keep his head down, he crossed the meadow and headed to the gangway. There were two men just inside who barely glanced at him as he passed, holding his breath.

A few steps in, one of them said, "Boss is looking for you upstairs, Quinn."

Kieran made a vague sound of acknowledgment. He paused for a second, waiting to see if either of them noticed.

They both turned back to each other and continued their conversation.

Okay, step one is done, Kieran thought. He glanced around the inside of the ship. The gangway opened into the foyer, and through there was the dining area, the study, the control room, and the kitchen. Along the far wall were the stairs to the lower deck, where the observation deck and Ariel and Santiago's room was. Three men were stationed atop that staircase, all armed with swords.

If these men think I'm Quinn, they're not going to understand if I try to get down that way, Kieran thought. *So Briar and the others will have to wait a bit. I just have to think of something to divert all the mercenaries away from the cabins. Then I can get Sebastian to help me.*

Kieran headed up the stairs to the top deck. All the while, he kept a count of the men inside the ship. There had been five downstairs, and as he emerged onto the top deck, he found four more gathered around the door to the crew cabins. As he approached, the one he'd seen giving orders earlier turned around and glared at him.

"Quinn—there you are. Took you long enough—we need this lock picked."

Kieran froze. On the one hand, it was great that they hadn't immediately realized he wasn't Quinn. On the other hand, Kieran had absolutely no idea how to pick a lock, nor did he have the tools to do so.

But he did have his own key to the door.

Doing his best to make his voice as nasal as possible, Kieran reached into his pocket and held it up. "One of the hostages had this. Said it goes to this door."

Immediately, the boss's eyebrows shot up. Even behind the fabric covering his nose and mouth, Kieran could see his sun-tanned skin turning red. Kieran's stomach flipped, and the blood drained from his face. *Shit, what did I say? Did I go too heavy on the nasally bit? This is why I don't do community theater.*

"Who said they could take the gags out of the hostages' mouths?" he demanded. He turned to the others. "Sanchez, Remi—with me. If those witches can so much as utter a magic rhyme, we're fucked. Quinn, you, Bernoff, and James get that door open and start searching." His eyes narrowed. "And keep an eye out for Sebastian. Elias wants that traitor in chains."

He waved to two of the men, and they ran after him as he marched back toward the main deck, cracking his knuckles as he went. Kieran eyed the two mercenaries who had been left by the door.

Okay—two on one. Not terrible, but not great either. Let's see if I can get a little help.

"Well?" one of the mercenaries asked, snapping Kieran out of his thoughts. "What are you waiting for? Open it."

Kieran grunted, not wanting to speak more than he had to in case these men were more familiar with Quinn's voice than their boss had been. He jammed the key in the lock, turned it, and opened the door.

"Finally!" one of the mercenaries called. He gestured to the other. "Come on, let's get this done. Boss might give us a raise if we find the Hilt fast."

The two men sprinted inside, one going for the door to Briar and Delilah's room while the other went to Sebastian's. Kieran's mind swam. *How am I supposed to warn Sebastian?*

The mercenary at Sebastian's door said, "There are spell runes inked on this one."

"Just wipe them off," said the other mercenary from across the hall. "That'll unlock it."

"Really?" The mercenary scoffed. "That's like locking the door but leaving the key in it. These kids must not know what they're doing."

Kieran took a sharp breath as the mercenary rubbed his sleeve across the runes, smearing them. *Uh-oh.*

At that second, the door to Sebastian's room flew open the second a mercenary got close. Two knives soared out at once, so fast Kieran could have blinked and missed it. One struck a mercenary in the chest. The other embedded itself in his colleague's shoulder. The chest-stabbed one immediately choked, blood sputtering from his mouth before he keeled sideways and hit the floor. The other one screamed, but the sound was immediately cut off as a shadow burst from the door, tackling him to the ground.

Sebastian, fangs out and extra-red eyes glowing, swiped his claws across the man's neck. The skin tore like tissue paper, blood pouring out. The mercenary choked, reaching for his throat with a quaking hand. He made a horrible gagging sound, bloody spittle leaking from the corner of his mouth as a last breath shook from his lips. The sight of it made Kieran's stomach churn.

Sebastian spun, teeth bared. His eyes locked on Kieran, and he tensed to jump.

"Wait, wait!" Kieran tore back the cowl. "Sebastian, it's me!"

The snarl on Sebastian's lips faded. All his eyes blinked at once. "*Kieran?* What are you wearing?"

"Quinn's clothes?" When Sebastian shot him a confused look, Kieran waved his hand. "Look, long story—the others are trapped downstairs on the observation deck, and there's no way I can take all the other mercenaries alone. Will you help me?"

The mercenary under Sebastian let out a final death rattle before he went still. Sebastian stood up, wiping his claws on the dead man's clothes. He pulled the throwing knife from the mercenary's shoulder. His eyes traced a droplet of blood that had begun to slide down the blade, glistening in the light.

After a beat, he asked, "Can I get a temporary pass on the animals-only rule?"

Kieran considered it. These men had raided his home and put his family in danger. They were using the people he loved most as hostages to get the Stave and Hilt. They'd been prepared to use their swords and ask questions later.

"You know what? I don't think the animals-only rule needs to apply to bad guys."

A smile broke across Sebastian's face, his white fangs bright in the setting sunlight. "Then lead the way."

Armed with six throwing knives each, Kieran and Sebastian headed down to the main deck. Sebastian had stolen the clothes off one of the men he'd stabbed, and they both had their cowls up and faces hidden. For the moment, Sebastian's fangs and extra eyes had vanished, leaving just a strip of pale, gold-toned skin and almost-black eyes peering out.

They paused before the bottom of the stairs. The boss was arguing with one of the men guarding the area, while two others stood by watching. Kieran didn't love their odds—especially since he could see magic flickering between one of the mercenaries' fingertips. He needed to draw some of the men away.

He put a hand on Sebastian's shoulder to stop him. Holding a finger to his lips, he gestured for Sebastian to follow him back up the stairs. He mouthed, *Follow my lead.*

Kieran cleared his throat and, in the most nasal voice he could manage, cried down toward the mercenaries, "Help! Monster!"

"Shit," the boss said. "Must be Sebastian—go, subdue him! Elias wants him alive."

Kieran gestured for Sebastian to follow him, and they ran the rest of the way up the stairs. At the top, Kieran pressed his back to one side of the opening, out of sight, and gestured for Sebastian to do the same. Moments later, three mercenaries darted up the stairs and onto the top deck. They breezed right past Kieran and Sebastian, coming to a skidding halt. They wheeled around, searching for their comrade.

Kieran nodded to Sebastian. "Now!"

At once, Sebastian pulled a knife from his belt and flicked it at one of the men. It struck him in the back, sending him toppling forward. Kieran, meanwhile, copied Sebastian's movement, flicking a knife forward. Unfortunately, instead of stabbing, it hit the second mercenary square in the nose handle-first. The shock of it, however, was enough to make him stumble back. He tripped over his fallen comrade, knocking him backward, so he slammed into a pile of supply crates. Kieran heard a *crack*—considering that the mercenary didn't immediately stand to fight back, Kieran feared it might have been his skull.

Meanwhile, Sebastian pulled his mask down to reveal his fangs. He jumped at the man Kieran had hit with the knife. Glistening white fangs sank deep into the man's throat. The mercenary began to scream, flailing. Sebastian, however, anchored him in place with both fangs and claws.

Just then, the third mercenary roared, and Kieran spun around as he bore down on him with his sword held aloft. Kieran grabbed a knife from his belt and threw it. The shot went high, whizzing over the mercenary's shoulder. Kieran stumbled back, grabbing for another one.

Before the sword could swing down on him, he blindly threw the knife. While it didn't stick, it did slice across the man's shoulder. He dropped his sword with a scream, stumbling and nearly tripping over Kieran. Kieran jumped back, magic sparking to life between his hands. Still, it wasn't enough—as he tried to summon more magic, it was as if something was stuck.

"Come on," he urged, trying to summon more power. "Just a little more—"

Before he could, though, a bolt of familiar green magic shot up from the stairwell and struck the mercenary in the side. He yelped. Vines suddenly appeared from the bolt, wrapping around him and pinning his limbs. As his legs snapped together, he hit the deck with a thump, writhing and screaming for help.

That, however, didn't last long—not as Sebastian finished

drinking from the other mercenary and launched another knife at the bound one's throat, piercing his voice box.

For a beat, everything went quiet.

Then two familiar figures stumbled up the stairs, gasping for breath. Delilah's eyes glowed green with her magic, while Santiago appeared to have armed himself with some mercenary's swords.

"Delilah! Santi!" Kieran cried. "You're okay! Where are Ariel and Briar?"

"Downstairs," Santiago said, pointing. "Briar brought down two of those men. Ariel went to the control room to get us off the ground, and Briar's fighting the last mer—"

"Briar *was* fighting the boss," a new voice came from the stairs. A moment later, Briar herself appeared, a cut on her cheek weeping blood. She wiped it away with her fist, eyes glowing with magic and mouth curved into a wicked grin. "Let's just say I won."

Sebastian wiped his mouth clean, meeting Kieran's gaze. "I'm beginning to like your twin more and more."

"Oh, thank goodness," Delilah said, going to Briar's side and wrapping her arms around her. "I was worried about you."

"Please," Briar scoffed. "That guy was nothing but dumb muscle. He didn't stand a chance."

Suddenly, the ground below them shifted. Kieran looked around and realized that the ship's wings had begun to beat, slowly at first, then faster and faster. After a second, they began to lift into the air.

"Looks like Ariel got to the control room," Santiago said. "Good. I was worried they were going to get distracted kicking as many of those mercenaries in the crotch as possible."

"They got two solid kicks in," Briar confirmed. "Really helped me stop that witch, honestly. Hard to cast spells when you're hunched over crying."

"Wait!" Kieran looked around in panic. "We can't take off yet! Seaweed is still on the ground—"

"Actually," Briar cut in, gesturing to the stairs. The blue-scaled otter appeared at her side, looking quite pleased with herself. "Seaweed is the one who saved us. She managed to sneak down the steps and chew through our restraints. Once the mercenaries left to deal with you, we were able to take care of the rest."

"B-but—I told you to keep watch outside!" Kieran said to the otter, hands on his hips.

Her only response was a little wiggle before she chirped and ran for Kieran, jumping to climb up his shirtsleeve and curl around his neck once again. Kieran sighed, giving her a little scratch under the chin. "I guess I can't be too mad, seeing as you saved everyone." To Briar, Kieran clarified, "So everyone's okay?"

Briar nodded. "Thanks to you and your familiar, yeah. You saved the day."

Thanks to you.

Kieran exhaled, smiled, then threw his arms around Delilah and his sister. They enveloped him in a hug, squeezing tightly.

For the moment, at least, they were safe.

CHAPTER FIFTEEN

Cleaning up the ship after the fight with the mercenaries was a deeply unpleasant experience. Two of them were still alive but knocked out, so Ariel brought the ship low enough to drop them off in the woods. It was the most kindness the pilot could offer them, considering they'd arrived fully intent on using Briar, Delilah, Santiago, and Ariel as bargaining chips to make Kieran give up the Hilt and Stave. And considering what the crew had learned from Sebastian about Elias's plans, the mercenaries absolutely wouldn't have hesitated to kill any of them to get what they wanted.

Still, human life was human life. It didn't feel good to know that people had died, even if had been in self-defense. It only made Kieran hate Elias more, knowing he'd paid all these people enough to kill or be killed. Kieran just felt lucky that, aside from a black eye for Ariel and a few cuts and bruises on everyone else, the crew had escaped unharmed.

As for the mercenaries who were dead, Sebastian volunteered to deal with them. While Kieran was grateful, the thought made his stomach churn. He'd never considered himself someone who could take another person's life. So far, he hadn't. And he truly didn't know if he'd be able to, even in the worst of circumstances.

Kieran had waited down in the study, staring out the window, while Sebastian finished his work. In front of him on the coffee table were the Hilt and Stave, looking strange and otherworldly in such a pedestrian setting. Seaweed had elected to leave the room as soon as Kieran pulled out the Hilt. He didn't blame her, considering what it had done to her. Plus, she deserved a nice nap on his bed for her heroism.

"Good to see you at least got the Stave out of all that."

Kieran glanced up to find Delilah entering the study, taking a seat on the couch. Her pink dress had been singed on the edges, and her curls were mussed and out of place, but she looked fine otherwise.

"Is Briar okay?" Kieran asked.

Delilah nodded. "She offered to help Sebastian up on the top deck. It sounded like she wanted to talk to him about something, so I decided to give them a little privacy."

Kieran's back straightened a bit at that. He was, at his core, quite a nosy person, even if he did his best to hide it most of the time. "Do you know what she wanted to talk to him about?"

Delilah shook her head. "No. But if I had to guess, it might be an apology."

"For what?"

"Assuming he couldn't control his curse," Delilah admitted. "I . . . think we were a bit too quick to judge him."

"You just wanted to keep everyone safe," Kieran offered. He pulled his knees up to his chest, hugging them. "I don't blame you."

Delilah nodded. "You all are my family. Sometimes I get a little too protective, I guess. Especially of you, after everything you went through with your curse."

Kieran chewed his lip, nodding. He thought back to the woods, where he'd seen all the different versions of himself. How he'd looked at what was supposed to have been his future, wherein he was nothing but a withered corpse. Another casualty of Pelumbra greed.

"I think . . . that'll always be a part of me," Kieran said. He looked up and met Delilah's gaze. "Life's kind of like a book, isn't it? You need all the chapters that came before to understand where the story's going. Acting like they didn't happen won't help. It's just a matter of honoring how they shaped your story so you can move forward."

"I like that." Delilah cracked a smile. "Since when are you so philosophical?"

"Since all of Verbena's tasks to get this stupid scepter required me to do nonstop magical soul-searching." Kieran pressed his fingers to his temples and sighed, staring down at the Stave and Hilt. "At least it's cheaper than therapy."

That made Delilah snort with laughter, and the levity was a welcome sensation after the day he'd had. He was tired on a cellular level, as if both his mind and his body had been dunked underwater and wrung out until there was nothing left.

And even if he wished it didn't, it made him think of Ash. It would be so nice to climb into bed with him just so he could be held by someone for a time so he wasn't shouldering the weight of everything alone.

He missed having that closeness. The last time he and Ash had had a quiet evening like that had been back in the fall, before Ash had stopped coming to the coffee shop and had started ignoring his calls. It had been an unseasonably cold day, and Kieran had spent the night at Ash's apartment. Kieran had cooked dinner for him and listened while Ash went on and on about a project he had at the library. It had been charmingly domestic, Kieran thought. As if they were playing house and acting like grown-ups. It was a peek into what the future could be.

But then it had turned into Ash asking Kieran about his career plans. Kieran had shot back something along the lines of *I'm seventeen, how am I supposed to know what I want to do for the rest of my life?* Ash's face had hardened in that way it always did when Kieran said things like that.

You'll have to grow up eventually, Ash had said. *You can't just wait around for someone to tell you what to do. You're not a child anymore.*

But he also wasn't an adult, he'd argued. Wasn't that the whole point of being a teenager? To try to figure yourself out? Besides, he'd spent his entire childhood trying to act like an adult to appease his mother. Didn't he deserve to mess around for a while and figure it out later?

Ash's answer had been clear: *Not if you want to be taken seriously.*

Maybe that had been the beginning of the end, Kieran realized.

Even if Ash had asked for a break only recently, he'd pulled away long before. The void he'd left had made Kieran all the lonelier, wishing constantly that he could have what they'd had back. And seeing Delilah and Briar so close hadn't helped. It was a constant reminder that his own relationship was failing. Maybe that's why he'd gotten so bad about comparing the two in the first place.

"You okay?" Delilah asked. "You look a little lost in thought."

"Oh! Yes, sorry. Just . . . thinking about Ash again."

Delilah's expression softened. "Do you miss him?"

His first thought was *of course,* but that gave him pause. *Did* he miss Ash, or did he miss the companionship? Both ideas felt true. He missed discussing the books he read with Ash, and the bike rides they took along the Gell River in the summer, and the evenings spent lazily kissing in bed until they fell asleep. But if Kieran was being entirely honest with himself, one idea outweighed the other.

"I do," Kieran said finally. "But . . . I'm not sure I miss him in the way I'm supposed to."

"Miss who?" a new voice asked: Briar.

Kieran and Delilah glanced up to find Briar and Sebastian stepping through the doorway. Sebastian was trying to smooth his hair down while Briar plopped down next to Delilah on the couch, leaning into the girl's arms as if it was the most natural thing in the world. Delilah embraced her and kissed her cheek. Sebastian took a seat beside Kieran, exhaling a heavy sigh.

"N-no one," Kieran said, suddenly feeling tongue-tied at Briar's question. Every nerve in his body had become hyperaware that Sebastian was sitting next to him, as if just his aura was enough to make Kieran sweat. Kieran's cheeks flared with warmth. Why was it so embarrassing to mention Ash around Sebastian? Maybe it was because Kieran knew how attracted he was to Sebastian, and that in and of itself felt like a betrayal of Ash. But being attracted to other people when you were in a relationship was totally normal, right? It didn't mean he was going to act on it. Sebastian was just a friend, after all. No reason to complicate things.

Desperate to change the subject before anyone could press, Kieran said, "So, um—everything . . . set upstairs?"

Briar nodded. "Yep. Got the deck scrubbed and everything. Not the most pleasant way I've spent an afternoon, but hey"—she gestured to the Hilt and Stave on the table—"it looks like it was worth it."

"I'm impressed that you found it so quickly," Sebastian said, eyes flicking to Kieran. "Those woods looked huge. I would have thought it would take days to find anything in there."

Kieran shook his head. "I, um. I had some help."

Everyone's eyebrows shot up at once, and it occurred to Kieran that he had no idea how to explain what had happened in the woods. Still, they deserved to know as much as he did, considering that he'd vanished for half a day while the ship was nearly seized by Elias's goons.

"There was a . . . spirit of some kind," he explained. "Not like Seaweed—something else. But it looked like me as a kid. I don't know whether it was a manifestation of the forest in the form of kid-me or the forest was able to take something that already existed in me and give it a physical form. Or, really, if it was something else entirely—who's to say? Whatever it was, it helped me find the Stave."

"Wow," said Delilah. "That's . . ."

"Magic is fucking wild sometimes," Briar said.

Kieran snorted a laugh. "Took the words right out of my mouth."

"I can imagine that was a lot to deal with," Delilah guessed. When Kieran widened his eyes and started nodding vigorously, Delilah asked, "Do you wanna talk about it?"

"Not really," Kieran admitted. "I'm just . . . exhausted. Still need time to process, I think."

"You can say that again." Delilah glanced around the room. "This whole day was a lot for all of us. I, for one, think we deserve a chance to relax."

"Did you have something in mind?" Briar asked.

"Maybe if we ask nicely, Santiago would let us raid his liquor cabinet. We could have a little party." Delilah's eyes moved to Sebastian. "After all, I think I speak for everyone when I say you're a member of the crew now, Sebastian. And it might be nice to get to know each other better without blood or swords involved."

Sebastian's face brightened a bit. "I'd like that."

"Perfect," Delilah said. A big smile warmed her face. "Not this evening, since we're all exhausted, but maybe tomorrow after dinner?"

"Definitely," Briar said.

"Sounds good to me," Sebastian agreed.

Part of Kieran would have preferred to curl up in a ball and sit in the dark for the foreseeable future, but that probably wasn't the best way to process his feelings. After all, he deserved to have a little fun with his friends after everything.

Finally, he nodded. "Count me in."

The next day, Delilah went into full party-planning mode, searching through closets and storage containers for anything they could use as decorations. Kieran did his best to help execute her vision, hanging strings of lights on the observation deck and helping to clean anything that hadn't been addressed since they'd taken off. He suddenly realized just how much of the cleaning his great-aunt Adelaide had done on their journey last spring, but with her absent this time around, it occurred to him that he needed to pitch in more.

That night, Santiago made an expansive dinner for the crew, breaking out a number of the dishes that had been served back at his family's restaurant in Esperona. They had plate upon plate of ham-and-manchego croquettes, chorizo-filled dates with a red wine glaze, custardy egg-and-potato pancakes, and fingerling patatas bravas with a garlic aioli. Santiago even let them enjoy a sangria made with some of his favorite red wine. Briar made a show of trying to fish the fruit out of her glass to eat while Santiago berated her manners, much to the delight of everyone else at the table. It also gave Kieran the chance to sneak scraps to Seaweed under the table.

Kieran kept an eye on Sebastian all evening. While he'd shared meals with them before, he'd always seemed tense—doing his best to deflect attention and eating as quickly as he could without seeming impolite. Now, though, he actually smiled and laughed as Briar shoved her entire fist into her wineglass and Santiago shrieked as if he'd been touched by a hot poker. A few times, he'd glance Kieran's way and their eyes would meet for a split second before they both turned back to the conversation at hand.

Kieran mentally berated himself for staring. It was hard not to, though. There was something enthralling about Sebastian's smile, his rounded cheeks growing redder and redder with each glass of sangria. Soon, his whole face was flushed, and his laugh had gone from a quiet chuckle to a full-throated howl.

And despite himself, Kieran couldn't stop smiling.

When they finished with dinner, Ariel and Santiago excused themselves to head for the control room. They explained that they were going to do some "route planning," to which Briar responded by muttering, "Oh, is that what we're calling it now?" Kieran nearly snorted the wine he'd just sipped up his nose.

Once they were gone, Delilah stood on her chair and clapped her hands. "Everyone, downstairs! I snuck a few bottles of Santiago's wine down there earlier and hid them between the couch cushions."

The four of them cleaned up the table before snagging their wineglasses and heading to the observation deck, with its glass walls that looked out over the land below. Seaweed was clearly tired of their loud chatting and refusal to feed her more; Kieran gave her one last bit of sausage before she vanished up the stairs.

Downstairs, they rearranged the chairs that had been set to look out the windows and arranged them in a circle. While Delilah poured wine, Kieran set up the turntable he'd grabbed from the kitchen. He thumbed through Santiago's collection of records, eventually settling on one with a song he'd heard Sebastian hum once or twice.

"Oh, hey," Sebastian said as the music kicked on and Kieran took a seat next to him. "I love this band. Did I tell you that?"

Kieran shook his head. "No. I just guessed."

Sebastian's smile grew, and Kieran turned his face the other way, hoping Sebastian wouldn't notice the rush of blood from Kieran's throat to his ears.

Delilah pushed Kieran's now-full glass back to him across the table. As he took it, she cleared her throat, pulling Briar from the conversation she'd been about to start with Sebastian.

"I," Delilah said, swirling her glass around in her hand, "think we should play a game. Something to get to know each other better, Sebastian."

For a moment, Kieran didn't recognize the look on Sebastian's face. His eyes had widened just a bit, and a vein in his throat jumped as he swallowed. Then it occurred to Kieran what that meant.

Sebastian was nervous.

"I . . . Of course," he said, tone not betraying any of what Kieran had just seen flash across his face. It was strange: The more time Kieran spent with Sebastian, the more obvious it became when he was trying to follow a mental script. "Did you have a game in mind?"

"Ever heard of Empty Glass?" Delilah asked. When the others shook their heads, she explained: "It's pretty easy. Everyone goes around and says something they've never done. If you *have* done it, you drink. The first one to empty their glass loses, and they have to answer one question the other players come up with truthfully, no matter what it is."

"Sounds easy enough," Sebastian agreed. His eyes slid to Kieran. "You wanna play?"

Kieran's throat had gone dry. He had to clear it before he said, "Y-yeah, I'd love to."

Across from them, Delilah and Briar exchanged a knowing look that Kieran couldn't even begin to explain.

"Why don't you start, Sebastian?" Delilah prompted. "Tell us something you've never done. It can be anything."

"All right." Sebastian cleared his throat, straightening in his seat and tucking his shoulders back. His eyes wandered the room for a moment before he said, "I . . . had never been on an aeroship before this one."

Kieran took a drink, as did Briar. Delilah cocked an eyebrow and asked Briar, "When did you go on one before we picked you up?"

Briar shrugged. "When I was on my own, between running away from Wrenlin and meeting you all. I did a little traveling around Celdwyn to try to avoid the Pelumbras' hunters. I stowed away on an aeroship at one point when I needed to get far away from them quickly."

"You never told me that," Delilah said, her jaw hanging open and an accusatory note in her voice.

Briar laughed. "I've got to a keep a little mystery, don't I?"

Delilah just rolled her eyes.

"Me next, right?" Kieran said. They nodded at him, and he put a fist under his chin and looked up as he tried to decide what to say. Should he say something that would help him get to know Sebastian or try to make Delilah and his sister lose? *Choices, choices.*

Maybe I can do both, he decided.

"I," Kieran finally said, "have never slept with anyone."

Delilah's and Briar's eyes slid toward each other, then back as they both took sips of their drinks. Delilah muttered, "Starting off strong, I see."

Kieran, meanwhile, was focused fully on watching Sebastian at his side. Much to his surprise, Sebastian left the glass on the table untouched.

Before Kieran could say anything, Delilah's jaw dropped. *"Really?"*

"I was homeschooled," Sebastian explained with a shrug. "Didn't have a lot of time to meet people my age. And my father kept me busy with training when I wasn't doing schoolwork—"

"Training for what?" Kieran blurted out before he could stop himself. *I really am too nosy for my own good.*

Sebastian shrugged again. "Oh, just general fitness, mostly. My father cared a lot about keeping us healthy."

If Kieran hadn't been looking, he wouldn't have noticed the tiny flutter Sebastian's fingers did as he said it. He narrowed his eyes. *Why would he lie about that? Was he training for something else? Or was he just doing other things with his free time? Weird.*

"All right," Briar said, moving on to her turn before Kieran could ask any more questions. "My turn. *I* have never been invited to a formal ball."

"But we went to the Pelumbra one last spring," Delilah pointed out.

"Sure, but we crashed that. Whole different story."

Delilah nodded her concession while Kieran and Sebastian

both took sips of their wine. Kieran explained: "My family let me attend their balls as a child, but only the masquerade one, so no one would ask questions about who I was. Plus, there were so many of my cousins running around that no one ever questioned the spare."

"Why would they want to hide you?" Sebastian asked, forehead wrinkled.

Kieran worried at his lip with his teeth for a moment. "They wanted to keep our curse a secret from people outside the family. If a witch who could smell magic—like Delilah—smelled it on me and figured out I was a Pelumbra, it would have been a massive scandal. But my mother wanted me to have a bit of normalcy, and she won that argument with my father. So they used the crowds and masks to their advantage, and I got to go."

Sebastian let out a low whistle. "Your family sounds . . . challenging."

"Understatement of the century," Briar said, a snorting laugh escaping her.

"What about you?" Kieran asked, hoping to deflect attention from himself. "Did your family go to a lot of balls?"

Sebastian shook his head. "My father was occasionally invited to them for his work. He brought me along. Hoped to introduce me to people in case I took up the family business."

Which was what, exactly? Kieran wanted to ask. At the same time, he worried that Sebastian might feel like he was being interrogated if Kieran kept needling for details. *I'll save it for later,* he decided.

"Well, *I* was never homeschooled," Delilah said, watching

with a smile on her face as everyone else around the table took sips of their drinks, Briar groaning as she did. "And I graduated with flying colors right before my Calling, for the record."

They went for a few more rounds, bringing up foods they'd never tried or places they'd never been. It seemed that Sebastian had traveled a lot, and Briar had covered more ground around Celdwyn than Kieran and Delilah had been aware of. Their glasses grew emptier and emptier, and when they were close to finishing, Delilah proposed that they refill them and continue the game, to which everyone agreed. And when they finished those, they did it again.

Kieran's thoughts grew watercolored as the wine settled warmly in his stomach. He became even more aware of Sebastian at his side, watching the way he smiled and laughed, the anxiety that had clung to him before melting away. Even as he tried not to, Kieran's mind began to fill with images of what Sebastian's hands would feel like in his hair, or tracing the curve of his bare spine. Typically, he wouldn't have let himself consider it. But now, with Sebastian's knee almost touching his, and the way his expression had grown so bright as he finally relaxed around them, Kieran couldn't stop himself. Even as Ash hung in the periphery of his mind, waiting to chastise him for his infidelity.

The wine was making it much easier to ignore that feeling, however.

In the current round, Delilah and Briar had elected to gang up on Kieran, mentioning all the things they'd never had as children, like silk pajamas, maids, cooks, and the like. Kieran took sip after sip from his glass, shooting them burning looks as it grew emptier and emptier. Sebastian laughed along at Kieran's expense, but for once, it didn't bother him. They were just friends enjoying their time together, simple as that.

The next turn went to Sebastian, who snuck a look at Kieran. He tapped the stem of his wineglass as he considered what he'd ask. Finally, he nodded.

"I've never been in love," Sebastian said plainly.

Kieran froze, staring at the final sip of wine in his glass. A few weeks ago, he would have instantly taken a sip. It had seemed so normal then: He'd been with Ash for months, so of course they were in love. Even if they'd barely spoken recently. Even if Kieran never felt that he could fully open up. Even if some days he wasn't even sure whether Ash liked him or found him irritating with his penchant for melodrama and overthinking.

But it wasn't as if Kieran had much of anything to compare their relationship to. Ash had been his first kiss, his first relationship. Besides that, he could only compare it to other people's relationships. It had been better than what his parents had, and far more committed than the brief relationships he saw his cousins have with locals in the town near their estate. It wasn't as good as Briar and Delilah's, but they were outliers.

Which, Kieran had decided months ago, meant that it was definitely love.

Right?

Delilah and Briar, meanwhile, both picked up their wineglasses, clinking them against each other before taking a drink. Briar, who had clearly been hit by the wine harder than anyone else due to her small stature, had started giggling and couldn't stop.

Kieran sighed. *Even if we never had anything like that.*

He stared at his glass, feeling Sebastian's eyes on him. *Did I ever really love Ash? Or did I just love the idea of having what Delilah and my sister do?*

After a long moment, Kieran sat back, leaving his glass untouched.

He'd expected Delilah or Briar to say something at that, but they were both too busy staring at each other. Delilah had Briar's hand in hers, tracing her fingers with her own. It didn't take a genius to understand that their thoughts had gone elsewhere.

Kieran cleared his throat to get their attention, but it was clear they were finished. They went around once more until Kieran had drained his cup, officially making him the loser.

Everyone else finished their wine as well, and Delilah set her glass down with a small smile. "I think we should probably get to bed," she said, nodding toward Briar, who had leaned against her and closed her eyes. To Sebastian, she said, "Thanks for playing with us. It was nice hearing a little more about you."

Briar hiccupped. "You're *way* less uptight than I thought. Like, you don't even have a stick up your ass. Maybe that's what Kieran likes about you."

Kieran flushed, shooting his twin a horrified look. Thankfully, Sebastian just chuckled.

"Thank you, Briar. I think."

Delilah stood, holding out a hand for her girlfriend. They

waved goodbye as they headed for the stairs, Briar giggling a bit too loudly as they ascended. Kieran felt a warmth in his chest that had nothing to do with the wine. Truly, he was so happy for both of them. They deserved a love like that.

And so, a voice in his mind reminded him, *do you.*

CHAPTER SIXTEEN

"They're really something, huh?" Sebastian said, breaking Kieran out of his thoughts as the sound of Delilah and Briar's laughter vanished up the stairs.

Kieran turned to meet his gaze. Sebastian's sharply arched eyebrows were up, a quarter smile quirking the corner of his lips. If Kieran hadn't known better, he might have laughed. Those eyebrows reminded him of little of bat wings. *I can see why whoever cursed him decided to go with vampirism.*

Kieran nodded. "*True love,* just like in the fairy tales. Sickly sweet, isn't it?"

"Not at all." Sebastian laughed. "It's kind of reassuring, in a way, isn't it?"

"I don't follow."

Sebastian gestured to the stairs where the girls had disappeared. "Well, if it exists for them, maybe it can for the rest of us too."

"How optimistic of you," Kieran said. He stood up, gesturing to one of the couches that had been set up along the windows to get a better view of the ground far below. "Wanna move to the couch? The view over cities is incredible, and I think we might be close to one."

Sebastian nodded, following Kieran's lead. The two crossed the floor side by side, hands nearly touching. They sat down next to each other, and Sebastian tilted his face down to better take in the lights below.

The aeroship had just left the flatlands outside the town of Maybury and were now approaching the towering buildings of Cestella City. The city lights glowed in shades of topaz and pink and blue, winking up at them as if the city itself were greeting them. Unlike up north, here, no snow decorated the sidewalks. Instead, some hearty cool-weather trees and bushes still clung to their leaves, framing the roads on either side. A few cars puttered down them with their headlights on. Not far from their own ship, other aeroships floated through the skies. With the languid flap of their metallic wings, they reminded Kieran of birds.

"Not bad, right?" Kieran said, sneaking a look at Sebastian.

Sebastian's eyes were rounded, the lights reflected in his near-black irises. His lips were parted in a smile, revealing the edges of his snowy teeth. Kieran's stomach clenched. Part of him waited to hear Ash's voice in his head telling him that this was a bad idea.

His brain had gone silent.

"No," Sebastian said, turning his gaze to Kieran. The joy in it was almost childlike. "Not bad at all."

Kieran's heart nearly launched itself into his throat. He could feel a hot blush in his cheeks. He felt lucky that the only illumination in the room was coming from string lights and the glow of the city below.

"You know," he said, and beneath the layers of tension in his body, something else gave way: an uncharacteristic boldness bolstered by wine. "I just realized that everyone forgot to ask me a question. The one I had to answer truthfully for losing the game."

"Hmm," Sebastian said, rubbing his chin as he considered it. "Well, that seems a bit unfair, doesn't it? Who am I to let you get away with such a transgression?"

Kieran's pulse thrummed. The air had suddenly begun to feel charged around them, as if any spark could ignite an explosion. Unconsciously, he moved closer to Sebastian, close enough to smell his cologne. Kieran could guess the layers of it: bergamot, grapefruit, and sandalwood. It reminded him of a summer night, heavy but warm.

"What's your question, then?" Kieran said, his voice coming out huskier than he'd intended. Typically, that would have made him turn bright red with an immediate shock wave of embarrassment, but for once, it didn't.

Sebastian angled himself so he was firmly leaning into Kieran's personal space. There was no way to ignore him, from the heat coming off his skin to the touch of his hand as it suddenly went to Kieran's knee.

The air was sucked out of Kieran's lungs all at once. Sure, he'd seen the way Sebastian had stared at him for a moment too long once or twice, but with him this close, Kieran's mind struggled to explain away what was happening. This wasn't something Just

Friends did. At least, not ones who were going to stay just friends for long.

I should tell him to move, Kieran thought, his eyes trained unwaveringly on Sebastian's lower lip. It was full and pouty, perfect for Kieran to nip at. *I should be loyal to Ash. I should . . .*

Sebastian took a breath, staring directly into Kieran's eyes.

"If I asked you to let me kiss you right now, would you say yes?"

Kieran felt like the ground had swooped out from beneath him. His heart lurched. When had he last felt like this? Had he ever, even with Ash's body wrapped around him? Because just now he couldn't seem to summon a single memory of a feeling that burned even close to as bright as the one growing hotter and hotter in his chest. He couldn't stop the truth from spilling out, voice choked with the weight of it.

"Yes."

The next moment, Sebastian's soft lips were on his. Kieran inhaled sharply as one of Sebastian's hands went to Kieran's thigh while the other pressed to his neck, nudging him closer. Kieran trapped Sebastian's lower lip between his teeth, nipping it gently. Sebastian hummed against the kiss. The touch of his fingers as they sank into Kieran's hair felt electric, a shiver running down Kieran's spine. Kieran failed to stop himself from smiling against the other boy's lips.

Sebastian broke the kiss, pressing his forehead to Kieran's so their noses gently brushed. His voice was thick, lower than Kieran was used to. "I didn't think you'd say yes."

"I wasn't allowed to lie," Kieran whispered.

"Well, then. Can I ask another question?"

"Sure."

"Do you want to do it again?"

Kieran's breath rushed out of him. "Yes."

Sebastian's eyes flickered with an emotion Kieran couldn't place. After a moment, it dawned on him: It was like hunger. Kieran's heart rate sped up. If they got closer, would it trigger Sebastian's bloodlust? Sure, he'd been able to control himself before when Kieran's blood had been dripping onto his face, but how could he know if it would be the same this time? Kieran barely felt in control of his own body at that moment—he couldn't imagine how much harder it must be for Sebastian with his curse.

Sebastian hesitated, pulling back. "Are you okay? You looked . . . afraid for a second."

Kieran tried to swallow, but his mouth had gone dry. "Sorry—sorry, it's nothing—"

"It's not nothing if it makes you uncomfortable. Tell me."

A wave of guilt washed over Kieran. Why did he find it so hard to communicate this sort of thing? Speaking up for himself had never been a skill Kieran excelled at, especially in the case of something like this. He'd hate to hurt Sebastian's feelings or make him think he was any less for his curse—

"Kieran," Sebastian said, eyes narrowing. "You're in your head. Tell me what you're thinking."

Before he could let himself get mired in anxiety, Kieran said, "Is it, um, safe? With your curse and everything?"

As soon as the words were out, Kieran winced. *You're going to hurt him, and he's going to hate you—*

Sebastian, however, didn't falter. His expression softened, though not in a sad way. There was understanding there, despite Kieran's feeling that he might hyperventilate. Sebastian reached out and cupped Kieran's cheek with his hand, tilting his face up to meet his eyes.

"I would never hurt you," he promised. There was a weight behind the words that made Kieran wonder if he was speaking about something more than just his curse. "I swear it. I've had time to learn how to keep that part of me in check. I would never bite you without your permission."

Kieran's eyes widened. Without . . . permission? He thought back to what Sebastian had said about when he bit Lila in Raven's Roost: *I can make it feel positive for whoever I'm drinking from.* Kieran's first thought was to emphatically deny he'd ever want that. That everything he liked was very safe and normal and didn't involve teeth.

His second thought, however, didn't fully support that.

"I . . . huh" was the only thing Kieran managed to say.

"Whatever I can do for you, just say the word," Sebastian said. He stroked a thumb across Kieran's jaw. "If it's a only a kiss, it's only a kiss."

Kieran found himself nodding before his thoughts could wander any further. "I think I'd just like a kiss for now."

Sebastian reached out for Kieran again. He pulled him closer, and they rearranged themselves so Kieran sat sideways in Sebastian's lap, his knees bent and feet on the couch. Feeling Sebastian's arms wrapped around him, resting low near his tailbone, was almost enough to completely erase his anxiety.

"I can manage that."

With that, Sebastian pulled him close once more. Kieran fell into his kiss as if it was the simplest thing in the world. While it was a bit stiffer at first than it had been before, Kieran felt his muscles slowly relax as he settled into the feeling of Sebastian's tongue teasing at his own and his hands slipping just underneath the waistband of Kieran's trousers. Everything about him was warm and sure and steady, and so much around Kieran wasn't.

And for once in his life, Kieran let himself simply enjoy that.

When Kieran awoke the next morning, Seaweed asleep on his chest, he wasn't entirely sure whether the night before had been a dream.

It had certainly felt like one. He'd spent more nights in a row than he'd like to admit wondering what Sebastian's lips would feel like on his. Each of those nights too he berated himself for thinking it. So when the moment had finally come, and it had been better than he'd imagined, it had immediately sent him into a spiral.

Even if Ash and I are on a break, we're still technically together. Does that make it cheating? If he finds out, will he still take me back?

Do I even still want him to?

Kieran pushed Seaweed off and hauled himself out of bed. She grumbled at him as he shuffled off to shower, doing his best to ignore the faint headache that had bloomed in the front of his skull. When he'd finished, he opened the drawer below his bathroom mirror and took out a small glass bottle of painkillers, tossing two in his mouth and swallowing them dry.

He'd love to blame the wine for last night. But he'd wanted to kiss Sebastian since the moment he'd laid eyes on him, if he was being honest. Really, all the wine had done was melt away his ever-present sense of impending doom for a few hours. And with it, his reservations about the whole thing.

Part of Kieran wished he could call Ash. Confess to what he'd done and apologize over and over until his bruised sense of self-worth stopped smarting. But what was that, ultimately? Did he want to apologize to Ash, or did he just want permission to kiss Sebastian again?

That definitely makes me a bad person, Kieran decided as he ran a smoothing serum through his hair to keep his curls from getting too frizzy. *Good people don't abandon the relationships they're trying to save just to kiss someone they barely know.*

I wish there was a rule book for this. Kieran sighed, staring at himself in the mirror. There were shadows under his brown eyes from sleeping only a couple hours, and a few small red bumps had appeared on his forehead. He moaned, pressing the backs of his thumbs against his closed eyes. *And now I have stress acne to top it off. Take me out back and end it.*

He set down the comb in his hand, deciding he needed to consult someone more experienced.

Once he'd gotten dressed in a pair of black pants, a white button-down shirt, and a blue sweater vest, Kieran headed to the door kitty-corner to his, leaving Seaweed to sleep on the warm spot he'd left on the bed. As he knocked, he glanced at the door to Sebastian's room. *I'm going to have to speak to him too.*

Did he regret last night? Kieran desperately hoped he didn't.

The door in front of him swung open, making Kieran jump as the sound yanked him from his thoughts. He jerked around to find Briar yawning, rubbing her forehead. Her short red hair was sticking straight up in the front in a perfect cowlick. If Kieran had to guess, she'd probably fallen asleep with her face buried in a pillow.

"You're up early," she grumbled.

"Is Delilah in there? I need to speak with her."

Briar said, "She's downstairs in the kitchen making croissants for breakfast with Santiago. Why?"

Kieran frowned. *Damn. I can't ask her about this in front of Santiago. He'll laugh at me, then tell Ariel, and neither of them will ever let it go.*

"Just . . . um . . ." Kieran's eyes unconsciously wandered over his shoulder, then immediately snapped back to his twin, cheeks warming. "I wanted to ask her some, um, questions about . . . things. And stuff."

Briar's gaze went to Sebastian's door for a moment, and Kieran watched as realization dawned on her face.

"Kieran," she said, biting back a laugh. She put a hand to her chest in mock surprise. "You little harlot."

Kieran shushed her. "Not so loud!"

Briar did little to cover her smirk. She stepped back and opened the door wider. "Come in. Delilah's busy, and I wanna know everything."

Kieran hesitated for a moment. Did he want to come clean about this to his sister? She might make fun of him for it, but he had to admit, it was better than keeping it to himself. He sighed and stepped over the threshold. While he didn't consider his twin to be a paragon of romantic knowledge, she was, at least, in a happy relationship. So maybe that counted for something.

"Fine, but lower your voice," Kieran said as he shut the door behind him. "I don't need Sebastian knowing I talked to you about this."

Briar scoffed. "Fine, fine. I'll do my best. Now sit."

Kieran nodded, then crossed the room to take a seat at the small table in the corner, identical to the one he had in his. Briar and Delilah's room was the largest of the crew cabins up here, with a four-poster bed and a big window behind it looking out at the sky. The room was a bit messy, with clothes stacked on a few of the chairs, but not dirty. Briar and Delilah were both cleaner than Kieran. He was, admittedly, a bit of a slob sometimes. He blamed it on the fact that he had had maids his entire childhood.

He sighed as he put his elbows on the table and hung his head. Briar took the spot across from him, steepling her fingers as if they were about to discuss a business deal.

"Let me guess. You told him you like him?"

"Not exactly. It wasn't so much talking as it was . . . kissing."

"Really?" Briar tilted her head, her brow furrowed. "I need some context. What happened?"

Kieran worried at his lip with his teeth for a moment before sighing and launching into what had happened last night after

Delilah and Briar had gone to bed. The whole time, Briar did little to hide the emotional journey her face was going on. Her smile turned wicked, and a few half laughs escaped her, especially when Kieran mentioned the truthful-question bit.

"I must admit," she said when Kieran had finished his story, "he sounds very smooth."

"He is! That's part of the problem. It all felt so easy. It shouldn't feel easy, right? Not when I dragged everyone to join my Calling for the express purpose of trying to get Ash back."

"Technically, we're here to get a panacea," Briar corrected. "What you use it for isn't our business."

Kieran considered it. She was right. While he'd been sure he was going to use it on Ash when they'd left Gellingham, that certainty had wavered—especially in the last few days.

"I mean, let's be honest," Briar continued. "Ash has been stringing you along for weeks now. Maybe months. He's just biding his time so he can muster up the courage to end it," she said, not even attempting to soften the blow. When Kieran winced, Briar asked, "What? You really think he's gonna change his mind? He's been done for a long time, Kieran. He's just too nice—or cowardly, maybe—to break your heart by making it official. Why waste your time on a guy like that when you can do better?"

"B-but—"

"No, no buts. There's no reason to defend him." It was odd to hear it said so matter-of-factly. Briar went on: "Plus, you're on a break. You're allowed to have some harmless fun. It doesn't have to be a whole new relationship."

Kieran blinked as he studied his twin's face. She was serious.

And really, why wouldn't she be? There was something to what she was saying that Kieran hadn't considered.

"I . . . guess I didn't think of it like that," he admitted.

"Of course you didn't. Because you're a hopeless romantic whose only knowledge of relationships comes from fairy tales. Runs in the family, it seems." Briar stood up, gesturing for Kieran to do the same. "Listen. I think I have something that can help you, but you can't tell anyone I gave it to you."

Kieran's eyes widened. *What in the world . . . ?*

Still, he stood, following his sister across the room. He had to step around the dress Delilah had been wearing last night, discarded in a heap on the floor.

Briar knelt in front of a trunk that had been pushed against the wall. She swiftly jammed a key in the lock. After it let out a *click,* she lifted the lid, then stepped back, gesturing inside.

"This," she said, "is my collection."

Kieran stepped forward, terrified of what she might be showing him. He peered inside gingerly, practically waiting for some kind of strange beast to jump out and bite him. Instead, however, he had to withhold a barking laugh as he realized what he was looking at.

Inside were at least fifty paperback romance novels, all with illustrated covers of couples in various states of undress. People of all genders clung to one another, hair windswept and chests exposed. A few even had humans held in the clutches of various half-human, extremely muscular beasts.

Kieran's jaw hung open, and he found himself unable to speak.

"There are a few in here that may speak to you," Briar said.

She reached inside and grabbed one featuring two men on the cover, one shirtless while the other wore a heavy trench coat. She handed it to him. "This one has a nice friends-with-benefits storyline." Kieran took it, and she shoved another in his hand. "This one has a relationship with three men. Just in case polyamory is of interest."

"I—" Kieran's shock silenced him for a beat. He could say with total certainty that he'd never considered anything of the sort. One partner was enough anxiety for him to deal with; he severely doubted he had the communication skills for two. "Briar, how many of these have you read?"

"Rough estimate?" Briar considered it. "A thousand, maybe? This isn't my entire collection, obviously. I have way more at home. If I'm not spending money on necessities, it's going to this."

Kieran was agog. Instead of elaborating, Briar handed him a third novel. This one pictured a shirtless, extremely built man, grinning with a mouthful of fangs and a trickle of blood running down his chin.

Despite himself, Kieran blushed. "Does Delilah know you have all these?" he squeaked. "In your . . . smut trunk?"

Briar snorted at that. "Of course. Sometimes I read them out loud to her when she's baking. She thinks they're hilarious."

"Oh." Kieran's eyes scanned the covers again, wondering just how many of them had been read aloud in their apartment while he was at work or asleep in his room. "Interesting."

"Listen," Briar said, getting to her feet as Kieran stood frozen with an armful of books. "Everything I know about relationships, I learned from these. If you're not sure what you want, fiction's a great way to figure it out. There are no unspoken romance rules you have to follow. You just have to figure out what *you* want. Does that make sense?"

Kieran frowned. He'd been asking himself what he wanted a lot recently.

"So . . . you don't think I'm a terrible person for kissing Sebastian?"

Briar scoffed. "Of course not. Granted, you should probably tell him that you're in a weird place with all the Ash stuff just so he knows what he's dealing with, but no."

"And I wouldn't be a terrible person if I wanted to kiss him again?"

"I don't think so." Briar pointed to the books. "I'm serious—read those. Think of it as a learning experience. A crash course in different kinds of relationships, if you will."

Kieran swallowed, the lump in his throat bobbing. He had, admittedly, never been one to consume this sort of literature. In fact, he'd read nothing but elegant love poetry about undying romance for most of his life. Maybe that was why everything else seemed so strange to consider.

Kieran held the books to his chest like a secret to keep. "I . . . I think I will."

Briar closed and locked the trunk. "Good. If you ever want more, just let me know."

"Noted." He nodded. "Thank you, Briar. Genuinely."

"Anytime. Now let's get out of here and see if breakfast is ready. I'm starving." Briar headed for the door, Kieran nodding in agreement as he followed. Then she paused.

"Might want to drop those off in your room first, though."

"Oh—sure." Kieran held them tighter. "Will do."

After he had tucked the novels under his pillow, he followed his sister down to breakfast.

Maybe Briar's right, he thought, eyes bright. *I just need a little perspective.*

CHAPTER SEVENTEEN

Down on the main deck, Delilah and Santiago had just finished cooking. Soon, the table was filled with the usual spread of fluffy scrambled eggs, pork sausage, golden pancakes, and—special for that morning—flaky chocolate croissants. Santiago put an upbeat jazz record on. While everyone loaded up their plates, Kieran took a head count.

Sebastian was missing.

Kieran froze in the middle of scooping eggs onto his plate. *Is he . . . avoiding me?*

Seeming to notice her twin's panic, Briar cleared her throat. "Should I go grab Sebastian from upstairs?"

That's not a bad idea. Then, at least if he's avoiding me, Briar can act as a buffer.

Kieran gave her a quick nod while everyone else agreed, consumed more by serving themselves than anything else. Briar nodded back to Kieran before she headed up the stairs.

The whole time she was gone, Kieran felt hyperaware of the seconds ticking by, as if he were on trial and not just sitting there adding hot sauce to his eggs. Shortly after, Briar returned. Kieran immediately met her gaze, his eyes wide, trying to silently communicate his panic.

Briar cleared her throat. "He's not hungry. Told me to save a chocolate croissant for later."

Kieran's stomach dropped. *He* is *avoiding me.*

"Too much to drink?" Santiago asked, unaware of the way Kieran's expression had crumpled as if he'd been slapped across the face. Santiago shot Delilah a hard look, eyebrows cocked accusatorially.

Delilah just laughed. "Sorry, Santi. I'll replace your wines next time we land for supplies."

Santiago crossed his arms and humphed. "You'd better. I quite liked what you stole."

Kieran barely picked at his food for the rest of breakfast, his head swimming. Meanwhile, Ariel and Santiago had a map spread out in front of them, chatting about which route to take back up north to find the Iceweave Coven, since there seemed to be multiple options. Delilah chimed in once or twice, as did Briar, but Kieran kept his mouth shut. He just pushed his eggs around, feeling a bit like he might vomit.

"What exactly do we know about the Iceweave Coven?" Briar broke in, her voice loud enough to snap Kieran out of his thoughts. "Because I've never heard of them."

"I have," Delilah said. She gestured to an illustration of the Slicetooth Mountains at the top of the map. "Some of them would pass through Kitfield when I was a kid, and they were the talk of the village. They always dressed so extravagantly, it was hard *not* to talk about them."

Kieran nodded. *Worrying about Sebastian can wait for a bit.* "The Pelumbras have some association with them, just because they live relatively close to the estate. They invited us to their winter solstice celebration every year, but the only ones who went were my older cousins, in their twenties. Apparently, it's quite a wild party. Very . . . hedonistic. Magical potions that trigger hallucinations, skyclad ceremonies, dances that end only when everyone collapses—that sort of thing. My cousins always spent months putting together their most lavish outfits for it."

"I'm surprised the Witches' Council is okay with that," Briar said.

"Oh, it's not." Kieran spun his fork around to point at the map. "That's why the coven lives on the border between Celdwyn and Mehana, to the north. Since their land straddles the two countries and the boundary isn't very well established, neither nation can claim them. They're basically their own city-state, where our laws don't apply."

Briar considered that. "Color me intrigued. Though, if the fashion is such a big part of it, will they even let us in? My entire wardrobe is black pants and button-down shirts." Her eyes flicked to Kieran. "At least you'll be okay."

Kieran glanced down at his clothes. "For your information, this is by far my most muted sweater vest."

"Exactly my point."

"Perhaps we can land and pick something up," Ariel suggested.

"It's going to take us twelve days or so to fly that far north—perhaps longer if I decide to take a different route to avoid the mercenaries. We'll have to get fuel at least once, maybe more. I could try to fit in a stop somewhere you could get something more appropriate for the celebration."

Kieran nodded his agreement. "Good call. Best to give Sebastian a chance to, ah . . . deal with his curse with something other than seabirds as well."

"Right—good point." Ariel made a few marks on the map with a small pencil, nodding. "I'll get the ship set for this path. In the meantime, it would be great if you witchy folks could do a sweep of the ship for anything those mercenaries left behind to make sure there's nothing they could have dropped that could track us. I doubt they would, but after that last ambush, I'm a little paranoid."

"I'll take a walk around and see if I can smell anything," Delilah agreed. She lowered her voice: "No offense to Sebastian, but it'll be a lot easier if he stays upstairs. That curse could cover up pretty much anything."

"I'll let him know," Kieran said. He took a small bite of eggs; swallowing it felt like a feat as his stomach roiled with anxiety. "I need to talk to him anyway."

Everyone at the table exchanged knowing eye contact. Kieran sighed. *These people are impossible.*

"In fact," he said, standing up, "I should do that now. Thank you for breakfast."

Santiago and Delilah nodded, and Delilah passed him a chocolate croissant. "Take that for Sebastian."

Kieran nodded, squaring his shoulders. Across the table, Briar caught his eye and mouthed, *Good luck.*

Kieran nodded his thanks and headed upstairs.

Raising his fist to knock on Sebastian's door was beginning to feel like a challenge on par with scaling the Slicetooths.

Kieran stood, staring at the dark wood, trying to tell himself that he was overthinking it. Maybe Sebastian really was just a bit sick. Maybe he wasn't avoiding Kieran on purpose.

Or, Kieran's traitorous brain offered, *he regrets last night and is about to tell you that he would prefer if you just went ahead and walked off the edge of the ship.*

Kieran gulped, the lump in his throat bobbing. *You won't know until you talk to him.*

Finally, before his anxiety could get the better of him, Kieran rapped twice against the door before hopping back, half convinced that the door was about to grow teeth and bite him.

There was a pause before Sebastian gruffly called, "Who is it?"

"Kieran?"

"Ah." Sebastian cleared his throat, then said, "It's unlocked."

Kieran's mouth felt like sandpaper. *Just* ah*? Nothing else? Oh, he definitely hates me.*

He reached for the handle, despite the way his heart had begun to pound, and turned it. He pushed his way inside, stepping as softly as he could, as if he were sneaking in. The room was dim, the curtains having been drawn to block out the sunlight. It gave the room an appearance of twilight. There was a stale scent in the air, as if dirty clothes had been left out.

Kieran's eyes fell on the bed, where he discovered a tangle of blankets and sheets. It took him a moment, though, to spot Sebastian buried inside.

Just the top of his head was poking out. Everything from the eyes down was cocooned in his fluffy dark-blue comforter. His hair stuck up at an angle, and what little of his skin was visible looked waxy and beaded with sweat. At the sight of Kieran, he reached up and pulled the blanket down so the rest of his face was visible and his voice unmuffled.

"I," he announced, looking like he was on the verge of vomiting, "am never touching wine again."

Instantly, Kieran's muscles all relaxed at once. *Oh, thank goodness, he* is *just super hungover.*

"Oh no." Kieran shut the door behind him and dropped the croissant off on the table before going to his side. "Are you okay? Do you need me to get you water?"

Sebastian nodded weakly. "Water would be great."

While Kieran rushed to the bathroom to fill a cup with water, Sebastian groaned and pulled himself into a sitting position. He barely moved as Kieran returned with the water, gently passing it to him.

A hand emerged from the blanket cocoon and took the water, raising it to Sebastian's lips. He barely got a few sips down before he stopped, once again looking green.

"I didn't realize you'd had so much," Kieran said, leaning on the bedside table. There was a hunk of wood on it, and a whittling knife beside it. If Kieran had to guess, it appeared Sebastian was carving it into the shape of a swan. "Honestly, I thought you had less than I did."

"I did." Sebastian's head hung. "It's just that, with my curse, if I don't drink enough blood, my body stops functioning quite as well. Apparently, I was low enough on blood that my liver decided to just *give up.*"

He suddenly had the dry heaves, and Kieran took a step back. With uncanny speed, Sebastian managed to grab a bowl on his bedside table that he'd clearly filched from the kitchen. Kieran looked away politely as Sebastian bowed his head and retched. After a few more deeply unpleasant sounds, Sebastian coughed, then spit the last of what was in his mouth into the bowl.

He sniffled, then wiped his nose with the back of his head. "Kieran, I need your help."

"Oh? S-sure. Whatever you need."

With grim seriousness, Sebastian said, "You need to kill me."

"Well, that seems a little dramatic for a hangover, don't you think?" Kieran reached out, and Sebastian stared at him for a beat before he seemed to realize Kieran was offering to take the bowl. "Let me clean that up. Maybe . . . maybe I can catch you a loose seagull to drain."

"Easier said than done." Half of Sebastian's face sank below the blankets. "I'll . . . survive. Maybe."

"That's the spirit." Without looking in the bowl Sebastian had thrown up in, Kieran said, "I'll go rinse this out and . . . maybe see if there are some plain crackers."

Sebastian nodded faintly, then sank back into his blanket cocoon.

Kieran turned for the door and headed toward the kitchen.

Once he was out of earshot, he breathed a sigh of relief. Clearly, Sebastian didn't hate him, so that was a win. Though he hadn't exactly brought up last night one way or the other. Considering how hungover he was, Kieran wondered if that meant he'd been drunker than Kieran realized. He'd seemed completely lucid last night, but he had proved to be a good actor in the past. Maybe he'd faked it.

Kieran sighed as he went into the kitchen, thankfully finding it empty. He quickly rinsed out the bowl and found a pack of unsalted crackers in the pantry. He hoped they'd be mild enough for Sebastian to keep down. Maybe he could convince Ariel to let them make a supply stop soon so Sebastian could feed on something larger than an albatross.

Or, he thought, *I could always offer to let him drink from me.*

He paused, the sound of the sink running the only thing to cover up the sputtering sound he made at his own intrusive thought. Sure, Sebastian had mentioned it last night, but he'd probably just been saying that because he'd had a few glasses of wine. Kieran doubted he'd really want to drink from him.

Right?

Once the bowl was clean, Kieran headed to Sebastian's room, only to turn back after realizing his mind had been so far away he'd forgotten to turn off the sink.

A few minutes later, he reappeared in Sebastian's room, setting the clean bowl down on his table with the crackers. Once again, Sebastian lifted his eyes from the blankets and gratefully nodded to Kieran before taking a cracker and nibbling on it.

Kieran gestured to the bed. "Is it okay if I sit down?"

Sebastian nodded, scooting over to make room for him.

Kieran, meanwhile, felt his heartbeat in his throat. Maybe he shouldn't even try to bring anything up right now, not when Sebastian was sick—

"I was meaning to ask," Sebastian started before Kieran's thoughts could grow any louder. "Are you feeling okay? About last night? I just wanted to make sure you didn't think I was trying to take advantage of you or anything."

Kieran blinked. He hadn't expected him to outright say it like that. With Ash, conversations like this were skirted around for days—typically, until Kieran's anxiety grew so intense he just blurted out his feelings at the dinner table, and Ash would argue that Kieran was blindsiding him. In the last months of their relationship, Kieran had simply not brought up anything that was bugging him, hoping Ash would stay if he kept his mouth shut. In light of that, Sebastian's openness felt incredibly refreshing.

"Oh—no, not at all." Kieran shook his head. "I kissed you because I wanted to, not because I felt pressured to. I just, um . . . How do I put this . . . ?"

"Feel like you're betraying Ash?" Sebastian guessed.

"Yes." Kieran winced as the word slipped out. He immediately began to backpedal: "Not that that's your fault or anything, I'm just—it's all a lot and—"

Slowly, Sebastian's hand left his blanket cocoon and came to rest on Kieran's knee.

"You don't have to make excuses," he said. "I just want to know what you're thinking. If you're holding back to try to preserve my ego, know that I'd much rather you be honest than nice. I can work with brutal honesty. I can't with half-truths."

Kieran could say with absolute certainty that no one had ever asked him to do that. Brutal honesty would have gotten him gutted at the Pelumbra estate. It probably would have cut off his relationship with Ash long ago too. Sure, it's how Briar operated—and Delilah, to some degree, though she was always much softer about it than Briar—but he'd always found it wildly intimidating.

Kieran swallowed the lump in his throat. His hands felt clammy, and his pulse was still thrumming. *Just be honest. He's not going to hate you.*

"I'm not ready for anything serious," Kieran admitted. When Sebastian just nodded, he added, "I like you *so much,* Sebastian. And I really, really enjoyed kissing you last night. But I also know that the last time I felt like this, I rushed into something too fast, and it didn't turn out well. So I need . . . time."

Sebastian nodded, his face giving away little more than casual agreement, plus a dash of still-lingering queasiness. He sat up a little more, sipping his water. "That's perfectly reasonable. Honestly, it would be a bad idea for me as well, considering the state of my life. But . . . I did really enjoy last night. Perhaps . . . we could make some sort of arrangement?"

Kieran thought of the smutty novels sitting in his bedroom next door. Was this what Briar had talked about? *I should have tried skimming those before doing this.*

Kieran's mouth was sandpaper dry. "Wh-what did you have in mind?"

"Maybe just . . . something casual." Sebastian shrugged. "We stay friends but with a little more of what we had last night added in. A way to clear our heads, I guess. Blow off steam."

Blow off steam? The concept gave Kieran pause, but then he blurted out, "With, um, sex?"

Sebastian, to his credit, didn't laugh directly in Kieran's face as that face turned the color of beet juice. *Kill me.* "Only if you want to. But I'm perfectly content sticking to kissing if that's what you're comfortable with."

"Yes," Kieran said, turning his face away so it was a little less obvious how hot his cheeks had become. There was just something about Sebastian's frankness that made him feel . . . flustered. Though not necessarily in a bad way. "A-about sticking to kissing, I mean. I don't think I'm ready for anything beyond that. But . . . I think I could handle something casual."

"That's good to hear." Sebastian managed a smile, even as he had to pause in his attempt to eat a single cracker. He'd still barely gotten a third of it down. "And . . . I'm glad you don't regret last night. I was up for hours hoping I hadn't scared you away."

"Not at all!" Kieran blurted, a little too enthusiastically. *Honesty is good, but let's not be too honest here.* "I . . . I really enjoyed it."

Sebastian met Kieran's eyes with little smile. "I did too. My only regret is this stupid hangover stopping me from doing it again."

Kieran's entire body flushed at once. Ash had never been particularly flirty, and it had frequently made Kieran question whether Ash was even attracted to him. Hearing Sebastian say it was almost enough to make him overlook the whole puke-bowl incident and lean in now.

Kieran cleared his throat. "Maybe later? When you're feeling better?"

Sebastian nodded. "I'll let you know. In the meantime, though, thank you for checking on me. That was thoughtful."

"Anytime." Kieran rubbed the back of his neck sheepishly.

"And also, ah . . . if you ever feel like you haven't had enough blood to deal with your curse, I . . . I might be able to help."

Sebastian's angular eyebrows shot up. Kieran wasn't sure, but it seemed as if he'd gone a little pink in the cheeks beneath the hangover pallor. "Really? I— Sorry, didn't expect that. That's . . . good to know."

"Of course." Kieran stood, reaching out to let his fingers brush Sebastian's arm as he did. "I should probably let you get some rest. But . . . my door's always open."

"Likewise." Sebastian smiled again. It was a subtle grin, not overly toothy or manufactured. Kieran decided he liked it. "I'll see you later, Kieran."

Kieran's heart nearly leapt out of his chest. Because if he knew one thing, it was what a promise sounded like.

And that was definitely a promise.

CHAPTER EIGHTEEN

Over the next week, Kieran fell into a routine on the ship. It almost felt like a return to normalcy. Even if the ship was far from his permanent home, between this adventure and Delilah's last spring, there was a familiarity to it that he hadn't realized he'd missed, living in Gellingham. He enjoyed getting to bug Ariel in the control room and help Santiago with meal prep in the kitchen. He spent afternoons reading with Briar and Delilah in the study, Seaweed snoozing in his lap like a cat. All in all, he hadn't realized how much he'd missed having the people he cared about the most all in one place.

Plus, it didn't hurt that he and Sebastian suddenly had plenty of opportunities to steal away whenever they desired. While Kieran had been nervous at first about the concept of kissing Sebastian again, it turned out to be incredibly easy. The first night after Sebastian had recovered from his terrible hangover, he'd casually asked Kieran if he'd be willing to help him with something on the observation deck after dinner. When Kieran had arrived—half believing that there was, in fact, some task Sebastian had needed him for—Sebastian had run his fingers through Kieran's hair before kissing him, slowly and gently. Kieran's breath had caught as he pressed closer to Sebastian, the feeling of his body enough to make Kieran's heart rate skyrocket. That gentle kiss had quickly ramped up to Kieran straddling Sebastian on the couch as he went back for more and more of his lips, feeling uncharacteristically bold.

The following week, they repeated the same thing: soft touches while passing in the halls and meaningful eye contact when they wanted to sneak away for a little privacy. Kieran felt downright giddy about the whole thing. Each night, he found himself with a pen in his hand, writing romantic passages that quickly turned into spells that sparked feelings of desire. He hadn't intended for that necessarily, but considering the way those thoughts tended to creep in as he wrote his spells, it wasn't a surprise. The more he wrote, the easier it became to cast. It seemed magic and words came to him easily these days.

It helped that Sebastian offered to give revisions on each new spell. Every night, Kieran would give him a new one to read. And every night, the two of them got too distracted to work as the warmth of Kieran's magic filled the room, lending a silver glow to them both. The feeling of it was overwhelming, as if Kieran might actually have a chance at calling himself a real witch. Especially because, inevitably, after a few minutes of reading, the journal wound up on a side table each night as Sebastian fell into Kieran's arms.

It was almost enough to help snuff out some of the crushing

guilt he felt anytime he thought about what Ash might say if he knew what Kieran was doing. But then again, as Sebastian had put it, Kieran and Ash were on a break. Even if they did somehow work things out when this was all over, Ash couldn't blame Kieran for stealing a few casual kisses from someone else while they were apart, right?

On the eighth day, however, fate decided to throw another curveball at the crew.

"I don't mean to scare anyone with this," Ariel announced at the breakfast table, "but I think you all should know: I heard on the radio that there's a blizzard heading for us." Everyone immediately sat up straighter as Ariel continued: "With hurricane-force winds. Which means that we won't be able to make the supply stop I had planned for this evening. We're safer flying over it instead of trying to weather it on the ground."

Instantly, Kieran noticed the color drain from Sebastian's face.

"Do we have enough fuel to stay aloft another day?" Delilah asked.

Ariel nodded. "We should be fine. So long as everything goes smoothly in avoiding the storm tonight, we can stop in Yarrowport in the morning. Easy."

Kieran, however, had been unable to take his eyes off Sebastian. The other boy seemed to be steeling his expression, staring intently at the untouched food on his plate. He pushed a clump of scrambled eggs to one side, a nauseated look crossing his face. Despite his best efforts, Kieran couldn't get a read on him as to why. *Maybe he's afraid of storms? I guess they are hard to stab, which seems like his general method of dealing with scary things.*

"But tell them the good news," Santiago pushed as he returned from the kitchen with a jar of honey to add to his tea. He dropped into his chair. "It's not all doom and gloom."

"Right! Yarrowport will be our last stop before the Slicetooth Mountains and the Iceweave Coven." Ariel nodded. "Which should get us there a day early. For once, I don't have to force this ship to tear itself apart to race across the country."

"Oh! That is great news." Kieran took a sip of his coffee, which tasted faintly of toffee and hazelnuts. "With any luck, we can be in and out quickly, then focus on how to reforge the scepter and get back to Verbena."

And figure out if I want to use that panacea on Ash or Sebastian, his brain reminded him.

He cringed.

At that moment, Sebastian stood, his breakfast plate mostly untouched. "I . . . need to attend to something. I'll be up in my room if anyone needs me."

He quickly rushed out of the room, dropped his dirty plate in the kitchen, then vanished up the stairs. As the sound of his footsteps faded, everyone at the table exchanged looks.

Briar cocked an eyebrow at Kieran. "What's his problem?"

"No idea." Kieran chewed his lower lip. "But . . . I'll see if I can find out."

When Kieran knocked on Sebastian's door later, he didn't respond.

Kieran lingered for a bit before he returned to his room and collapsed on the bed. He picked at his fingernails. He told himself Sebastian had fallen asleep. But as the day wore on and the clouds below the ship grew darker, swirling like a gyre of shadows and sea-foam, his worry began to spike. Sebastian hadn't so much as shown his face since breakfast. And with the daylight seeping away with the thick swath of clouds beneath them, it was beginning to seem more suspect.

"He just needs time, right?" Kieran asked Seaweed as she stood on her hind legs to look out the window, staring at the darkening clouds. "I'm sure he's fine."

The muffled squeak Seaweed let out did little to calm his racing mind.

When Sebastian didn't show up for dinner, Kieran decided that was the final straw. First, because that meant he probably hadn't eaten all day—which couldn't be good for him—and more important, because if Sebastian was allowed to ask for brutal honesty from Kieran, he was allowed to ask for it back.

As soon as he was done with dinner, Kieran marched up the stairs. Normally, he didn't consider himself confrontational, but despite himself, he was, well, worried.

He squared his shoulders, then rapped on Sebastian's door.

"Sebastian?" Kieran called. "It's me. Can I talk to you?"

There was a long pause. For a moment, Kieran had a sudden new fear: What if in attempting to give him privacy, Kieran had missed something, and Sebastian was in some kind of bodily danger? Maybe if he hadn't eaten any food all day, his curse was getting worse—

"Kieran," a gruff voice called. It sounded as if the inside of his throat must be completely dry. "Don't open the door. Not until we land."

"What?" Kieran wrinkled his nose. "Sebastian, what are you talking about?"

"I—" He cleared his throat, but it didn't seem to help. "I was planning on hunting when we landed for the supply stop. As long as I got a big enough animal, I'd be fine. But now I—I don't think it's safe for any of you to be around me."

A chill went up Kieran's spine. *Of course.* Sebastian hadn't been able to drink any blood for days now. Kieran had noticed he'd seemed a little more distracted over the last day or so, but when he'd asked about it, Sebastian played it off as a lack of sleep. Now that Kieran thought about it, though, he should have known. They were flying high enough that there were very few—if any—birds around, and without them to snack on, Sebastian had to be starving.

Kieran's pulse sped up, and his hands grew clammy. Even if he wasn't saying it out loud, he knew what Sebastian meant: He may be in control now, but if he didn't drink soon, he'd wouldn't be for long.

Kieran's shoulders set. For once in his life, he didn't question himself at all as he called through the door, "Let me in. I think I can help."

"That's not a good idea—"

"I don't care." Kieran stood firm, even as his knees started to feel a little weaker than he'd prefer. At the spike of emotion, the magic in his chest began to react, and for once he had to push it down. "Please, Sebastian. Let me help."

There was a long pause. Kieran wondered if Sebastian was simply electing to ignore him. Then he heard footsteps on the other side of the door, so light they were almost imperceptible. A lock clicked, and the door opened, just barely enough to give Kieran room to come inside.

Sebastian waited on the other side, his body blocking the entryway. His thick black hair hung over his eyes, lank and listless. Heavy shadows were like bruises under his eyes. At first, Kieran thought Sebastian was having some sort of breakout, but then he realized the lumps on his upper cheek were, in fact, the red eyes Kieran had seen the other night, beady and unlidded like an insect's. As Sebastian breathed through his mouth, Kieran caught sight of the matching sets of fangs on the upper and lower parts of his mouth; his fingers had turned spindly and black like a spider's legs.

As soon as there was open air between them, Sebastian winced, taking a step back. He clapped a hand over his nose and mouth. For a moment, Kieran was offended—he'd showered just recently—until he realized it was his blood that Sebastian was smelling.

Sebastian, voice muffled by his hand, said, "This is a bad idea, Kieran. You should go."

"And let you starve? No." Kieran stepped inside, then shut the door behind him. His pulse thrummed. While this was far bolder than he usually felt, strangely, he wasn't paralyzed with anxiety. This wasn't some stolen kiss that made his brain go dark. This was Sebastian's well-being—something he'd recently found himself caring about more and more.

Kieran took a step closer to Sebastian. Even in this form,

starved and fraying, he was still breathtaking. His lips were just as soft despite the fangs behind them. To see him there, beneath the visage of his curse, was to understand the meaning of grotesque beauty.

"Drink from me," Kieran said. He'd never heard his voice come out quite so certain. In an odd way, he was suddenly reminded of his father—how steadfast he was, unable to be moved by even the most powerful forces. While he wanted to emulate very few of his father's traits, this wasn't a bad one.

"I can write a spell to help keep your mind clear," Kieran promised before Sebastian could open his mouth to argue. He reached into his back pocket, pulling out his well-worn journal and a pen. "That way you won't lose control."

Sebastian, to his credit, looked absolutely mortified. "I—You're not kidding."

"Of course not." Kieran began penning a paragraph comparing lucidity to the blade of a knife. His magic stirred easily, even now. He absently asked, "So where's the best place for you to bite me? Neck? Wrists? I guess there's also that big artery in the thigh." He paused as the mental image of Sebastian's face against his bare thigh flickered through his mind, and he immediately felt his face grow hot. "Okay, maybe not—"

"Neck," Sebastian interrupted. He tried to swallow, but it seemed his mouth was still too dry. "Neck is easiest. And . . . lying down helps too. That way there's no risk of your collapsing."

Lying down? Kieran didn't take his eyes off the page as he wrote, even as his palms began to sweat. *This is turning into that one book Briar let me borrow.*

"I—I think I can do that," Kieran said. He had only a few

words left to write before his spell was done. The feeling of his magic rushing through his hands and through the pen was enough to slow his pulse and help him stand straighter. It was as if someone had turned his blood into soda water. It was both electric and soft at the same time, almost like a phantom kiss that sent a pleasant shiver down his spine.

"There." Kieran drew the final period and passed the spell to Sebastian to read. While Sebastian's eyes moved across the page, Kieran added, "Let me know if that helps. In the meantime, should . . . should we put a towel down?"

Sebastian paused in reading, nose wrinkling. "On the bed?"

Kieran's face lit up with a burning blush. It was almost enough to throw him off, but he quickly explained: "Well, mind you, these sheets are very expensive. One thousand thread count. It would be a shame for them to get all . . . bloodstained."

Sebastian just stared at him, his primary eyes wide. Kieran found it comforting that he could at least do that, even if the bloodlust was burning him from the inside. It seemed the spell had helped. "Out of anything you could fixate on . . . you're worried about *stains*?"

"I cannot stress enough how many hours of making lattes it would take for me to replace these," Kieran shot back.

"Well . . . I guess that's fair." Sebastian nodded. "I'll grab a towel. And, uh—thanks for the spell. It helps."

Once Sebastian's back was turned, Kieran exhaled, doing his best not to go into a spiral. Was this dangerous? Almost certainly. Could he get hurt? Yes. But at the same time, part of him felt oddly happy that Sebastian had agreed. It seemed vulnerable, in a way, to let Kieran see this part of himself that he seemed so desperate to hide.

Outside, Kieran heard the wind whistling. As he went to Sebastian's bed, he glanced out the window. The blizzard had begun. While they were flying high enough to avoid the brunt of it, Kieran could still see crackles of lightning skittering across the clouds below. They were so thick they looked almost solid enough to walk on. The way they moved felt too slow and relaxed, considering the wreckage lightning and snow like that could cause below.

Sebastian returned from his bathroom with a towel. Seeing Kieran's expression, he said, "You can still say no. You really don't have to do this."

Kieran shook his head. "I'm sure—really."

Sebastian studied him a moment longer, as if trying to read his face for signs of hesitation. Kieran wouldn't necessarily call what he was feeling fear—more like anticipation. Ultimately, he trusted Sebastian. Even if he hadn't been forthright about his secret—and there certainly seemed to be more Kieran didn't know about him—Kieran was inclined to believe he wouldn't hurt him on purpose. He'd been so gentle the last few days, letting Kieran take the lead when they snuck away together to kiss on the observation deck. It had made Kieran feel confident in a way he hadn't before.

Sebastian handed Kieran the towel, and he laid it out over the pillow. Kieran lay back on it while Sebastian slid onto the comforter, straddling Kieran's hips with his knees. Kieran looked up at him, noticing how all of his eyes were trained on Kieran's throat. He could imagine what it must look like, his jugular pulsing with each rabbit-quick beat of his heart. For a moment, Sebastian's eyes seemed to glaze over, their red glow growing brighter. His lips parted, revealing the edges of his fangs.

He hesitated.

"It's okay," Kieran promised. "Really."

Another long second passed before Sebastian nodded, closing his primary eyes. Gently, he leaned down, using his spiderlike fingers to brush away a loose curl that had fallen over Kieran's neck. They were sharp, and Kieran had to stop himself from cringing. With one long finger, Sebastian gently pushed Kieran's chin to the side, exposing his throat.

As soon as he did, his restraint seemed to fall away. So fast that Kieran barely had time to make a sound, Sebastian was on top of him, fangs piercing his throat.

Kieran gasped as pain cut through him like an electric shock. He squeezed his eyes shut, hand fisting around the comforter as he winced. His body tensed until the pain was suddenly replaced with a warm sensation, and he didn't feel the punctures in his neck anymore. Instead, it was just low heat and the gentle kiss of Sebastian's lips against Kieran's skin. If he hadn't known better, he might have assumed it was nothing but a kiss. The heat of Sebastian's venom quickly spread through Kieran's body with each pump of his heart, melting away his sense of fear. Sebastian had been right—it *was* pleasant. Far more than Kieran ever would have guessed. He slid one hand into Sebastian's hair while the other went to his back, feeling the warmth coming off him in waves.

Sebastian drank for only a few more seconds before pulling away from Kieran's throat, gasping for breath. The extra eyes had vanished, and his normal ones had returned to dark brown.

He rubbed a hand over two ruby drip lines on either side of his mouth, wiping most of it away. "Thank you," he whispered. He pressed a kiss to Kieran's cheek, then moved his legs so he sat beside him, still trying to catch his breath.

Kieran gingerly touched his neck and felt puncture marks from Sebastian's top and bottom fangs, though they didn't seem to be bleeding. Something about Sebastian's venom made the blood clot faster.

"Are you okay?" Sebastian asked. Kieran realized he hadn't responded when Sebastian had spoken before, and nodded, his head still cloudy from the euphoria that had consumed him.

"I—I think so." His nose wrinkled. "Should I disinfect this? Or put some ointment on it? I wouldn't want to get an infection—"

Much to his surprise, Sebastian sputtered a laugh. When Kieran looked at him, wounded, Sebastian explained: "The holes will close on their own in a few minutes. The venom helps with that. There shouldn't be any marks or anything either."

Kieran breathed a sigh of relief. He could just imagine Briar's face if she knew what he had done, and how much she would rib him for it if she ever found out. "That's probably for the best."

He sat up, feeling a little lightheaded but otherwise unharmed. He pressed his back against the headboard, letting his shoulders slump. Looking sideways at Sebastian, he added, "Did you get enough to last you until tomorrow?"

Sebastian nodded. "I'll still need to hunt in a few days, but . . . I should be fine for now. Truly, I cannot thank you enough, Kieran. You . . . really saved me from myself."

"From your curse," Kieran corrected. When Sebastian tilted

his head to the side in confusion, Kieran said, "You are not your curse. That's something Delilah really hammered home back when I still had mine. It's better to remember that it isn't your fault that you have one, so you don't define yourself by it."

Sebastian pushed a lock of hair out of his face. "But . . . what if it was my fault?"

Kieran's brow wrinkled. He couldn't imagine why Sebastian would think that—in all his experiences with curses, the people who cast them were the villains, not the people being cursed. It was why he harbored so much self-hatred for what had happened with Ash.

"Unless you cursed yourself, I don't know how it could be."

"I . . ." Sebastian trailed off, waving his hand. "Maybe you're right. But . . . thank you, Kieran. Genuinely."

And while Kieran smiled and nodded at that, in the back of his mind, all he could think of was that single statement:

What if it was my fault?

CHAPTER NINETEEN

The next morning, Kieran woke to the ship landing in Yarrowport, one of the largest cities in Celdwyn's northwest region. As he went down to breakfast, all he could think of was last night. Images of Sebastian's fangs flickered through his mind, along with the rush he'd felt after they were in his neck. But also, the look on Sebastian's face as he asked what it would mean if his curse was something he'd brought upon himself. Every piece of the experience had felt intimate in a way Kieran hadn't anticipated, and he couldn't claim to have disliked it.

Kieran wondered how far he could push Sebastian to open up. It wasn't that Kieran was simply nosy. He just really, genuinely wanted to know more about Sebastian. Even the tiniest details, the briefest childhood stories, the quickest glimpses into his mind were suddenly things Kieran found himself yearning to hear about. Really, he'd listen to Sebastian read his shopping list over and over if it meant simply getting to hear his voice.

Which was, perhaps, not a great sign, if he was being honest with himself. They were just friends. Friends who kissed a lot, sure, but just friends.

Maybe I'm getting in over my head here, he thought, letting out a heavy sigh on his way down the stairs to get breakfast.

After they'd eaten, everyone prepared to go on their individual errands. Kieran told Seaweed to stay on the ship, despite her squeaks of dismay. He feared she was simply too conspicuous to bring along. Instead, he told her to guard the ship in case any more intruders arrived. She hissed a bit at that but didn't try to follow as he headed for the gangway.

Yarrowport grew out of the lowlands surrounding the Gell River, the skyscrapers limited to a small cluster that made it look like the smaller stepsister of Gellingham. While Ariel and Santiago set out for supplies, Kieran, Sebastian, Delilah, and Briar elected to head to the shopping district to find clothes for the Iceweave Coven's winter solstice celebration. While Briar and Delilah went off into a store where Delilah could look at dresses, Kieran and Sebastian went to a different one featuring an array of colorful men's formalwear.

"Is this too much?" Kieran asked Sebastian as they thumbed through the racks. He held up a long dark-blue coat with embellishments in emerald, sapphire, and topaz beads that looked like peacock feathers. It was the kind of thing Ash would have laughed at him for considering, calling it too garish.

Sebastian didn't even blink. "For the Iceweave Coven? Definitely not. Plus, that color suits you."

Kieran beamed. "Really?"

"Mm-hmm. Although"—Sebastian reached out and turned the price tag to face Kieran—"it might be a bit outside our budget."

Kieran's eyes widened. It certainly was. He might be able to afford it . . . if he skipped a month's rent. Before he could respond, however, an anguished cry interrupted them.

"Damn it," a masculine voice cried, "this is all wrong! Perdita's going to kill me."

"Only if the customer doesn't first," another voice responded. "Isn't that the jacket for his wedding?"

Kieran and Sebastian turned to find two employees examining a suit jacket that appeared to have been tailored by a drunk person wearing a blindfold. Even on the hanger, it was obvious that the sewing was haphazard, fabric bunched in some places and stretched to the point of nearly ripping in others. The jacket appeared to be vintage, with silvery embroidery in the lapels and sleeves that looked like leaves.

"Hmm," Sebastian said. "That's one way to kill the excitement for your wedding day."

"No!" said the more flustered of the employees—a dark-skinned man wearing fine leather shoes—as he opened the jacket to look at the inside. "There's an iron burn mark! I told the tailor not to use an iron on fabric this delicate!"

"Unless you know how to turn back time," said the other employee, a redhead with freckles splashed across his nose, "we're in deep shit."

At that, Kieran straightened. Was this issue any of his business? No. But could he help? Possibly. He couldn't turn back time, by any means—he had no idea if any witch was capable of that kind of magic—but he might be able to try something else.

Mind made up, Kieran set down the jacket he'd been looking at and closed the distance between himself and the employees. Sebastian cocked an eyebrow but didn't say anything, hanging back instead. It occurred to Kieran that Sebastian wasn't the type to speak to strangers unless he absolutely had to.

Kieran, however, was the complete opposite.

"Afternoon, gentlemen." Kieran raised a hand to wave. "I couldn't help but overhear that you're having a bit of an issue over here. I think I might be able to help."

"Are you a tailor?" the redhead asked. "Specifically, one who knows how to work with this fabric? It's some rare blend from Fenshi, and our guys already damaged it. Just taking out the seams is gonna tear it like tissue paper."

"Not a tailor, unfortunately," Kieran clarified. He reached into his pocket and withdrew his journal, flipping it to a new page. "I'm a witch. And I might be able to write you a spell to help, if you're interested."

"Really?" The man with the leather shoes brightened. "How much will it cost?"

"Nothing. I'm still an apprentice—haven't passed my Calling yet. I couldn't charge you for it even if I wanted to." Kieran pointed back toward where Sebastian stood. "But I wouldn't say no to a discount on the peacock jacket."

Leather Shoes choked on a scoff. "A discount? Hell, I'll *give* it to you if you can actually fix this thing."

"Adam, are you sure this is a good idea?" the redhead asked.

The more stressed employee—Adam—widened his eyes. "You have a better plan? Because I don't know about you, but I *really* don't want to lose my job."

The redhead pursed his lips, then sighed. He held the jacket out to Kieran.

"Go for it. But please just . . . don't make it any worse."

Kieran smiled as he took it. "Not sure I could if I wanted to."

While the shop employees exchanged looks, Kieran set the jacket down on a side table and began to write. He described the garment, from the silver threads to the crystal buttons, envisioning what it would look like in perfect condition. He described how the fabric's glossy texture would reflect light, and how it would slide perfectly over the groom's shoulders on his wedding day. He wrote of how it would look just as brilliant as the day it was first sewn, gleaming and crisp and fitting as if it had been made specifically for the owner. All the while, his hands glowed silver, the pen sparking faintly as he scratched the words onto the page.

And when he was done, he read the passage aloud, folded the paper into the shape of a pocket square, and tucked it in the jacket's breast pocket.

For a tense second, the two employees peeked over Kieran's shoulders, eyes rounded. At first, nothing happened. Kieran's stomach twisted. Then, though, silvery light began to glow from the pocket. In the space between breaths, it began to glow so brightly that Kieran and the others averted their eyes, hands held up to block out the light.

When they looked back, they found the jacket lying before them, looking glossy and bright, as if it had been made that very day.

Kieran's heart swelled.

"He did it!" Adam cried. He threw his hands in the air, then pulled the other employee into a tight hug. "We're not getting fired! Oh, this is a miracle."

The other employee, though, looked less convinced. He pulled a measuring tape from his pocket and laid it down on the jacket. His lips moved as he silently said the measurements to himself, cross-checking them with a tag that hung off the hanger. As he did, his eyes grew wider and wider, mouth hanging open.

"It's . . . exactly right!" His face jerked up to meet Kieran's gaze. "You did it. I—I can't believe it!"

Kieran didn't even realize how big his smile was until his cheeks began to ache. He'd done it. No fumbles, no mistakes—just a perfectly executed spell. Sure, he'd offered partly to get the jacket, but most of him had simply wanted to give it a shot. He'd never been able to casually help a stranger with his magic before. It was so simple, and yet Kieran felt that he could do anything in that moment.

Suddenly, a realization hit him: *I don't want to lose my magic.*

It was such a simple thought that it didn't strike him as big at first. Then, like a crashing wave, it swallowed him all at once. He *wanted* to use magic. To be a true witch. At the beginning of this journey, he hadn't cared if his magic was taken away. It had felt more like a burden than a gift—proof that he was as weak and unskilled as his father always said. Now that he had a handle—no matter how basic—on it, it felt strange to consider a life without it.

Before he could fully process the thought, the employees had pulled Kieran into a hug. He stood, nonplussed, before gently patting their backs as they showered him with praise. He craned his neck to look over his shoulder and saw Sebastian biting back a laugh.

"The peacock jacket is all yours," Adam said. "And anything else, if you want it. We cannot thank you enough."

"Anything, huh?" Kieran called to Sebastian, "We're in luck."

The sight of Sebastian's smile was enough to make Kieran feel as if he'd cast a thousand perfect spells at once.

Maybe I'm not such a bad witch after all.

Once Sebastian had picked out a crisp suit for himself, he and Kieran left the shop in high spirits. It was a cool afternoon, and Yarrowport was bustling. As they stepped around people on the sidewalk, Sebastian reached out and took Kieran's hand. "That was incredible back there. You should be proud," he said as Kieran turned pink at his touch. Sebastian noticed, quickly adding, "Oh—sorry, I can let go if you like. Just don't want to lose you—in the crowd, I mean."

Kieran's eyes flicked to their hands for a quick second. He'd never done something so . . . casually romantic with Sebastian before. He couldn't say he disliked it.

Before he could respond, though, Kieran spotted something strange. There, on the edge of Sebastian's coat sleeve, was a silver beetle. Its body glinted with a metallic sheen, and tiny clockwork mechanisms whirred on its back. Kieran halted, and people behind them cursed as they had to swerve out of the way to avoid running into them.

"Kieran, did you—?" Sebastian started.

As quick as he could, Kieran dropped Sebastian's hand and attempted to snatch the insect. The second he did, its wings buzzed, and it managed to fly out from between his fingers before they closed. Kieran grabbed for it once more but missed.

"That's a listening bug!" he cried. He followed it with his eyes as it buzzed over the crowd, heading for an alley nearby. Kieran grabbed Sebastian's sleeve. "We have to—"

At that moment, the bug buzzed toward a figure standing at the edge of the alleyway. They wore all black and had chestnut-colored hair that was shaved entirely on one side and long on the other. They lifted a pale finger, and the bug landed on it.

For a brief second, they turned and looked at Kieran. They had androgynous, fey-like features: sharp, high-set cheekbones, a small upturned nose, luminous pale skin, and icy-blue eyes. For just a moment, they gave him a close-lipped smile.

At Kieran's side, Sebastian went stock-still, his eyes wide.

The figure gave them a wink before they ducked into the alleyway out of sight.

"Come on!" Kieran cried. He grabbed Sebastian's hand and pulled him in that direction. "We can't let them get away!"

Sebastian seemed too stunned to move for a moment, but when he came to his senses, he followed Kieran's lead. They shoved through the crowd as quickly as they could. People cursed at them as they passed, but Kieran didn't care. If Elias was going to send a spy after them, he was going to confront them before they escaped.

As they stumbled into the alleyway, Kieran called, "Hold on!"

What they found, though, was a completely empty side street. Kieran's eyes darted around, looking for any sign of movement, but there was nothing. He rushed down the alley, cursing as he checked behind trash bins and storage crates the local businesses had left outside. Nothing.

"How could they just disappear?" he asked, spinning back to Sebastian, who seemed rooted in place at the end of the alley. "They were right . . ."

Kieran trailed off as he found Sebastian squinting at a small piece of paper in his hand. He asked, "What's that?"

"Nothing," Sebastian said coolly, crumpling up the paper and shoving it in his pocket. "Trash that got loose. I'll recycle it in the next bin we see. That was . . . quite an escape, though."

"Seriously. Must be a witch or something to get away that quickly." Kieran straightened his coat. "We'll have to check each other for more of those bugs before we board the ship. Don't want to accidentally bring one with us and compromise our location."

"Right. Of course." Sebastian squared his shoulders. "Let's find Briar and Delilah and head back. Don't want them boarding the ship with bugs on them."

Kieran nodded, and they changed course for the dress shop. Luckily, it wasn't long before they found Delilah and Briar. They checked each other over for more listening bugs before heading back to the ship, and didn't find anymore. While that was a relief, Kieran couldn't help but notice something: Sebastian didn't throw away the note.

He probably forgot about it, Kieran told himself. *No big deal.* He was probably just overthinking it.

Right?

A few days after their stop in Yarrowport, the landscape below began to turn white. At the sight of layers upon layers of snow, Kieran realized they'd made it nearly to Celdwyn's northern border.

Towering pine forests created a blanket across the jagged Slice-tooth Mountains, the drooping tree branches weighed down by snow. In the sun, the entire landscape sparkled. Kieran couldn't look at it for too long without red spots appearing in his vision. The air too had grown significantly colder. Every trip outside meant feeling the bite of the cold against skin, the chill sinking all the way to the bones in seconds flat.

As the ship approached the Iceweave Coven's airfield, Kieran felt an uncharacteristic sense of calm. For the first time in his life, he felt genuinely sure of himself. He'd managed to get the Hilt and the Stave, which in and of itself was significant. Plus, his magic had begun to feel like a strength. And while he hated to admit it, that someone like Sebastian—who only a month ago had seemed so out of reach and impossible for Kieran to even carry on a conversation with—had agreed to any sort of romantic arrangement with him felt like proof that maybe, just maybe, he wasn't quite as hopeless and pathetic as he used to feel.

The ship let out a groan as it gently came to rest in its spot at the Iceweave Coven's airfield. Though the festivities for the solstice wouldn't start until the next day, aeroships were lined up all across the snowy landscape. Kieran also noted, as he stepped out onto the main deck with Seaweed around his neck, that the airfield was impressively loud. Music drifted through the air, along with peals of laughter from witches sitting on the decks of their ships. They wore fine fur coats and sipped mulled wine. The sound of all these people talking and laughing and playing their music made Kieran feel like he was back in downtown Gellingham. Down below, even more witches chatted as they made their way toward the impressive structure looming across the field.

It was a castle made entirely of ice. Massive ice crystals shot out of the earth in jagged spikes, bunched together in clusters to resemble turrets. It had an aurora-like glow to it, pale greens and blues and yellows undulating just beneath the ice's surface. Paths had been carved through the thick blanket of snow so nearly six feet of fresh powder framed them. All around the airfield and the castle were thick pines, though these seemed even taller than the ones Kieran was used to. Some were nearly ten stories high, taller than the castle itself. The snow appeared pillowy and stark white, unmarred by footprints other than small animal trails.

When Kieran exhaled, his breath frosted in the air. Though he wore a heavy coat, he shivered. The chill turned the tip of his nose pink and numbed his fingers, which he shoved in his fur-lined pockets. Seaweed squeaked and shivered against Kieran's neck.

"Ready to get going?" called Delilah.

Kieran turned to find her and Briar headed for him, bundled in their coats. Delilah appeared to be much more comfortable than Briar, whose teeth were chattering despite the heavy woolen coat she had on. Delilah had an arm around her to share body heat.

Kieran nodded. "Should be. Have you seen Sebastian?"

"He's downstairs with Ariel and Santiago," Briar managed through her rattling teeth. "Can we please join him? My nose is gonna freeze off if we stay out here."

Kieran bit back a laugh and nodded. "Lead the way. You wanna come, Seaweed?"

The otter spirit just curled around Kieran's neck tighter as a response. Part of Kieran thought it might be a bad idea to bring her out in public, but then again, this was a gathering of witches. He doubted that Seaweed would stand out too much.

He scratched her under the chin. "I'll take that as a yes."

After gathering the rest of their party—and getting Briar a spare scarf to wrap around her face—the crew made their way to the airfield. Even out in the cold, witches were dressed in extravagant coats; some were decorated with crystals, while others wore colorful fur from creatures Kieran couldn't even begin to name. The cold air smelled of pine, incense, smoke, and something more skunklike that Kieran wasn't familiar with. Most people seemed to ignore Kieran and the crew as they made their way down the path to the castle, boots crunching in the snow. Kieran wondered if they realized Seaweed was alive and not just a statement scarf.

They passed even more witches sipping beverages as they closed the distance to the castle entrance. Kieran's eyes wandered to the wine that everyone seemed to be drinking.

Delilah explained: "That wine's enchanted. I can smell magic in it—and considering that we're the only ones with real coats on, I bet it's some kind of warming spell."

"How much trouble do you think I'll get in if I steal someone's glass?" Briar grumbled, shivering as if she might shake out of her skin. "Because I'm freezing to death."

"I suspect you won't have to wait long," Kieran said as they stepped over the threshold of the castle's huge arched front doors. Even Seaweed lifted her head at the sight. "Look."

He pointed ahead to the open foyer. A grand chandelier dripping with ice crystals hung from the ceiling, casting warm light on the room. At the center was a massive fountain flowing with mulled wine. Witches held their cups under the cascade to refill as they chatted with one another. All around them were statues made of ice, all in strange, abstract shapes that glowed with the same aurora light as the castle itself. Music floated from every open hallway, blending with magical smoothness. Guests wore extravagant outfits with plunging necklines, hand-beaded crystal details, colorful capes, and hats covered in plumage and flowers. If he weren't here with a purpose, Kieran could have enjoyed hours upon hours of simply watching these witches glide across the floor as the chandelier light caught on their gem-covered ensembles.

Once they stepped inside, a uniformed man in a plainer uniform—a double-breasted blue coat and matching slacks—stepped up to them.

"I don't recall seeing your faces yet today," he said, offering them a pleasant smile. "Have you come for the solstice celebration?"

Kieran nodded. "Yes. In fact, we were hoping to speak to someone in charge. We're here on business—"

"Business?" the man repeated. He barked a laugh. "No one comes to the Iceweave Castle for *business.* The solstice is a time of revelry! Celebration! The coven has little interest in *business,* I assure you."

Kieran hesitated. It occurred to him that he wasn't going to get far around here being prim and proper. Considering that guests were already laughing with drunken mirth before the sun had set, he needed to change his approach.

"I— Well, that makes sense, I suppose. It is a party, after all." Kieran managed a weak laugh. "In fact, if I could just speak to the head witch about the festivities planned for the next few days—"

"Ah! Well, if it's a breakdown of the festivities you're looking for, I can assure you that much is a surprise." The man winked. "Until this evening, of course. The opening ceremony will begin in the grand hall just after sunset. Guests will be provided with a meal, a show, and a preview of what's in store. I'm sure if you still need to speak to the head witch then, you'll have your chance. Though, if I'm being honest, she likely won't be in a state for questioning."

"Noted." Kieran nodded to the man. "Much appreciated. We'll . . . look around, in the meantime."

"Don't forget to try the wine!" he called as Kieran and the others stepped away to start their exploration. "It's enchanted! Should help you warm up!"

"Maybe I won't turn into an icicle after all," Briar muttered. She met the others' eyes. "Well? Wanna get some wine?"

Kieran swallowed. As much as he knew he needed to keep his head clear for the night ahead, a single glass shouldn't hurt. Not as much as the cold did, anyway.

He nodded.

"Let's go."

That night, as the sun vanished behind the Slicetooth Mountains, Kieran and the crew were swept up in the Iceweave Coven's revelry.

After enjoying some mulled wine and feeling its warming enchantment spread across his skin, Kieran decided to socialize.

Witches from all over—including outside Celdwyn—had come for the event. He learned all about their spellcasting, their covens, and even met a few familiars. Seaweed hopped off his shoulders to sniff them, seeming perplexed. When the other witches asked if she was Kieran's familiar, he paused.

Seaweed, however, chirped happily at the title. Kieran grinned. She might not be a traditional familiar, but she was a being made of magic who helped Kieran, so she wasn't far from one. Considering that nothing about Kieran's relationship with magic was traditional, maybe that made the title an even better fit.

As the sky darkened, he and the others wandered deeper into the castle. It boasted a twisting maze of hallways and stairwells, and each room they discovered featured some new activity. Briar got to try her hand at a ledrith sparring match with a few witches from Esperona, while Delilah sampled pastries from a group that had come all the way from one of Kitfield's neighboring towns. Others had games, which Ariel and Santiago immediately excused themselves to try.

Soon, Kieran, Seaweed, and Sebastian found themselves alone, the others having all found other rooms to occupy their interest until the opening ceremony. They took a left turn into a small room that appeared to be full of different enchanted tinctures. They elected to forgo those, instead taking a seat on cushions in the corner of the room, grateful for the chance to escape the crowd.

"So," Sebastian said, taking a sip from the glass of mulled wine he'd been nursing for nearly an hour. Kieran suspected he was trying to avoid another incident like his hangover on the ship. "Any ideas on where the Crown might be?"

Kieran's eyes flicked back over his shoulder to the hallways, and he sighed. "No idea. The only thing Verbena told me about the Crown was that the coven has it. And considering how massive this castle is, it could take weeks to find anything in here. Our best shot is trying to persuade the coven to tell us where it is. Maybe we can make some kind of trade for it."

Sebastian shrugged. "That's not a bad plan. Easier than stealing it. Though . . . that might not be impossible."

Kieran asked, "What do you mean?"

"I suspect that if we worked together, we might be able to manage a heist."

Kieran couldn't stop himself from barking a laugh that nearly woke Seaweed. "Are you joking? I have the stealth of a drunk ox. Plus, it has not escaped me that underneath all these fancy rugs, the floors here are ice. I fear that the moment we start trying to move quickly, I'll wind up on the floor with broken bones and a bruised ego to boot."

Sebastian cracked a smile. Kieran's heart squeezed at the sight of it. "Give yourself a bit more credit. You seem quite adept at sneaking around the ship with me at night to avoid waking up the o—"

Just then, someone said, "Well, would you look at that. Sebastian Feng in the flesh."

Instantly, Sebastian's entire body went stock-still. His sunny expression vanished. Kieran watched his face harden, returning to the muted mask he'd worn nonstop when they first met. He angled his body so he was in front of Kieran, and his eyes briefly flickered from brown to red.

Standing there at the entrance of the room was the person he'd seen back in Yarrowport, arms akimbo. Instead of black, they were dressed in a blue jumpsuit with a slit down the center of their chest that went nearly all the way to their belly button. The shaved side of their head was decorated with swirling blue and silver paint that resembled the night sky. They also had a big smile on their face, which was in sharp contrast to Sebastian's glare. Seaweed hissed at them from Kieran's shoulders.

"Sad we didn't have a chance to chat back in the city," they added. "I would have loved to catch up, but you know how work is. No socializing on the job."

Sebastian cleared his throat, voice coming out in a monotone. "Hélène. I wasn't sure it was you back there. Guess my suspicions were correct. The new hair is a . . . statement."

While Sebastian's tone was cold, the person—Hélène—just kept smiling. They ran a hand through the long part of their hair, pushing it back behind an ear decorated with numerous silver piercings. "Thank you. My current assignment didn't call for subtlety, so I had fun with it."

As soon as the word *assignment* left their mouth, Sebastian's jaw twitched and Kieran saw the muscles in his arms tense.

"Who sent you?" Sebastian asked, maintaining his casual tone, even as Kieran saw his fingers flexing in and out of a fist. He shifted to block Kieran from view even more. "Elias, I assume?"

At that, Hélène's eyebrows shot up. "Oh, please. Always so wrapped up in work, aren't you, Seb? I'm not on the clock right now—no reason to spoil the party by talking shop." Their eyes fell on Kieran. "But then again, I am being a bit rude, aren't I? You must be the one I saw back in Yarrowport. I'm Hélène. Sebastian and I used to, ah . . . work together."

Work together? Kieran's head tilted to the side. *Why does that statement feel so loaded?*

"You tried to put a listening bug on Sebastian," Kieran said, fighting to keep his voice even. "And you work for Elias. So what do you want from us? To capture us? Kill us? There are a lot of witnesses here for that."

"Pfft—you're no fun either. Like I said, I'm off the clock," Hélène repeated, seemingly on the verge of a laugh. Their eyes moved to Kieran, looking him up and down. He might have assumed they were checking him out if it weren't for the glint in their eye. That made it feel a bit more like they were a jungle cat preparing to sink its teeth into his neck. "Clearly, neither of you knows what it means to enjoy a party. I suppose I should get going before one of you pops a blood vessel. See you around, Seb. Stay sharp."

Something about those parting words seemed to make Sebastian tense up even further, and for a moment, Kieran wondered if he was going to attack. But before he could, Hélène stepped out of the room, vanishing into the network of hallways—so quietly that Kieran found himself wondering if they'd cast a spell to silence their steps.

Kieran put a hand on Sebastian's arm. His muscles were still tensed, and from the distant look on his face, his thoughts seemed to be absolutely swimming.

"What in the world was that?" Kieran asked. "How did you know them?"

Sebastian set his jaw. He straightened, seeming to realize he could relax, and exhaled through his nose as his shoulders fell. After a beat, he met Kieran's eyes, expression unreadable.

"That," he explained, "was my ex."

CHAPTER TWENTY

Kieran didn't have a chance to ask Sebastian if he was serious, because the next moment, the chime of a bell resonated through the icy halls of the palace.

"Honored guests," a low-pitched woman's voice said, echoing from the walls themselves. "Please join us in the banquet hall for our celebration's opening ceremony. All are welcome, and we look forward to seeing your beautiful faces."

Immediately, a flurry of movement began outside the room Kieran and Sebastian had settled in. They stood and went to the entryway, where crowds of witches were making their way to the banquet hall. After a quick exchange of looks, the two stepped into the crowd, following the witches forward. They wound up pressed in on either side by moving bodies, Kieran doing his best to keep his elbows out so they didn't shove him and Sebastian into each other.

Under his breath, Kieran whispered, "I thought you said you'd never been in love."

Sebastian nearly slammed to a halt, only continuing when the crowd behind them pushed. He started, "I never *loved* Hélène. In fact, I barely tolerated them. It was purely physical outside of work—"

"And what was *work,* exactly?" Kieran arched his eyebrows, looking at Sebastian askance. "Because when they brought it up, you seemed really worried—"

Sebastian glanced over his shoulder briefly, then lowered his voice. It was so quiet Kieran had to strain to hear it over the din. "I *was* worried, Kier. Hélène isn't someone you want to tangle with, and if they're working for Elias, it means we're in danger."

Kieran repeated, *"Danger—"*

"Oh, thank goodness, there you are," a familiar voice interrupted. Kieran felt a hand brush his elbow. He looked up to find that Delilah had slid in at his side, clasping Briar's hand on the other side. "I didn't realize this was going to turn into such a crowd. Let's keep an eye out for Ariel and Santiago."

Kieran's eyes darted between Delilah and Sebastian, his question for Sebastian still on the tip of his tongue. When his eyes met Sebastian's, he shook his head, then mouthed, *Later.*

While Kieran managed to smooth his expression and nod, all he really wanted was to scream.

It didn't take long for them to run into Santiago and Ariel in the hallway, who joined their trek to the banquet hall. They turned into a hallway where the ceiling tapered off, revealing an open view of the ice spikes that composed the apex of the castle. The soaring space sat in the very center of the castle, the rest of it built up around the ballroom-like hall.

Pale, silvery lights bobbed in the air over the tables. Each was decorated with centerpieces made of ice, ivy, and white roses. Crisp white cloths covered each table, and the chairs gathered around them appeared to be antiques, with fine woodwork and soft velvet cushions. Staff walked around with trays of drinks and food, greeting diners with sunny smiles as they took their seats. Soft music came from a band seated at a stage at the center of the room, elevated so they looked out over the hall. The entire space smelled of mulled wine, roses, and burnt sugar.

Getting tables was something of a free-for-all. Kieran spotted one that was empty and led the others over to it. All the while, he found his eyes wandering the hall, looking for Hélène's half-shaved head. Kieran had seen Sebastian face down dozens of mercenaries and never once show anything but mild annoyance. But with Hélène there had been something . . . different, some understanding of their skills that Kieran simply couldn't grasp as an outsider. It was the first time he'd sensed any hesitation in Sebastian at all.

They took their seats. Briar immediately loaded a small plate with meat skewers as a waiter walked by with them. She offered one to Delilah before digging in, unaware of anything else. Not long after, more food was brought out, the staff stopping at each table to offer different dishes. Kieran found himself taking food but only nibbling at it, his stomach still twisting as the image of Hélène's face burned in his brain.

He wanted to tell himself it was simply because of Sebastian's comments about their work and skills, but if he was being honest with himself, that wasn't it. Because he was beginning to realize that the writhing ball of emotion in his gut didn't just come from fear.

He was, despite his best efforts, *incredibly* jealous.

Which I shouldn't be, he reminded himself as he took a sip of water, the condensation cold on his fingers. *He said himself that he never loved them. Plus, Sebastian and I are just friends who kiss sometimes. It's not like we're together. I have no reason to be comparing myself to someone he was in an actual relationship with.*

Kieran snuck a peek as Sebastian cut a slice of beef with razor-like precision. When he took a bite, his eyes flickered to Kieran. He cocked his head in question. The way the magic lights shone on him made his eyelashes cast spindly shadows over his sharp cheekbones. Somewhere along the way, it seemed he must have brushed up against someone wearing something sparkly, because there were a few silvery metallic flecks in his black hair that Kieran yearned to reach out and brush away.

Just as he wanted to take Sebastian back to the ship and kiss him until his lips ached. As he wanted to know his every secret, to be the confidant he could always trust to understand him, no matter how dark or unwieldy those secrets were. He wanted more than just stolen kisses and whispers whenever everyone else had gone to bed. He wanted to be here, now, holding Sebastian's hand in front of all these people so it was obvious that he was his.

Kieran felt his cheeks flare pink at the thought. "Sorry," he muttered, looking back to his own plate. "Nothing."

Sebastian stared for a moment before going back to his meal.

Shit.

For a moment, it looked like Sebastian was going to say something. Before he could, though, a booming voice cut through the din.

"Honored guests!" called an excited feminine voice. "Please turn your attention to the center stage!"

Kieran and the others found a woman—maybe in her mid-thirties, if he had to guess—standing at the center of the stage. She wore a dramatic ball gown that resembled a wedding dress, aside from the pale-blue bodice. A cream-colored fur stole hung over one shoulder, while the other was bare. She had dark-brown skin and wore her black hair in two Afro puffs atop her head. Nestled between them was an intricate silver crown decorated with sapphires.

Kieran squinted. The shade of silver looked so familiar he paused. It looked a bit like . . .

Kieran's breath caught. *No way.*

"Welcome, all, to the kickoff of the Iceweave Coven's annual winter solstice celebration!" cried the woman, her smile broad. She was elegant and vibrant, magical light seeming to twinkle around her as if she were a planet surrounded by stars. Her eyes glowed with dark-blue magic, ocean-deep and powerful in a way that gave Kieran pause. "I am Philomena Goldenday, Witch Queen of the coven. As you enjoy our opening banquet, I wanted to give you a rundown of all the events planned for our celebration. Starting off, of course, with the various rooms in the castle . . ."

She kept talking, but all Kieran could focus on was her crown. Seaweed too had gone tense in the shoulders at the sight of it. It couldn't be what he thought it was, right? There was no way that *the* Crown was right there in front of him, sitting atop the Witch Queen's head. It just happened to be the exact same metal as the rest of the scepter, in the exact spot they'd been told to get it . . .

I can't just steal that off her head. She's powerful—maybe even more powerful than Briar. I suppose I could ask her for a trade. But what in the world would a queen trade for her crown? Maybe—

"Which brings me," Philomena said, drawing Kieran out of his thoughts, "to the week's final event." She reached up and took the crown from her head, then gently held it out in front of her with both hands. "Every year, the coven offers our guests a chance to win a single favor from us, which we'll grant regardless of the size of the request. But to earn that favor, you must complete a great hunt."

Suddenly, the crown in her hands rose into the air, shining with silvery-blue light. Philomena continued: "This crown represents said favor. Starting tomorrow at dawn, it will be hidden somewhere in the ice caves beneath the palace. Your task, then, is simple: Find where we've hidden it, and the coven's favor is yours. Any witch who wishes to try their hand at recovering it should meet here at first light. Then, at my word, the hunt will begin. Magic of all sorts is allowed in the hunt. We only ask that no one take the life of another hunter. Should that occur, you will be immediately disqualified. But, barring loss of life, you are free to use all the tools at your disposal to win."

The crowd exploded into murmurs as witches began discussing how they could potentially get their hands on the crown. Kieran, meanwhile, felt his stomach plummet. There had to be hundreds of—maybe even a thousand—witches in this ballroom alone. How in the world was he supposed to find the Crown before all of them? Nearly everyone in attendance was older than him, and certainly more skilled at magic. And if the only rule was that they couldn't kill, that left a lot of room for what they *could* do.

"Which concludes the summary of our events," Philomena finished, seemingly unfazed by the crowd's growing murmurs at the introduction of the crown hunt. She placed the crown back atop her head. "The coven wishes you a pleasant evening, and an even more pleasant solstice. Now, enjoy the feast!"

And with that, she snapped her fingers, and vanished into the air like water vapor.

As soon as she was gone, the room grew rapturous. Every witch suddenly scrambled to make their plan for the hunt tomorrow. Kieran's skin chilled despite the enchanted wine he'd drunk. There were simply too many of them, and not nearly enough of him and his friends. It didn't help either that when Kieran glanced around the table, everyone was staring at him.

Waiting for him to make a plan.

I can't, that familiar, terrified voice in his head said. *I can't—I can't—I can't—*

Kieran stood suddenly, making his friends flinch.

"I need to get some air," he said.

And before anyone could stop him, he turned on his heel and nearly sprinted from the banquet hall.

Kieran hadn't intended to wind up on a balcony overlooking the Iceweave Coven's snow-packed territory, but after a few wrong turns caused by his desperation to get out and some poorly planned trips up the stairs, that was exactly where he found himself.

It was massive. Kieran guessed at least forty people could fit on it. Unlike most of the castle, the balcony was made of stone, jutting free from the cutting geometry of the castle's ice spikes. The sky had turned midnight blue, and the stars were clearer than Kieran had seen them in ages.

The view, however, did little to calm his racing thoughts. He went to the edge of the balcony, leaning against the thick stone banister that stopped him from plummeting sixty feet to the ground. His head hung, breaths coming out in short rasps. Seaweed gently nuzzled against his chin, but it didn't help. The air was cold enough to sting his throat and lungs. He felt as if he might pass out. His heart was squeezing and pulsing in a way that made Kieran think he may be on the verge of a heart attack. Each inhalation felt forced, and his fingers were shaking as he tried to hold on to the banister. The cold air was the only sensation that cut through his panic; it kissed the sweat-soaked arch of his brow and the back of his neck, stinging where it touched.

The back of his throat constricted and burned as tears pricked his eyes. How in the world was he supposed to beat all those people to the Crown? Sure, he'd been able to get the Hilt and the Stave, but Elias had been the only other one looking for them at the time. There'd been no competition, no need for him to come up with some grand plan that would somehow save the day when all appeared lost. He couldn't do that.

Just when I thought I might have a chance. I'm going to lose my magic. I'm going to lose my chance at breaking Ash's curse.

I'm going to lose everything.

"My," a low voice said from behind him. "Quite a view from up here."

Seaweed whipped around and growled as the wine's warming

enchantment evaporated all at once. Kieran turned just as a short, heavyset man came to stand beside him. He wore a finely tailored gray suit that matched the streaks of silver in his brown hair. He settled in beside Kieran with ease, as if they were old friends who had had heart-to-hearts out here plenty of times before. Seaweed bared her teeth at him but didn't move to attack.

Kieran could barely get the name out: "Elias."

The man nodded politely. His skin appeared chapped from the wind, redder than it had been back in the mushroom forest. There was something jovial about him—Kieran wondered if he'd been anticipating this moment for some time.

Kieran, meanwhile, felt his dinner moments away from reversing course. He didn't have the Hilt or the Stave with him—they were safely locked away back on the ship—but that didn't mean that Elias wouldn't do something to him to get them. After all, his mercenaries didn't seem to care about keeping Kieran alive. For all he knew, Elias could be seconds away from seizing him by the shoulders and pushing him over the banister to his untimely death.

"It's been too long, Kieran," Elias said, as if they were old business partners sharing a glass of whiskey. "You've given me the runaround for a while now, haven't you? That pilot of yours is quite proficient at shaking off my men. Not to mention"—he gestured at Seaweed—"I suspect that little monster has been eating my listening bugs, considering the crunching noises I've heard the second they land."

Seaweed growled again, seemingly waiting for Kieran to give her permission to attack. He, though, was too frozen to even consider it. Not when he felt ready to dissolve into a quaking puddle of anxiety and terror.

"What do you want, Elias? To finish what your mercenaries keep failing at?"

Elias chuckled. "Goodness, I would have expected a Pelumbra to keep a stiff upper lip at a moment like this. My dealings with your family have always been so . . . rigid. Very serious folks. Never even wanted to stay for a drink when I had them over back in Gellingham. Your father especially. Tell me, has he ever smiled?"

"You didn't answer my question," Kieran said, ignoring the statement entirely. He didn't have the wherewithal to argue over how like or unlike the Pelumbras he was. "What do you want?"

Elias smirked. "Perhaps you're more like him than I anticipated. Pity—I would have liked to simply chat. You've impressed me immensely these last few weeks."

Kieran blinked. *Impressed him?*

"You handily disposed of all my mercenaries," Elias went on. His eyes had gone to his hands, examining the rings he wore on each finger. Kieran wondered if they were enchanted. "And you turned my assistant against me. I had to hire a new one, and on such short notice too."

"A new one?"

"I heard you met them earlier," Elias continued conversationally, even as Kieran's muscles all stiffened at once. "Handsome young thing, aren't they? Hélène, I mean. And so good at their trade too. Better than Sebastian, I might argue. And certainly with more flair."

Kieran's mouth went dry. "Their . . . trade?"

"Oh, my boy." Elias chuckled, hand over his heart as if the laughter was simply too much to contain. "Sebastian still hasn't told you? Perhaps you aren't as close as I first thought. Well, in that case, I suppose all I can offer you is a bit of advice."

While the first part came out breezily enough, his voice turned cold on the final words. Kieran's hands were clammy, bile crawling up his throat. He found himself unable to speak.

"Tomorrow, when that hunt for the Crown begins," Elias began, casually turning his hands over as he adjusted the placement of his many rings, "a second hunt will also kick off. While I'm off securing the Crown, my dear Hélène will be looking for you. I've told them to avoid deadly force, if possible, but I question their restraint."

Kieran's heart stopped for a moment. He really hoped he hadn't heard that right. Because if he had, that meant Sebastian's ex might try to kill him tomorrow.

Unfazed by the color draining from Kieran's face, Elias continued: "Of course, that can be prevented. If you would prefer not to risk it, I'll happily take the Hilt and the Stave from you in exchange for your life. After all, it would be a pity to die over . . . what was it? Some petty little curse you cast? Seems a bit too small to throw away your life for, if you ask me."

Kieran sputtered, "How did you—"

"I have my ways. Remind me—what was your beau's name? Ashmont Bartelle? He seems perfectly nice. Safe, even." Elias chuckled to himself. "Much safer than Sebastian and his bloodlust, that's for sure. If I were you, I'd head home, where you belong. Go find an easier way to break Ashmont's curse, say you're sorry, get your happily ever after. Then you can go back to your simple little life of making coffees and worrying over the electric bill. No more dabbling in a world that's far too sharp for a soft young man like yourself."

Hearing Ash's name come out of Elias's mouth was almost enough to push Kieran over the edge. Seaweed began to growl again. Magic sparked at Kieran's fingertips as he spat out, "If you lay a *finger* on him—"

"Oh, come now. I'm a reasonable man, Kieran. I don't just go around hurting teenagers for fun." Elias straightened, tucking his hands into his pockets as he turned to face Kieran fully. "I'll give you the rest of the night to think about it. If you'd like to make the trade, meet me here tomorrow before first light with the Hilt and Stave. And bring Sebastian, if you wouldn't mind. He has a broken contract we need to discuss."

Elias cracked his knuckles, though his face remained unchanged. "If you don't, I suppose I'll see you in the ice caves. Pity the coven will have to clean up the mess."

With that, Elias tipped his head pleasantly to Kieran, then took his leave. "Goodbye, Kieran," he said over his shoulder. "And good luck. You'll need it."

CHAPTER TWENTY-ONE

After standing on the balcony, nonplussed, for nearly half an hour, Kieran decided to return to the ship. His rabbit heart had been kicking against his ribs nonstop as the resting panic twisted him into tighter and tighter knots. Elias's threats floated through his mind, each punctuated by the image of the man's sempiternal shit-eating grin. If Kieran were braver, he would have sicced Seaweed on Elias and thrown a punch right into those pearly teeth.

But he wasn't brave. He was a sniveling, pathetic little creature who was in way, *way* over his head. And he needed to get out of there before panic consumed him and he turned into nothing but a quivering, shaking lump. He needed somewhere familiar where he could lock the doors and feel safe, and this castle was about as far from that as he could get.

He told himself that Elias's grace period applied to his friends as well. He wouldn't risk Kieran's compliance by hurting one of them tonight. At the moment, as much as he'd love to go find them and make sure they were okay, the animal part of his brain had taken over. He needed to hide. He needed to pull the covers over his face and squeeze his eyes shut until he could think normally again and not like a creature being hunted for sport.

When he made it back to the ship, it was clear everyone else was still at the castle. His sweaty fingers shook and slipped on the locks as he latched every door and window on the ship, listening for footsteps. When he was done, he went down to the observation deck. The windows that usually showed views of the world below were now completely covered by snow, leaving the deck dark and enclosed. Exactly what Kieran needed.

He grabbed a blanket, pulled it around him, and tucked himself into a corner while he tried to catch his breath and not burst into tears.

Ten minutes passed. Seaweed hopped off his shoulders and rubbed her face against his leg, chirping. He reached down and stroked her head. Slowly, Kieran started regaining control over his brain. He took deep breaths, counting to ten over and over, telling himself that he was safe. Gradually, his heart rate started to calm and the shaking in his hands stopped. As he sat with his head between his knees and the blanket pulled over it, the ache in his chest dissipated, as if the hand that had been squeezed around his heart was finally letting go.

It did, however, leap right back into action as he heard a voice whisper, "Kieran? Is that you?"

Kieran's face jerked up, dislodging the blanket from his head. Standing there was Sebastian, his suit jacket removed and his shirt untucked. At the sight of Kieran, his eyes widened. Without a moment's hesitation, he closed the distance between them. Seaweed scampered away as Sebastian knelt before Kieran as if he were an altar to be prayed at.

Sebastian's hand cupped Kieran's cheek. His touch was so gentle it nearly made Kieran's eyes well up. He couldn't remember the last time he'd been handled so carefully, like a baby bird whose bones might snap with any wrong movement.

"What happened?" Sebastian demanded, his eyebrows bent with cold, quiet rage. "Did one of those witches hurt you? Give me a name and I swear on my life I'll—"

"Elias," Kieran said, the back of his throat tightening once again. *Don't cry. Don't cry.* "He's here. He found me up on the balcony, and he told me that he hired Hélène to replace you. H-he said they're going to be hunting me during the crown hunt tomorrow."

As soon as the words were out of Kieran's mouth, Sebastian's face went ghostly white. His fingers pulled away from Kieran's cheek as they balled into a fist. His nearly black eyes began to burn, suddenly shifting to red. His mouth curled into a snarl, and Kieran watched his fangs snap free of his gums.

"I," Sebastian said, voice still perfectly composed even as his fingers began to sharpen into claws, "am going to drain that man until he's nothing more than a *husk*."

Kieran caught Sebastian's shirt by the sleeve. Sebastian looked back at him, the smaller, spiderlike eyes beneath his primary ones glinting in the low light.

"Sebastian," Kieran said. "Wait."

Sebastian paused, studying Kieran's face. "Elias can't send Hélène after you if I kill him firs—"

Before he could stop himself, Kieran burst out, "Look, I—I need you to tell me the truth, okay? The entire time I've known you, you've been . . . skilled at certain things that stood out. Darts, knife throwing—it's always felt a little suspect. Plus the discussions about your family business, your training, and then Hélène . . ."

Sebastian, to his credit, didn't jump to defend himself. Instead, he averted his eyes, some of the anger draining from his expression. "I never planned for you to find—"

"You're an assassin," Kieran said, "aren't you?"

Sebastian's jaw closed on the words he'd been about to say. Part of Kieran had expected him to deny it. Instead, it was like the wind had been knocked out of him. All at once, the rage that had burrowed into him dissipated, his extra eyes and fangs vanishing until only the boy was left, refusing to look Kieran in the eye.

"That's why Elias hired you in the first place, right?" Kieran asked gently. "You weren't his research assistant—you were his bodyguard."

Another long pause spread before them. Suddenly, the two feet of space between them felt cavernous. Regret bubbled up in Kieran's chest. He resisted the urge to grab Sebastian and apologize for bringing it up. Maybe he should have kept his theory to himself, let Sebastian tiptoe around it for a while longer.

When Sebastian finally met Kieran's gaze, the fire in his was gone. His eyes looked . . . empty. Ashamed, as though he'd been caught doing something unforgivable.

"I never wanted to be one," he said, wincing, as if simply saying it was driving a spike deeper and deeper into his chest. His hair hung in his eyes. "I never even got a choice. And the minute I tried to be something else, I wound up cursed."

Kieran studied him: shoulders hunched, brows low, eyes downcast. Shame practically radiated off him in waves. Seeing him like this made Kieran ache from the inside.

"Sebastian, I don't want you to think I'm judging you, I just—"

"No," Sebastian cut in. He sighed. "You're right—you deserve to hear the truth. Are you . . . willing to hear me out?"

"Of course."

"Right, then." Sebastian exhaled. "I guess I should start at the beginning . . ."

"It all began," Sebastian explained, "when my parents came here from Fenshi."

He and Kieran had moved to one of the couches, sitting together with their knees brushing. Kieran had wrapped a blanket around both their shoulders in lieu of Seaweed warming his neck, as she'd scampered off. When Sebastian had cocked an inquisitive eyebrow at him, he didn't react. Instead, Kieran had simply prompted him to continue.

Sebastian sighed, acquiescing. "Back in Fenshi, my father's family were some of the most elite assassins in the country. They were hired by high-profile clients to carry out hits on significant people—government officials, celebrities, that sort of thing. But when my father was my age, he got a different kind of target. She was an heiress to a silver baron's fortune, and her younger brother hired my father to kill her so he could take the fortune for himself when their father died. Unfortunately, as my father told it, the second he saw her through his spyglass, he couldn't bring himself to hurt her. He wound up warning her that she was a target and offered to help her escape the country. Which is how my parents met.

"Once they got to Shui City, my father swore he'd find reasonable work—something safe. But at that point, my mother was already pregnant with me, and he'd had no luck finding another trade. Right around the time I was born, my father found his way into Celdwyn's assassin circles. It was either do that or let my mother and me starve, so he did what he had to."

When Sebastian hesitated, Kieran placed a hand on his knee and nodded.

Sebastian went on: "I think he had to admit to himself then that he was never going to have a traditional life. Not when the money was that good and he was that skilled at the work. As I grew up, he decided it was only fair to train me in the family business.

"Turned out I was just as good as he was. I could hit a bull's-eye with a throwing knife by the time I was five. I took to it like I was made for it. The only problem was, I . . ."

He ran a hand through his hair, and for the first time, he coughed out a small laugh. It didn't feel lighthearted by any means—more self-derisive, if anything.

"My father said I was too soft," Sebastian finally admitted. "At thirteen, when I had my first kill, he found me crying afterward. I couldn't stop seeing the blood on my hands even after I'd scrubbed it off and washed my skin raw. He told me I needed to learn to compartmentalize, to remember it was nothing but a job. But at that point, it wasn't just a job to me. I was a piece of metal my father had sharpened into the perfect knife. He taught me where to find the most tender, delicate parts of a person and how to carve the life out of them, just as most fathers teach their sons to catch a ball. I never had a chance at being anything other than that.

"It was stupid to think I could change my fate," he said softly. His hands had begun to shake, and Kieran wondered if he could still see the crimson stains beneath his fingernails. "I'm still a knife. I was made to cut, to spill blood as quickly and efficiently as possible. There's a certain irony in the fact that blood used to horrify me and now it's one of the only things I think about."

"Was . . . was it one of your targets who cursed you?" Kieran asked gingerly.

Sebastian shook his head. "No. Honestly, I would have preferred if it had been. It was . . ."

He trailed off. Kieran raised his eyebrows.

"Fuck it," Sebastian muttered. When he next met Kieran's eyes, it almost looked as though he was trying not to laugh. "You know what? I've gone this far—you might as well know."

"My father died about a year ago," he went on. "A job got away from him, and he wound up with a knife in his eye socket. My mother was already gone—she passed away from complications after my sister Lisha was born—so I had to start taking more jobs to support Lisha and my other sister, Mei. Each time I got one, I could feel myself just . . . dissociate. With every new kill, I felt a piece of myself die with them. I was miserable, but I had to keep doing it so my sisters had food on the table and a place to sleep.

"But then, around seven months ago, I was coming home

from a job when I saw the police chasing this group through Shui City. One of them was a witch, and she did an incredible stunt—ledrith, I think? She was able to use magic to create dust clouds that completely threw off the police, and the whole group managed to get away. I was so impressed that she could do that without hurting them, it got me thinking how much easier life would be if I had been born a witch. So between jobs, I started researching more about witches. Specifically, how to become one."

Something about that story tickled a memory in Kieran's mind, but he decided not to bring it up now. "The only way I know of is being born one."

"Sure, but there had to be a first witch, right?" Sebastian shrugged. "Everywhere I looked, there were always mentions of the first witch getting her powers from nature. It took me a while, but I realized that the most likely candidate was a magical vein, and I found out that there had been evidence of one in the woods outside Gellingham. I decided I was going to try to tap the vein and use the magic to turn myself into a witch."

Kieran jolted back. He'd never heard of anyone trying to turn themselves into a witch. It sounded ludicrous. "You— What? *How?*"

"Well, I started spending a lot more time in the woods, for one thing. Took me a while to find the vein, but when I did, I knew I had to be close. My training taught me never to jump right into a situation, though—I needed to know how the vein worked before I tried to take its power. For days, I watched that area, trying to figure it out. That's when I first saw that witch."

Kieran's eyes widened. "Verbena?"

Sebastian nodded. "At first, I thought she was just a strange old hermit. But then I saw her use the scepter. She was able to channel the vein's magic like it was her own. After a few more days, I decided that if I wanted to take that magic, I'd need the scepter to do it."

Kieran's heart began to speed up. "Verbena told me she broke it into pieces because someone tried to steal it from her. But—you wouldn't—"

Sebastian's face fell. "I was desperate, Kieran. I didn't think she'd catch me. The last thing she did with the scepter was use the vein's magic to curse me. Said I needed a punishment equal to my crime. She decided the best thing to give a thief was a curse that makes him steal life to live. Hence, vampirism. Specifically, vampirism that can be cured only with a panacea. A grave punishment for a grave crime, I guess."

Kieran's jaw had gone slack. "B-but she was so kind to me—"

"Because you're the kind of a hero who popped directly out of a storybook, Kieran." Sebastian's expression hardened, eyes shifting back to his hands. "Look at yourself. You're kind, handsome, as charming as the stars, and completely selfless. Me? I'm a murderer who tried to steal my way out of a life of killing people and wound up turning into an even worse monster. The fact that you have any interest in me at all—"

Without thinking, Kieran reached up, cupping the sides of Sebastian's face in his hands. The skin was soft and grew warmer at Kieran's touch. He tilted Sebastian's face up until they were eye to eye. Sebastian's lips remained gently parted, his dark eyes sparkling.

"You're not a monster," Kieran said, his gaze unwavering. "And

I'm not a hero. We're people who made mistakes, but we made them with the best intentions. You just want to be more than what your family made you, right?"

Sebastian nodded.

"Me too," Kieran said gently. He stroked Sebastian's cheek. "And it's hard. It's so, so hard not being the person your parents created. But we're both trying, aren't we? To make things better? Doesn't that mean something?"

Sebastian went quiet. Gently, he reached up, taking Kieran's hands from where they rested on his face. He pressed a kiss to Kieran's knuckles. Involuntarily, Kieran shivered.

"You're aware that any sane person would be frightened in this scenario, yes?" Sebastian asked. "Most wouldn't react well to learning that the person they've been traveling with has been hiding the fact that they're a bloodstained killer."

He wasn't wrong. But also, this was Sebastian. Kieran had watched him nonstop since the day they met in the woods, studying him as if he were a poem in a language Kieran didn't know but yearned to translate. Each day had felt like learning a new word until the sentences had finally started to come together, telling the story of a boy who kept himself carefully hidden beneath his calculated facade. How, underneath it all, he just wanted to take care of his family, make a better life for himself, and talk about the properties of different woods until the night sky turned pink. His father might have shaped him to kill, but that didn't mean that was all he was.

"I think we deserve second chances," Kieran finally said. He reached out, putting a hand on Sebastian's knee. "Maybe you're right that it's foolish of me to think so, but I do."

"Really?" Sebastian asked. "After everything I've done? You barely know the half of—"

Kieran cut him off with a kiss, his hand gently gripping Sebastian's hair as he did. Sebastian hummed against his lips, and Kieran pulled him closer. Sebastian's lips were soft against his, as tender as a summer peach. Kieran pulled away, pressing his forehead to Sebastian's.

"I know so."

CHAPTER TWENTY-TWO

That night, Kieran gathered everyone at the dining table to discuss his and Sebastian's plan. The crew had returned not long after Sebastian had. With Kieran's support, Sebastian had elected to tell the rest of them his secret. The only person who seemed surprised was Delilah, while everyone else exchanged nods, as if it made perfect sense, which, in retrospect, it did. Sebastian's ability to take out the mercenaries had been a strong clue, but at the time, it had seemed too ridiculous to be true.

"As long as you're on our side," Briar had said, shooting Sebastian a looked with her eyebrows cocked, "I have no complaints."

After a bit more discussion, everyone agreed, though Kieran couldn't help but notice that Delilah hesitated a bit more than the others. He made a mental note to talk to her later about it. Even if she didn't agree, Delilah was Kieran's best friend—he wanted to hear her opinion, even if it was different from his own.

From there, Sebastian laid out everything he knew about Hélène and their unique approach to the trade. They favored a bow and arrow and tended to stick to attacking from a distance. Sebastian drew up plans that would best throw them off, and Briar suggested some magical solutions as well. All the while, Kieran watched, half impressed and half hot in the cheeks, as Sebastian took command of the planning. There was something he found wildly attractive about assertiveness—perhaps because he struggled with it so much himself.

When Sebastian paused to ask what everyone thought, they agreed. They wanted to keep the group small to minimize the chances of detection, so Ariel and Santiago would stay behind to keep an eye on things on the ship. Briar and Delilah would use magic to help bolster their stealth while Sebastian acted as Kieran's personal bodyguard. All Kieran had to do, then, was find the Crown.

Easier said than done, of course. But oddly enough, not impossible. Especially with Sebastian, Briar, and Delilah at his side.

I am going to owe them big-time after this, Kieran thought as he closed his eyes to sleep that night. *In the meantime, we just have to get through tomorrow.*

He fell into a dreamless sleep.

The next morning, hordes of witches gathered back in the Iceweave Palace's grand banquet hall, all awaiting their chance to hunt for the crown. The tables from the night before were still out, but the centerpieces had been replaced with glowing blue orbs that floated a few inches from the tabletops. As the final witches made their way into the hall, buzzing with anticipation, Kieran caught his reflection in one of the orbs, Seaweed perched atop his shoulders. He shivered.

They had a plan. A good plan, even. But considering that Kieran had blown off his meeting with Elias, he was decidedly not safe. Not until Hélène was dealt with anyway.

Kieran felt Sebastian, at his side, weave his fingers between Kieran's and squeeze. That small touch was enough to melt the tension in Kieran's shoulders ever so slightly.

"Wherever they are," Sebastian said under his breath, "I won't let them hurt you. I promise."

Kieran nodded, swallowing his trepidation. Half hoping to convince himself, he whispered, "I know. We can do this."

Just then, the doors to the banquet hall closed of their own accord, making a few people jump. On the central stage, a glowing blue light flashed before the Witch Queen, Philomena, appeared from the ether. She wore a simpler gown than the night before, skintight and creamy yellow with a white fur ruff.

"Welcome, all," she called, eyes glowing blue as magic amplified her voice, "to our grand hunt! My crown has been placed deep in the caves by members of the coven. Your job, then, is to find it. As a reminder, you'll be owed one favor by the coven if you find it. Any magic is allowed, except for deadly force, which will result in immediate disqualification."

The Witch Queen went on to describe more rules, but all Kieran could focus on was scanning the room. He hunted for Hélène among the crowd but came up empty. Clearly, they knew how to hide themself well. Sebastian too seemed to be struggling to pinpoint them, even as he allowed the extra eyes beneath his primary ones to open. As soon as they appeared, they vanished, and he cursed.

"Which brings us," Philomena continued, "to the beginning of our hunt. You'll notice that each table has been given a transportation orb. Upon touching one, it will transport you to a random location within the ice caves. When I give the signal, everyone in your party should lay a hand on your orb, and the hunt will begin."

Kieran's eyes widened as he glanced at each of his companions. Seaweed had fallen asleep around his shoulders, seemingly uninterested. Sebastian hunted for Hélène, while Delilah and Briar exchanged a look. Briar had her hand on the small of Delilah's back, while Delilah closed her eyes, taking a deep breath. Her gray eyes opened and fell on Kieran.

"Ready?" she asked.

Kieran gulped. "As I'll ever be."

Onstage, Philomena said, "Everyone, gather around your orb! Prepare to start in three . . . two . . . one!"

As soon as the final word was out, Kieran and his friends palmed the orb. A clawing, cold burst of energy shot up his arm, and before he could even gasp, the floor vanished beneath him.

Half a second later, he landed on a new floor, the air knocked out of his lungs and his heart racing. He heard Seaweed squeak with annoyance at being woken up. He reached up to pet her as his vision returned, slowly clearing from the center outward.

All around him were crystalline ice walls. Aurora-like bands of green, blue, and purple light undulated beneath the surface. The ground was tightly packed snow that crunched under Kieran's boots. As he turned his head, he realized that the tunnel was arched, curving softly in different directions. A few sconces had been added to the walls, offering additional pale light.

As he studied the walls, his companions came to their senses around him.

Briar shivered, wrapping her arms around herself. "Well," she said, looking around, "this is . . . going to be hard to navigate."

Sebastian, meanwhile, withdrew a knife from his belt and approached one of the walls. With a swift flick of his wrist, he used it to chip a small bit of ice away, leaving a small mark on the wall. Nodding, he said, "We can mark our path to make sure we don't backtrack. Granted, others might have the same idea, so we want to choose a way to mark it that stands out to us . . ."

He kept talking, but Kieran found himself zoning out as he stared at the aurora. Seaweed sniffed at the ice, eyes narrowed. It was strange—the movements didn't seem random. While they flowed like water, there was an element of purpose to it. As if all the light was flowing downstream toward something.

Kieran stepped a bit closer. While those same rivers of light flowed just beneath the ice on all the walls, the one going down the hall on their left was much brighter and swifter.

Kieran pointed and, cutting Sebastian off, said, "The aurora—most of it is going that way. I think it's magic being attracted to more magic. If I had to guess, I'd bet if we follow the brighter, more concentrated aurora, it will lead us to the Crown."

The others paused, all studying the walls. Delilah began to

nod absently while Briar let out a low whistle. Sebastian's knife gently scraped against the ice as he mentally traced the path of it, nodding.

"You're right," he agreed. He met Kieran's eye over his shoulder. "Well done, Kier. I didn't notice that."

"Me neither," Briar agreed, while Delilah nodded as well.

Kieran flushed. "Oh, um—thank you. I think if we start that way, we'll be on the right track."

He pointed down the tunnel with the most light, and the others nodded. Sebastian returned to Kieran's side as they'd planned, while Delilah stayed behind him and Briar remained at his other side. Keeping his chin up, Kieran let himself focus solely on the light, even as his heart began to race.

"Come on," he said to the others, fighting back the anxiety that had begun to claw at him from the inside. He squared his shoulders, setting his jaw. "Follow me."

As Kieran led the way through the tunnels, he kept his eyes and ears open. So far, they hadn't run into anyone else. They had, however, avoided a few traps. One had been a snare—a bigger version of the sort used to trap rabbits. They'd been able to step over it easily but heard someone yelp behind them not long after. Another was a pit covered with a thin layer of snow-dusted ice that would collapse under the slightest weight. Seaweed had fallen into that one, only to use her magic to float back out, grumbling.

Now the only sound was their footsteps crunching in the packed snow and the faint sound of their breathing. Kieran pulled his coat tighter around himself, though the chill going up his spine had little to do with the cold.

Just as he went to navigate down another long passageway, a sharp yelp echoed down the icy path. He immediately moved closer to Sebastian, who skidded to a halt with a hand on his knife. Sebastian held a finger to his lips. Delilah and Briar pressed themselves to one of the icy walls, Delilah with a protective arm over Briar. Seaweed growled against Kieran's ear.

A beat passed. Kieran heard whispered cursing down the passageway. Sebastian met his eye, then crept toward the passageway entrance to peek in. Kieran followed. He was a few inches taller than Sebastian, which meant he could peer over the top of his head.

Around the corner, an older witch—maybe in his forties—was submerged up to his waist in the snow. He had black hair and a dark beard, both dappled with silver, and pale skin. Around his top half was a cage made of icicles. When Kieran tilted his head upward, he saw more icicles hanging from the ceiling, each one glowing with more aurora light. Each time the older witch struggled, he sank deeper into the snow, the icicles flaring brighter blue.

"It's another trap," Kieran realized aloud.

"How are we supposed to get by?" Briar asked, fighting to see around Kieran's shoulder.

"Let me test something," Sebastian said.

He bent down and scraped up some snow in his hand. Packing it into a ball, he turned it over once before he launched it at the ground near the trapped witch. The witch yelped in surprise. For a moment, nothing happened.

Then, for a flashing second, the packed snow floor suddenly glowed with light. Instantly, it was replaced with clear water. The trapped witch cried out, managing to free an arm before another second passed and the ground turned back into snow. As it did, more icicles fell from the ceiling where the snowball had fallen, creating another cage around the spot.

"Who's there?" the trapped witch cried, trying to twist his body to see them. "Whoever you are, get over here and help me! I swear I'll give you something in return!"

"He's lying," Sebastian muttered under his breath. "But unless you all have some idea of how to get past this without setting off the trap, we might need to find a way around."

"Hold on," Briar said, cracking her knuckles. She stepped out from behind Kieran, planting her feet firmly in the snow. She shifted into a ledrith stance, her eyes beginning to glow pale blue. "I can handle this."

Briar took a breath, then swung her arms, blue light crackling between her palms. She kicked into the air, then slammed back to the ground, fist colliding with the snow. Instantly, a thick green vine shot out of the earth. It rocketed down the passageway before colliding with the wall, where it bit into the ice with teethlike thorny protrusions. It was thick enough to act almost like a balance beam across the snow, resting about a foot above it.

Briar shot a smile at Delilah, who quietly offered her a round of applause.

"Wow," Sebastian said. "That was incredible."

"I try." Briar hopped up on the vine, then gestured for the others to follow. It seemed solid under her weight, though, considering that she was tiny, Kieran found himself feeling less than confident. "Go slowly and make sure to keep your balance."

"I can go next," Delilah offered, seeing the hesitation on Kieran's face. To Briar, she said, "If I fall, fish me out of the snow?"

"I can manage that," Briar said.

With a nod, Delilah followed Briar, stepping up onto the vine. Briar took a few more steps forward to allow Delilah enough room. She was a bit shakier than Briar, clearly less sure of her own balance. Briar held out a hand for her. Delilah took it, letting Briar lead her a few more feet down the vine.

"All right," Kieran said. "Me next?"

On his shoulders, Seaweed chirruped before hopping down onto the vine, seeming ready to show her friend the way. She took a few steps forward before craning her neck to look at Kieran.

Sebastian nodded. "I'll catch you if anything happens."

Kieran felt himself blush. A swooning fall into Sebastian's arms didn't sound so bad. His arms were, after all, nicely muscled beneath his woolen trench coat.

Focus, Kieran, he chided himself. *You can ask Sebastian to carry you around bridal-style when you're not actively in danger of being assassinated.*

"Right, okay." He took a breath. "Here we go."

Kieran stepped up onto the vine, testing it to see how stable it was beneath his boots. It had a tiny amount of give but didn't seem to be in danger of coming loose anytime soon. He took a few tiny steps forward. His heart raced. Blood rushed in his ears. He held his arms out on either side of him, hoping it would help maintain his balance. Up ahead, Seaweed, Delilah, and Briar made their way past the trapped witch, ignoring his cries for help.

Sebastian stepped up onto the vine behind Kieran. "Don't worry, I've got you."

The five of them continued down the vine, holding their breath with each small step. Almost as soon as Delilah and Briar passed the trapped witch, his eyes locked directly on Kieran. He waved his free arm, eyes wide and wild like an animal trapped in a snare.

"Hey!" he called, arm flapping wildly. "You there, young witch! You must help me out of here—please! I—I can help you find the crown; you just have to get me out of here!"

Kieran paused. Even though Sebastian had said he was lying, Kieran hesitated. Was it really such a bad idea to help a witch in need? Sure, this was a competition, but he had to be freezing. Kieran was almost next to the man now, the vine steady beneath him. Maybe if he just offered him a hand—

"Kieran," Sebastian warned. "Don't—"

Just then, the trapped man managed to jerk himself up enough to shove a hand through the bars of the icicle cage. The hand went straight for Kieran's ankle. Long fingernails clawed at his pant leg. Seaweed snapped her teeth at the man but was too far away to reach him. Kieran yelped, nearly stepping off the vine as the man closed his fingers around—

A flash of silver shot through the air. Kieran gasped as the hand that had been about to grab him was pinned to the vine by a throwing knife. As blood bubbled from the wound, the older witch screamed loud enough to shake the icicles overhead.

"Damn you!" he screamed, fiery eyes landing on Sebastian, who stood with a second knife at the ready. "You bastard—"

Suddenly, a nearby icicle fell from the ceiling, exploding in a burst of icy shards. One stabbed the trapped witch in the shoulder. He cried out, and as he did, more icicles shook loose, hurling themselves downward.

Shards of ice exploded around them.

"Run!" Sebastian cried.

Immediately, the four broke into a sprint as icicles dropped from the ceiling. Each burst on impact, glittering shards flying like shrapnel. Briar nimbly ducked to avoid falling chunks of ice while Delilah ran after her, clumsily trying to repeat the same movements without falling. Kieran barely dodged out of the way of one that sailed past him and embedded in the vine. The impact was almost enough to throw him off balance. His arms flapped in a desperate attempt to steady himself. He managed it after a few steps. At his heels, Sebastian cursed as he caught a shard in midair that had nearly struck him in the eye.

Kieran had almost reached the end of the vine. In front of him, Briar jumped off and landed, catlike, in the snow, where the passageway split into three more. Delilah too stumbled but managed to leap her way to Briar's side. Seaweed was on their heels. Kieran was so close, just one step away. If he could only—

An icicle at his side plummeted to the ground, shattering.

Kieran threw up his arms, protecting his face. He felt ice hit his sleeves painlessly. *I'm fine, I'm fine—*

Hot agony jolted up his leg as a shard flew past, slicing his calf.

Kieran yelped. His knee gave out. He grabbed at air, unable to find an anchor as he fell.

At that moment, something slammed into him from behind, knocking him forward. The next second, he was rolling over the snow, the cry in his throat fizzling out. When he finally came to a stop, he gasped, his vision slowly swimming back.

Sebastian looked down at him, and Kieran realized he'd tackled him. The sound of the falling icicles tapered off, leaving just the sound of their panting breaths. Sebastian reached out, brushing hair out of Kieran's face. "You okay?"

"Ice spike," Kieran managed, wincing. "Cut my leg. Hurts."

"I think we can handle that." Sebastian's face moved to Briar and Delilah, a few feet away. "You two okay?"

"Yep." Delilah groaned, rubbing a spot on her arm. Kieran wondered if she'd taken the impact of an ice spike there.

"Peachy," Briar agreed, dusting herself off.

"Good." Sebastian looked down at Kieran. "I'm gonna help you up, okay? You can lean on me for a bit while we get out of here. Then we can wrap it to stop the bleeding."

"Okay," Kieran managed. He could feel the cut, but it didn't hurt as much as he thought it should. *Must be the adrenaline.*

Sebastian stood, then used both hands to help Kieran straighten. Kieran winced at the hot pain, though it wasn't so deep he couldn't stand. Especially as Sebastian pulled Kieran's arm around his shoulders, letting him lean on him, and Seaweed brushed against Kieran's leg as if offering to help support him.

"Come on," Kieran said, meeting Delilah's and Briar's eyes. "We have to keep going."

With a quick nod, the girls agreed, and they set off down the next tunnel.

CHAPTER TWENTY-THREE

As the five continued their winding journey deeper and deeper into the Iceweave Palace's caves, they began to hear voices. They'd caught up to some of the other parties. Each corner they skirted revealed a new group of witches. Most seemed to be nonchalant, participating purely for fun. A few even carried flasks with them, clearly not wanting the celebratory vibes to end. A few of them saw Kieran and his companions, but they simply waved and moved on.

Soon, though, they caught up to the more serious competitors. As the five made their way down one passage, they overheard a shouted greeting, quickly followed by a pained yelp, one tunnel over. Kieran immediately tensed, holding tight to Sebastian. The sounds of muffled expletives and explosions came through the walls. Luckily for Kieran, Delilah had been able to wrap his calf well enough for him to walk on his own, which made it easier for them to sneak past. All the while, he kept an eye out for chestnut hair.

Seeming to read his mind, Sebastian whispered, "I don't think Hélène would try anything here. The passages are narrow, and they're outnumbered. They'll wait until they have a better opening."

"Have you seen any sign of them?" Kieran asked.

Sebastian paused, worrying at his lip with his teeth. "No, but that doesn't mean they aren't here. Stealth has always been their weapon of choice."

"Comforting," Briar muttered under her breath.

"Hey," Delilah said, coming to a halt. She pointed up ahead. "Hold on. What's that?"

Kieran tore his eyes away from Sebastian and followed Delilah's finger upward. There among the icicles was a small handle-shaped piece of metal. Ribbons of greenish light danced around it, seeming to disappear around its edges. Kieran tilted his head as he took a step closer, examining it. Indeed, as he traced the aurora, they all seemed to be disappearing around it.

"Good eye, Delilah," Kieran said. "Maybe we should check it out."

"What if it's another trap?" she asked, cocking a brow.

Kieran bit the inside of his cheek and rubbed his chin as he considered. This was the first place he'd seen the aurora act like this, like water flowing into a basin. If his theory was correct that the magic was being drawn somewhere, he had to imagine it would look something like this.

"I don't think it is," he finally decided. "I know that's probably not the most comforting assessment, but I really think we should try."

"If there is a trap," Briar started, stepping into a balanced, ledrith-ready pose, "I'll do my best to stop it."

"Appreciate that." Kieran glanced between Delilah and Sebastian and asked, "Can one of you boost me up? We should see if it opens to anything. If it does, I have a good feeling it'll get us to the Crown."

Sebastian nodded, dropping to a knee and interlocking his fingers to make Kieran a platform to step on. Delilah joined at his side to help while Briar kept her eyes peeled on the tunnel. After a moment's hesitation, Kieran stepped up. Sebastian grunted as he hoisted him upward.

Even as he swayed a bit, Kieran managed to thread his fingers through the handle. He tightened his grasp as Sebastian's hand vanished beneath him. As his entire body weight pulled down on the handle, he felt something give way.

Which was how he wound up dropping to the floor, hand still tight around the handle, as a set of icy stairs unfolded above him like the entrance to an attic.

Kieran landed on his feet, his calf throbbing. He managed to stay upright as Sebastian's hands went to his hips to steady him. The stairs, meanwhile, hung there, ready to be ascended.

"Ow," Kieran said, wincing. When Sebastian started to say something, Kieran added, "I'm fine, really. Maybe a bit bitter that they didn't think to put in a nice stepping stool here, but fine."

Seaweed chirped, eyes wide as she straightened up on Kieran's shoulders. A second later, he heard the echo of voices. Sebastian's hand went to his knife while magic began to spark at Delilah's and Briar's fingertips. Kieran froze, unsure what to do.

"They're coming around the corner," Sebastian whispered. "Get up the stairs, now!"

Kieran didn't need further prompting. Wincing at the pain in his leg, he dragged himself up the stairs, Seaweed on his heels, as the voices grew closer. He'd just reached the top when one of the new voices rang out.

"Hey!" a stranger called. "Look what we have here!"

"Go!" Sebastian cried. "I'll hold them off!"

Kieran scrambled the rest of the way up the stairs, barely able to move out of the way as Seaweed, Briar, and Delilah followed. Below, Kieran heard a shout. He spun around to find a flash of green light colliding with Sebastian's arm. On impact, it sizzled, and Sebastian spat a curse. Kieran caught a glimpse of an angry red burn on Sebastian's gold-toned skin.

Kieran held out a hand. "Sebastian! Come on!"

Sebastian's eyes met his for a moment, and he nodded. Gritting his teeth, he grabbed a knife from his belt and launched it at someone. Then, as they let out an agonized cry, he scrambled for the stairs. A second bolt of green light narrowly missed hitting him in the side. His hand snagged Kieran's, warm to the touch.

With a grunt, Kieran used his full strength to haul Sebastian up the final stretch. The two fell backward as another flash of green light hit the stairs where Sebastian had been seconds before. While voices ricocheted around the tunnel in a cacophony, Briar's eyes glowed blue. Just as Kieran spotted the edge of a boot heading for the stairs, Briar held out a hand. A vine shot out of the light enveloping her fingers. It hooked onto the bottom step and, when she wrenched upward, yanked the stairs back up into place.

It slammed closed, and the voices below went quiet.

"Fuck that," Briar whispered under her breath, still holding the

vine in her hand. She dropped it, and it coiled around a nearby ice spike. Kieran hoped it would hold if other witches tried to grab the handle and yank the stairs back down. Briar, meanwhile, rubbed her shoulder as if she might have pulled something. "Ouch."

"Agreed," Sebastian said, grimacing. To Kieran, he said, "Thank you for that. Saved me another magic acid burn."

"Anytime," Kieran replied, chest still heaving from the effort. Seaweed chirped, rubbing against Kieran's uninjured leg supportively.

"At least there's some good news," Delilah said. Everyone craned their necks to look at her, and she pointed upward. "Look."

In his panic, Kieran hadn't had much of a chance to look around at the room they'd entered. All he'd caught sight of before was the same aurora light in a bigger, wider space than he'd been in before. Now, though, he realized he'd been right to bring them up here.

The cavern they found themselves in was massive, with a soaring ceiling that went up three stories. The room was domed, and the ceiling was covered in more icicles, all shining with ribbons of light. The ground was the same packed snow as in the rest of the ice caves, the only evidence of the entrance they'd come through a faint circle in the snowpack. At first glance, Kieran didn't see any other ways into the room or—more disconcerting—ways out.

As he tilted his head to look for doorways or passageways, his eye caught on something glinting. While he had noticed the icicles at first, he had missed the one with a faint, silvery band around it.

A silvery, gemstone-dotted crown that drew the ribbons of light toward it.

Kieran jumped to his feet and pointed. "There! That's it!"

While everyone spun to look, he ran toward it, Seaweed at his side chirping excitedly. The Crown was about two stories up, certainly too high for him to reach. If he could just knock the icicle down, or maybe hover a few feet in the air . . .

"Why don't we use fire?" Briar asked, pointing to the ice. "We can melt the ice until the Crown slides off and falls right into our hands."

"Smart." Kieran waited until Briar caught up to him to ask, "Remind me how to cast that spell with ledrith?"

"Watch," Briar said, placing her feet apart and holding her hands at her sides. Over her shoulder, she added, "Delilah, you too—we could use the help."

Delilah gave a nod, as did Kieran. He copied his sister as she swung around, kicking herself upward, and sailed through the air. As she punched, a bolt of fire shot at the Crown. Instantly, the icicle began to melt, water dripping melodically against the floor. Kieran watched Delilah cast the same spell, and the Crown slid partway down the icicle.

All you have to do is try, Kieran reminded himself. *No one's going to call you less of a witch if you can't manage this.*

He took a deep breath, ran the movements back through his mind again, then gave it his best effort. While he was shakier than Delilah and less confident than Briar, as he punched upward, a bolt of fire exploded from his fist. It hit the icicle, melting away the last of it that was holding on to the Crown.

Soundlessly, the Crown slid off the icicle, plummeting toward the floor. Kieran ran to snag it out of the air.

Which was exactly the moment that a massive *boom* echoed through the room.

Kieran yelped, jumping back as the Crown clattered to the floor. Shards of ice and snow exploded into the air on the opposite side of the cavern. The sparkle of snow in the air began to clear, revealing the cause of the explosion.

Someone had blown a hole in the far wall.

"Well," a familiar voice called out. Elias Barclay stepped into the cavern with a broad smile on his face, his eyes immediately locking with Kieran's. "Looks like we're right on time."

Kieran barely had time to process what was happening before Sebastian was in front of him, knocking something out of the air. Kieran watched in horror as an arrow—sliced in two by Sebastian's knife—fell to the ground at Kieran's feet. Seaweed hissed at it, bristling.

From behind Elias stepped Hélène, their expression unreadable. While they had seemed pleasant yesterday, any warmth in their expression was gone. Now they wore all black, a crossbow held aloft. Their eyes went straight to Kieran as they prepared to fire another bolt in his direction. If they had any hesitation about putting a crossbow bolt between his eyes, it didn't show.

Elias, however, held up a hand to stop them. As he did, more people emerged from the blown-open passageway—more mercenaries. Kieran counted as they entered: six in total. Which meant Elias had double the people they did, not counting Seaweed.

"Looks like you beat us to it," Elias said, gesturing to where the Crown sat at Kieran's feet. "I'm impressed. But then again, you do always seem to have something up your sleeve, don't you, Kieran? It's a pity you didn't elect to meet me this morning. It would have been lovely to work something out."

"You finished with your little speech?" Hélène asked, eyes

unwaveringly on Kieran. "Because I, for one, would like to get this contract out of the way."

"Hélène," Sebastian said, stepping between them and Kieran. He twirled a dagger between his fingers. "Whatever he's offering you can't be worth the regret you'll feel later."

Hélène sighed. "Seb, you of all people know that jobs aren't personal. It's just money, right? Same reason you worked for Elias. Same reason Elias is trying to get his stupid scepter. We don't have a choice if we want food to eat and a roof over our heads."

Sebastian hesitated at that, his grip on his dagger loosening. Kieran felt his chest ache. Having grown up in such an affluent family, he barely knew how to wrap his head around the threat of poverty. Only recently had he known anything about struggling with money. But granted, he'd had Delilah and Briar's support while they all tried their hands at living in that terrible apartment back in Gellingham. He hadn't needed to support himself and his siblings as Sebastian did. He hadn't had to sacrifice his morals just to put food on the table.

"What about you, Elias?" Sebastian asked, gaze sliding to his former employer. "You know what Verbena did to me when I tried to steal the scepter. What makes you think she won't oppose you?"

"I'm not afraid of a geriatric witch who hasn't taken a shower in at least a decade," Elias said, sounding as if he was on the verge of laughing at such a question. "And I've already figured out how to subdue her. Once I've done that, I'll use the scepter to take the vein's magic and turn it into panaceas—ones that will be able to do more than just break a curse, mind you. These will be *true* panaceas, able to cure any ailment that has befallen someone, magical or medical. Do you have any idea how much people will pay for a cure-all? I'll be richer than anyone else alive, including that scam artist Klaus Hammond."

"At least my father has some semblance of a moral compass," Delilah snapped. "All you care about is yourself."

Elias scoffed. "Ah, so you're the daughter he mentioned. Naturally, he'd find a way to be a thorn in my side without being here himself. Then again, I didn't come to discuss Klaus. I came for the Crown." His eyes traveled down to Kieran's feet, where the sapphire-encrusted crown sat. "And I suspect you won't be giving it up willingly."

"Correct," Briar snapped.

Kieran's fingers had begun to itch as magic traveled from the well in his chest down his arms. On another day, he might have tried to reason with Elias. Try to talk through what their options were, see if they could reach some kind of agreement. But diplomacy went only so far when the man in front of him had preyed on the vulnerability of someone Kieran cared about.

Kieran reached down to the ground, snagging the Crown. "Try me."

With that, he spun, punched out a fist, and launched a fireball straight at Elias.

Immediately, the room exploded into a cacophony. Mercenaries sprinted toward Kieran and his friends while Delilah and Briar stepped into ledrith stances. Delilah fired off an electric bolt at a mercenary while Briar summoned vines to encase another. Sebastian yanked Kieran sideways as Hélène fired off another crossbow bolt in his direction. It got close enough to slice Kieran's temple, a hot bead of blood dripping down his jawline. Seaweed snarled and sprinted in Hélène's direction, teeth bared.

As soon as Kieran was out of the way, Sebastian whipped around and launched a knife at Hélène. They jerked their crossbow sideways so the metal jammed into its wooden side. Without a second's hesitation, they fired off three more shots at Kieran. Kieran was barely able to slide out of the way of two. A third one, though, sliced across his hand. His grip on the Crown went slack.

The Crown clattered to the ground as Kieran howled in agony. Hot pain shot up his nerves as if the wound had been dipped in boiling oil. Blood speckled the snow below him. He clutched the injured hand with the other, moaning as he squeezed his eyes shut. Pain clouded over every thought.

Especially as Hélène managed to fire off another shot straight into Kieran's shoulder.

He cried out. Sebastian looked as if he was about to shatter his own jaw, so tightly were his teeth clenched. With a roar, he ran for Hélène. The other assassin spun, bobbing and weaving through the mercenaries. As they did, fangs snapped free from Sebastian's gums and his fingers twisted into those spiderlike claws.

For the first time, Hélène looked horrified. Before they could speak, though, Seaweed sank her teeth into their leg, and they cried out in shock. Sebastian used the opening to pounce, attacking them with a swipe of his claws.

Kieran, meanwhile, had begun seeing double. Where Delilah and Briar had previously been fighting four mercenaries, suddenly there were eight, then sixteen. Kieran's head swam, and a strange, numb feeling overtook him. He staggered sideways, trying to summon magic. As he did, though, he found the well in his chest empty. It was strange—he hadn't felt that kind of emptiness since his curse had all but hollowed him out from the inside.

"Kieran!" Delilah cried as she grabbed a mercenary's wrist and sent an electric jolt up their arm. "What's wrong? Are you—"

Kieran, however, didn't hear the end of her sentence. His vision began to swim, and the world turned watercolor in front of him. All the fighting seemed to slow to a crawl. Sebastian had sliced his claws across Hélène's chest as they trained their crossbow at him. Seaweed's mouth was stained with their blood. Briar punched a man in the jaw as he went for Delilah, who was busy kicking away another one. Some mercenaries had fallen, though based on the rise and fall of their chests, they were simply knocked out instead of dead.

Finally, Kieran saw Elias smirking, standing back near the passageway he'd blown open. As Kieran's vision began to close in at the corners, black swallowing the scene around him, the last thing he saw was the glint of those snowy white teeth beneath the aurora light.

Poison, Kieran realized as his last shred of focus went to the crossbow bolt in his hand. *The bolts were dipped in poison.*

His knees gave out, and he slipped into darkness.

CHAPTER TWENTY-FOUR

In his dreams, Kieran was on a beach.

He might have believed it was real if not for the fact that there was something too watered down about the way the sunlight felt on his skin. The quiet rumble of the waves made it clear it was simply his brain trying to re-create something it was only half familiar with. The only beach he'd ever been to was in Kitfield, Delilah's hometown, right after they'd visited to celebrate the end of her Calling. This one looked similar, with white sand that sat at the edge of a leafy forest, the trees verdant as if in mid-spring instead of the dead of winter.

Despite that, though, Kieran's skin felt cold. He shivered even as the sun beat down on him from above. He felt feverish and dizzy, sweat making his hands and forehead clammy.

"Kieran," someone called. "Over here!"

He did his best to shake off the nausea that was roiling in his guts. He put a hand up to block out the sun, squinting to see who had called his name. Slowly, a figure came into focus. She was tall and lithe, with white-blond hair and dark-brown eyes, like Kieran's own. She wore a loose sundress, and her smile was serene. Instantly, the ill feeling that had come over him vanished.

"Adelaide!" he called, eyes brightening at the sight of his relative. "Is that you?"

Adelaide Pelumbra stepped closer and swept Kieran into a hug, just as she'd done his entire childhood. For most of his formative years, Kieran had thought Adelaide was nothing but another employee of the family, splitting her time between cleaning duties and teaching some of the younger Pelumbras magic. She'd remained eternally youthful due to a geas—a combined curse and blessing—that had rendered her unable to speak. He'd only discovered that she was something like his great-aunt a couple generations removed when he'd been on Delilah's Calling and they'd found a way to end her geas. Since then, Adelaide had been using her newfound voice to upend the Pelumbras as much as she could—revenge for the years they'd kept her silent.

"Oh, I've missed you so much," she said, squeezing him tighter before pulling back and resting her hands on his shoulders. She was tall, nearly looking Kieran in the eye. "Look at you, all grown up."

Kieran couldn't help but laugh. "I'm glad it looks that way, at least."

Adelaide's smile turned a bit more winsome. She gently patted Kieran's arm and said, "Why don't we sit down for a moment? We should chat."

Kieran hesitated for a moment, his mind reminding him that this was a dream. Although he did still feel that coldness on his skin and the sweat on the back of his neck. If it was truly a dream, wouldn't he feel fine?

"Right," he said, cutting through his own thoughts. "Let's sit."

Kieran followed Adelaide to a blanket that had been spread out on the sand. They sat side by side, staring out at the cerulean waves as they lapped at the shore, sea-foam pushing back and forth with the ebb and flow of the tide. In another life, Kieran would have liked to stay here, just watching the water sparkle in the sun, not having to worry about anything. As he considered that, though, a thought struck him.

"Adelaide," Kieran asked, half joking, "am I dead?"

Kieran had been hoping she'd laugh that off as absurd, but instead, her lips pressed into a thin line. Immediately, that heavy, sick feeling in his stomach seemed stronger. He felt the color drain from his face as she rubbed her hands on her legs, exhaling.

"Not dead," she finally said. "But . . . dying."

Kieran jolted back. *"What?"*

"Here." Adelaide held out a hand to him. "I can show you, if you like."

Kieran's eyebrows rose. *My own untimely demise? This should be interesting.*

Gently, he took her hand.

Almost instantly, all the things he'd been feeling—the sweat, the cold feeling on his skin, the churning of his stomach—increased tenfold. The beach vanished, and the world around him turned into an impressionist blur. He could feel hands on him, holding him up. When he blinked, he saw Sebastian looking down at him as the world rushed past.

"Stay with me," Sebastian said, his fingers brushing back blond curls that had stuck to Kieran's sweat-soaked forehead. "I've got you, okay? I'm not going to let you go. Just focus . . ."

Kieran couldn't. The strain on his body was simply too much. His muscles had all gone rigid, shaking as the poison coursed through them. He felt cold—so, so cold. When he tried to open his mouth, the only thing that came out was foamy spittle.

Instantly, the scene vanished, and Kieran was back on the beach with Adelaide.

He jumped to his feet, gasping for breath. Adelaide's face pinched into a frown, her eyebrows bent upward in sympathy.

"No—no, you have to send me back!" Kieran cried. "Adelaide, please, I can't die! Not after all this! Not when finally, *finally,* I feel like I'm not completely useless. A-and now that . . ."

He trailed off, but the words in his head were clear enough. *Now that I have Sebastian.*

Because as much as he'd tried not to admit it, he had fallen for him. From the first moment he'd laid eyes on him, something had been different. Every conversation they had felt natural, no need to push things along with the kind of stilted conversation starters he'd gotten so used to with Ash. Being with him felt exciting but comfortable; every day he got to wake up and see Sebastian's face was another he looked forward to. When they were together, Kieran felt that he could be someone special—not because he was with Sebastian but because Sebastian could see it more than he could.

And he achingly, *desperately* didn't want to lose that.

"Please," he repeated. Adelaide bit her lip as he added, "For the first time in my life, I don't hate being Kieran Pelumbra. I *want* to keep living. I want to fix my mistake with Ash, and I want to tell Sebastian how I really feel. I want to move out of that shitty apartment in Gellingham and make something of myself. Just please, please, give me a chance. I can't lose this life when it's finally the one I want."

Adelaide came to stand beside him. She wrapped her arms around him, pulling him into a hug. She exhaled, patting his back.

"It's not going to be easy," she told him. "You're not in great shape."

"I don't care," Kieran insisted. "Whatever it takes, I'll do it. I'm not afraid—not anymore."

Adelaide's gaze softened. She nodded, seeming to mull over his words.

Then she said, "I'm proud of you, Kieran. Truly. Remember that."

Darkness consumed him once again.

When the darkness finally faded, Kieran felt as if he'd only been gone for seconds. Upon opening his eyes, though, he saw that that wasn't the case.

He was back on the ship. It was dark out, but someone had turned one of the lamps on in his bedroom. Kieran found himself lying in his bed as if he'd just woken up from a normal night's sleep, Seaweed snuggled up beside him. The aching pain in all his muscles, though, was proof it had been anything but. Even lifting his head hurt, as if he'd been turned into one giant bruise that went all the way from skin to bone.

Sitting to his left, flicking through a book, was Sebastian.

Kieran shot up without thinking about it. Seaweed squeaked

in protest. Instantly, pain hit him from every direction, and he winced and cursed as his body screamed at him for moving too fast. At the same time, Sebastian's face jerked up from his book, and he closed it. Kieran couldn't help but notice it was the one with the shirtless vampire on the cover that Briar had lent him. If he hadn't been in the most physical agony of his life, he might be embarrassed by all the pages he'd dog-eared.

"Kieran?" Sebastian sputtered. He put the book down and hopped to his feet. His hands hovered over Kieran, as if unsure what he could possibly do to lessen the pain. Gently, he put a hand on Kieran's back and said, "Lie down, okay? The poison should be gone, but it's still going to hurt for a couple days."

Slowly, Kieran leaned back against Sebastian's hand, letting him lower him to the pile of waiting pillows. He grimaced, but the warmth of Sebastian's touch helped a bit.

"I'll get you some painkillers," Sebastian said, straightening. "Those should at least numb some of the—"

"Wait." Kieran held out a hand. "Hold on. Tell me what happened."

Sebastian paused for a moment. Then he said, "After the painkillers. I'll be right back."

Kieran opened his mouth to argue, but Sebastian was already in Kieran's bathroom rummaging through the cabinet. He returned a few seconds later with a cup of water and a few small tablets, which Kieran tossed back and swallowed with a grimace. His mouth felt dry, and the water was a welcome relief to his scratchy throat. He drained the entire glass before lying back with a groan.

"Okay," he managed after a moment. "Start from when I passed out."

Sebastian waited a beat, assessing Kieran's condition. When Kieran didn't immediately start vomiting blood or something, Sebastian sighed and nodded.

"Hélène's crossbow bolts were dipped in a powerful paralytic poison," he explained. "It would have stopped your heart if they hadn't been carrying the antidote—typical assassin procedure, just in case someone wrestles your weapon from you. But it took me and Seaweed too long to subdue them, and by the time I gave it to you, you were already paralyzed and struggling to breathe. I wasn't sure if you were going to pull through."

Kieran managed a weak chuckle. "You and me both."

Sebastian, however, only nodded solemnly. "Once I gave you the antidote, that seemed to help. But at that point, Briar and Delilah were the only ones fighting the mercenaries. Briar got hit with a spell, and when Delilah tried to help her, Elias managed to knock her out. Briar went *berserk*. Trouble was, it was her against four. She didn't stand a chance."

"But she's okay, right?" Kieran's eyes widened. "And Delilah? Please tell me they're—"

"Briar is fine. Bruised and angry but fine." Sebastian grimaced. "But Delilah . . . I'm so sorry, Kieran, but Elias took her. And the Crown."

"Took her?" Kieran repeated in horror. "Why—"

"As a hostage," Sebastian explained. His inky hair fell in his eyes as his gaze went to the floor. "Elias told us that if we want her back, we have to bring the Hilt and Stave to the Pinwhistle Forest vein and exchange them for her."

Kieran's entire body went cold all at once. He imagined Delilah tied up somewhere, bruised and bloody from the fight. Elias had no reason to treat her well. She was his rival's daughter, after all. So long as she was alive, he could use her as a bargaining chip, regardless of how ragged and injured she was.

Fire ignited around Kieran's heart, licking at his ribs as rage built within him. Elias could poison him twenty times over, but hurt his best friend?

"Elias," Kieran snarled, "is a dead man walking."

"Briar shared a similar sentiment," Sebastian said, unfazed by the waves of fury rolling off him. "She hasn't been taking it . . . well, exactly."

"Where is she?" Kieran asked. He could only imagine what Briar's unfiltered rage could have amounted to in the time he was unconscious.

"She's been on the top deck since we got back a few hours ago," Sebastian said. "She's, ah . . . taking it out on some crates. Loudly. With a lot of fire. Frankly, it's good the wood this ship was built with is heat resistant."

"I need to talk to her," Kieran decided, starting to sit up again. Even as his muscles screamed their displeasure, he simply gritted his teeth and pushed through it.

Sebastian held out his hands. "You should probably wait for the painkillers—"

"I'm okay," Kieran insisted as his feet hit the floor. The full-body ache only throbbed more as he straightened. He was still wearing the same clothes from earlier, now with holes in the shoulder where the bolts had pierced him. He could feel the bandages that had been applied there and on his hand. He wondered if Sebastian had been the one to do it. "Really."

Sebastian went to his side, gently putting a hand on his back. "If you need to, you can lean on me."

Even in a state of full-body agony, Kieran wasn't exactly going to say no to more of Sebastian's hands on him. He gratefully leaned into him, immediately feeling something in his muscles loosen. Together, they made their way to the door, and Sebastian led him down the hall. Even before they got to the door to the main deck, Kieran could already hear screaming.

"That's not a great sign," he whispered.

"At least she'll be happy to see you're up." Sebastian reached out and pushed open the door. "Come on."

After a few hobbling steps forward, the scene opened up in front of Kieran, and he froze. Debris from shipping crates littered the deck, scorched at the edges. There was a dusting of ash across the entire deck, and a few smoldering embers winked out in the wind. The air smelled of burnt pine and smoke.

Standing near the crow's nest was Briar, her eyes glowing blue as she fired off two more plumes of flame at another crate. She was screaming, voice raw and hoarse as if she'd been doing it for hours. As she slammed the crate with another spell, it exploded, spinners of wood and sparks raining down around her. Her knuckles were bruised and bleeding, clearly having punched more than one rigid surface.

"Briar!" Kieran called, having to summon up what felt like half the energy in his body just to yell.

She paused, turning to look at him. In the light from the dying fires around her, Kieran saw the ash coating her skin, and the pale tear tracks that cut through it on her face. The light in her eyes flickered out, leaving the normal blue of her irises. The whites were bloodshot, and her cheeks and nose were red. She was panting, the sound ragged in her scream-raw throat.

"Briar," Kieran said a little quieter. "I'm so sorry."

Briar sniffled, her chin trembling. She closed the distance between herself and her brother, then threw her arms around him, pulling him into a fierce hug that made his sore muscles ache even more. Still, Kieran wrapped his arms around her, holding her tightly as her shoulders began to shake with sobs.

"She's gone," Briar said simply, voice choked by tears. "He took her. That motherfucker *took her.*"

Kieran rubbed her back. "I know. I'm so, so sorry."

"I'm gonna kill him," Briar said, gritting her teeth through the sobs. "He's drawn his last fucking breath, you hear me? When I get my hands on him, I'm going to shatter every bone in his body one by one and grind him into a *paste.* I'll burn him inch by *inch* until there's nothing left but ash. I'm going to . . . I'm gonna . . ."

She broke down, sobbing too hard to speak.

"He's not getting away with this," Kieran promised her, holding her tightly. His throat and sinuses burned as tears welled in his eyes; the next time he blinked, two of them rolled down his chin. "I swear it. I *swear it.*"

For a moment, Briar simply cried, fingers tight around her twin's coat. Her entire body shook. It was as if she was going into shock, unable to control the violent sobs. All the while, Kieran just held her, blinking away his own tears.

He'd failed Briar and Delilah both. Thinking about it felt like a spike straight to the heart.

"I can't lose her," Briar whispered.

"I know." Kieran squeezed her tighter. "But we're not going to. We're going to find Elias and get Delilah back, okay?"

"And that Crown," Briar said. She pulled away from Kieran, setting her jaw. Her expression was fierce but firm. Something about it reminded Kieran of a white-hot blade that had just been tempered. "We didn't come this far not to complete the scepter."

"It doesn't matter compared to—"

"It does, though." Briar met his eyes, unflinching. "Delilah and I swore we were going to help you do this, so we're going to do it. We're going to get it, finish your Calling, and make things right. And if Elias winds up in a shallow grave, well, I guess that can't be helped."

"I wouldn't be against that," Sebastian muttered, having politely stepped aside to let the twins have their moment. "Anything you want me to do, I'll do it."

"Any experience with skinning people alive?" Briar asked.

Sebastian held out a hand and wiggled it. "A bit."

"Fantastic. We'll need that." Briar swiped her sleeve across her face, rubbing away the ash and tears. To Kieran, she said, "I'm . . . I'm relieved you're okay too. Things didn't look great back in the ice caves."

Kieran shrugged. "Another thing to add to the list of things that almost killed me but failed. I'm okay, I swear. Just sore."

"Good. We'll need you in fighting shape when we land tomorrow." Briar cracked her knuckles. "Ariel said that we should be able to get there by sundown. Then we can finish this."

"Gladly," Kieran muttered. He asked Sebastian, "You still with us? Even for this? Hélène may well still be working for Elias, and we might have to fight them again."

"Oh, don't worry. There's no way they're recovering from their injuries enough to fight tomorrow." At the look of horror on Kieran's face, Sebastian reached out and gently took his hand, giving it a gentle squeeze. "But that isn't important. Where you go, I go. Simple as that."

Kieran's eyes flashed to Sebastian's fingers—the ones that twitched when he was lying.

They remained perfectly still.

"Guess it's settled," Briar said. "We save Delilah, then we finish your Calling. Deal?"

Together, Kieran and Sebastian echoed, "Deal."

CHAPTER TWENTY-FIVE

That night, as the poison worked its way out of Kieran's system, he found himself lying in bed in a cold sweat. Something told him he just needed to get through this like a bad hangover, except instead of a headache, it was a full-body ache, as if he'd been rattled around in a cocktail shaker like a loose ice cube. If he could sweat it out, he'd be fine.

He did, however, really need something to quiet the grumbling in his stomach.

With an exaggerated moan, he pulled himself out of bed and made his way down to the kitchen. It wasn't terribly late—most of the other crew members were still awake—but after the day they'd had, everyone had squirreled away in their separate corners of the ship in anticipation of tomorrow.

Kieran shuffled into the kitchen, yawning, and went to the pantry. There were plenty of ingredients, but he didn't know much about cooking. He'd learned some basics—making toast and pasta—since leaving his family's estate, but for the most part he just leeched off whatever Delilah prepared back at their apartment. They'd made a deal early on that if he took on some of her cleaning duties, she'd cook for all three of them. It had worked swimmingly.

Kieran's chest ached. *We'll get her back. We have to.*

Ultimately, he elected to throw together a sandwich, which he wrapped in cloth to take back to his room. He took a few bites as he made his way down the hall.

As he was passing the study, though, he heard the phone start to ring.

He let it go for two rings. Who could possibly be calling them? Could it be Elias, hoping to discuss the hostage exchange? Something personal for Ariel or Santiago?

It rang again, and no one was rushing to pick it up. Realizing he was the only one hearing it, Kieran swallowed the bite of sandwich he'd just taken and went inside. He took the phone off the receiver, uncoiling the cord as he did.

"Hello?" he said.

The voice that responded felt like a punch to the stomach.

"Kieran?" Ash asked, his voice as clear as it had been that day back in the noodle shop. "H-hey, um. It's me. I was hoping you'd pick up."

"Ash? Wait—can you *hear me*?"

"I can." Ash paused for a moment. "Loud and clear."

Kieran's heart felt as if it was about to beat out of his chest. How in the world could Ash hear him? Hadn't the curse made it so Kieran was completely imperceptible to him? Using a phone wouldn't get around that, unless . . .

There's no way. I haven't even gotten the panacea yet. How could it have . . . ? Maybe the phone is a loophole?

Unsure of what else to say, he whispered, "Wow, um. Huh. It's . . . been a while."

Sounding a bit unsure, Ash said, "I tried phoning your apartment a few times. When no one answered, I figured I should make sure you were all okay. Klaus was the only person I could think of who might know where you were, so I tracked him down. He let me know you were back on the aeroship doing your Calling with everyone."

"Y-yeah, I am." Kieran felt like he was about to throw up. How was this even possible? "Did he mention the, um . . . the goal of my Calling?"

"He did," Ash said. "You're finding a panacea, right?"

Kieran opened his mouth to confirm when Ash added, "I assume you wanted it to break the curse you put on me."

Kieran froze. Time seemed to slow to a crawl as his heart hammered in his ears. Over and over, he'd told himself that Ash had no way of knowing he'd been cursed. The only thing it impacted was his ability to perceive Kieran, so theoretically, he never had to know what Kieran had done. Kieran had hoped that it was a secret he could keep longer, only admitting to the shame of it when he had a solution. He'd spent nights turning over in his head how Ash would react, and every option had been terrible. The fear and guilt around it had felt like an infection he couldn't shake, always there lingering bitterly in the back of his throat.

It occurred to Kieran, as the seconds ticked by, that Ash was waiting for him to speak.

All he could think to say then was "I'm so sorry, Ash. Truly."

"Why didn't you tell me?" Ash asked. Kieran had expected him to be more accusatory, but really he just sounded . . . hurt. Kieran couldn't blame him.

"The curse made it so you couldn't perceive me. I tried to find you at the library the day after I accidentally cast it, but no matter how hard I tried, you couldn't hear me. I—"

"So that's what it was," Ash said, mostly to himself.

"Yeah," Kieran said, wincing as he admitted it. "It was an accident, I swear. After you said we should take a break, I went home and wrote a poem about it. I wound up accidentally channeling magic into it, and the next day I went to find you and . . . Well. You get the picture."

"But you could have sent a letter," Ash pointed out. "Or had Briar or Delilah tell me. If you'd wanted to, you would have found a way."

Kieran went quiet again. As much as he wanted to make another excuse, Ash was right. He'd been trying so hard to keep this under the rug that he hadn't even considered finding a way to admit his mistake to Ash.

"Yeah," Kieran finally admitted, voice thick. "I would have. But I was too much of a coward to admit I'd made such a big mistake. I thought if I could just fix it without your ever knowing, it wouldn't be a big deal. That was wrong of me."

Ash exhaled, seeming to mull over Kieran's words. Faintly, he said, "Do you know how I found out?"

"Klaus told you?"

"No, actually. Which was part of why I was so surprised this afternoon when I felt the curse break."

For a moment, so many emotions rushed through his mind

at once that all Kieran felt was numb. He thought back to the poem he'd written weeks ago. It had highlighted his insecurity, his self-hatred—all of it. He'd just needed somewhere to put his worst thoughts, and it had manifested into the curse.

Those same thoughts he'd so fiercely rejected in his vision with Adelaide.

"I suppose you didn't need a panacea after all," Ash finally said after a long pause.

Kieran's breath caught in his throat. This whole time, all he'd been focusing on was finding the panacea to fix his mistake. He hadn't even considered trying to break the curse without one. That wouldn't have worked to fulfill his Calling, so he'd put all his efforts into finding the panacea.

What had he written in that poem?

Maybe in a different time . . .
When I'm worthy of your tender heart,
When I'm confident, sure, and skilled,
You can see me again.

Huh. I guess I am a lot more confident now.

"I guess not." Kieran twisted the phone cord around his finger, then untwisted it, trying to think of what to say. Finally, he settled on "Are you . . . angry?"

Ash hummed softly. Then, gently, he said, "It was an accident, wasn't it?"

"Very much so," Kieran confirmed, nodding even though he knew Ash couldn't see him. "After *my* curse? I would never, *ever* do that on purpose. I think that's part of why I was so ashamed.

I never wanted someone to have to deal with anything like that. The thought that I had done that to you, even accidentally, was probably the most horrified I've ever been with myself."

"That's . . . good to hear. And considering I didn't even know I was cursed until it was broken, I suppose I really can't be too mad. I only wish you'd told me."

"You're right. I should have found a way to." Kieran sighed. "You know, I . . . I realize now I wasn't a very good partner to you. Even before the curse. I think I was just so desperate for love that I didn't want to let you go even when things weren't working, you know?"

Ash was quiet at the end of the line. Kieran had spent night after night wondering where he was at with everything. Had Ash gone home and felt instant regret after that night downtown? Had he been relieved? Kieran had no way to tell.

Finally, Ash said, "I . . . think I was the same, honestly. And I still like you a lot, Kieran. Just . . ."

"Not as your partner?" Kieran guessed. "It's okay, I feel the same way. Maybe . . . maybe we could agree to just be friends?"

This time, there was no hesitation on Ash's end. "Yes—absolutely. When you get back, I'd love to hear about whatever it is you did to break the curse, and about your Calling too. It must have been quite an adventure so far."

Kieran almost wanted to laugh. Ash didn't know the half of it. "Maybe we can get coffee when I'm back in Gellingham? I'll tell you all about it."

"Yeah—that would be great." Ash paused, then added, "I'm . . . really proud of you, Kieran. I hope that's not weird to say. But you just sound . . . better, I guess. And I'm happy for you."

"Thank you. That means a lot. We'll be in touch soon?"

"Sounds good. Good luck out there, Kier. Bye."

"Bye, Ash."

The line went dead, and Kieran put the phone down. Part of him had expected to feel worse talking to Ash again, but it had been . . . nice, in a way. He'd spent so long worried about what would happen when Ash found out about the curse that he hadn't even considered it could go that smoothly. It was like a weight off his shoulders that made it possible to take a deep breath for the first time in weeks. Simply put, he'd done it. He'd fixed his mistake—which left only three more things to do.

Save Delilah. Get the panacea. Keep my magic.

Well, maybe four:

Live happily ever after.

Sebastian opened his door to find Kieran standing outside, breathless from having sprinted up the stairs as fast as he physically could.

"It's broken," he burst out before Sebastian could even ask. "The curse I cast—it broke this afternoon. I—I don't know exactly how, but I think it had to do with my realizing I'm not completely useless as a person."

Sebastian blinked. He'd pinned back the longer parts of his hair, and his hands were covered in sawdust. He wore a little apron over his clothes, and he held a whittling tool in one hand. The room smelled of aromatic cedar.

"I— Wow. That's great news." Sebastian stepped aside. "Come in—I was just finishing up a project I've been working on. Tell me more."

Kieran stepped over the threshold, taking in the state of Sebastian's room. He was, Kieran had to admit, much tidier than Kieran was. Everything was neatly arranged, from his freshly folded laundry to his throwing knives and a whetstone beside them. The only area with a mess was the table beneath his window, which was covered in wood shavings and loose whittling tools. At the center of it was a reddish piece of wood half carved into the rough shape of an anatomical heart.

"Oh, wow," Kieran said as he took a seat on the other side of the table. He pointed to the heart. "Sebastian, that's incredible. How long have you been working on that?"

"Hmm. A week, maybe? The red cedar's a bit hard to work with, but I like the color. Grabbed some the last time we stopped." Sebastian shook his head, sitting down on the other side of the table and quickly sweeping his project to the side. "But—more important—how did you find out the curse broke?"

"I was downstairs getting something to eat and I heard the phone ring. Turns out it was Ash." At the sound of the other boy's name, Sebastian tensed a little. Kieran continued: "He told me he felt it break this afternoon. He . . . didn't even realize he was cursed until it did. And we had a chance to talk, and—"

"He wants you back, doesn't he?" Sebastian interrupted.

Kieran's eyebrows shot up. In retrospect, he had made it clear early on that that's what he wanted. Upon reflection, it was hard for him to pinpoint the exact moment he'd *stopped* praying that Ash would change his mind. The last few weeks had been such a whirlwind, it felt as if he'd blinked and suddenly the world's axis had shifted entirely.

Or perhaps he was the one who'd changed.

"He . . . no. He doesn't." Kieran offered a small shrug. "Somewhere along the line, I think I realized I didn't want him to take me back either. We actually talked about how it's better we just stay friends in the long run. We . . . weren't good for each other, I think."

"Really?" Sebastian's jaw hung open for a moment before he shook his head. "Sorry, it's just—you made Ash out to be so smart. Clearly, that isn't the case if he didn't want you back."

For a moment, Kieran was too stunned to speak. Sebastian, meanwhile, looked perfectly casual, as if what he'd just said was the most obvious statement ever spoken.

He added, "As much as I know how much you wanted to fix things with him, I am, selfishly, a bit relieved that it isn't happening."

Kieran's mouth went dry. What did he mean by *relieved*? Was he trying to look out for Kieran as a friend, not wanting him to be in a relationship that wasn't healthy? Or was it more? Kieran had convinced himself that Sebastian just wanted to be a brief blip in his life—someone he used to blow off steam with, like Hélène.

Maybe that wasn't the case.

Kieran guessed: "Because . . . you don't want me to go back to a bad relationship?"

"Of course not," Sebastian said. Kieran felt himself deflate for a moment before Sebastian added, "You deserve far better than that. And because I . . . well . . . um . . ."

Kieran's eyebrows shot up. Sebastian was avoiding his gaze, cheeks having flushed pink. Kieran's heart thumped hard against his ribs. He felt the edge of the precipice before him, like that night on the observation deck when Sebastian had closed the distance between them, squashing any thoughts Kieran had that he wasn't attracted to him. Now, though, it felt deeper. Whatever it was Sebastian wanted to say, it was heavy on his tongue.

"It's just that . . . you're different from anyone else I've ever met," Sebastian finally said. Dusting his hands off nervously on his apron and keeping his gaze turned from Kieran's, he added, "My whole life I've felt like I had to play a role. The perfect son, the perfect brother, the perfect assassin—I never got to just be *Sebastian.* In fact, I'm not sure I ever really knew who Sebastian was until recently. But with you, here, I finally feel like I can be *someone.* Not a tool for others to use, but a person. I never have to follow a script with you, Kieran. It's made me quite . . . fond of you."

"You know," Kieran said softly, "I've grown quite fond of you too."

Sebastian straightened in his seat, finally meeting Kieran's eyes. From the arch of his eyebrows, it was clear Sebastian hadn't been expecting him to say that. Sebastian opened his mouth, then closed it again, clearly struggling to find the words.

Which was exactly the moment when Kieran realized he had to be the one to push them over the edge.

"I want to be with you, Sebastian," he said, reaching across the table to thread his fingers through the other boy's. "If you'll have me."

Sebastian made a faint choking sound, looking somewhat dumbstruck. He studied Kieran's face as if hunting for something that would prove the statement had been a joke. When he didn't find anything, he stared for a beat longer, nonplussed.

Then he burst out, "Kieran, I don't deserve you."

Now it was Kieran's turn to stare. "You don't mean that."

"Of course I do! I mean—look at you. You're an incredible person who cares so deeply about others you'd risk your own magic to fix your mistakes. I'm a killer with a violent curse to match—"

Kieran shook his head. "I don't care what you think you deserve, or what you think you're worthy of. I care about what you *want,* Sebastian. So tell me."

For a beat, Sebastian choked on his words again. It occurred to Kieran that this kind of vulnerability couldn't be easy for him—he didn't have any sort of plan to execute, as he typically did. Just as Kieran was about to ask again, Sebastian met his eyes, expression wild, as if he were about to leap off into the abyss.

"You," Sebastian finally said. Something about the word itself seemed to surprise him, making his face turn even deeper pink. The air grew more and more charged with every word. He gently added, "I want you, Kieran. Not just as a friend. I want all of it. I want all of *you.*"

Kieran's heart nearly exploded.

The next moment, they rose from their chairs in tandem. Kieran grabbed Sebastian by the belt loop and pulled him against him, pressing a firm kiss to Sebastian's lips and scraping his fingernails through his hair. Each move of his lips only drew Kieran closer, every point of contact crackling with electricity. Sebastian's lips parted, and Kieran felt his tongue swipe his own. Immediately, it sent a shock of heat through him. He kissed back harder, wanting nothing more than to feel every inch of Sebastian against him. All the while, Sebastian's words repeated over and over in Kieran's mind: *I want all of* you.

Maybe it was time Kieran stopped lying to himself.

"I need you to know," he said, pulling away just enough to nudge his nose against Sebastian's, "that I was lying to myself, pretending I wanted something casual. I don't think I *can* be casual with you. Hell, seeing Hélène nearly sent me over the edge the second I realized they're your ex."

"Trust me, there's nothing between Hélène and me anymore." Sebastian studied Kieran for a moment, kissed him again, and nodded. "What about Ash? You sure you're done with him?"

Ash. Not long ago, hearing his name would have thrown off Kieran's entire center of gravity. Now, though, it felt more like the accidental prick of a needle while trying to thread it, or the dull pain of a mostly healed bruise. Somewhere along the way, the deep ache that had accompanied his memory had dulled.

Kieran exhaled, and it felt like a weight lifted off his shoulders. "Ash moved on a long time ago. I think it's time I did too."

He pulled Sebastian back into their kiss.

And for the first time in a long time, all Kieran felt was joy.

CHAPTER TWENTY-SIX

The next day, an hour before sunset, the aeroship landed back in the airfield outside Gellingham. It was strange seeing the city come into view again. While the gilded skyscrapers looked the same as they always did, seeing it now felt different. When Kieran had left, he'd felt trapped by the idea of staying in the city. Simply walking through downtown would serve as a reminder of all the ways he had felt inadequate since moving there. Now, though, he had only one thing on his mind: getting Delilah back and making Elias pay for taking her in the first place.

A good night's sleep had managed to quell the side effects from the poison, leaving only a distant ache in Kieran's leg from where the ice had sliced it. The wound had felt deeper than it actually was, but it still ached with each step. With the dull roar of pain gone, Kieran's brain jumped, over and over, between last night's conversation with Sebastian and his anxiety about Delilah, like a strange game of emotional Ping-Pong.

"You ready for this?" Sebastian asked as the ship came to a halt in the airfield. The two of them, along with Briar and Seaweed, had gone out onto the main deck to watch the landing, scanning the snowy terrain. They'd woken up early, doing their best to plot out their plan of attack. Kieran had been grateful for Sebastian's levelheadedness—without Delilah around to be the voice of reason, he and his twin had needed that.

"I'm going to make Elias regret the day he was born," Briar said through her teeth.

Seaweed growled in agreement from her perch on Kieran's shoulders.

"That's the spirit," Kieran said. "Come on—let's grab our things. We don't want to keep Delilah waiting."

Not long after, the three of them said goodbye to Ariel and Santiago. Santiago made them promise to be back before the next morning; otherwise, he'd have Gellingham's entire search and rescue force looking for them. Ariel, meanwhile, offered a particularly heavy wrench to Briar, just in case she needed something to hit Elias with other than spells. Briar considered it for a moment, then threw it in her pack.

"Do you have the Hilt and the Stave?" Sebastian asked Kieran as they headed down the gangway toward the trolley that would take them to the Pinwhistle Forest trailhead.

Kieran nodded, hooking a thumb toward his pack. "In here, along with a few of your throwing knives. Once we get the Crown from Elias, we should be all set."

"Get Delilah, get the Crown, create the panacea, pass your Calling," Briar said. She nodded. "Easy, right?"

Kieran tried to swallow, but his mouth had gone dry. It was going to be anything but easy, but at least he wasn't doing it alone.

"Right." Kieran nodded, making himself stand a little straighter and holding his chin high. "Come on. Let's go get Delilah back."

By the time Kieran, Sebastian, Seaweed, and Briar arrived at the vein, the sun had set. The moon was full and glowing with pale light. An eerie silence hung between the barren trees. Even at the point where the vein's magic turned the landscape lush and green, it seemed as if there wasn't a single living creature around for miles. The only living things were the towering pink mushrooms and the strange light they cast on the mossy forest floor. It was beginning to feel as if they'd be hunting for hours.

At least, until a muffled voice cried out in pain.

Briar immediately bristled. *"Delilah!"*

Without a second thought, she sprinted off into the mushroom forest. Seaweed immediately followed on her heels. It was all Kieran and Sebastian could do to scramble after her, trying not to slip on the mossy rocks or into the babbling brook at their feet. Any lingering pain in Kieran's body vanished as adrenaline shot through him. The climb was uphill, and Kieran felt sweat immediately wet his brow and the back of his neck, even with the cool chill on the wind.

Seconds later, they burst through a copse of towering mushrooms into a clearing. Here, the brook widened into a large pool, the rocks having dammed it. The water was opaque, icy pale blue like snowmelt. A small waterfall poured into it. Even from this distance, Kieran could feel a magical charge coming off it like heat from a flame.

It would have been a beautiful sight if it weren't for the massive iron chains that had been hammered into the rocks. They wrapped around a small, elderly woman who was probably only five feet tall. Her face was smeared with dirt, and her hair was in tangles. The chains pinned her against the rocks, and everywhere they touched her was raw and red from her struggling to escape.

"Verbena?" Kieran gasped.

Her eyes blinked open weakly. She barely seemed strong enough to lift her head.

"You," she whispered, voice small. "You must run—it's not safe here. This pool is full of the vein's raw magic, which will twist the mind and body without the scepter to control it—"

"Not now, Verbena," a low voice said. "Give us a moment to speak before you start making demands."

Elias Barclay stepped out from the mushrooms, holding a chain in his hand. At the sight of him, Seaweed bared her teeth and growled. Six mercenaries flanked him. He was dressed in a nice suit, and Kieran might have laughed at how absurd that choice was for a magic forest if he weren't so horrified by the scene in front of him. The chain in Elias's hand was attached to a pair of handcuffs made of a strange material—wood, Kieran realized.

"Hawthorn," Sebastian said, as if reading Kieran's mind. "To block magic."

Elias pulled the chain, dragging another figure into the light. As soon as the glow from the mushrooms illuminated knotted brown curls, Briar let out a sharp gasp.

"Delilah!" she cried.

Delilah looked up to reveal a fresh black eye that had left one side of her face swollen and bruised. Tracks of dried blood went from her nose to her lip, which was split. Her dress was torn and mud-stained. Her wrists too appeared red and raw.

She croaked, voice hoarse and pained, *"Briar."*

Instantly, Briar jumped for her before Kieran could think to stop her. She leapt over the rocks in Delilah's direction, eyes burning with twin blue flames as her magic awoke and unfurled in her chest, sparking at her fingertips. The mercenaries on either side readied weapons.

As Briar lifted her hand to fire off a spell, Elias yanked Delilah closer to him, a knife seeming to appear from nowhere as he pressed it to her neck.

"Not a step closer," he told Briar pleasantly, as if this were little more than a joke to him, "or this goes in her throat."

Briar skidded to a halt, her eyes rounded. Delilah tried her best to pull away from the knife's kiss. It nicked her skin, a small droplet of ruby-red blood dripping from the wound onto the collar of her dress.

Briar froze. She growled a curse, then added, "Fine! Damn it, what do you *want,* Elias?"

Elias smirked. "Ah—there we go. Cutting to the chase. That's what I like about you Pelumbras—no dillydallying."

Elias reached into a bag at his hip and withdrew the Crown. Still holding the knife to Delilah's throat, he waved it in the air, grinning.

"Our deal still stands," he said, his eyes moving from Briar to Kieran. "You give me the Hilt and the Stave; I give you your friend back. Then we can all go home, no fuss." His gaze fell on Sebastian. "I'll even forgive your breaking your contract, Sebastian. Consider it an act of goodwill."

"And if we don't take your deal?" Briar cut in, her focus still solely on Delilah.

Elias exhaled a laugh, tapping the knife against Delilah's throat. "Well, your friend here won't be walking away. Or . . . any of you, really. With all the money I'm about to get with this magic, I can make any sort of investigation disappear before it starts. Klaus might be a pain in my neck, but then again, he hasn't broken a curse in nearly a year. His limelight is fading—and will go dark the second I take his chance at a panacea away. So really, I have nothing to lose, unlike all of you. So tell me: Do we have a deal?"

Kieran's heart thrummed. He stared across the clearing into Delilah's bloodshot eyes, seeing the way she was fighting not to shake. He'd never seen her so scared; she was always the one to put on a confident face for everyone else. Now, though, there was nothing but raw terror in her eyes.

"I should mention," Elias said, tapping the wooden cuffs around Delilah's wrists, "that all of us are wearing hawthorn protection, so your magic won't be able to touch us. I suspect that will put you at something of a disadvantage, no?"

Kieran ground his teeth, feeling magic burn in his chest. It wouldn't help him here, not with the hawthorn. Any spell he cast would turn into nothing but sparks the second it got close to Elias and the mercenaries. It simply wouldn't work.

But he had an idea of what would.

Kieran exhaled, letting his body relax. He put on his best

timid, nervous voice—the one he'd always used as a child with his mother. "I guess you're right—this was a bad idea from the start. I'm not willing to risk our lives for a panacea. I accept your deal."

"What?" Briar said, jaw agape. While Kieran dropped his pack and unzipped it, she started, "You can't—but we agreed—"

Elias lowered the knife from Delilah's throat. He grinned. "I knew you were a smart boy, Kieran. Now, just toss the Hilt and the Stave this way, and you'll be out of here in no time."

"Of course." Kieran reached into his pack, hands tightening around a hilt. "Just toss it, you said?"

"That will be fi—"

In one fluid motion, Kieran withdrew Sebastian's spare throwing knife and flung it straight into Elias's shoulder. The impact sent him reeling, the chain in his hand dropping as he bellowed a scream. Delilah scrambled backward out of his reach.

"Now!" Kieran cried.

Shock froze Briar in place, but Sebastian immediately leapt into action. He grabbed two knives from his belt and flicked both at Elias. One hit him square in the chest, but the other missed him as a mercenary shoved him out of the way. Elias roared and stumbled, barely keeping his footing as blood stained the front of his collared shirt. At the same time, the other mercenaries charged.

"Briar!" Kieran called. "Use Ariel's wrench to break the chains around Verbena! Seaweed, help her! Sebastian and I will hold them off!"

Briar nodded, swinging her bag around and pulling it free. A mercenary advanced on her. She whipped around and slammed the wrench into his temple with a *thwack.* He stumbled, eyes fluttering, then collapsed. A second one tried the same, and Briar struck him with a similar powerful hit. While this one didn't fall, he did cry out and jump back. Seaweed immediately dove at him, ripping at his ankles with her teeth. Briar, meanwhile, used the distraction to scramble over the mossy rocks surrounding the pool, making her way to Verbena.

Kieran jumped back as another mercenary with a dagger ran at him. His mind raced—he was out of knives, and if he couldn't hit them with magic, what could he use? He grabbed a large fist-sized rock and launched it forward. The throw went wide. *Shit, shit, shit—*

"Kieran!" Sebastian called. He had shifted into his vampiric form, fangs shining in the moonlight. He stabbed his clawlike fingers straight into a mercenary's solar plexus. "Duck!"

Kieran looked up just in time to see a knife flying at him. He tried to duck but stumbled back and hit a mushroom. The mercenary's blade nicked the side of his face and embedded itself in the mushroom stalk behind him, making the whole thing shake.

Suddenly, Kieran had an idea.

He spun and pulled the knife from the mushroom. As he did, an arrow struck it an inch above his head. He jumped behind the stalk just as another arrow pierced it. Pulse thrumming, Kieran took the knife and began sawing at the mushroom stalk. Arrows and knives sailed by as he hacked at it, two mercenaries bearing down on him. They were barely five feet away, then four—

The mushroom stalk began to wobble, and just as the two mercenaries were about to reach Kieran behind it, he stepped back and kicked the stalk with his heel. Instantly, the giant mushroom toppled forward. The mercenaries barely had time to yelp before it slammed to the ground. One mercenary was entirely pinned beneath it, struggling even to scream, while the other would up with a leg trapped.

"Well done!" Sebastian shouted. He held the final mercenary against his chest. The man in black looked deathly pale, which made sense, considering the blood on Sebastian's face.

Kieran felt a warm flutter in his stomach. He bowed as if he'd just completed a spectacular solo onstage. "Thank you."

"Guys!" Briar called. Kieran found her and Seaweed standing beside Verbena, Seaweed holding a piece of iron chain in her mouth. Briar had managed to break the rocks the chains had been anchored to with Ariel's wrench and was in the process of unwinding them from around the old witch's body with the lake spirit's help. "The pool!"

Kieran and Sebastian both spun. There, at the edge of the pool, was Elias. He was bleeding heavily from where Sebastian's knife had pierced his chest, and Kieran suspected his heart may have taken the hit. Blood dribbled from the corner of Elias's mouth, and his face was sweat-slick and chalky.

"Very clever, Kieran," he spat out, meeting the boy's eyes as he tried to reach the pool. "But I'm not giving up that easy."

"You fool!" Verbena cried. "You cannot control raw magic on your own!"

But the next moment, Elias used what little energy he had left to pull himself to the lip of the pool. With an agonized cry, he managed to slip into the water.

For a beat, everything was silent. But then the pool lit up with blinding blue-white light. Kieran had to throw a hand over his eyes to protect them from the flash.

Verbena screamed.

The ground beneath their feet began to shake. Kieran had to fight to keep his footing, blinking away red starbursts. As they cleared, he saw a dark shadow rise from the pool. Seaweed squeaked in horror.

It was maybe three stories tall and absolutely hulking. It had thick shoulders and long arms like an ape and a face deformed by patches of mushrooms growing out of it. Moss coated its body, more mushrooms growing out of it and glowing with a faint pinkish light. Sparks collected around the thick, gnarled fingers. Kieran recognized that sideways smirk on the creature's face, even twisted by raw magic. When Elias spoke, his voice sounded deeper, croaking almost like a bullfrog.

"You," he said, holding up a massive finger and pointing at Kieran, "are not leaving this forest alive."

Kieran's heroic response was to half yelp, half squeak, *"Shit."*

He dove behind another mushroom just as an electric bolt of magic shot from the monster's finger. It hit the cap, and shimmery spores rained down. Kieran scrambled out of the spore cloud, heart punching at his ribs.

Across the clearing, Delilah slammed her wooden handcuffs against the rock, busting them to splinters. Finally free, she stepped into a ledrith stance and shot twin fireballs at Elias. They struck him in the side, but they barely seemed to do anything.

Elias fired off another spell at Kieran, who sprinted as fast as he could to get away. He had to dive forward to avoid the bolt of magic, landing hard on the mossy rocks. The wind flew out of him with a gasp. The spell whizzed through the air above him, and Kieran craned his neck to see it strike a mushroom.

At first, nothing happened. Then a blood-red blight bloomed out from where the bolt had struck. The mushroom began to instantly wither as the blight spread. It was as if the blight was sucking the life out of it, making it decay more and more as the seconds passed.

"Kieran!" Sebastian cried, then pivoted on his heel and sprinted in Kieran's direction.

Kieran struggled to get back on his feet, shouting, "Sebastian, no!"

Elias fired another magic bolt at Kieran. Time seemed to slow. Kieran locked eyes with the magic flying in his direction. The bolt would be impossible to dodge, even if he tried to roll out of the way. He had no way to block it.

He closed his eyes. *Please just make it fast.*

But the impact never came. Instead, Kieran heard a pained yelp a few feet in front of him. His eyes flew open just as he saw the light from Elias's spell fade.

And Sebastian, standing between him and Kieran, collapsed.

"No!" Kieran cried.

Just then, Kieran's focus was pulled away by a clattering as the chains holding Verbena, whom Briar and Seaweed had managed to free, fell to the ground. The witch's face was contorted into a mask of rage, her body pulsing with pinkish light. She held up her hands.

Suddenly, all the mushrooms around them lit up with a similar light. The ground shook, and Elias cried out as it collapsed beneath him. Rocks shot up out of the earth, stabbing through him and skewering him in place. It seemed that even without the scepter, she alone still had some control over the vein's magic. Verbena descended on him, firing bolt after bolt of magic at him as he cried out in animal agony.

None of that, though, registered with Kieran in light of the weak wheeze that escaped Sebastian's lips.

"No, no, no," Kieran choked as he dropped down to his knees beside Sebastian. He gently cradled the other boy's head. The bolt had struck Sebastian in the chest, burning away a portion of his shirt. The skin beneath began to discolor as the same reddish blight that had hit the mushroom began to spread from the center of his chest. It turned the skin into the same blood-red blight, which crept across his torso, spreading slowly as the seconds ticked by. Kieran could imagine it reaching deep into Sebastian's tissue, consuming him from the inside as it spread.

Kieran was helpless to stop it.

When Sebastian spoke, his words came out choked: "I guess we're even now."

"Sebastian, I don't know what to do." Kieran's eyes welled with tears as he ran a thumb over Sebastian's cheek. The blight was spreading up his shoulder, reaching for his neck. "I don't know any healing magic—"

"It's okay," Sebastian said. He offered Kieran a weak smile. "Just . . . keep holding me."

"Stop it! You can't give up," Kieran said, tears choking him. They dripped down his chin as it wrinkled with a sob. "Just stay with me, okay?"

Behind them, Elias let out a pained roar as Verbena's attacks on him grew more brutal. Chunks of the moss-covered soil that made up his new body rained down as Verbena hit him with concentrated blasts of air that acted like knife cuts, flaying Elias alive. Her expression didn't change as she cut him to pieces, watching him fall apart into nothing but mud and plant matter.

"You have to find my sisters in Shui City, okay?" Sebastian said. His voice was growing hoarser as the blight climbed from his shoulder to his throat. "Mei and Lisha. Find them and tell them how much I love them."

"No," Kieran said firmly. He grabbed Sebastian's hand, feeling how cold the skin had become, and squeezed it. "You're not done. You're not—"

"Kieran," Sebastian said gently. His dark eyes met Kieran's own. "Do you remember what I said? Back when we were playing that truth-telling game on the ship? About how I've never loved anyone?"

"Seb—"

Sebastian weakly lifted his free hand, pressing it to Kieran's cheek.

"That's not true anymore," he whispered.

Kieran's heart twisted in his chest. The blight was creeping up Sebastian's jaw now, the color draining from his skin. Even now, he was so beautiful it made Kieran's chest hurt. His breath was becoming ragged, and Kieran feared the blight had reached his lungs.

"Please, Sebastian," Kieran begged, shoulders shaking as he cried. "Don't do this."

Across the clearing, Elias let out one final cry as his entire body crumbled into nothing, collapsing, inert, in a heap.

Verbena stared daggers at the creature. She exhaled, then turned away from him, walking in Kieran's direction.

At the sight of her, Kieran cried, "Verbena! Please, you have to help him—I'll give you whatever you w—"

"Hold now, child," she said, cutting him off. She crossed the distance, coming to stand over them. She examined Sebastian as the blight crawled up his cheek, turning the skin red.

"Ah," she said, meeting Sebastian's eyes. "I remember you. The little thief."

Kieran stiffened. Would Verbena even be willing to help someone who had once tried to steal from her? Considering that she'd cursed him, Kieran couldn't imagine she'd be understanding. She hadn't exactly asked what his motivations were—

Then, though, her face softened as she looked between Sebastian and Kieran. To Sebastian, she said, "You've changed since then, haven't you? Not so selfish anymore."

"He wasn't selfish then either," Kieran heard himself say.

Verbena's eyes went to him, and he instantly froze. Realizing he'd already put his foot in his mouth, he elected to simply push on. "Sebastian tried to steal the scepter because he was trying to get magic to help his sisters—to make a better life for his family. It was never for his own gain. And I know you have no reason to believe me, but *I* know *him.* So please, you have to help him. I'll do whatever you want in exchange."

Sebastian started, voice quieter than before, "Kieran—"

"You know," Verbena said, voice creaky, "you are quite the unusual person, Kieran Pelumbra."

Kieran blinked. "I'm . . . What?"

"I've lived a long life," Verbena explained. "In these woods and beyond. I've seen how people take and take and take, draining every magic vein of its power. It's why I was so drawn to you in the first place. You were willing to sacrifice yourself for someone you didn't even know."

Her eyes fell to Sebastian. "This boy tried to steal from me, like so many others before him. I never would have expected him to give up his own life for someone else as you did. Perhaps I've . . . misjudged."

"Does that mean you'll help him?" Kieran's hand tightened around Sebastian's.

Verbena stared at Kieran for a long beat. She seemed to be looking past him straight into his soul, examining far beyond his words. All the while, Kieran clung to Sebastian, silently praying that this creature could find it in her heart to forgive him.

Finally, she said, "Perhaps we can make another deal, Kieran Pelumbra."

Kieran straightened. "Yes—of course, I'll do anything."

Verbena nodded. "Then so it shall be."

She held out her hand, and suddenly, Kieran saw that the bag he'd discarded on the ground began to move. It unzipped, and from inside, the Hilt and the Stave floated out. From across the glade, the Crown floated toward Verbena's hand. All at once, the pieces joined together. The gaps between them closed, and a second later, Verbena held a slim silver scepter in her hand.

She stood, taking a few steps back. She examined the scepter for a moment before she took a breath and held it aloft with both hands. As she did, it began to glow silver like moonlight.

Then, in one fluid motion, she stabbed it into the earth.

All around them, the scene began to change. New pools of water suddenly opened up, paths of stone connecting them all. Clouds of steam rose from them, creating a glittering mist in the moonlit air. The towering mushrooms shrank, becoming small bundles as the base of massive trees that grew out of the ground in their place. The air grew colder, and Kieran realized that the obvious divide between the magic vein and the forest around it vanished. Now the pools simply looked like hot springs in the middle of the woods, blending in nicely with the rest of the nature around it.

Verbena pointed to the nearest pool and met Kieran's eyes. "Submerge him there."

Kieran nodded. He reached beneath Sebastian and, with Briar's help, lifted him. The twins lowered him into the pool together as the blight covered half his face and his breathing grew shallow. They submerged him. Kieran's heart felt like it was about to break through his ribs.

The second the water closed over Sebastian's face, the blight washed away. The skin beneath went from bruised back to normal in seconds. Color returned to Sebastian's cheeks. His eyes flew open, and he jolted, flying upward and taking a gasping breath. He coughed violently for a moment, and suddenly, an oily black ball flew out from between his lips. The second it touched the water, it melted into nothing.

Sebastian stood, completely drenched. He touched his face, stared at his hands. He flexed his fingers, and when nothing happened, his eyes widened.

"The water's a panacea," he said, in awe. He met Kieran's eyes, a smile spreading across his face. "The curse is broken."

In that moment, it was as if Kieran's body moved of its own accord. One moment, he was at the edge of the pool, and the next, he was jumping inside, throwing his arms around Sebastian and holding him tightly against him. He pulled back enough to press a kiss to his lips, though he was smiling so much it was mostly teeth. Sebastian laughed and kissed him back, wet fingers knotted in Kieran's hair.

"It's like Wyvern Springs," Delilah realized with a gasp as she looked around at the pools. "This is what happened when the Hammond family was entrusted to look after the water because of its magic."

Verbena nodded. "You understand, then, what I'm about to ask of you."

Kieran stopped kissing Sebastian long enough to refocus on Verbena. She gestured to the space around her, looking between the four of them.

"I've synthesized the magic to create this panacea spring—its water will break any curse. You may use it for whatever you like, including to pass your Calling. Beyond that, a place this powerful will need to be protected. I'd like you all to be the ones to do it."

Briar seemed on the verge of laughing. "Us? But—we're just a bunch of kids. How are we supposed to protect this place?"

"With this," Verbena said, holding up the scepter. She turned and held it out to Kieran. "You'll be able to use it to channel the vein's power as you see fit."

Kieran's eyes widened. "You . . . want me to be the vein's guardian?"

Verbena nodded. "I told you when we first met that my family has guarded this place for generations. Unfortunately, I never cared to continue the family line." She chuckled. "You, however, have proven to be a worthy successor. Of course, I will stay for some time and train you in the art of protecting this place, but I have no doubt you'll take to it easily—especially with your friends at your side."

Kieran didn't even hesitate. "Okay—deal."

Everyone turned to him, eyes wide in shock.

"Kieran, this is a huge responsibility," Delilah said.

He shrugged. "All this time, I've had no idea what I wanted to do with my life. I've never felt that I had a purpose, you know? But if I can help with this"—he gestured to the spring—"then maybe I've finally found one."

"I'll help," Briar offered. When Delilah spun on her, wide-eyed, she shrugged. "What? We can manage, can't we?"

"You could always make a home here," Verbena said. "In the woods. The forest will take care of you so long as you care for it."

"I never really liked the city much," Briar admitted.

"I . . . suppose that might not be so bad," Delilah said. She looked at Kieran. "You sure about this?"

Kieran considered it. He'd spent months in Gellingham feeling useless, floating through his life as if he were just another leaf on a river he had no control over. This, though? It was a purpose. A life he could see himself in, standing here with the people he loved, making a future that felt solid and defined.

"Yeah," he finally said. He turned to Verbena. "I'm sure. We'll protect this place any way we can. Thank you, Verbena. For everything."

The old witch nodded. "And thank you for proving to me that perhaps there's some good in this world after all."

With that, the old witch passed the Scepter of the Woods to Kieran. Instantly, its magic shot up his arms, and Kieran gasped as he felt it sink into his chest, connecting with his own magic. A faint silver glow surrounded him and the scepter. Seaweed chirped before running up to him and jumping onto his shoulders. With his familiar and his magic surrounding him, Kieran felt a warmth he hadn't before.

"Well," he said, turning to look at his friends, "it looks like we have some planning to do."

CHAPTER TWENTY-SEVEN

On the evening of his eighteenth birthday, Kieran found himself watching Sebastian's sisters tear him to pieces.

"You look like you're going to a business meeting," his sixteen-year-old sister, Mei, said. Her inky-black hair was in a long braid down her back, tied off with a ribbon, and she wore a stylish skirt and a button-down shirt. The outfit was nice, but not overly formal, unlike what her brother had chosen.

"I want to make a good impression," Sebastian shot back, straightening his tie for the umpteenth time. "And most good impressions start with looking the part."

"Of what, a tax collector?" eight-year-old Lisha shot back from where she was sitting on the couch beside Kieran.

While Sebastian blushed, Kieran couldn't hold in his laughter. Now that he'd known Sebastian's sisters for a few months, it occurred to him that they had a lot in common with Briar—namely, their ability to absolutely eviscerate their brother at the drop of a hat. Mei and Lisha, though, managed to do it even more sharply than Briar most days. They may not have been trained assassins like their brother, but that didn't mean they weren't well-versed in cutting deep.

Sebastian sighed. "I'm meeting Kieran's aunt Adelaide tonight—it's essentially like meeting the parents. I can't make a fool of myself."

Kieran smiled. The four were getting ready to head to the Pinwhistle Forest, where the twins had elected to throw a joint birthday party for Kieran and Briar. People had come out from all over Celdwyn, including Adelaide, both of Delilah's parents, and Ariel and Santiago.

Their pilot and chef had just returned from Esperona, where Santiago had introduced Ariel to his family. They'd sent piles of postcards detailing their adventures and describing all the finest foods and wines they'd sampled. Kieran, in turn, had written them enchanted letters: When Ariel and Santiago read them, it was as if they were actually witnessing Kieran's memories along with him. Kieran showed them the springs in the Pinwhistle Forest, Verbena, and even the day when Kieran had brought the Witches' Council to see the springs. They spent hours examining the waters, taking samples, and discussing what to do. After they determined that Kieran had, in fact, found a panacea, they announced that he had officially passed his Calling. They also agreed to help protect the vein in any way they could. They insisted, though, that Kieran and the others never tell another soul of its properties, lest it be drained of its power, to which the four friends agreed.

And Kieran's magic, for all its faults, was still flickering proudly in his chest.

"She's gonna think you're a weird small businessman," Lisha shot back at her brother, breaking through Kieran's thoughts. Seaweed sat in her lap, letting the girl stroke her like a pet cat.

Sebastian put his hands on his hips. "A *weird small businessman*? Come, now."

As much as Kieran was enjoying seeing Sebastian's slow roast, he stood up from the couch, crossing the floor to reach his boyfriend.

"Hold on," he said, placing a gentle hand on Sebastian's arm. "I have an idea of how to fix this."

"It better not be kissing again," Lisha grumbled.

Kieran's cheeks flared red. Earlier, when he and Sebastian had met up in Shui City, Lisha had made the unfortunate mistake of not knocking while the two of them were enjoying a private moment in Sebastian's bedroom. Lisha had screamed so loud the neighbors had come over to make sure no one was being murdered. Kieran was just relieved he'd been wearing pants at the time.

Now he and the Feng siblings were all in the kitchen of Kieran, Delilah, and Briar's apartment in Gellingham. The whole place was full of boxes, most of the trio's belongings packed away in preparation for their upcoming move. With some financial help from Klaus—in exchange for a small amount of panacea spring water—they'd been able to have a second cabin built in the woods beside the one Klaus had been living in during his time studying the vein and had left to Delilah and Briar. The second one was Kieran's.

"Take the jacket and tie off," Kieran said to Sebastian, "so it's just the button-down and suspenders. That way it's formal but not *too* formal. Oh, and, ah . . . you could always unbutton the first two buttons on your shirt. Or three, if you feel really adventurous."

"No," Mei chimed in, glaring at them. "No buttons undone until marriage."

Sebastian scoffed at her. "You don't get to tell me what to do."

"Well, Mom would want me to say the same thing," Mei argued.

"Yeah!" Lisha agreed. "Mom's gonna haunt you if you unbutton your shirt!"

Kieran held up his hands. "All right, all right. Understood. Buttons all buttoned, zippers all zipped. Now we should get going. We don't want to be late for the next trolley."

The girls and Seaweed got up from their seats to get their things, and as they did, Sebastian nodded toward Kieran gratefully. He mouthed, *Thank you.*

"Anytime." Kieran looped his arm through Sebastian's and flashed him a grin. "You look great, by the way."

Sebastian's eyes flickered from Kieran's face down to the peacock jacket he had on. It was the one he'd gotten in Yarrowport. It looked a bit ostentatious but also very much in line with what Kieran typically chose to wear on a night out.

"You too. You always have good taste in clothes." Sebastian leaned in close to him and whispered, so quietly there was no way his sisters could hear, "Plus, that collar's doing a great job of hiding your hickey."

Kieran turned bright pink. Even with his curse broken, Sebastian still had a habit of biting.

"Okay, let's go!" Lisha called, marching toward the door. "Don't wanna be late!"

Kieran and Sebastian exchanged a look, snorted with laughter, and headed out.

When Kieran and the others arrived at the party, they discovered that Delilah had truly outdone herself.

The springs were decorated with layers and layers of lights, both hovering near the ground and sparkling in the trees. Paper stars were affixed to the branches, and a sign reading HAPPY 18TH BIRTHDAY, BRIAR AND KIERAN! hung over a table boasting carafes of hot cocoa, coffee, and mulled wine. There were also fires burning in firepits around the springs, seeing as winter was still holding tightly to the region three months after that first blizzard had hit the city. People wore heavy coats over their party clothes. There would be time later for everyone to return to the cabins and warm up, but for now, they seemed perfectly happy enjoying the scenery of the spring—and the enchanted warm drinks.

Already, the area was filled with guests. Kieran recognized a few of Briar's friends from the gym where she'd been teaching ledrith recently, along with some of the witches with whom Delilah had been rubbing shoulders as she continued her freelance cursebreaking work. Ariel and Santiago were helping to hand out drinks, along with a warm stew that Santiago had cooked up. Delilah stood by the fire chatting with her mother, who had made the trip up from Kitfield, while Briar was with Adelaide at a different fire. As Kieran, Sebastian, and his sisters approached, Ash turned from the fire he was standing at with Klaus and waved.

It was still a bit odd to see him simply as one of his friends, but Kieran had begun to feel rather good about it.

"There you are!" Briar called, waving, as Adelaide just smiled. "We were wondering where you were!"

"Sorry, we missed our trolley!" Kieran jogged in his twin's direction, Sebastian and Seaweed following while Sebastian's sisters went to grab hot cocoa. "Everything going well here?"

"I'd say so. Though one of my ledrith friends asked me to introduce her to Adelaide to maybe try asking her out, and it was a little awkward explaining that she's, y'know, ten times our age."

"What can I say?" Dressed in a rich blue peacoat, Adelaide adjusted the matching hat over her pale hair and smirked. "I look good for my age."

Kieran said, "Oh—yes! Adelaide, this is Sebastian—the one I told you about on the phone."

"And that's Seaweed," Briar added as Adelaide's eyes wandered to the otter-like creature at Kieran's side. "She's Kieran's familiar."

Adelaide smiled at both, reaching down to scratch Seaweed's chin. "It's an honor to meet you both. Always exciting to have new additions to the family."

Kieran gently took Sebastian's hand, and the other boy stiffened. Sebastian's palm was clammy, and it occurred to Kieran that, as usual when it came to meeting new people, his boyfriend was nervous.

"It's good to meet you, Adelaide," Sebastian said, offering her a deep bow. "I've been looking forward to meeting more of Kieran's family."

"Well, the great news is, you can stop with me—there aren't many Pelumbras worth meeting." Seeing the way Sebastian hesitated at that, Adelaide just laughed. She straightened from petting Seaweed and patted Sebastian on the shoulder. "Kieran's told me all about your adventure together. It's a pity I couldn't join you."

"But who else would take care of ruining the Pelumbra family in the meantime?" Briar pointed out.

Adelaide looked more than a bit proud of herself. "You know, I meant to tell you both about the last time I saw your father. Oh, he was boiling mad . . ."

Kieran and the others fell into Adelaide's story just as they always did. When she was finished, Kieran and Sebastian excused themselves to get drinks, hoping to warm up a bit. As the night went on, Kieran introduced Sebastian to more of the guests, feeling pride well in his chest as he got to say they were together. Sebastian and Ash even spoke for a bit and seemed to get along swimmingly. As most guests got too cold to stay out, Briar and Delilah led them to the trail to head down to the cabins, where they could warm up and sit on the furniture that the two of them had managed to move from their old apartment to their new home. Seaweed joined them, seemingly excited to curl up in her usual spot in front of the fire.

Soon, the only people left outside were Kieran and Sebastian. They cleaned up everything, the only step left being carrying out the trash, to be disposed of elsewhere. When they'd finished, Kieran invited Sebastian to sit down with him on the lip of one of the hot spring pools. The two dipped their feet in, the water warm and silky with minerals. Kieran leaned his head on Sebastian's shoulder, and Sebastian tilted his head to rest against Kieran's. After a moment, Sebastian lifted his head and pressed a kiss to Kieran's hair as if he'd forgotten to before, then laid his head back down.

"So," Sebastian said, staring out at the water, "what's next for us?"

Kieran couldn't help but laugh. "Oh, did you want my five-year plan? Because I have one now, for the record. Now that I've gotten better at magic, I was thinking about writing a book."

"Really? About what?"

"Adventures. Magic." He waggled his eyebrows and added, in a faux-sultry voice, *"Romance."*

Sebastian sputtered a laugh. "Do you need an editor? Because I might be willing to offer my services, if you asked."

"Naturally. Who else would be there to tell me how often I use *just* as a crutch word? Plus, you're the reason I switched from poetry to prose in the first place. Turns out I like telling stories more than trying to wrestle with rhyme schemes."

"One could argue that poetry can tell a story too, but I understand what you mean." Sebastian bumped his shoulder against Kieran's. "Do you think you'd want to write up here by yourself or . . . have some company?"

"As in . . . have you move in with me?" When Sebastian nodded, Kieran's eyes widened. "Wait—really? You'd want to live with me up here?"

Sebastian nodded. "Of course—if you're willing. I know it'll be tight quarters with me and both my sisters, but they'd love to get out of the city. Maybe not for a few months—since you still need time to get settled—but sooner rather than later. I'm in love with you, Kieran. You're the best thing that's ever happened to me. Sure, we don't know how things will change in the future, but right now, I feel like this is the best choice. It'll keep Mei and Lisha safe, and I'll get to be with you—there's not much else I could ask for."

Kieran couldn't bite back the goofy smile warming his face. It was only recently that Sebastian had started using the word *love.* Every time Kieran heard it, he wanted to bounce up and down like a child and kiss Sebastian until he couldn't breathe.

"Plus, it's . . . good for me, I think, to be farther from the city. Keeps me away from my old job." Sebastian ran a hand through his hair, which had started to get longer in the last few months since they returned to the city. Kieran found it ridiculously attractive, so Sebastian hadn't cut it. "I want to stay far away from that part of my life now. Break the cycle, you know?"

Kieran nodded. "Intimately, yes. I just . . . I hope you realize how proud I am of you."

Sebastian's nose wrinkled a bit as he smiled. Kieran resisted the urge to lean in and kiss it. "I'm proud too. Of both of us. We've come a long way."

Sebastian's eyes flickered to Kieran's lips as he said it, so Kieran took it upon himself to lean in and kiss him. Kieran felt the warmth coming off Sebastian, yearning for it. Kieran kissed him once, twice, three times before pulling back, nudging his nose against Sebastian's.

"You know," Sebastian said, face pink, "I don't want to gossip or anything, but when I was helping your sister pack the other day, I found something hidden in her dresser."

Kieran gagged. "Oh, gross—"

"Not like that!" Sebastian barely held back his laughter. He gently shoved Kieran. "It was a velvet box. With a ring inside."

Kieran's jaw dropped. "*What?* You're kidding."

"I'm not. She made me promise not to tell Delilah. Sounds like she's not going to use it anytime soon but wanted to have it *just in case.*" Sebastian shook his head, smiling. "If I were a betting man, I'd say it'll be on Delilah's finger before spring is over."

"I don't know. I think Briar's got a little more self-restraint than that." Kieran paused, considering. "It'll be early summer, on the anniversary of the cursebreaking."

"Did she tell you that?"

"No—just a twin hunch." Kieran laughed. "Of course they'd get engaged at *eighteen years old.* When do you think the wedding will be? Before we turn twenty?"

Sebastian shrugged. "Who knows? If it works for them, it works."

Kieran nodded at that. He swirled his foot in the other direction, grateful for the warmth the steam offered as it rose out of the spring. He thought back to a few months ago, when Ash had pointed out Kieran's insistence on comparing their relationship with Briar and Delilah's. For once, Kieran didn't feel that he had to do that. Even now, when it seemed as if they were about to take a big step and he wasn't.

But then again, he didn't feel that he needed to. He didn't have to prove to anyone that his relationship was valid. What he and Sebastian had was just for them, and he liked it that way. It made everything feel so much more natural to move on their own timeline without outside influence making Kieran feel inferior for no reason.

Sebastian broke the silence. "Do you think about it much? The future, I mean?"

"Oh, yeah—nonstop. That's just the way my brain works." Kieran rested his hand atop Sebastian's where it was waiting, open-palmed, beside him. "But . . . I guess I'm not scared of it anymore. It feels like I'm going somewhere, you know? I can't exactly say *where* yet, but . . . I think that's okay."

"I do too." Sebastian squeezed the hand. "I'm just happy you're in it, Kieran."

"Listen, I'm *extremely* hard to get rid of. Many have tried and failed. I'm not going anywhere." Kieran stroked Sebastian's fingers with his own. "Not when I'm this embarrassingly in love with you."

Sebastian leaned in and kissed him again, then pressed his forehead to Kieran's.

"I love you too, Kier."

And as they fell into each other's arms again, Sebastian pressing kisses down Kieran's jawline as he laughed, the lights seemed to glow a little brighter and the dying fires sparked anew once more.

Because for the first time in both their lives, they'd finally found home.

ACKNOWLEDGMENTS

When I sat down to write this book, I was thinking a lot about how romance is portrayed in teen media. Often, teen characters will start dating one person and suddenly, boom, that's their soulmate, despite how uncommon that is in real life. A lot of that is wish fulfillment, sure. Maybe life would be easier if love was a "one and done" situation for most of us. That said, for this book, I wanted to move away from that idea. After all, I've already written that story for Delilah and Briar. When it came time to write Kieran and Sebastian's story, I wanted to focus a bit more on the messiness of teen relationships: the fickle feelings, the intense ups and downs, and the reality that most of the time, people *don't* wind up with their first partner. Along the way, I had a truly ridiculous amount of fun. Therefore, I owe a huge amount of thanks to everyone who helped make this fantastical gay romp of a book happen.

First, as always, my amazing, patient, extraordinary agent, Erica Bauman: Thanks for sticking with me for over half a decade. Your support, insight, and willingness to meet me for margaritas whenever I'm in New York are always appreciated.

Next, shout-out to the incredible editors who helped shape

this project into what it is: Hannah Hill and Ari Lewin. You both are rock stars, and I'm so glad that I had the unique delight of working with both of you. Thanks to Makena Cioni as well for your assistance, especially during Hannah's maternity leave. In addition, massive thanks to everyone else at Delacorte Press and beyond who worked on this book and helped get it into readers' hands. Y'all are the best.

To my friends, family, and wonderful partner: Thanks for sticking with me and always being supportive of my career. It means the world to me that you're still out here reposting my silly Canva graphics and attending my book events. I love you dearly. Special shout-out to my D&D group for letting me occasionally steal a detail or two from our campaign to put in my books and vice versa (I'm not saying my hapless blue wizard with a strength score of 5 and an otter familiar is Kieran, but he's not *not* Kieran).

Finally, thanks to you, the reader. More and more, reading is becoming a radical act in the face of book bans and rampant anti-intellectualism. With that in mind, I am incredibly grateful to everyone who reads my books—especially the queer kids. You're the reason I do this, and I love you immensely. Here's to many more. ♥

ABOUT THE AUTHOR

KAYLA COTTINGHAM (they/she) is a former teen librarian and *New York Times* bestselling author of sapphic horror and fantasy novels. Originally from Salt Lake City, Kayla lives in Boston, where they love to go hiking in the woods, play RPGs, and snuggle on the couch with their ridiculously large black cat, Squid.

kaylacottingham.com